WINTER FIRE

WINTER
FIRE

William R. Trotter

A DUTTON BOOK

DUTTON
Published by the Penguin Group
Penguin Books USA Inc., 375 Hudson Street,
New York, New York 10014, U.S.A.
Penguin Books Ltd, 27 Wrights Lane,
London W8 5TZ, England
Penguin Books Australia Ltd, Ringwood,
Victoria, Australia
Penguin Books Canada Ltd, 10 Alcorn Avenue,
Toronto, Ontario, Canada M4V 3B2
Penguin Books (N.Z.) Ltd, 182–190 Wairau Road,
Auckland 10, New Zealand

Penguin Books Ltd, Registered Offices:
Harmondsworth, Middlesex, England

First published by Dutton, an imprint of New American Library,
a division of Penguin Books USA Inc.
Distributed in Canada by McClelland & Stewart Inc.

First Printing, February, 1993
10 9 8 7 6 5 4 3 2 1

 REGISTERED TRADEMARK—MARCA REGISTRADA

LIBRARY OF CONGRESS CATALOGING IN PUBLICATION DATA:
Trotter, William R.
  Winter fire / William R. Trotter.
    p. cm.
  ISBN 0-525-93581-9
  I. Title.
PS3570.R596W56   1993
813'.54—dc20   92–28952
                                                              CIP

Printed in the United States of America
Set in Janson
Designed by Eve L. Kirch

PUBLISHER'S NOTE
This is a work of fiction. Names, characters, places, and incidents either are the
products of the author's imagination or are used fictitiously.

Dedicated to Mary Lustig and Betsy Nolan, two ladies whose faith in this novel exceeded the bounds of reason.

In the cold my song was resting
long remained in darkness hidden.
I must draw the songs from Coldness,
from the Frost must I withdraw them . . .

Shall I ope my box of legends,
and my chest where songs are treasured?

—The *Kalevala*, Runo I

One

Around midnight, the gale temporarily stopped blowing, the clouds thinned, and the auroral glow began to bleed through the sky again. On the rare clear nights, when the stars burned like white cinders, the aurora could be spellbinding, weaving fugues of light across the star-dusted void. On cloudy nights, when it was diffuse, seeping into the folds of the clouds, its light could be ghastly—a pale, sulfurous lime that made the tundra look as though it were paved with bone. A tricky light, too, that curdled shadows where no shadows had a right to be; the kind of light that made sentries see infiltrators in every dip and wrinkle of the ground. But sickly and treacherous as it was, it was somehow less depressing than the attenuated grey murk that passed, in these latitudes, for daylight. As November came on, even that would fade; by midwinter, the land would be gripped in perpetual night.

But for a couple of days yet, it would still be October. Along the Rhine the woods would be turning—the colors of apples and quinces and doubloon gold against a vaulted blue sky. In Mannheim, the concert season would have started. Ziegler's replacement—a talented but still shallow interpreter who reminded Erich of himself, ten years ago—would of course be presiding on the podium. The fellow had plenty of ambition, Erich thought ruefully, and if the war lasted another two or three years, the orchestra would stop regarding him as a replacement.

Erich tried to shut off this line of thinking. It always led to a burning sense of frustration, of helplessness, coupled with an acute awareness of his own selfishness. He was only one of millions whose lives and careers had been split in two by the chasm of war. What right did he have to feel sorry for himself?

Every right, came the reply. The exact same right as every other poor freezing bastard in the division.

Poor bastards like Corporal Eberbach, who stood on the other side of the foxhole, fussing with a belt of machine-gun ammunition. Did it make any difference to Eberbach that his platoon commander had chosen to stand this watch, rather than simply order another enlisted man to pull the duty while Erich slept in the comparative warmth of the platoon dugout? And if it didn't make any difference to Eberbach, then what the hell was Erich doing here?

No doubt about it: leading a platoon of soldiers was a lot trickier than leading an orchestra. Erich's being here in a forward outpost, rather than snug inside the dugout, really made sense only if his presence elevated morale. But how did one determine that, exactly?

"Well, Eberbach . . ." He had almost blurted out something like: "How am I doing so far, old chap?" But now he had opened a conversation with a man with whom he had absolutely nothing in common but their present shared misery.

"Do you care for music, Eberbach?"

"What kind of music, *Herr Oberleutnant*?"

"There are only two kinds of music: good and bad."

Erich realized at once what a fatuous, indefensible remark that was. Would Eberbach call him on it? Would he know? Care?

"In that case, *Herr Oberleutnant*, I certainly prefer the former."

Actually, that was not such a bad reply. Erich warmed to

the man at once. "Come on, now, tell me what you like. I was a musician in civilian life, myself."

"Yes sir, I know. I heard the other officers talking about it."

Erich waited. He knew what Eberbach meant by that: most of the officers who knew about his past felt that Erich was not only too old to be leading a platoon of twenty-year-olds, but that he was too soft, too intellectual, too much the offspring of wealth and privilege, even to be good cannon fodder. Which was the main reason he had nearly killed himself, in training and in combat, trying to prove them wrong.

Eberbach needed coaxing. "All of us were different things in civilian life, Corporal. That's why we all hate being here."

Eberbach laughed, a brittle hack, and reached forward for the tenth time in as many minutes to work the cocking lever of the MG-34, making sure the lubricant had not frozen. The long thin barrel poked between two ration crates packed with snow that had been watered down and was now as hard as granite.

"I like American jazz," Eberbach finally said.

Silence descended again and Erich suppressed his irritation. Why had he ever started this conversation? After a few seconds he surrendered to another one of those reveries that came so easily, and so dangerously for those who yielded wholly to them, from the intense cold.

"Lieutenant!"

Eberbach was shaking him. "Snap out of it, sir!"

"Sorry, Corporal. Drifted away for a minute."

"Yes sir," Eberbach replied in the flattest of voices, then went back to fussing with his machine gun.

Overhead, the trapped auroral light dimmed inside returning clouds. The wind picked up once more, and Erich drew a swaddling of scarves up to the bridge of his nose. A new wall of clouds was thickening to the north, always to the north. A Russian flare went up in the darkness to the east, throwing the cloud wall into sharp relief. The flare hung like a sputtering blob of grease. By its light, the frozen Litsa River glowed like a ribbon of diamonds.

"I wonder if that flare means they have a patrol coming in . . ."

"I doubt it," said Erich. "They're probably just trying to get a look at the weather."

"I'd rather not see it coming."

A sudden burst of wind slapped at their cheeks, sent probes of cold deep into their chests. An icy powder brushed their faces, burning and thickening.

"Shit, here it comes again." Sometimes Erich thought God had saved this place for the last day of Creation, and then He had run out of ideas.

"We won't have to spend the winter here, sir, will we?"

"We will if our relief doesn't show up soon. They're way overdue now, and if the snow gets too thick, they'll never find the trail markers. They could keep wandering until they hit Russian lines."

"Yes sir. I heard the Hundred Thirty-eighth lost a dispatch rider that way last week. Got disoriented and rode straight toward Murmansk. They fired rifles in the air to warn him, but he couldn't hear over the motorcycle engine. It's easy to do—no landmarks at all except for that damned river."

One of the worst things about being a platoon leader, Erich thought, was having to make all these trivial decisions. It was obvious to him that he needed to go back and find the relief column and guide it forward through this blizzard. But that would leave Eberbach alone with a weapon that was supposed to be served by two men, in weather that was getting worse by the minute.

"Eberbach, go back to the platoon bunker and wake up somebody who doesn't owe you money. When you get back with him, I'll go find our missing brethren and lead them to the promised land."

"It's okay, sir, let the poor fuckers sleep. I'm wide awake, and there doesn't seem to be anything cooking on Ivan's side of the river."

"I'm not worried about the Russians—they're no more likely to do anything on a night like this than we are. I'm worried about frostbite. The temperature is going to plum-

met, and we're all dressed more for a Tyrolean ski party than
for arctic exploration. Just stay alert, will you? If you start
feeling drowsy, go to the dugout and get a couple of guys to
relieve you—tell them it's on my direct order."

Eberbach seemed to smile; his mouth was invisible behind
its wrappings, but his cheeks rose like chapped apples and the
flesh around his eyes crinkled.

"I'll be fine, Lieutenant. Don't worry."

But Erich did. He was now paid to worry about Eberbach
and every other man in the platoon, and he didn't like it
much.

Erich self-consciously patted Eberbach's shoulder, took a
deep breath, and hoisted himself out of the shallow machine-
gun pit and into the rolling punch of the wind. The gale
raked his exposed flesh, making the inside of his nostrils burn
and the roots of his teeth throb. He pulled a scarf over his
nose and narrowed his eyes to slits. The air sacs of his lungs
began to ache. He made himself as small as possible, presenting a round, humpbacked shape to the wind, and began to follow the trail markers—cairns of rock spaced at ten-yard
intervals—toward the battalion command post. The fresh
snow was already deep enough to squeak under his boots and
the auroral light had faded. He walked along, bent and tortured, into a scream of wind whose first howl had been voiced
on the polar ice cap. He fought for footing against a sudden
uppercut of wind. Christ, it was still *October!*

The distance from the front line to the battalion command post was a quarter mile, and by the time Erich had
covered two-thirds of the distance, the storm had turned into
a blizzard. Sheets of gale-driven snow blew horizontally,
scourging the land like white bullwhips, and the wind, rushing
through the cracks in the rock cairns, moaned and shrieked.
Erich had a vision of snow devils, paper-white little dervishes,
writhing inside every cyclonic twist of snow.

Situated in the lee of a knocked-out tank, the command
post was nothing but a hole that had been punched into the
tundra with high explosives. The tank was an old French
Somua-35, captured intact in 1940, that had blown its treads

on a Soviet mine back in August. No spare parts had ever come up the four-hundred-mile Arctic Highway from the railhead at Rovaniemi, so the tank still sat there, a cubist igloo, serving as nothing more than an armor-plated windbreak. A pit had been blasted behind it, walled with rocks and roofed over with the wing of an antique Polikarpov biplane that had somehow escaped the Stukas in June. It had been discovered, intact and loaded with fuel, in the middle of the tundra; various slices of its wings and fuselage had been parceled out for use in the construction of strong points and a first-aid bunker. A faint edge of light showed through the tarpaulins; the snowflakes it illuminated looked as hard and fat as walnuts. If it were not for the wind, Erich thought, you could actually have heard them plop when they landed.

Erich stepped inside, inhaling warm but fetid air. He felt ridiculously like a supplicant. If a gulf separated a platoon commander from his men, just as big a one separated anyone who served on the front lines—regardless of rank—from anyone who served behind them. He felt an absurd flush of contempt when he looked around at the sleeping men, a response made even pettier by the envy he also felt. There lay the battalion commander and his adjutant, asleep on makeshift bunks, snoring roughly. Their radioman was tinkering with the field stove. The place was lit by greasy lanterns, and the fumes from the stove smelled as though a small animal had just fallen into the flames.

"If that's coffee, Sergeant, I certainly would appreciate a cup. There's a blizzard coming on out there."

"Yes sir, as opposed to the balmy weather we've been enjoying."

There was insolence in the man's tone, but Erich didn't know whether to respond to it or not. None of the other officers present were awake, and there was no guarantee their sympathies would be with him if they were. So he chose to pretend he had not heard the radioman's response.

"I asked if there was coffee."

The man poured him a cup. Erich's tongue touched fire, and he forced down a scalding swallow.

"It's pretty vile stuff, Lieutenant," the man said, having waited until Erich was committed to drinking it. "Gave me the squitters real bad, sir."

Erich discreetly put the cup aside. The last thing he wanted, at twenty below zero centigrade, two hundred miles from an indoor toilet, was diarrhea.

"Any word on the relief columns?"

"Got a call from the Hundred Thirty-eighth about half an hour ago—they've already been relieved. I guess the weather's slowing down our people."

Erich nodded, puckering against the seared place on his tongue. Just as quickly as it had taken a sour turn, the conversation had become comradely. Either he was overinterpreting what was said to him, or the subject matter had served to unite him with the other man. Both of them wanted to leave this terrible place.

"Did you learn exactly who the lucky chaps are who are relieving us?"

The sergeant ruffled through a stack of message flimsies. "*Ja*, here it is: Schorner's Sixth Mountain Division."

"Good unit. Austrian *Jägers*, mostly. I hope to Christ they brought more winter clothing than we did. Well, I'd better go look for them. Why don't you make a fresh batch of coffee for the officers?"

The sneer on the sergeant's face told him that the Austrians would have to make their own coffee.

Outside, the hot breath knocked from him by the impact of the storm, Erich could feel the oppressive weight of the sky. He could almost stretch on tiptoe and touch it, but it would burn his hands, blacken them with a cold that could kill almost as quickly as fire. He felt sorry for the Austrians, blundering through this howling darkness, lurching from roadmark to roadmark, sandblasted by the wind, but he was not doing this for them.

He backtracked along the main supply route for ten long minutes, and then he remembered leaving Eberbach alone at the outpost. He turned around and went back to the command post, and was just moving the tarp aside from the entrance when, at the edge of his vision, he spotted a recognition flare, grainy and distorted through the snow. He pulled the tarpaulin aside and reached in.

"Hand me that flare gun, Sergeant, and wake the colonel—they're here!"

Erich fired an answering flare, and five minutes later was astonished to see a gigantic top-heavy reindeer materialize out of the swirling murk, towing a supply sled in the center of which sat a grizzled man with two icicles depending, walrus-like, from his nostrils. The reindeer halted with its muzzle a foot from Erich's face. The animal wore a glazed, bovine expression and the steam from its nostrils carried a barnyard fragrance. Erich wanted to hold his face close to the animal and grow warm, just for a moment, in the smell of hay. He peered around the trembling antlers.

"Are you from the Sixth Mountain?" he yelled.

"No, we're from the North Pole and I'm bloody Saint Nicholas! Are you part of the Hundred Thirty-second Regiment?"

"We are. Welcome."

The driver struggled free of the sled, slapped the reindeer on its rump, and extended his hand. "Colonel Prausnitz, Hundred Twenty-ninth *Jägers*. I need to get my men under cover as soon as possible."

Erich saluted and introduced himself. "I'll have to guide your men to the front lines, Colonel—until you know how to keep track of the markers, it's easy to get lost."

Erich could now discern a long ghostly column of shrouded men and pack-burdened beasts, shuffling miserably in place. He peered more closely at the column.

"Colonel, what sort of animals have you got there?"

"Mules."

"Mules? In Finland? Where did you acquire mules?"

Prausnitz managed a thin, haggard smile. "Athens," he said.

"Athens, *Greece*?"

"Yes. We started out with about two thousand animals, but the last time I counted we were down to about half that."

"You'll lose the rest of them within a week. I hope they taste better than reindeer."

"They don't; in the past three days, I've tried both. Well, Lieutenant, let's move on and get these men into some warm bunkers."

After a quick conference in the command post—dispositions made easily on paper that would take two hours to accomplish on the ground—Erich retraced his route eastward. Several inches of new snow had accumulated since he had left the line and the cairns were hard to see. But anyone who was going to stay here for the winter would have plenty of time to make larger ones.

Before he led the Austrians forward, Erich inspected a few of them closely. They looked unspeakably wretched, as though wondering what collective sin they had committed that was so heinous as to warrant their being sent to this place. As the column lumbered into motion, Erich suddenly felt a distasteful but very real desire to shatter any remaining illusions these men might have. He was a veteran of this place; he'd been scooping rocks out of the permafrost to make bunkers with while these sods had been basking on the steps of the Parthenon and flirting with black-eyed Greek girls. With a lecturing, classroom tone that must have seemed, under the circumstances, needlessly cruel, he walked alongside Prausnitz and told him what he and his men were in for.

"About those 'warm bunkers,' Colonel . . . you have to understand what we're up against. The treeline stops more than a hundred miles south; up here, there's only tundra and scrub. If you dig down in summer, you hit water first, and below that, permafrost. After the first snows, the soil turns to iron. When we used up all our extra explosives, we used brush and rocks and pieces of metal cannibalized from disabled vehicles. The Reds do the same, but they're twenty miles from their supply base, not four hundred."

They had reached the front line. Erich led Prausnitz to an almost invisible dugout. A plate of new snow broke as he lifted the tarp to reveal a cramped, reeking hole. A dozen grimy faces peered out at the new arrivals like disturbed badgers.

"My God," said Colonel Prausnitz, "you live in caves!"

"No," said Erich. "It's worse than that."

Twenty minutes later, with the relief unit parceled out and his own company assembling on the trail, Erich took two of the Austrians back up to the forward machine-gun pit to relieve Eberbach. The snow had tapered off by that time—just vicious little stingers of it remained, driven by the fitful wind—and Eberbach was still standing faithfully behind his machine gun, staring into the void over no-man's-land. Snow mantled his helmet and a thin pointed ridge of it lined the barrel of the MG-34.

"Hey, Eberbach! Time to go! The relief column is here!"

Erich went over to embrace the machine gunner, and his arms encountered iron. A Russian flare—how did they always know when a relief was taking place?—sizzled skyward, and its light was given back by the open sightless marbles of Eberbach's eyes. The face was peaceful with sleep. At the touch of Erich's hands, the frozen body fell one way and the machine gun fell ponderously in the opposite direction, pressing a clean blue hole in the snow.

Two

The snow had stopped, but the world had greyed out all around them; there was no demarcation between sky and land. Distance was articulated in a few places by sullen outcroppings of red granite; otherwise everything blended into a directionless, unmeasured, putty-colored void. The road itself was defined only by the column of trudging men and steaming horses. This so-called "highway" turned out to be no modern *autobahn*. One and a half lanes wide, it was made from crushed, steamrollered rock. You could not pave roads this far north, one of the engineers said during a rest stop, because the spring thaws were so violent the paving material cracked.

Erich's unit had been marching for four days, ever since Prausnitz and his Austrians had relieved them, and still they had not reached the treeline. The Arctic Highway was the sole supply line to the Murmansk Front, and traffic moving north, toward the lines, took priority over anything moving in the other direction. Whenever a supply column appeared out of the murk, Erich's battalion moved to the side of the road and waited stoically until it passed—waited without shelter, immobile, for up to an hour. Only the wounded and the most important baggage had been loaded into trucks—trucks which presumably waited somewhere down the road. Everything else went on foot or was drawn behind horses, including the artillery. Every day more men came down with frostbite. Eight men were required, working in four-man relays, to carry a single stretcher case. Every night more horses died or simply refused to start moving again in the morning; there were no tents for them and precious little fodder. Thus, each day, the internal weight of the column grew, its pace slowed. Yesterday, Erich estimated, they had covered only ten miles during the short period of gloomy daylight.

During the first hours of the march, Erich's unit had been swept by a mood of rejuvenation. Men who had been too tightly wrapped inside their personal cocoons of physical misery to do more than growl sullenly at their comrades suddenly began to crack jokes, even sing; a general communal effort was made to look and act like soldiers, rather than half-frozen troglodytes.

Erich even felt an unaccustomed pride when he dressed his revitalized, smiling platoon into the line of march, passing by each man and pausing long enough to say something suitably optimistic and good-humored. Most of them responded in kind—after all, the new lieutenant was leading them out of this frigid hell and taking them to some place where there would be shelter, warm food, and possibly even mail. It did not matter that Erich personally had nothing to do with their being relieved—they still looked upon him, that first morning of the march, with a gratitude he was happy to accept.

There was even some pale, watery sunlight to bless them in the early hours of their withdrawal to the south. Erich began to feel so good, as he strode along at the head of his platoon, that he had no trouble putting Eberbach's death behind him. His worst feelings had come in the frustrating, seemingly interminable interlude between packing up for the move and actually being given the order to start; even then, brooding about the matter, Erich could not pinpoint any wrong decision, any oversight on his part that made him the cause of the corporal's death.

After all, no one had prepared them for this ghastly climate. The entire Murmansk offensive was supposed to have been concluded, victoriously, long before the first snowfall. No one had equipped them with proper clothing, shelter, or adequate supplies of hot food. No one had lectured them on the special problems of arctic warfare. They had all been forced to improvise everything, and to learn from harsh experience what effect these conditions had on mind and body.

It had been this hard-won feeling of expertise that had compelled Erich to linger, just for a few minutes, to lecture Prausnitz about the facts of life on this front. Surely, those few minutes had made no difference to Eberbach—from the look of him, the man had been dead for quite some time. Probably he had dozed off, without any preliminary yawns or drowsiness—something that had happened to a number of frostbitten men in the regiment—and hypothermia had set in massively. Erich *had* ordered the man to seek help if he felt himself getting drowsy.

Such was his reasoning as he started the march south, reveling in the muted glow of the morning sun, savoring the illusion of warmth it provided. With all his being, he wanted to put the whole appalling arctic episode behind him.

But by the end of the second day, when it had become clear that his regiment had only exchanged a stationary ordeal for a mobile one, every bit as cold and debilitating, all he could really focus on was the need to keep putting one foot in front of the other.

His legs had turned into columns of lead, cored with pain. The pain was friendly in a certain sense, and he had to monitor it continually, for if it stopped, or if it did not return after a rest period, that would mean the onset of frostbite. If he looked up, let his eyes go deep into the marbled grey emptiness around him, he became dizzy. Late yesterday, he had briefly hallucinated that the column was walking upside down within an upturned globe of crystal—the disorientation this had caused had made him fall. Now, to prevent any similar accident, he kept his eyes on the snow-brushed greatcoat of the man in front of him, intently studying the cracked surface of the leather cartridge pouches, matching the other man's pace.

The other men, and probably the horses too, marched the same way, studiously contemplating one another's backsides.

Erich had tried to summon memories of warmth and comfort, but they refused to come forth. All he could get his brain to do, besides monitor his body for the signs of frostbite, was to replay over and over again his own personal newsreel, beginning with his induction into the army and continuing through the early weeks of the Murmansk campaign, as he had seen it during the summer, when he had been moving in the other direction, confident that victory was only days away.

When his draft notice arrived, Erich went through the same emotional progression as a man who has just been told he has a terminal illness: despair, anger, and final resignation. Until the moment that letter arrived, Erich's future had seemed rich with possibilities no matter who won the war. He had risen from provincial obscurity to the brink of an international career. Suddenly, there was nothing in front of him but a chasm that could swallow him and his career without a trace.

He raged; he wept; he went on a three-day binge that reached its tawdry climax when he cynically seduced a young music student who had an obvious crush on him, using her as he would a whore and coldly dismissing her afterward.

More than any other factor, sheer self-loathing finally drove him to a state of acceptance. After all, he reasoned, he had for many years acquiesced, through an elaborate private moral calculus, in the known and guessed-at excesses of the Nazi regime simply because, at bottom, he shared that regime's belief that Germany should be invincibly strong, the shield of European values against the Bolshevik hordes. Had he not lost his own father to those same barbaric forces?

He sent flowers and a letter of apology to the girl, drafted his letter of resignation to the orchestra, and took a week's leave to get his personal affairs in order, before reporting for induction on the specified day.

In one sense, he was better prepared for basic training than most people his age. Conductors get a lot of exercise just by doing their jobs; that, and Erich's years of alpine trekking, had kept him in top physical condition.

Much harder to take than the physical regimen was the psychological ordeal of adjusting to the military way of doing things. He had built his career upon the individuality of his musical interpretations and the unfaltering motivation of his ambitions. To the army, his individuality did not exist and his ambitions were without the slightest relevance. He endured a thousand petty cruelties and degradations from drill instructors younger than he was, men whom he would have deemed utter brutes in civilian life, because he knew that the training they forced down his throat would improve his odds of getting through the war alive.

By virtue of his age and background, Erich qualified for officer candidate school, where the same system inflicted the same injustices and cruelties on better-educated men and then rewarded them by giving them the authority to make life-or-death decisions regarding the men under their command.

After being commissioned as a second lieutenant, Erich was assigned to the Second Mountain Division, because someone had read his file diligently enough to see that he had alpine experience and could ski. Since the mountain units were regarded, by the public at least, as elite formations, Erich was not displeased with the assignment.

He joined the division, at Kirkenes, shortly after the termination of the Norwegian campaign, in which the unit had distinguished itself during the battle for Narvik. Erich was one of the first replacement officers to arrive after that engagement, and he had the unfortunate luck to be assigned to a regiment whose commander was a tone-deaf professional soldier, filled with contempt for civilians-in-uniform, especially those who came from occupations which he deemed unmanly. Conductors, evidently, he regarded as just slightly less suspect than male ballet dancers. Unfortunately for Erich, the commander's prejudices also colored the attitudes of many of his fellow officers.

Those early weeks of garrison duty in Norway were leisurely. The weather was warm and Erich never even saw a pair of skis, much less put them on. In late May, the pace suddenly changed, and Erich's regiment began a period of intensive special training. Time and time again, his platoon assaulted mock pillboxes and practiced long-distance marches through the wilderness. Since there were also increased security precautions against Russian spies and infiltrators, it did not take long for everyone in the division to figure out what was going to happen.

There had nevertheless been a certain unreality to the actual start of hostilities against the Soviet Union. For diplomatic reasons, no German combat troops had been allowed inside Finland until hostilities had actually started, so before Erich's unit could assault the Russians, it had to wait behind the Norwegian border, then cross Lapland. At 0200 hours, June 22, 1941, Erich had stood just inside Norway, emotionally primed for battle, on the western side of a comic-opera roadblock—a candy-striped pole between two huts—while half a dozen Finnish customs guards drank coffee, chainsmoked, and kept glancing at their watches.

At 0231, the officer in command of the Finnish border guards raised the candy-cane pole, bowed to the waiting Germans like a doorman, and said: "All right, you can come in now; the war has started."

At that same moment, all along the Soviet Union's western border, more than seven thousand pieces of artillery and two thousand aircraft were ripping the night apart. By contrast, there in the Arctic, as the Second Mountain Division began its transit of Finland, men marched to the sound of birdcalls, and the wind coming off the open tundra was sweet with heather and tart with the aroma of cloudberries.

On the map it looked easy enough. Only sixty miles separated the eastern border of Finland from the Soviet Union's only ice-free northern port: Murmansk. Hitler had correctly surmised that Allied aid to the Russians could only be sent to that place, and could not be used in battle until it had been transported down the long railroad line to Leningrad.

From Norway, the German Mountain Corps would attack due east and simply bash through to Murmansk. The mountain divisions were considered strong enough to do this on their own, without much air or armor support except for a few squadrons of Stukas and some captured French tanks that had been reconditioned. Intelligence reports indicated that there would be little need for overwhelming firepower. Opposing the Germans were badly trained Siberian and Mongolian troops, ill-motivated conscripts for the most part, led by officers who still kept one eye on their backs because of the recent purges. Finland's Arctic Highway carried the Mountain Corps close to the border, and beyond the border—on the far side of a single flimsy line of bunkers and trenches—captured Russian maps clearly showed two suitable roads leading to Murmansk.

But the Siberians and Mongols had died hard in their pillboxes. Each position had to be burned out or Stuka-ed before it could be captured. Lacking heavy artillery, Erich's regiment had manhandled antiaircraft guns close to the fortifications and slathered them with fire while flame-thrower teams and satchel-charge squads worked in close. Thousands of Soviet border troops died; only two hundred, mostly injured, were taken prisoner.

Once through the border fortifications, the Germans had driven hard for the two roads. Everything hinged on those roads—without them, no sizable military force could long be sustained on the open tundra. The terrain was inhospitable and mostly coverless. Quicksand bogs were common. Clouds of mosquitoes and midges, so dense they resembled fog from a distance, appeared out of nowhere. When attacked by them, horses panicked and ran braying into the hills; wounded men writhed and bucked as the insects fed beneath their bandages. The landscape seemed to swallow both German divisions, and Murmansk was still thirty miles away.

When the campaign had been planned, the Mountain Corp's staff assumed that Soviet cartographers used the same map symbols as their Western counterparts. After days of fruitless patrolling, after scanning hundreds of bleak aerial photos, the Germans came finally to understand that the dotted lines on those captured Russian maps, the "roads" that would permit the Germans to sustain their advance, in reality represented the routes of seasonal reindeer migrations.

General Dietl, commander of the Mountain Corps, nevertheless ordered an all-out assault, and it almost succeeded. But he lacked the punch to break that final crust of enemy resistance, for his Stuka wings had been transferred south to take part in the stupendous battles raging along the approaches to Leningrad. On the final day of the German attack, Erich became platoon commander when the C.O. took a Degtyarev round through the lungs.

Winter descended early and harshly. Snow fell on the lines outside Murmansk as early as September 29. On October 9, the first gale came down from the polar north, picking up force as it roared over the unimaginable wastes of the Barents Sea, paralyzing all movement when it struck. The Mountain Corps scratched holes in the rock-hard soil and gave up all thought of advancing farther into Russia. And now, a burned-out husk of the elite formation it had been in June, it was being withdrawn.

Erich was startled out of his reverie by the noise of a shot. He looked to his right. A few yards from the road, a *Feldwebel* had just put a Luger bullet through the forebrain of a horse with a broken leg. As the horse flopped to its side, the blood on its muzzle already congealing in the cold, Erich could count the animal's ribs. The horse had been carrying mortar ammunition, and in a few moments the shells were passed out to the men in the column. Erich stuffed two rounds into one of his coat pockets and tried to forget about the extra weight that now pulled his steps to one side, upsetting the carefully maintained center of gravity he had worked out for himself during the march.

He felt a wave of pointless anger rising inside himself, and he let it come. Just when a man had worked things out, balanced all the elements of his discomfort in such a way as to keep functioning, something was always forced upon him that queered the equation, made it necessary for him to start all over again. The fear and horror of combat were bad enough, but he had come to realize that a man could be undone, ground to a powder, by an accumulation of small indignities, small unanticipated increments of pain, the one additional discomfort that could not be borne—like the one grain of sand that tips the scales microscopically out of plumb. Suddenly there you were: the limit. Your limit. He could feel the brittle impress of it, as though he were leaning against a pane of glass, just one additional burden away from its shatterpoint.

He snarled under his breath, closing his hands around the mortar shells in his coat, feeling their fins scrape two fresh raw lines of irritation into his skin, deepening the trace with every step, every new beat of friction that came up from the iron-hard roadbed.

Twenty meters from the road, he saw a broken-down truck. He turned to the man beside him and said, in a voice loud enough to carry to most of the platoon: "I'm going into that truck and take a shit. Anybody got some spare paper?"

A private two ranks back passed up a folded square of newspaper. Erich thanked him and broke ranks. Once inside the truck's cab, he pulled the two mortar shells out, opened the door on the far side, and dropped them into a snowbank.

After all, he reflected as he trudged back to his place in line, it would not do to set a bad example for the men. Several marchers noticed, when he rejoined their ranks, that Lieutenant Ziegler was laughing to himself, but no one had the energy to ask what was so funny.

Irony was what was so funny. The irony of a man aspiring to the most dictatorial of civilian occupations who had always tried to suppress within himself a schoolboy's anarchistic delight in flouting authority.

Erich got his first conducting job, a "bottom rung" position as *répétiteur* with the Municipal Theater in Frankfurt, when he was nineteen. Better educated than most aspirants to the podium, he was still enmeshed in a system that, perhaps wisely, forced those who held such aspirations to learn the practical aspects of their craft in humble, indeed sometimes humiliating, circumstances. Although Erich chafed at this system, he understood its virtues and applied himself diligently, rehearsing choruses and soloists for opera productions, and, if he was lucky, getting to direct the offstage band during crowd scenes. But in his off hours, he could journey to hear the orchestras in Berlin, and occasionally to Dresden or even Leipzig, where the already-legendary Wilhelm Furtwängler was conductor of the famed Gewandhaus Orchestra.

By holding his ambitions, and his tongue, in check, Erich laboriously worked his way up to the relatively august post of third assistant, and achieved a signal success in the spring of 1932, when both the principal and assistant conductors of the municipal orchestra fell indisposed and he was called to lead his first public concert. The program had long been chosen: Pfitzner's Three Preludes from *Palestrina*, the second piano concerto of Rachmaninoff, and the Ninth Symphony of Schubert. Erich had two days to prepare, but he was more than ready.

Erich would later remember little of the event itself, for it passed in a dreamlike state. At least he felt no stage fright, protected from it by the conviction that he was about to do what he had been born to do; when he actually strode to the podium, gave the downbeat, and heard the orchestra come in together, in tune, and with feeling, all he could think was: Well, it *works!*

He was not even conscious of the applause at the end, which was generous if not rapturous, and scarcely aware of the embraces and handshakes backstage. The moment that he remembered with diamond-bright clarity, however, came when the dressing room was almost empty and he had relaxed enough to light his first cigarette since intermission. He glanced up from the smoke and saw standing at the door a tall, broad-domed gentleman with immense penetrating eyes and long, gangling arms, whom he recognized immediately as Wilhelm Furtwängler.

"Maestro, I . . . I did not know you were in the audience!" Erich stammered.

Furtwängler smiled knowingly: "And a damned good

thing you didn't, I'll wager. I happened to be in town, auditioning a singer for one of my concerts next season, and saw an unfamiliar name on the program tonight. One needs to keep abreast of the competition, you know, so here I am. My congratulations, young man. You did exceedingly well for your first time. The Pfitzner work was especially lovely, I thought."

"I heard the composer rehearse it in Berlin, many years ago, and it made a deep impression. How was the Schubert?"

"You won't be ready to do that properly for another ten years. But if you don't keep trying, you'll *never* be ready to do it. No matter: you will keep doing it, I know. You've tasted blood, now. So, good luck to you, and if I can ever be of service, here is my card, and my private number in Leipzig."

Despite generally decent reviews and a good response from the musicians, Erich was not scheduled for an orchestral concert the next season. By successfully stepping in for the regular conductor, he had aroused that colleague's suspicions, and so he was consigned to the same routine for yet another year.

Two months into the season, suffocating under that routine and acutely conscious, despite his youth, of time slipping away from him, he learned that the assistant conductor of the Bremen Opera had fallen seriously ill and would be unable to fulfill his duties for a year or more. He heard this from a sympathetic orchestra member, confirmed it with a few telephone calls, and was on the next train to Leipzig, where he solicited, and obtained, a letter of recommendation from Furtwängler. Armed with this, he booked air passage to Bremen, and was first in line when the job officially came open. It transpired that the principal conductor of the Bremen Opera was a Furtwängler admirer, and Erich was engaged on the spot, beating out ten older and more experienced musicians who applied, in some cases, only hours later.

During the winter of 1932–1933, he labored in Bremen. On one hand, he was pleased to be in a more prominent location, working with a slightly better orchestra and with regular conducting assignments every week; on the other hand, he was stuck, all that spring, conducting performance after performance of the wildly popular operetta *The Merry Widow*. Erich had no prejudice against light music, and at first was simply delighted to have a solid, responsive orchestra under his command. He conducted the first two performances as enthusiastically as if he were doing *Die Meistersinger.* By the end of the fourth performance, he was completely bored by the operetta, and tended to wave his stick without much enthusiasm. By the time he stepped out to do the tenth performance, he felt as though he were entering Purgatory in a tuxedo, and during one of the spoken-dialogue sections of the work, when he had nothing to do, he drifted off into daydreams, envisioning himself in the pit at Bayreuth, or standing, proud yet humble, before the Berlin Philharmonic. Gradually and at first unconsciously, he realized that the scene had gone on rather longer than usual; this insight was followed by the horrifying realization that the singers had repeated their cue lines several times, and he had not yet brought the orchestra in. He rallied his wits and had just lifted his baton, when the leading tenor, who had become red-faced with rage, suddenly threw his hat at the orchestra pit, shouted, "To hell with you, if you don't want to conduct it!" and stormed offstage.

There could be only one consequence for such a lapse, and Erich found himself, jobless, back in Berlin. Too ashamed to contact Furtwängler again, he sought help from his father's old friend, Hans Pfitzner. The old composer had heard of the incident in Bremen, but he dismissed it with a smile and a wave of his hand, saying: "It only proves you were not cut out to be a conductor of operettas—something you already knew when you were six years old."

Using his connections to the utmost, Pfitzner managed to land Erich in the competition for the post of conductor of the municipal orchestra in Lübeck, a medium-sized city north of Hamburg. There were four finalists, each better known than himself, but Erich got the job, largely on the strength of the orchestra's enthusiasm for his magnetic and unorthodox style of leadership.

Lübeck's orchestra was old enough to have some sense of

pride and tradition, and if it was, in the final analysis, a provincial ensemble, it was a good one, and under Erich it became better. During his first year he planned a full eight-concert season, won good notices for his work, and increased the season to ten concerts the following year. He was so happy to be doing what he had always wanted to do that he paid only scant attention to developments in the world beyond the concert hall, although he did scan the papers with more than usual attention on February 1, 1933, the day after an odd little man named Adolf Hitler was installed as chancellor of Germany.

By 1937, Erich was a seasoned orchestra conductor, with a portfolio of good reviews and several widely reported premieres to his credit. In the spring of that year, he learned that the prestigious Mannheim Orchestra was looking for a new conductor, and that a man was required who was both steeped in the basic repertoire and knowledgeable about what the competition guidelines ambiguously termed "contemporary developments in the world of German music." Assuming this last bit referred to musical developments, Erich chose as his competition piece Hindemith's *Mathis Der Maler* symphony, a challenging but accessible work he had already led, to acclaim, in Lübeck.

He arrived in Mannheim at the appointed time and registered for the competition. When he informed the judges that he wished to conduct the Hindemith work, he was startled to see their expressions of unease.

"What's the matter, gentlemen? Is there a law against conducting the music of one of Germany's finest living composers?"

"Not yet," muttered the man who grudgingly took his application. Another official took him aside a few minutes later and gave him some friendly advice: Perhaps Herr Ziegler would get a clearer idea of how things were if he attended the panel discussion that evening at the municipal concert hall?

Erich had been prepared to do some last-minute studying that night, but he knew the Hindemith score well enough already, so he decided to follow the man's advice—clearly, something was amiss here.

The panel discussion was entitled "The Cleansing Flame—New Arts for the New Reich!" The panelists consisted of Hans Johst, a notoriously corrupt theater critic from Berlin; Adolf Hauptmann, a barely competent painter of romantic genre subjects, and a sleek, oily-haired young man named von Golzer, who was introduced as "one of the Reich's most promising young conductors." Erich had never heard of the fellow, but he knew, vaguely, of the other two men: hopeless mediocrities who had suddenly been given elevated status and bureaucratic power within the new National Socialist regime.

Each man in turn addressed himself to the subject of "artistic purification" in the theater, the visual arts, and music. There was a great deal of anti-Semitic rhetoric and much castigation of modernism, which, by convolutions of logic Erich found impossible to follow, was equated with the dreaded Bolshevik Menace. While Erich had every reason to share the Nazis' hatred of Bolshevism, he thought the connecting logic of their argument transparently spurious.

Things did indeed become clearer when the tall, almost cadaverous von Golzer rose to speak. He condemned all music written by Jewish composers, going all the way back to Mendelssohn, for its nefarious racial impurities, and attacked even more vehemently the "decadent, degenerate" styles of Hindemith, Schoenberg, and a host of other living composers. It surprised Erich not one bit to learn, from the leaflet he picked up at the door, that von Golzer was another finalist for the Mannheim conducting job.

At his first rehearsal the next day, Erich addressed the orchestra in a voice loud enough to carry to everyone who might be sitting in the darkened auditorium. "Gentlemen, my name is Erich Ziegler, and I am a conductor, not a politician; you are my colleagues and you are artists, not politicians. It may be true that, as the American gangsters would say, 'the fix is in,' but I am asking you, as proud German artists, to play with me today, and at the concert, a magnificent work by one of our nation's greatest living musicians, and to play it with all your hearts. Are you with me in this?"

There was a moment of silence, and then, emerging from the back rows of the violins, there came a rhythmic tapping of bow against music stand; the sound spread throughout the orchestra until it became a raucous din. Dimly aware of a certain amount of consternation in the hall behind him, Erich conducted one of the finest rehearsals of his career, aware that the orchestra was giving him one hundred percent cooperation.

His performance, too, was considered, by the musicians at least, the finest of the competition, even though the auditorium, at its conclusion, was spotted with pockets of nervous silence. The next morning, the new music director of the Mannheim Orchestra was announced. To no one's surprise, it was von Golzer, who had conducted some hyperthyroid Wagner performances, accompanied by some of the worst mugging and most exaggerated gestures Erich had ever seen from a colleague.

That night they bivouacked near a pile of raw lumber, hauled up from the tree line near Ivalo, the first Finnish settlement big enough to be shown on a map. There was enough for one big bonfire, although it took several splashes of petrol to kindle self-sustaining flames from the frozen wood. Erich reckoned that the wood, and the gasoline needed to ignite it, amounted to a full truckload—just to keep the horses in his company from freezing to death for one night. The supply columns devoured themselves as they moved north. God alone knew what dribbles of food and fuel finally got through at the far end, in that bitter and forlorn place they had left.

By the time the column fell out for the night, many of the packhorses were close to death. Groups of men clustered around the shivering animals, removed their burdens, then pushed them as close to the fire as they would go. Several animals, no longer strong enough to stand on their own, were supported by soldiers—literally held upright by dozens of hands, until the fire thawed them out and they could stand without help. One bony nag fainted as soon as it was left un-attended. It fell into the flames and began shrieking hideously. A dozen cursing men fought through its hooves, pulled it free, and finally shot it; then they butchered, roasted, and ate it.

When the horses had been thawed, it was the men's turn; they clustered around the fire. A crude meal was prepared in one of the tents, a roll call taken, and a frostbite inspection announced for any man who could not distinctly feel both feet. By the time Erich had finished his duties, he was dizzy.

Three days later, the column finally reached the tree line, just north of the Lapp settlement of Ivalo. Here were log huts, hot food, ample firewood, a field hospital, and the first sacks of mail to reach the unit since August. Erich had a packet of letters from his family and, rather surprisingly, a birthday card signed by fifteen members of the Mannheim Orchestra; it pleased him greatly to know that they missed him enough to make the gesture. After reading through the letters twice, and luxuriating in the first hot shower he had taken in two months, Erich slept for fourteen hours.

He was awakened by the urgent pumping of a *Feldwebel*'s hand on his shoulder. Swallowing against the dryness in his throat, he struggled upward in darkness until a flashlight beam smote his eyes.

"Sorry to waken you, *Oberleutnant*, but you're wanted right away at regimental headquarters."

"Christ, it's the middle of the night!"

"A little past oh-seven-hundred, sir; it's morning, I'm afraid."

For a moment, he had successfully forgotten where he was. He snarled at the sergeant, cursing him, then regretted it. What a difference, he thought, a hot shower and a full night's sleep makes: yesterday, he would not have entertained any regret. He apologized to the man for snapping at him, then said: "I'll be along as soon as I get my boots on, pro-vided you can tell me just where regimental headquarters hap-pens to be. There are a hundred cabins in the woods out there."

"It's the big hut on the road, south of here about a quarter mile, sir. The one with the staff car and the motorcycles in front."

When Erich entered the building, a smartly dressed staff sergeant saluted him crisply.

"You're expected, sir," the man responded after Erich identified himself. "That second door on the left—please go in."

Erich marched on strangely clean-swept planks past a line of flickering switchboards and bespectacled clerks pecking at typewriters. Everything here seemed efficient, busy, purposeful; yet at the other end of this pipeline, Prausnitz and his wretched Greek mules would be huddled in their rock-walled pits, cursing their luck and wondering when someone was going to send them some timber, some mail, some proper winter clothing.

He squared his shoulders, tried not to think of how shabby his uniform must look, and knocked on the door before him. Whatever they wanted him for, it was going to be a surprise, and surprises, in the army, were not usually to be desired. At least there was one thing in his favor: it was not likely that they could assign him to any place worse.

"*Kommen Sie!*"

A square-jawed officer with salt-and-pepper hair rose to meet Erich. A bank of cigarette fog hung over the room at breast height. The officer's desktop was covered with one-to-one-million-scale maps of Finland and the Baltic regions of the Soviet Union. Long sinuous lines ran the length of the maps, punctuated with sharp little arrows, all dated to show the front line, from the Barents Sea to Estonia, at various stages of the campaign's development since June. A sawed-off 88-mm shell case, overflowing with yellowed cigarette stubs, served as both paperweight and ashtray. The officer, a colonel, extended his hand and bowed slightly.

"Good morning, *Oberleutnant*. I'm Klatt, Intelligence, Army Group North, attached to Falkenhorst's Norwegian Command. I trust you've been able to recover from the rigors of your recent march?"

Erich searched the man's face. The smile Klatt put on for

him seemed warm enough, and his slightly mannered way of speaking was probably what one encountered in most intelligence officers, in most armies. Almost against his will, Erich found himself enjoying the prospect of polite conversation. He would never again take even the most modest pleasures of civilization for granted.

"As well as could be expected, *Herr Oberst*. It's amazing what a difference hot food and clean sheets can make."

"Just so. Did you know, Lieutenant, that during the Winter War, the Finns listed enemy field kitchens as the highest-priority targets for their raiding parties? Even ahead of radios, observation posts, or ammo dumps? Can you imagine—handing out a medal to a man because he single-handedly knocked out a kitchen!"

"Yes sir, I think I can understand that very well." Instantly, Erich's guard came up. Another rear-echelon asshole, after all. "Where I've just come from, Colonel, a hot meal can mean the difference between finding the will to keep on living, or just wandering off into the snow and falling asleep."

Klatt's expression changed. He noted the sharpness of Erich's reply, but instead of bristling at it, holding up the shield of his rank, he seemed to slump a bit in his chair.

"I had heard it was bad up there, but everything I've seen and heard since you people arrived yesterday has made the picture worse. You and your men, I'm afraid, were victims of over-optimism generated a thousand miles away. I'm in a position to pass the truth on to those in power, but I cannot make them act upon it."

Klatt observed Erich for a moment with sympathetic hazel eyes, appraising him just as intensely as Erich was appraising him. Abruptly, he tossed the cigarette pack across the table, sat down, and opened a dossier.

"Sit down, Ziegler, and have a smoke. Take the pack, if you like. I have your army records here, and I've spent some time going over them. Let me just touch on a few points with you. You are thirty years old, unmarried, and you are by profession a musician, correct?"

"Yes, *Herr Oberst.* More precisely, a conductor. I am, or rather I was, director of the Mannheim Orchestra."

"A fascinating profession. Let's hope the war gets over with soon, so you can return to it."

Klatt turned his eyes back to the dossier, made a notation, tapped ash into the shell casing.

"You were assigned to a mountain division because you are an alpinist and a skier. And according to this information, you are something of an expert on Finnish culture."

"Sir?"

"It says right here: 'has special knowledge of Finland and its culture.' Is that true or not?"

Erich had the distinct feeling that he was being nudged toward an affirmative answer. He had been in the army long enough to know the smell of special duty. Whatever they wanted him to do, it could only be better than squatting in a cave three hundred miles north of the Arctic Circle.

"Not long before the war, I wrote an article about one of the symphonies of Sibelius, the Finnish national composer. During the course of my research, I naturally learned something about the country."

Klatt chuckled dryly: "Paavo Nurmi and all that, eh?"

"Sir?"

"Paavo Nurmi, the Olympic runner. Surely you remember?"

"Oh yes, of course. Seems a long time ago."

"Indeed it does. There's nothing in your file about it, and I feel compelled to ask: You don't by any chance speak the language, do you?"

"Finnish? I'm afraid not, sir."

"Not surprising. Nobody does. Bloody gibberish. Well, it's not that important—all their officers seem to speak German anyhow. You will make an effort to learn at least conversational Finnish, though, won't you?"

Erich sat straighter in his chair; a sudden vision had entered his mind of staff duty in Helsinki—by all accounts a clean and civilized capital.

"I take it, then, that I'm being considered for a new assignment here in Finland?"

"Come around to this side of the desk, Ziegler, and I'll show you what's being considered."

Viewed from above, the upper half of Finland had an outline similar to a bear's hide nailed on a wall: two long forepaws with a round head between them. The left paw reached into the narrow rugged curve at the top of Norway; the right paw reached northeast, toward Petsamo, a dismal but strategically vital port on the White Sea, hard by the nickel mines on the Rybachi Peninsula. That paw had been amputated in 1940 when, as part of the settlement of the Winter War, the Soviets had annexed it all the way down to the shoulder. Now, thanks largely to the exertions of the German mountain troops, the paw had been grafted back on, swollen with newly occupied territory.

Just to the right of the line marking the farthest German advance, the ice-free port of Murmansk was circled in red. Like a great artery, a thick red line ran due south from the port, through wilderness, to the White Sea port of Kandalaksha, thence along the White Sea coast, then south again, through a region filled with irregularly shaped lakes, until it tied into the rail network that fed Leningrad—a total distance of 850 miles.

Klatt tapped the long red line with his forefinger. "The Murmansk Railroad. The sole lifeline from Russia's only year-round overseas port. If the United States enters the war, which in my opinion is only a matter of time, it is through Murmansk that any significant Allied aid would come to the Russians. We can make them pay dearly for it, of course, but if they're willing to lose a lot of ships, enough will get through to make the Reds a lot harder to defeat.

"If we are able to take Moscow before Christmas it won't matter so much ... but if we aren't, there will be another, even larger campaign next spring. We have hurt the Reds terribly, but in order to crush them for good, we must prevent Allied aid from making up any of their losses.

"The problem becomes one of how to do that with the resources on hand. Here, on the Arctic Front, we have Dietl's Mountain Corps, of which your own regiment is a part. You know at first hand the reasons why they haven't taken Murmansk. Two hundred and fifty miles to the south is the German Thirty-sixth Corps. They have advanced to within fifty miles of their objective, Kandalaksha, but they're unable to advance farther for the same reasons your people could not: terrible weather, no roads, and terrain that seems to consist entirely of obstacles to military operations.

"Down on the Leningrad Front, on September third, the Finnish Karelian Army reached the Murmansk Railroad and since then has managed to cut about one hundred forty miles of line. Unfortunately, our aerial reconnaissance indicates that the Russians are already building a spur line around that bulge, and when it's finished, the Finns' accomplishment will be negated. It seems that the only way to knock out Murmansk completely is to drive all the way to the White Sea, and utterly cut the port off from the Russian mainland.

"The only force in a position to do that is here, in the middle of Finland, the Finnish Third Corps. At last report, they were still creeping forward here and there. We have no operational control over them, only advisory and liaison roles with the various divisional headquarters. The Finns insist the Third Corps is not strong enough to cut the railroad, but is that true, or are they simply holding back for political reasons? And if they aren't strong enough to do it now, could they be *made* strong enough, with a modest infusion of German firepower?"

Klatt's finger moved south again, came to rest on the besieged city of Leningrad.

"It is not common knowledge yet, but the führer has decided not to assault Leningrad directly. We have a noose drawn tight around the city, and he feels that we can now simply starve them into submission. I hope he's right. But in case things don't work out, it will become necessary to attack the city after all, and in that case, it will be vital to have the Finns assault from the north and northwest, so that the defenders will be stretched as thinly as possible.

"At the moment, however, the Finns show no inclination to press their advance very far beyond the positions they hold today. They've recaptured all the land they lost to the Russians in 1940 and have driven some distance beyond the old border, to good defensive ground. Now they're just digging in, and Mannerheim's headquarters is resisting all our arguments for renewed offensive action.

"The point of this lecture, Ziegler, is that if things do not go as well for us next year as we plan, we may have to light a fire under our Finnish friends, to get them to look beyond their own national objectives to the greater goal of crushing Bolshevism once and for all. And if the present Finnish government balks at that, well, it may become necessary to encourage those who would like to replace Mannerheim and his clique."

Erich's mind was strained from trying to visualize the reality behind those looping arrows of grand strategy, moving across the map along invisible vectors of political will and national pride. It required some effort to relate these lofty considerations to his immediate memories of the Arctic Front's desolate squalor.

"You mean, we would engineer a *coup d'état?*"

"I mean that we would look with favor upon the assumption of power by certain irredentist elements in the Finnish Army that are known to be more sympathetic to the goals of National Socialism than Mannerheim and his cronies. There's a summary in these notes I'm going to give you about the activities of some shadowy Fascist groups—the Lapua Movement, the Greater Karelia Society, they all have names like that. We don't know how large they are, or how influential, or how serious. And we need to know these things in case circumstances change."

Klatt looked Erich in the eye and flipped a casual index finger in his direction.

"In order to take military advantage of any changes in the political situation, we need reliable information, firsthand information, often of the kind that cannot be obtained by formal methods. Perhaps someone who is already familiar with the Finns, someone who is basically sympathetic to them, might be able to work his way closer to them than a trained intelligence operative could do. We need someone who can gain their confidence—they're such a damned taciturn lot, don't you agree?—and, so to speak, take their temperature periodically. Orally, of course, ha-ha!"

Klatt laughed at his little joke.

"You're sending me to the Finns as a spy?"

"Oh nò, no, my dear lieutenant . . . or perhaps only in the most casual sense. A spy goes around counting gun emplacements and fuel dumps—we already know all of that stuff. What I want from you are informal reports on the *feel* of things: morale, political trends, opinions about Germany and about the war in general, about the Russkies, about the Finns' own will to fight. Officially, and in fact as well, you are also to be a liaison officer without portfolio, attached to the entire Third Corps' zone of operations. You will send regular monthly reports on conditions as you see them: what the Finns need in the way of equipment, how their tactics work, how they keep warm, how they design their latrines, and what they talk about over coffee. Especially that kind of information.

"Of course we do have a regular staff team at General Siilasvuo's headquarters, but that's where they have to stay. You, by contrast, will have, as it were, a roving commission, and you are under direct orders to report only to myself, and through me, to OKW Headquarters. You can go anywhere you like and see anything there is to see, and you'll have the papers to open any door. If you find a door they *won't* open, I want to know about that, too. The only time I want you to be loitering around their headquarters is when you put your reports into the mail pouch. Otherwise, I want you out with the troops, although that does not necessarily mean you'll have to stay in the front lines all the time—just follow your nose and send me any pertinent information, no matter how trivial it may seem. It's our job here to sift through it all and spot the important things, and believe me, sometimes they can seem minute to the untrained eye."

"If my eyes are so untrained, *Herr Oberst*, why do you entrust them with such a sensitive task?"

"Frankly, because I can't get anyone more expert than yourself. We're a low-priority front up here. But you'll do, I think, Ziegler, because you're not only intelligent, you're also generally sympathetic to the Finns—at least, you find their music congenial, and that's a key that might help unlock their culture, their way of *regarding* things. I want you to be like a sponge: soak it all up as you see it, then squeeze it back out for me onto paper."

Erich crushed his cigarette and studied the map once more. The land bordered by the Finnish Third Corps' zone of operations appeared to encompass about twenty thousand square miles of lake and forest, mostly uninhabited and virtually roadless on both sides of the border. It did not look any more hospitable than the fells of Lapland, but at least it was closer to civilization, and there would be plenty of firewood.

"Come, come, Ziegler, you've done your bit up here and you have a good combat record. I'm offering you a chance to perform a signal service for the Fatherland as well as a statistically better chance of staying alive long enough to resume your musical career."

"I don't mean to give the impression that I'm hesitant, sir. It's just . . . a lot to digest so suddenly. Of course I shall accept."

"Excellent!" Klatt reached into his desk and pulled out a thick buff envelope. "These are your official orders, including travel passes and special authorizations signed by both General Dietl and a member of Mannerheim's own staff—there is enough weight behind those signatures to get you into Heaven, if necessary. Your other orders, the 'unofficial' ones, are not of course written down, but you may consider them just as binding as the ones that are. You'll find inside as well a generous supply of Finnish marks, which you are free to spend at your own discretion, for the purpose of making friends and doing favors. The job also comes with a promotion to captain—the insignia are inside the packet; we'll catch up on the paper formalities later on."

Erich accepted the documents and shook hands with the colonel.

"Good luck, Captain Ziegler. I've arranged for a driver from the Third Corps to pick you up tomorrow morning at oh-eight-hundred hours—given the supply mess, you'll get there much faster by car than by train. Oh, there is one final thing . . ." Klatt reached into a wooden box lined with straw and held out a fine-grained presentation case embossed with a gold foil swastika.

"You should know that the führer himself has approved of this arrangement and that he is aware of your name. In fact, he selected you from a list of several candidates, largely I think on the basis of your musical qualifications. He adores classical music, I'm told, at least of a certain kind. Anyway, this was sent to you from OKW Headquarters, with his compliments."

Inside the case were two bottles of good brandy. Erich, who had not enjoyed a drop of alcohol for five months, turned the bottles under the light, examining them as though they were Mayan artifacts.

"I . . . don't know what to say, *Herr Oberst.*"

"I shall pass it along that you said 'thank you,' ha-ha-ha!"

Erich thought about sharing the bottles with someone, but he had no real friends among the other regimental officers, and if he just passed both bottles along to his platoon, there wouldn't be enough to do anyone any good. So he stayed in the cabin he had been assigned and methodically drank both bottles, which rendered him very drunk indeed.

About midnight, he stepped outside to urinate, got slugged by the cold halfway through his piss, and, quite unexpectedly, began weeping at the thought of Eberbach's death, convinced, with the ironbound logic of the inebriated, that if Eberbach were still alive, which might be another way of saying "if Erich Ziegler had been a more responsible platoon leader," the two of them could have killed the brandy together and this sudden pit of loneliness would not have opened up inside Erich.

In that moment his thoughts turned from Eberbach to a

far deeper wound, the killing of his father years earlier. On that very day he had decided to become a conductor. That was why he hated the Bolsheviks. As he lurched back toward the cabin, Erich mused over that day that had changed his life.

His father had been recognized throughout Europe as one of the great authorities on Greece and Rome, and his children, of whom Erich was the youngest and most susceptible, were indoctrinated from birth with a philosophically lofty, yet practically functioning overview of Western culture. His father was a product of a world and a time when no one was embarrassed to start the word "art" with a capital "A."

In his book-lined study, behind locked glass doors, Erich's father kept the artifacts he could not bring himself to donate to a museum: a metope frieze depicting the abduction of Europa, taken from the temple dig at Selinus, and a slightly cracked but still breathtaking amphora dug gently from the soil of Olympus itself. Elsewhere in the room were a number of classical *objets* (copies, to be sure, but the best that could be obtained): Apollo, curly-haired and self-consciously noble of brow; Hephaestus, vain, bearded, and smiling foxily to himself; and a rather massive bas-relief of the three Graces, deep in earnest conclave with one another. This was a piece that the famed director Max Reinhardt had once dubbed "Three Critics Comparing Notes for an Opening-Night Review."

The house of Professor Ziegler, director emeritus of the university's classics department, became known as one of those places where one went to see the cream of Berlin's artistic life. Poets and dramatists gave readings, painters came to sketch, musicians to give recitals.

Best of all, to young Erich, were the musicians. His mother had started piano lessons for him when he was five, and Erich had found the lessons tedious but tolerable. Only two years into them, however, he began to reveal a sudden and quite surprising facility for improvisation—whenever the mood was on him, awkward yet compelling melodies could be heard emanating from the drawing room, broken by sudden thunderous chord progressions, as though the boy was exploring the extremes of the instrument's expressive range and his own sensibilities.

Wilhelm Ziegler saw this musical flowering in his son and rejoiced; a devoted amateur all his life, he secretly worshiped those who practiced what he perceived as the most divine art of all. And could any nation on earth match Germany for its heritage of great musicians?

Wilhelm frequently took the children to operas, ballets, and concerts. While Erich's older siblings, Rosa and Oskar, went along dutifully, it was clear that neither of them possessed the depth or intensity of interest shown by Erich. Eventually, the concertgoing became a ritual shared almost exclusively between father and younger son.

One evening, Wilhelm gently patted his son's shoulder. "Listen to me. Tomorrow you and I shall enjoy a rare privilege. The composer Hans Pfitzner is rehearsing Beethoven's Ninth with the Philharmonic, complete with chorus, and he's gotten us passes into the hall. You have never heard this symphony before, have you?"

"No, Father. But I like Beethoven very much."

"Yes, I know you do. And so I envy you the discovery you will make tomorrow!"

The next morning, while Erich was dressing for the rehearsal, his brother, Oskar, and two of Oskar's friends were watching with binoculars from a second-story vantage point, keeping score of the various armed detachments they saw in the street and the number of cannon, armored cars, and ambulances that passed. "There goes a battery of seventy-sevens!" Oskar would cry, while one of his friends noted the fact under the proper column of data. "Now the Bolshies will catch hell!"

Since January 5, 1919, Berlin had been a city in turmoil. Rallying under the Spartacist banner, the city's numerous left-wing parties—ranging from disciplined Bolshevik cadres led by dozens of would-be Lenins to the politically muddled workmen who took up rifles because they could no longer afford bread—had seized all government buildings in the center of the capital. Machine guns mounted on the Brandenberger Tor had been firing down Unter den Linden. All was chaos and confusion; and on the outskirts of the city, battalions of the counterrevolutionary Freikorps were rumored to be assembling, with field artillery, to crush the uprising.

His mother, Adelheid, pleaded with her husband not to take Erich out of the house during such a dangerous time, but Wilhelm had spent an hour on the telephone that morning, ascertaining which parts of the city were dangerous and which were quiet, and he had mapped out a route which, he explained confidently, would get them to and from Philharmonic Hall in perfect safety.

When Adelheid insisted that the situation was still too violent and unpredictable for any route to guarantee safety, Wilhelm got as angry as Erich had ever seen him.

"Damn it, woman, my son is not going to miss his first chance to hear Beethoven's Ninth just because a bunch of verminous Bolshevik rabble have thrown up a few barricades! The Freikorps are already advancing into the city, and by the time the rehearsal is over, this whole grotesque uprising will be over as well. Now, our taxi will be here in five minutes, so I would appreciate it if you made sure that Erich has his shoelaces properly tied."

Berlin that morning was an even greyer city than it usually was in midwinter. Erich sat close to his father, bundled against the chill, and counted the blocks that went by. He had memorized the time it took to go from their house to every major concert venue in the city, and he was impressed by the devious route his father had selected. As Wilhelm had predicted, they avoided all roadblocks, although it seemed to Erich that every time he raised his eyes to look around, he saw groups of armed men, some wearing coal-scuttle helmets, others wearing civilian overcoats and workmen's caps. How, he wondered, did you know who was on which side? Sometimes, in the hazy distance, he saw smoke rising from buildings and heard, even through the rolled-up windows, the crackle of small-arms fire.

At the home of the Berlin Philharmonic, however, all was normal, all was apparently as it should be: the musicians unpacking their instruments, the concertmaster onstage, tuning, and the conductor in his Green Room, smoking a last cigarette before it was time to begin.

Hans Pfitzner had been a guest in the Ziegler house several times, so Erich recognized him right away: a tall, stoop-shouldered man with a sharp eagle's profile and long, spatulate fingers that made him appear to be sculpting the air when he conducted. Although his primary fame rested on his compositions—his *magnum opus*, the opera *Palestrina*, had premiered, triumphantly, only two years ago—he still had to make much of his living by conducting and teaching.

Pfitzner embraced Wilhelm when father and son entered the room. Kneeling, his bony knee joints cracking, he held out his long arms to Erich. "My young friend, you have grown since I saw you last!"

"Maestro, that was only two weeks ago," replied Erich, proud that he knew the proper form of address.

"In two weeks, an ambitious young man can grow a lot, if he tries! Now, Erich, your father tells me you have never heard the Ninth Symphony of Beethoven."

"No, sir."

Pfitzner smiled with much the same conspiratorial expression that Wilhelm had used the night before. "In that case, I envy you the discovery you are about to make."

This was a final rehearsal, so the conductor rarely interrupted things. The orchestra knew the music, and so did the chorus and the four soloists. Minor technical flaws were allowed to pass—what Pfitzner was after was the long arc of the symphony, the flow of its lines, the big bones of its physical power. So what Erich got to hear, to his measureless delight, was virtually a private performance, one given by the entire Berlin Philharmonic and the choir of St. Hedwig's Cathedral, just for the honorable Professor Ziegler and his spellbound son.

His father had to lead him backstage when the rehearsal was finished, for Erich only dimly perceived his surroundings. In the Green Room, Maestro Pfitzner was drying himself with a towel and helping himself to glass after glass of cold water.

"How did it go, Wilhelm?"

"Wonderfully, Hans."

Again, the conductor knelt and looked into Erich's face. "And you, young man, are you inspired now to write some music of your own?"

"No, Maestro. Because no one could ever write such music again."

"Well, then, perhaps if you study hard and master an instrument, you can play in this orchestra one day."

Again Erich shook his head. "I don't want to play in the orchestra. I want to conduct it."

Pfitzner laughed and rumpled the boy's hair. Wilhelm looked down at his son with a puzzled expression. He had never heard this ambition voiced before.

"Why a conductor, Erich?" he asked.

"Because then, I could *be* all the composers that I love, at least while I was conducting their music!"

Pfitzner thought this reply astonishingly perceptive from one so young, and said so. Still ebullient from the rehearsal, he suggested that they conclude the afternoon with tea and pastries. "I'm staying at the Kaiserhof Hotel, just a few blocks away. They have a good tea room there, with marvelous éclairs. Has Beethoven given you an appetite, Master Erich?"

"Yes, Maestro, he has!"

Both men lit cigarettes as they exited the concert hall, Erich between them, and began to cross the street. Ahead of them walked a slump-shouldered man in a threadbare overcoat—Erich would remember him clearly, down to the pattern of tweed in the cloth, down to the way he clutched two loaves of bread under his arm, probably all he could afford for his family due to rampant inflation.

A taxicab had stopped at the intersection, and behind it stood a horsedrawn cart. In the middle of the intersection, Erich heard what sounded like a string of firecrackers and saw the man in the overcoat begin to dance, small puffs of dust popping out from the back and side of his coat, the loaves of bread spilling from his hand. In an instant, his father's arms, surprisingly fierce, wrapped Erich tightly and hurled him behind the taxicab, just as the vehicle's windshield exploded in a bright cloud of glass. Pfitzner moved fast, too, belying the gawkiness of his tall, bony frame. The three of them huddled in a knot in the shadow of the vehicle, while bullets struck the pavement and whined off into space. Through the crack between the spare tire and the trunk, Erich could see the man in the overcoat, a look of astonishment frozen on his face, a loaf of bread at his side now soaking up blood like a long, thin sponge.

"Who's firing?" cried Pfitzner. "And for God's sake, why are they shooting at *us!*"

"Not shooting at us," puffed Erich's father, pointing down the avenue behind them, where a Freikorps detachment was wheeling a pair of field guns into position. In the opposite direction, where the rifle fire had come from, a Spartacist unit was holed up in an office building with provocative red flags hanging from the second-story windows and a flimsy barricade of carts, mattresses, and flour barrels piled around the entrance.

The two artillery pieces roared, so loudly that Erich clapped his hands over his ears and buried his head against his father's shoulder. After a dozen salvos, the Spartacist position was in flames and the red flags came down, to be replaced by a white one. Out came the ragged defenders, throwing their rifles into the street ahead of them. They looked exhausted, hungry, and terrified.

Wilhelm Ziegler turned his son's head and forced him to look at the dead man in the overcoat, then turned him around to face the helmeted, hard-eyed men of the Freikorps detachment.

"This is a hard lesson to learn right on top of Beethoven, boy, but one you must never forget. When there are barbarians everywhere, you must pick something to stand for and then be willing to fight for it. Otherwise, you'll just end up like that poor man, dead in the street, between two fires."

Erich did not see what was so barbaric about the disciplined Freikorps men until he realized that they were backing a truck into the street with a machine gun mounted in the back and that they were going to shoot down the unarmed Spartacists. He hid his eyes while the machine gun roared, and when he opened them again, there was a ghostly silence on the street, so profound that he could hear the last spent bullet casing land on the pavement, with the tinkling sound of a tiny bell.

The commander of the Freikorps unit, a lieutenant fearsomely decked out with crisscrossed bandoliers, three stick-grenades in his belt, and a broom-handled Mauser pistol in his hand, motioned for them to stand, indicating that all was clear. Wilhelm rose first, dusting off his trousers with slow, dignified motions.

Somewhere in the burning office building a hundred yards away, a dying Spartacist fired one last shot, aiming at the Freikorps commander. His bullet was intercepted by Wilhelm Ziegler's throat.

In the fifteen seconds of life remaining to him, Wilhelm struggled to rise, gesturing fervently at his son as though something urgent and profoundly important had just popped into his mind, but Erich never learned what it might have been because the flow of blood carried away his father's final words. All Erich heard was a ghastly phlegm-clotted sound, followed by one last pathetic sigh of relinquishment.

Three

Acrid coffee smote Erich's tongue like a branding iron. When the liquid reached his stomach, it triggered a gag reflex that required some effort to repress. He had a snarling hangover, and after the march down from the fells his body was in no condition to deal with such disagreeable symptoms.

The prospect of a long ride in a stuffy car with a total stranger, which had yesterday seemed rather agreeable, now loomed before him as another ordeal. He prepared as best he could, forcing down several mouthfuls of bread in order to put something between the coffee and the lining of his stomach.

Klatt had been looking after him. When the headquarters orderly had prodded him awake at 0700, his bag had already been packed, the document folder neatly positioned on top; his uniform had been cleaned and his boots and sidearm belt polished to a gloss.

By the time the same orderly came in from the mess hall kitchen, toting a musette bag full of sandwiches and two warm bottles of beer—"Compliments of Colonel Klatt"— Erich had managed to put down a passable breakfast and had recovered from the most purgatorial effects of the brandy. He rewarded himself with the day's first cigarette. There was just time enough to savor it before the orderly reappeared for a third time.

"*Herr Ziegler,* the Finnish driver is here."

Outside it was still dark. Of course. Erich paused at the door of the mess hall, taking a final look around, breathing deeply. For once, the cold felt good; it peeled away one more layer of his hangover. He drank in the chill bluish clarity of the predawn air, sucking in lungfuls of icy vapor like a diver equalizing pressure. In the gloom around him, lanterns burned like medieval candles, their reflections glazed against surfaces of ice. Men crunched by, swaddled in greatcoats, trailed by plumes of breath. A supply column was moving up the Arctic Highway: horses' hooves chimed softly on the ice, runners sighed beneath sledges full of ammunition—the most mechanized army in the world was, on this front, reduced to moving its supplies the same way the Mongols had done in the Dark Ages.

Swinging away from the supply column, Erich saw the waiting staff car, an aging Ford camouflaged in whitewash. He noted with some relief that it was a four-door model; if he outranked the driver, he could at least manage some additional sleep on the back seat. Behind the steering wheel, in a pool of shadow, bobbed a glowing cigarette tip. Erich had never had his own staff car before, and because of the nature of his new assignment, he wanted to start off doing things by the book. Should he stand there and wait for the driver to notice him, should he rap commandingly on the window to get the man's attention, or should he establish an informal tone from the start by simply sliding into the back seat?

As he approached the car, the driver met him halfway by emerging, throwing a parade-ground salute, and smartly swinging open the rear door. Erich slid in. The car was, to his relief, not overheated, although the air was thick with the smell of coarse tobacco. The driver returned to his seat and spoke in the throaty voice of a heavy smoker.

"*Hyvää päivä, Herra Kapteeni! Puhettiko Suomea?*"

"I beg your pardon?"

The man switched to passably good German. "I said:

'Good morning, Captain. Do you speak Finnish?', which of course you do not, as I expected. Not surprising. Nobody does except us Finns, and even we sometimes don't know what to make of it. No matter—I'll teach you a few words as we travel. My name is Eino Pekkanen, master sergeant. I'm your driver, obviously, until we get to where we're going, and after that I'll be your unofficial *aide-de-camp*, guide, translator, Finnish teacher, whatever the situation requires."

"Your German is good, Sergeant."

"You'll have no trouble on that score, sir. All the officers speak it and most of the noncoms as well. Everyone who wants to graduate from high school has to be fluent in a second language—otherwise, commerce with the outside world would be impossible."

"I see. Well, I suppose it would help if I could learn at least enough to read the signs—wouldn't want to take a wrong turn and end up in Russian lines."

"No sir, for a fact you would not. But it happens sometimes, out in the forest, where there aren't any signs."

"How do you know where the enemy is in such terrain?"

"You can smell him sometimes; trees don't smell like sweat and garlic. And sometimes you can just feel where he is."

Erich offered the man a cigarette. "Okay, Sergeant, where are we going and how long will it take to get there?"

"First, you have to present your credentials to General Siilasvuo at his headquarters in Oulu, over on the Bothnian coast. Then, unless he wants to send you somewhere else, you might as well set up shop with my unit, the Third Division, about a hundred fifty kilometers due east of Oulu—that's about forty kilometers inside the Russian border. It should take three days by car, barring really bad weather or any unpleasant incidents. Speaking of that, Captain, do you have a weapon?"

"Only my sidearm, why?"

"Better take this into the back seat with you, just in case. I've got another one up here."

Pekkanen handed him a heavy, stubby submachine gun, a 9-mm Suomi with a seventy-round drum magazine. Erich carefully placed the weapon on the floor, muzzle pointing toward the door.

"Just in case of what?"

"Oh, the Russians have started dropping parachutists behind the lines, just like they tried during the Winter War. Mostly Finnish-speaking Karelians, a lot of them from old-time Bolshevik families that got booted out after our civil war in 1918. They're nothing more than a nuisance—most of them come down in the middle of bloody nowhere and just wander around until they freeze to death. Still, this is the only supply route in this part of Finland, and it's only a matter of time until even the Russians figure out that it's a good target for a raid. By the way, the safety catch is behind the trigger guard and if you have to use it, aim low—the barrel jerks up like a sonofabitch when the gun's on full automatic."

Having digested that information, Erich informed the sergeant that, parachutists or no parachutists, he was going back to sleep. As he drowsed, lulled by the purr of tires on snow, he remembered the music of Sibelius, and made a silent wish that, when he awoke, the landscape would look like Sibelius's Finland, not like that bleak lunar place he had come from.

Erich opened his eyes to full daylight. When he sat up, he was surprised to see that the forest had temporarily yielded to open piedmont. They were driving beside a wide lake, distantly fringed by a line of blue-black trees. A small cluster of farm buildings and fishing shacks nestled on the shore. The scene was a study in grey: the sky, softly lit, was the color of a gull's belly; the lake water was a tone darker, shaded with a touch of aluminum blue and skimmed with thin eggshell-white plates of ice; the farm buildings were a rougher, seasoned, woolly-textured grey, streaked with the season's first tentative snowfall. Long plumes of smoke, curling fantastically in the air, spoke of occupancy. The only dramatic change in color within the panorama framed by the car window was the dark jagged line of the distant forest, a long horizontal brushstroke.

Gradually, the road followed the curve of the lakeshore

until the water narrowed and the forest closed in again: majestic blue-green firs and massive arctic pines, their boughs dusted with snow. The trees were closely spaced and the ground between them was a mass of matted, snow-softened undergrowth. It was possible to see individual trees only to a depth of four or five meters back from the road; beyond that, the dense interweave of snowy branches seemed to blot the daylight so that the deeper reaches of the forest were thick with an impenetrable marbled gloom.

This was the way Erich had expected Finland to look. He had been almost offended to find himself in that country, yet stuck in the barren, lunar terrain of Lapland, where nothing grew larger than a few niggardly stands of waist-high shrubs. He liked the idea of these vast northern forests, so much deeper, darker, and wilder than the woods of mainland Europe.

"Sergeant Pekkanen, how long have I been asleep?"

"It's a little past midday, sir. We've come about a hundred kilometers. Would have come farther, but we had to pull over a few times for supply columns to pass."

"Lunchtime, then."

He handed Pekkanen one of Klatt's sandwiches and fumbled in vain for some means to open the beer bottles. At the Finn's suggestion, he removed the magazine from his Suomi and used the steel feeder lips as an opener. That worked perfectly. Erich handed a foaming bottle of pilsner to the driver, saying: "You're a fountain of esoteric but useful knowledge, Sergeant."

"Yes sir. I guess that's why they gave me this job."

After refueling at a supply depot in a tiny village called Sodankylä, they continued down the Arctic Highway, bearing south and slightly west. They crossed the Arctic Circle at dusk and by nightfall they were in the little city of Rovaniemi. In peacetime the gateway to Lapland, it was now transformed into a garrison town of much bustle and officiousness. True to their advance billing, the papers Klatt had given Erich worked wonders. One glance at the signatures thereon was enough to transform the bureaucratic hostility of a quartermaster into virtual fawning; within moments, they were shown to warm billets, VIP ration cards clutched in their hands. A few discreet inquiries also netted them a bottle of fiery Swedish *aquavit*, which the two men took to a table in the officers' mess after supper. They had found each other to be agreeable company during the long, monotonous ride and, having exhausted their stock of small talk about the war, they now proceeded to speak of personal matters. Erich sketched his own background quickly, concentrating on his musical career. Pekkanen seemed especially interested when Erich mentioned his discovery of the Finnish composer, Jean Sibelius; although he professed to have little knowledge of classical music, he certainly knew who the composer was. Everyone in Finland did, he told Erich.

Erich finished his own narrative rather hurriedly, for he was much more interested in what his companion had to say. After all, he had been inside the borders of Finland since late June, but Pekkanen was the first Finn he had seen since the border guards who had waved him in on the day the campaign began.

Erich learned that his new companion was slightly older than himself, thirty-two, and that he was a reservist, a Winter War veteran who had been recalled during the general mobilization of May 1941. In peacetime, Pekkanen was a foreman in a locomotive repair shop in the industrial city of Tampere. His father, Erich was surprised to learn, had been in one of the Red militia units during the Finnish Civil War of 1918, and had died in a prison camp during the influenza epidemic of the following year—along with thousands of other internees. Pekkanen's voice betrayed no residual bitterness when he spoke of these things.

"But wasn't Field Marshal Mannerheim, the same *generalissimo* who's running the show in Finland today, the man responsible for those deaths?"

Pekkanen shrugged. "No one was responsible; everyone was responsible. It was terrible in those days, Captain. In the remote parts of the country, there was cannibalism. The war was bitter, but it did not last long as such things go. As for

Mannerheim, no question but that he has ice in his veins, but his way of handling the whole business was quite pragmatic: shoot the Bolshevik leaders and send everybody else back to work as soon as possible. But the flu epidemic struck while things were still chaotic, during the winter, when there was already no food to spare and people's resistance was low. Most of those who were in the internment camps just stayed there—they had no way to travel and many of them had no homes to return to. And they died there by the thousands. My father, if he had survived that winter, would have returned to his factory and resumed life as he had left it when he picked up a rifle. But he would have fought politically for the same ideals he fought for in the Red militia.

"It's hard to describe the mood of those days. We were a brand-new country, and all of a sudden we were free. There was a feeling in the air that we finally had a chance to shape our own destinies, after centuries of being either a Swedish vassal or a Russian doormat. Now we were *Finns*, all of us, Red and White alike."

Pekkanen leaned forward and took a stubby, murderously harsh Klubbi cigarette from the pack on the table.

"You know, when the Russians invaded in 1939, they brought with them into the forest whole brass bands and truckloads full of propaganda posters. They actually expected a workers' uprising inside Finland, actually believed some kind of huge fifth column would spring up to greet them. But it didn't happen. All the die-hard Bolsheviks left the country in 1918, after Helsinki was recaptured by the Whites; they resettled in Leningrad or in Soviet Karelia. All that was left here were *Finns*. And Finns will never submit to the Russians, never! The Russians are pigs!"

"Brave pigs, Eino," amended Erich, using the Finn's first name to signal the informality he already felt for the sergeant.

Eino swallowed some liquor and thought it over. Then he struck the table with a large red-knuckled fist. "Okay, brave pigs! But still pigs!" The two men clinked glasses and drank to the brave pigs.

Eino Pekkanen had mild blue eyes that never seemed to

lose their placid clarity even when the rest of his features showed strong emotion. The long winters had fatigued the flesh around those eyes, however, and given him middle-aged pouches and lines. His sandy hair was thinning in two even crescents back from his lined forehead. He also had quite a capacity for liquor; had their supply been adequate for the task, he showed every sign of being able to drink Erich under the table. Like rational men, however, they nursed the bottle until closing time, and woke up relatively free from after-effects.

From Rovaniemi they drove to the port of Oulu. The lead-grey expanse of the Gulf of Bothnia—peppered here and there with small armed cutters and intracoastal steamers—stretched out on their right side for most of the journey. Once in Oulu, they reported to the headquarters of the Finnish Third Corps, General Siilasvuo commanding. As they parked, just before reentering the embrace of military protocol, Eino turned to Erich and said: "Captain, I know those magical documents of yours can get us a nice bed for the night, but if you'd permit me to ask a favor . . . There is a family living not too far from here, in the forest, the widow of a friend of mine who was killed in thirty-nine, and her children. I haven't seen them for more than a year, and I know they could put us up for the night. It isn't far out of our way, and it would mean a lot."

"Well, all right, provided I'm not required to stay here overnight for some reason."

Erich was welcomed decently but perfunctorily, and given still more travel papers and passes, sufficient in their authority to permit him to obtain transportation, provisions, and assistance anywhere within the Third Corps' sector, provided no overriding military priority got in the way. He was introduced to General Siilasvuo—a tall man who radiated wintry authority—and then left pretty much to fend for himself.

Armed with Erich's papers, Eino shepherded him to the Finnish quartermaster depot and had him outfitted in a snow-suit, a sheepskin vest, fur-lined gauntlets, and waterproof boots made from reindeer hides. They also bluffed their way into possession of two loaves of bread, some crackers, a wedge of utilitarian cheese, and a few grams of coffee. These, Eino assured Erich, would be treasures indeed to the family they were about to visit.

Winter night was full upon the forest when they reached their destination—a backwoods homestead far down an ice-covered wagon road. The last few kilometers had been like a journey through a dreamworld: the road glistening arrow-straight between two dense walls of trees, utterly black except where they were mottled with snow—a landscape whose rhythm, as it flowed by on either side of their headlights, was so unvarying as to verge on the hypnotic. Although Eino assured him that this was a community of some two hundred woodsmen and their families, Erich saw no sign of habitation until they reached the slightly decrepit cabin, its few small windows softly lit by oil lamps.

As they crunched over the patchy snow, Eino called out a greeting. His words drifted off into the trees on ghostly hints of echo. Erich, following behind, found the dark looming forest oppressive, like something out of Grimm. He was relieved when the cabin door opened and a weak shaft of light shot out across the snow.

Then Eino ran forward and embraced a woman in the doorway. Behind her stood two children—a boy perhaps eight and a girl verging on adolescence. Erich shuffled into the cabin, which was agreeably warm and smelled pleasantly of porridge, and was introduced. At a table made from scrubbed pine planks, the woman placed two extra bowls. The bread and cheese were parceled out, and the coffee, which the woman regarded as though it were the dust of jewels, was prepared on the hottest part of the stove.

As they ate, Erich, who could take little part in the conversation, studied the sturdy, heavy-breasted woman. She was now of indeterminate age, but clearly she had once been a beauty. Her clear blue Nordic eyes remained vital, but the rest of her face showed the effects of grief, hardship, and too many endless winters.

After dinner, the children retired quietly to a curtained alcove. There was a single remaining bedroom, and the woman insisted that Erich sleep there.

"But where will she sleep?" he asked Eino.

"Where she always does—that platform behind the stove."

Erich looked where Eino pointed and saw an alcove large enough for two built into the firewall behind the hearth. A thin mattress and a down-filled comforter were neatly spread inside this domestic cave.

Inside his own small room, in addition to the bed, Erich found a hand-carved chest of drawers and a floor-to-ceiling tile stove. While Eino brought in a box of kindling and lit a fire inside the grate, Erich studied a small framed photo of a dark, strong-featured man with a stubborn trace of Mongol in the slant of his eyes. Eino's friend, no doubt, and the woman's husband.

"Just stoke the fire and throw a few fresh logs on before you go to sleep, Captain. The tiles will hold the heat until morning. I . . . I'll be up for a while yet, talking."

"I understand, Sergeant. Please thank the lady for me."

Erich crawled into the soft, voluptuous space beneath the comforter and shivered for a moment until the sleeping bag began to take his body heat. Once that had happened, he was submerged by comfort and passed into sleep quickly.

When he awoke, there was only a faint glow in the tile stove's grate and a deep chill in the room. He had neglected to reinforce the fire before falling asleep. But something other than the cold had wakened him. He listened to the night. A strong wind had begun to move through the forest. It washed over the wilderness in long mournful sighs.

Then something rap-rapped on his window. A dry tapping, just as though a private signal were being given by a cautious forefinger. For a disconcerting moment Erich thought it actually was someone seeking his attention, or perhaps some night-thing that dwelled here in this chaos of trees and bogs and nameless lakes. For, lying there in the darkness and cold, listening to the myriad crepitant forest sounds on the threshold of hearing, he could not doubt that the forest was alive out there, a vast alien organism, each tree forming a cell. It was a deliciously spooky thought, and Erich was heartened to discover that sixteen weeks of combat duty had not utterly dried up his capacity to experience wonder. Indeed, the chill in the air reminded him of that night so long ago when he had first crossed into the world beyond the known.

After Wilhelm Ziegler's death, the family moved to Munich, where they were taken in by Wilhelm's wealthy younger brother, Rudolf, an executive with the Bavarian Motor Works corporation. In addition to his luxurious town house on a street near the botanical gardens, Rudolf owned a big chalet-style "summer house" on the shores of the Tegernsee, one of the most picturesque lakes in all Bavaria.

That summer, Erich started the process of becoming, as Uncle Rudy liked to say, "more Bavarian than the Bavarians." During his childhood, he could only explore the territory close to the house, or go on family excursions to see the most famous sights, to visit what he thought of as "the guidebook places." As he grew older, he went farther and stayed longer. In time, he roamed the breadth of the Bavarian Alps, from Oberammergau in the west to unsurpassed Berchtesgaden in the east.

The basic tenor of these odysseys was established early, during the family's second summer at the Tegernsee, when Erich was a week away from his tenth birthday.

He had started walking after lunch, and by twilight he had covered several miles of shoreline. He was making a pilgrimage to one of his favorite places: a partly ruined Benedictine monastery that had been founded in the eighth century and had flourished as a center of learning for almost a thousand years, with one major interruption in the tenth century, when it was sacked by Hungarian invaders. The family had visited the place several times already, for one of the buildings had been converted into an attractive restaurant, and the dark, earthy beer—brewed on the premises by men whose families had passed on the secrets of the beverage for generations—

was, so Uncle Rudy averred, the finest to be had in all Germany.

When Erich came out of the forest, he skirted the restaurant and headed instead for his favorite part of the grounds, a partly ruined chapel whose stone walls still bore traces of the fires the steppe-riders had set nine hundred years ago. He had long wanted to come here alone, for he was certain—in the same way he was certain about becoming a conductor—that something would be revealed to him if he did, something that he would not be able to see if he was with the family.

A tremendous lavender stillness held the last fading light above the lake. A few lanterns showed on its surface, where boats glided homeward for the night, and lamps burned at a tourist hotel a mile to the south. But now that Erich had put the commercial part of the monastery behind him, he might as well have stepped back into the Middle Ages, so still, so hushed and timeless the air had become. He felt a deliciously keen sense of anticipation compounded by solitude. He sat on ancient rubble and breathed the deep mint green scent of the forest, waiting, but unsure what he was waiting for.

Time passed, until he could see only the sharp-cut outlines of the great peaks across the water. Suddenly, his skin prickled—not unpleasantly—and he realized that there was someone else beside him. An old man, bearded but straight-backed and firm of step, had come forth from inside the ruined building and now stood, quite comfortably it seemed, at the boy's side.

"Good evening, sir," Erich said, with the respectful inflections he had learned at home.

"*Ja*, it is that, young man. A beauty of an evening. We were drawn to this spot, I think, seeking the same view and the same silence."

"I like the restaurant, and my uncle says the beer is wonderful, but the spirit of the place is *here*, and not inside where all the people are."

"You are wise beyond your years, boy. Wiser than you probably know. When the ghosts come to say prayers at the monastery, this is where they come."

"What ghosts, sir?"

"Take your pick. These mountains are full of wandering spirits. In the twelfth century, the great troubadour poet, Walther von der Vogelweide, composed some of his greatest love lyrics here, in a place without women! He had no time for poetry when he was near the real thing, you understand!" The old man laughed, a deep and contented rumble that put Erich utterly at ease. Clearly, this encounter was what he had come here to experience. He did not doubt it then, or ever afterward.

"What other ghosts, grandfather? Tell me!"

"Aside from the poet? Well, the greatest of them all, as well as the saddest, is the ghost of poor King Ludwig. By the end of his reign, they called him a madman, and said that he had died by his own hand. Don't believe it—the bankers and politicians had him killed. They say he bankrupted the state by building castles and palaces, but the only ones he hurt were the rich. To the poor, he was not 'the Mad King' but 'the Dream King,' and on moonlit summer nights, he dressed himself as Siegfried and rode through the forest, giving gold to any poor family that offered him hospitality. In the winter, he went about in a great gold sleigh drawn by six Arabian horses as black as midnight, accompanied by outriders dressed in ermine robes and carrying immense sputtering torches that dripped fire like the tails of comets."

"I can almost see him," whispered Erich.

"When I was a child, I *did* see him! He had the eyes of a prophet, a great dreamer of dreams, someone not of this earth. No wonder he fell under the spell of Richard Wagner!"

"When I grow up, I shall be the conductor of a great orchestra, and I will dedicate a Wagner concert to the memory of the Dream King!"

"A conductor, eh? To be a great conductor, you too must be willing to dream great dreams—and I sense that you already do. But have you the kidney for it, boy? Timid men do not become great conductors. Just remember something that the great Gustav Mahler said: 'Where music is, the Demon must also be!' "

"What did he mean by that?"

"You'll know when you find your own demons."

"Where would I find them?"

"Don't worry; they'll seek you out. But if you want to know what one looks like, you might try visiting the Tatzelwurm Gorge, east of here near the Austrian border. It is one of the most interesting places in these mountains, I promise you."

More time must have passed than Erich realized, for there was a sharp new moon sitting above the lake now, and it glittered on the old man's eyes, turning them into the white, pupil-less orbs of a statue. With his beard and slightly mischievous expression, Erich realized with a start, his companion looked not unlike the statue of Hephaestus in his father's study.

Erich's attention was distracted at that moment by a rude but familiar sound: the squawk of the horn on Uncle Rudy's car. Suppertime had come and gone several hours earlier. Frantic with worry, Rudolf had been telephoning everyone within walking distance of the house, trying to ascertain whether anyone had seen young Erich. As it happened, one of the restaurant cooks had spied the boy earlier, just at twilight, while making a trip to one of the outside storage lockers.

His uncle's anger did not surprise Erich; he had been prepared to pay a price for this adventure. Two other things did, however, surprise him: one was the lateness of the hour— almost closing time at the restaurant—and the other was the fact that, when he turned around once more from the distraction of the horn, the old man had vanished.

"I was talking with someone old and wise," he answered when his uncle sharply questioned him.

"And where is this old, wise person?"

"He must be inside the chapel, Uncle. He was here only a moment ago."

But there was no one in the ruined chapel, and no one by the shore. Only the upturned hulls of pleasure boats, lined neatly against a thin beach of snowy pebbles, and beyond them, shimmering lemony slices of moonlight on the ebony surface of the lake.

"Well, who was this person, then? What was his name?" demanded Rudolf, brusquely propelling his errant adoptive son toward the waiting car.

"He was a ghost, I think," said Erich, totally in earnest. "These mountains are full of them, you know."

Setting his teeth against the chill, Erich rose from the womb-like warmth of the bed and stoked the fire with fresh chunks of split birch. Fully awake now, he went to the clear black square of the window and peered out. The night was winter-dark and moonless, with a snow-filled sky luminous and heavy above the treetops. The troll that had been tapping his window, he discovered, was a tiny ice-sheathed twig growing from a birch. He opened the window and grasped the tip with his fingers—his hand feeling as though he had dunked it into a bucket of ice water—and snapped it off so that it would not disturb him again.

Back in bed, he watched the newborn fire shadows dance on wooden rafters. Outside, in the kitchen, Eino was still talking softly with the woman. After a time, their voices stopped. Dimly, Erich heard them climb together into the sleeping cave above the hearth. The sounds that followed were discreet, yet clearly they were the sounds of a desperate, inevitable intimacy. Erich drifted to sleep half-embarrassed and half-envious. He awoke, to a chill blue daylight, with the first erection he had experienced in weeks.

Snow began to fall at midday: fat, wet flakes that piled up quickly on the trees. They were driving now due east, across the narrow waist of Finland, along a deserted road, through woods denser than any they had yet passed through—trees so thick, so uniformly spaced, that they seemed regimented, planted that way on purpose. It seemed, sometimes, as though the road lay at the bottom of a narrow, straight-walled canyon. The heavy, silent monotony of it might well have been perceived by someone else as oppressive, but to Erich, the sheer verticality of it was a refreshing contrast to the raw,

open tundra he'd been staring at for months. There was no
doubt in his mind now—his emotions this morning confirmed
it—that some dormant element of his spirit had come back to
life last night, when he was wakened by the tapping on his
window. Some new muscle drove the engine of his heart,
some instinctive response which took a deep Spartan pleasure
from this unpopulated forest world.

"Only another hundred kilometers to go, Captain. If we
weren't on the back roads, we'd already be seeing some military traffic."

In fact, except for a single horse-drawn cart they had
passed shortly after leaving the widow's cabin, they had seen
no traffic of any kind. They were greatly surprised, therefore,
when they suddenly encountered another auto. They had
stopped to urinate by the roadside and were reentering their
own vehicle when a large sedan bore down on them from the
opposite direction. The car was unmarked, but only a high-
ranking officer or government official would have access to
such a vehicle, so both men watched curiously as it neared
them.

It did not pass, but slowed on the icy road and made a
careful turn onto a side road, previously invisible, that led
south, into the depths of the forest—an area which, according
to the map Eino had been using, contained no habitation of
any kind.

At the wheel was a Finnish army officer with a blunt,
beefy face. In the back seat was an elderly man wrapped in an
overcoat trimmed with fur. As the man's face came into profile, Erich gasped. Hatless, the man seemed to be totally bald.
His head was like an outcropping of granite: large, finely
shaped ears set low beneath an immensely powerful forehead
where proud veins bulged. The nose was sharp and prominent
above a mouth, downturned, that seemed chiseled by a sculp-
tor's blade. It was a face that Erich had stared at every night
during the writing of his article, on the cover of an orchestral
score from Breitkopf and Härtel.

The car vanished into the trees.

"Eino—what's down that road?"

"According to the map, nothing but more forest. That road's not even marked."

"If you don't mind, I want to follow that car for a while."

Eino shrugged and turned on the ignition. "Any reason why the captain is so curious?"

"Didn't you recognize that man in the back seat?"

"The old fellow with the bald head? I didn't pay that much attention. Should I have?"

"Yes, I think perhaps you should have. Unless I'm very much mistaken, that man was Jean Sibelius."

Four

Erich vividly remembered his first encounter with a work by the great Finnish composer. After he had stayed in Lübeck for another three years, he was invited back to Mannheim in October 1937 to guest-conduct the orchestra. The opportunity came about quite suddenly due to the illness of Sir Thomas Beecham, the celebrated English maestro, who had been scheduled to lead that concert but was felled with stomach flu during his first day in town.

Sir Thomas had insisted on programming the one-movement Seventh Symphony of the Finnish composer Jean Sibelius, a relatively new work by a composer who had not been fashionable in Germany since the Great War. The regular Mannheim conductor had no trouble with the other works on the program, but took one look at the Sibelius score, declared that he neither liked nor comprehended it, and refused to direct it.

Beecham, who was very keen on giving the Sibelius work its first German hearing one way or another, expressed great indignation when informed of this situation. Surely, he declared, some itinerant maestro could be "rounded up" to substitute for Mannheim's "decrepit *Kapellmeister*" in the Sibelius. The Mannheim orchestra's manager dutifully made dozens of phone calls, but none of the conductors he spoke to would or could take the assignment.

And then someone remembered the young conductor who had caused such a commotion during the 1934 competition, yet whose magnetism on the podium had impressed virtually everyone in the ensemble. Where was he now? In Lübeck, someone else remembered; there were airline flights from Lübeck to Berlin, from Berlin to Mannheim—if the fellow accepted, he could be at work studying the score by that evening. A long-distance call was put through and the situation was explained to Erich, who accepted the challenge eagerly.

But as he sat on the connecting flight to Berlin, he began to have doubts. He was familiar with only a few of Sibelius's early, crowd-pleasing tone poems, and he had heard a couple of performances of the Second Symphony on the BBC wireless concerts, but that was all. The composer simply was not popular in Germany any longer, and Erich had absolutely no idea what his later works sounded like. He would have twenty-four hours to become familiar with an entirely new symphony, of unknown difficulty. Well, it was an opportunity to trump an old humiliation and—who knew?—sooner or later, the Mannheim post would become vacant, and that oleaginous creature von Golzer would not be in his way a second time.

That evening, Erich ensconced himself in the Mannheim Orchestra's library, preferring that location to any other that had been offered to him; he plugged in a hot plate for coffee and got down to work. When he opened the score of the Sibelius Seventh, he experienced something akin to actual panic. The work was scarcely a decade old, which made it, from a musical point of view, very contemporary indeed. It was cast, moreover, in a single movement of approximately twenty minutes' duration. Ten o'clock came, then eleven; Erich made a second pot of coffee and opened a fresh pack of cigarettes. The more he studied this curious work, the less he knew how to start preparing to conduct it. The conventional benchmarks of symphonic sonata form were conspicuously absent, or were present only by allusion. He searched in vain for the "starting points" his training had taught him were basic to any piece of music called a symphony: exposition, development, recapitulation, coda. This Finn, he concluded, certainly had his own way of doing things.

After a peremptory rattle on the timpani, the work began with a simple ascending figure—little more, really, than an enriched scale—that started in the low strings, was picked up and floated by the woodwinds, then augmented by remote, mysterious horns. It was not a "melody" by any means, not even a motif, just a kind of musical cell which, once stated, was then transformed and elaborated upon in the manner of a somber mosaic; moods changed often in the developmental passages, one flowing into the other, the whole edifice gradually coalescing into a chorale-like central climax dominated by a massive pileup of brass sonorities, which then ended in a long sustained wash of sunset colors in the massed strings.

And yet ... there were moments scattered through the piece which stirred his imagination, which conjured refreshing visions of stern, hyperborean landscapes. The horns and trombones of the climax were undeniably noble, almost Brucknerian, and the string passages were marvelously atmospheric. Throughout, the orchestration was subtle and showed the easy confidence of genuine mastery.

By midnight, although Erich was still not sure *how* the symphony worked, he was convinced that it did, absolutely on its own terms and beholden to no other discernible influence in all musical history. As he rested his eyes for a moment, he turned from the score itself to the half-tone picture of the composer on its cover: a craggy bald head, powerful eyes, a high brow deeply cut by vertical creases, a thin and stoic mouth—the visage, he guessed, of a man in his mid-sixties. The fellow looked as granitic, and as enigmatic, as his music.

Then he noticed, for the first time, the characterizing subtitle Sibelius had given his Seventh Symphony, almost as a signpost for its future interpreters: *Fantasia Sinfonica.*

A fantasia? One did not often encounter that musical term in a symphonic context, although it cropped up fairly often in solo works. Erich was feeling the effects of a long, strenuous day, and he had trouble bringing into focus a textbook definition of the word. He paced the room and lit another cigarette. Well, he reasoned, he was in a music library, so there should be a musical dictionary somewhere, should there not?

There was, over in a dusty corner crammed with general reference works.

"*Fantasia:* A species of music in which the composer yields to his imagination and gives free scope to his ideas, without regard to restrictions of form."

He glanced again at the composer's likeness and whispered: "All right, old man, I think I have you now."

He reopened the score and read it again, from an entirely different point of view. He would stop forcing it to be the kind of symphony it patently was not; he would simply conduct it as a rhapsody, a dark and mysterious poem, and let it flow outward, manifested in the motions of his baton, directly from his emotional responses to the score, not from any intellectual considerations of its architecture.

He read through the score two more times—switching at 1 A.M. from coffee to brandy—then took a taxi to his nearby hotel and fell almost at once into a deep but dream-embroidered sleep, from which he was awakened only by repeated rings of the telephone, one hour before his first and only day of rehearsals.

It was so very odd sometimes, he reflected as he walked onstage, this matter of chemistry between conductor and orchestra. There was always that wary moment when orchestra and putative leader got their first look at one another, and drew conclusions, so it seemed, from the vibrations in the air between them. He had been before these men only once before, and yet there was an almost palpable sense of harmony between them from the moment he stepped onto the podium. He did not have to go through the time-honored ritual of guest-conducting, proving his basic competence before a stageful of hard-nosed, cynical professionals. Instead, the atmosphere was bracingly businesslike. He felt as though he were returning to an orchestra which had once been "his" and was about to become so again.

He told them that it was a pleasure to work with them again, and said that he, too, had found the Sibelius work problematical at first, but that the key to it lay in its subtitle, a plain enough signpost from the canny old Finn, at least for those who chose to read it for what it was.

"Forget that this is not Mozart or even Bruckner. It is what it is: Sibelius, and if we just let the music take us where it wants to, we shall get there and find the trip invigorating. Very well, gentlemen, let's begin. Timpani, please: this opening figure—would you play it not loudly, but with clarity and just a shade more force than you might be inclined to use from its appearance on the page?"

By the end of the first run-through, the orchestra had overcome its initial skepticism and was really digging into the score. Erich tolerated, even relished, the rawness of some of the playing, for this was music born of the earth and close to it. There would be time later to polish and refine, although not very much. By noon, he was reasonably certain that things were going as well, or better, than he could have hoped.

After lunch, they went back to work on the Sibelius, this time with confidence and even a bit of anticipation. It was clear from their expressions that some of the older and more jaded players still had misgivings, but he encouraged them with personally targeted nods and brief smiles that punctuated his beat, trying telepathically to kindle in them some of the fire he heard from the younger men.

By the end of the second rehearsal, the overarching shape of the work was firmly in place. He worked for thirty minutes on isolated passages, adjusting balances and dynamics, asking for accents here, a certain inflection there. Then a third run-through, this one almost without stopping. When it was done, he smiled at them, thanked them, and told them that the rehearsal was over.

No one moved. After an uneasy moment, the concertmaster said: "Maestro, we still have time enough to run through it again, if you wish."

Erich stopped putting on his coat, one elbow dangling, then replied to the orchestra as a whole: "No, gentlemen, let's

save something for the concert. A rhapsody must sound spontaneous to sound good, and I think we're at the point where
it's proper to stop. Go home and relax until concert time, just
think a little bit, please, about what we've done today, and
when we play this piece tonight, give me just a little bit more
all the way through it, and the thing will go splendidly. Thank
you all for a wonderful rehearsal."

When he strode onto the stage that night, there was only
polite applause. Beecham's cancellation, and the unusual arrangement of a dual substitution, had made the morning paper, of course, but few in the audience had ever heard of
Erich Ziegler; Lübeck was a long way from Mannheim. The
orchestra, however, faced him on the edge of their seats, giving him their fullest attention. He felt confident of them and
of his vision of the work about to be performed, although he
knew it to be, inevitably, imperfect.

He opened the score and waited for that ideal moment of
silence, when the latecomers had been seated and the coughing
and rustling of programs had died away, when the downbeat
must be given. His glance flickered up from the score to the
hovering timpanist, his sticks poised above the drumheads in
white-knuckled fists. And when it came, the downbeat went
out to the men through Erich's eyes, far more than the motion
of his wrist.

The whole performance went like that. Erich knew that,
had he chosen to, he could have led the entire work with his
eyes alone. He could feel some kind of radiance flowing from
his eyes, a bandwidth of communication that he had never,
until this performance, been able to control with any degree
of reliability. It came from deep within him, and, more important, it seemed to come from deep within the music, a com-
mingling of essences, projecting outward. He scarcely glanced
at the score; unconsciously, he had already absorbed it in a
way that bypassed simple memorization. It seemed to have
become part of his cells, his fluids, the firing of his synapses.

He did not so much beat time in the conventional sense
(he was later told) as project some mysteriously compelling
physical analogue of the music. He even gave cues with his

eyes, using both hands, not just the traditional left one, to sculpt timbres and nuances of dynamic range, while the baton hand moved not bar by bar, but in the contours of much longer phrases, whole paragraphs of the composer's singularly bardic discourse. Surprised by this new, improvisatory style, the orchestra's ensemble suffered for a few moments. There were ragged entries and hesitations, but Erich met each one with glances that solicited, or encouraged, or communicated disapproval, all at light-speed. By midway through the symphony, the orchestra had accepted this new style and adjusted magnificently to it, falling under the spell—as he would later hear it described—of the force emanating from him, giving him everything that his eyes asked them to give. They started to play with the abandon of gypsies, yet their discipline grew even sharper, so that they phrased like the rise and fall of a single collective breath.

Then came the symphony's chorale-like climax: horns and trombones piling up and up over turbulent strings, forming a crushing bronze-colored wave of sound, and that climax took on a stark urgency so fierce that Erich's hands began to tremble from the act of shaping and controlling it, so that the resolution, when it came, seemed to well up like a cry coaxed from the earth itself.

When the final string chord faded into nothingness—a long diminuendo like the last ferruginous streak in a dying autumn sky—Erich felt his "possession" drain from him, replaced by numbness. He took his bows, several of them, and was moved to see that the orchestra was applauding him even more vigorously than the audience—a great many of whom, however much they might have been pleased by the intensity of the performance, were still quite unsure as to what the music itself was about. But all of this seemed to be happening at some distance, on a remote plane which he might as well have been observing through a thick pane of glass. He knew that he had been in a strange and hypervivid place for the past twenty minutes, in a state he had reached occasionally before during performance, but never so intensely, for so long, or with such a sensation of control.

*   *   *

The road that plunged into the forest was a narrow track that snaked around pewter-colored bogs and then straightened between melancholy stands of spruce and high-trunked pine. They drove two kilometers before encountering any sign of human habitation. Finally, after rounding a long graded curve that hinted of higher ground ahead, they were confronted with the unexpected sight of a candy-striped gate pole across the road. Three men—two privates and an officer—stood behind the gate, stonily regarding the approaching car. They wore the field-grey tunics and woolen caps of the regular Finnish Army, and both privates carried Suomis, held alertly at port.

The officer stepped to the edge of the barrier and raised his hand. Erich recognized him as the man he had seen in the vehicle they had been following. He was powerfully built, stocky, in his late thirties, with the bearing—arms hanging just so from his broad shoulders, thumbs automatically aligned with trouser creases—of a career officer. He had what Erich would come to recognize as a classically Finnish face: round, with full cheeks offset by a thick, aggressive jaw line, lips that were full but not sensual, and eyes that seemed disproportionately small in relation to the rest of his face; intelligent blue eyes couched not in fat, but simply in extra flesh—a function of the long winters and the lifelong need to squint through falling snow, eyes that retained in their shape and cast the faintest whisper of Central Asia, an echo a thousand years old. He wore the shoulder tabs of a major.

Eino stopped the car ten meters from the gate. "It appears that we've blundered into some kind of installation, sir, although I'm damned if I know what it could be, way out here."

Erich rolled down the window and gathered his documents for inspection. The Finnish officer glanced perfunctorily at Eino, who clambered out of the car and stood awkwardly at attention. A brief exchange in Finnish, during which Erich heard his own name and rank embedded in a rush of umlauts and polysyllables. The major nodded, both to signify understanding and to dismiss Eino. Then he tossed

Erich a crisp salute and bent his head into the car. The man smelled of wool and, incongruously for the place and time, cologne.

"Good day, Captain. I am Major Rautavaara, in command of security here. I'm sorry to inconvenience you, but I'm required to examine your papers. I suggest we do our business in my office rather than out here in the snow. There's coffee in the guard hut, and my boys will look after your driver while we're gone."

Erich now counted a squad of six enlisted men at the gate and inside the guard hut, where a pot of coffee hissed atop a glowing iron stove. Gratefully he accepted a mug, then followed the major to a larger cabin, set back in the trees about fifty meters from the road. Inside were two rooms: a communal barracks for the squad and a private room for the major, furnished with a pine-plank bed, a desk, and a bureau. A large map of central Finland filled one wall; on another hung framed portraits of Marshal Mannerheim and Adolf Hitler.

Erich was brought up short by the sudden appearance of the führer, whose visage had been conspicuously absent on the front lines in Russia. His feelings about the Nazi leader had always been mixed. There was undeniably something unscrupulous about his rise to power, and the cultural policies Hitler's henchmen promulgated—the ritualized book burnings, the proscription of Jewish composers and performers, the enthronement of *kitsch* in the visual arts—offended Erich's taste and smacked of fanaticism.

But so far, Erich had been able to reconcile himself to these excesses as a trade-off for the strength, stability, and prosperity Germany had enjoyed throughout most of the previous decade. He had seen the consequences of anarchy, when his father had lain bleeding to death in a Berlin street, and he was willing to put up with certain imbalances and annoyances if that was what it took to keep his beloved country from ever again knowing such chaos.

Besides, the more unreasonable of Hitler's policies would surely prove to be transitory, the product of historical pressures and external threats. Once Germany was secure from such threats, more moderate policies, overseen by more reasonable men, would surely evolve. If nothing else, the basic decency and common sense of the German people would insist upon it.

Still, the sight of the two national leaders' portraits, so carefully hung against the wall of rude logs, was a surprise as well as a study in contrast: the handsome, aristocratic Finnish baron—once an officer in the Tsar's household guard—and the *parvenu* dictator who had clawed his way up from the beer halls. They seemed unlikely bedfellows to Erich, each with radically different reasons for attacking Russia. Other than the peculiar and transitory circumstances that had made cobelligerents of their two nations, the two men had almost nothing in common. Mannerheim, from what Erich knew of him, was a haughty old monarchist who found himself leading a socialist democracy, while Hitler—a man of the humblest origins—now commanded the entire Prussian officer caste.

Noticing Erich's quizzical gaze, Rautavaara smiled and said: "Finland's great leader and Germany's great leader, side by side. We make good partners in this war, don't you think? You can have the Ukraine, we'll get back our stolen provinces in Karelia, and Stalin is *kaput.*"

"You speak excellent German, Major."

"Should do. I trained in Germany when I was fresh out of officers' school—keeping abreast of new developments, you know. Now, you enjoy that coffee while I read through this impressive stack of documents."

Erich did. The major's room was warm and woody-smelling, Spartanly comfortable. Rautavaara studied the papers scrupulously, his pale eyebrows rising once or twice in appreciation of the weight of their signatures.

"You realize, of course, that I'll have to make a phone call or two to verify that these documents are genuine?"

"It's your duty, Major."

Erich helped himself to more coffee while the major made several telephone inquiries, not one word of which—except for his own name—Erich understood. When he was finished,

Rautavaara handed the documents back to Erich with a warmer smile than he had shown heretofore.

"These are certainly in order. And they'll get you into just about any place you might wish to be. What interests me is why you should show up *here* . . . "

"I've really no idea where 'here' is, Major. My driver and I had stopped to relieve ourselves, and when I saw the car drive by, the one you were in . . . well, you see, in civilian life, I was a musician. A conductor. And—I know I could be ridiculously mistaken—but I could have sworn that the gentleman in the car with you was Jean Sibelius."

Again, Rautavaara smiled. "Would you like to meet him? It's almost dinnertime up at the big house—since he hates telephone calls, I'll drive up there and see if he's in the mood to meet an admirer. He usually is. Or was, until the war. The flow of visiting journalists and pilgrims has dried up for the duration, I'm afraid. If you'll excuse me for a minute, I'll drive up and see. When I come back, I'll try to answer your questions."

A sudden rush of emotion made Erich dizzy. He held his posture until the major had left the room, then steadied himself by leaning against the man's desk.

For months, he had despaired of his career; for an entire year, he had been utterly shut off from the world of music. Yet here, in the middle of nowhere, he was about to meet a great composer whose work he had championed before an indifferent audience. For the first time since his call-up, Erich felt that old, obsessive sense of destiny, felt an upwelling of his own individuality, which had been battered into submission by the army. This meeting could not be a coincidence; it was a turn in the road he was meant to take, a thing meant to happen.

Rautavaara returned shortly, bearing fresh coffee. He offered it to Erich, who accepted, and followed it with an open pack of Klubbi cigarettes. Erich took one and smoked it in shallow puffs; the tobacco was black, Russian, and savagely strong.

"He's out walking by the lake. One of the girls will ask him and call us back in a few minutes."

"So . . . what is Sibelius doing here, Major? I thought he lived on an estate just north of Helsinki."

"The world-famous Järvenpää. Yes, normally he does. But these are not normal times, Captain. Consider Finland for a moment. We are a poor country with a severe climate tucked away in the farthest corner of Europe, struggling to raise our standard of living and struggling not to be swallowed alive by the Russians. Except for the forest, we have virtually no natural resources. Our literature is extensive, but except for the *Kalevala*, quite unknown, and the best of it fiercely resists translation. Per capita, we have more artists, more scholars, more theaters, more hospitals, and more bookstores than any other country in northern Europe . . . but no one knows any of that.

"What *do* they know about us? They know Sibelius's music. To the outside world, he *is* Finland. He put us on the world map. Until his music started being played abroad, people regarded us as barbarians who dressed in bearskins and practiced pagan magic. Then, suddenly, there came this powerful, original voice out of the North, and people began to think of us instead as 'brave little Finland.' Sibelius instilled a love for this landscape into the hearts of people who have never set eyes on it. He's a national institution by now—*the* national institution. In the eyes of the world, he is the beating heart of this nation."

Erich had not realized these things, and said as much. "In Germany, we would never regard a living composer that way. The closest thing to it would be Wagner, and he's been dead for quite some time."

"In Finland, it's different. A person in America may love Wagner's music, but when he hears it, he just hears 'Wagner,' not 'Germany.' When Americans and Englishmen hear Sibelius, they hear Finland; they close their eyes, and they *see* Finland. They don't really know us, as a nation, but they think they do. Do you believe for one minute that we would have experienced such an outpouring of sympathy during the

Winter War if his music had not predisposed people toward our cause?

"Thanks to Sibelius, there is an enormous reservoir of goodwill toward this country, which might otherwise not exist. And so now, for reasons the outside world seems unable to grasp, we find ourselves cobelligerents with Germany, which is in turn at war with England, which is the country in which Sibelius has enjoyed his greatest foreign success. It may well be that one fact—the popularity of that old man's music—which has kept the British from declaring war against us, and which may well restrain them from taking any significant action if Russian pressure does force them to declare war."

Erich thought that this major had a remarkable grasp of some fairly elusive issues, as well as an articulate way of expressing them, for all that the man looked like a professional wrestler. He could not help contrasting this officer with officers of the same grade he had recently served with in the Mountain Corps.

"I must admit, Major, I would never have considered these matters to be so bound up in one composer of symphonic music. You speak of him as though he were an element of your foreign policy."

"Even more than that. You see, Captain, when you examine these things in context, Sibelius looms as more than just a great composer—he becomes a strategic weapon. And so his life becomes much more than just the life of one old man. His value as a national symbol, as a propaganda object, cannot be calculated. You yourself knew exactly where Järvenpää is—be sure that the Russians, too, have it pinpointed to the centimeter. They could try to kill him with a massive bomber strike, or they could try to capture him and hold him hostage, perhaps by means of a large-scale operation involving parachutists. We could not deter such a thing unless we surrounded Järvenpää with interceptors, flak batteries, and a battalion of crack troops. Obviously, with our military resources stretched to their limits, it is not practical to do that. Therefore, a much simpler solution: very quietly, we moved the composer from

Järvenpää and secluded him here, hundreds of miles to the
north, in the middle of nowhere."

"Any reason for this particular place?"

"As a matter of fact, Sibelius chose this place himself. It's
a lodge where he used to come when he was a young man,
back before the turn of the century. It was half in ruins when
we took it over, but it's quite commodious now. Here he stays
for the duration of the war, quite secure, his every need taken
care of, guarded by a single squad instead of half the Finnish
Army. Of course, as far as the outside world knows, he's still
residing at Järvenpää—which has been placed off limits to
journalists for the duration. His mail, his telegrams, even his
phone calls, are all routed to this place."

"And does this place have a name?" asked Erich.

"He calls it 'Tapiola,' after Tapio, the mythological god of
the northern forests."

"I think I've seen that name before. Did he write a piece
of music by that title?"

Rautavaara looked at him rather sharply, causing Erich to
redden and feel a sudden wave of anxiety; had he unwittingly
said something that gave offense? His mind was in a turmoil,
for he desperately wanted this portal to open for him, now
that he stood before it.

"I think that is the case," the major finally replied, before
actually giving Erich what sounded like a clear warning. "I
should emphasize to you, before you meet him, that he's very
reluctant to discuss his current musical activities, so you'd best
confine your questions to the published works."

A field telephone buzzed in the other room. Rautavaara
excused himself, and when he returned he was smiling.

"It's all arranged. Uncle Janne would be happy to receive
you. I'll drive you up there myself, and have the boys fix some
lunch for your driver."

"Uncle Janne!" Was this gruff-looking but ever-so-precise
officer a relative? Had Erich already penetrated the composer's innermost circle? He clenched his hands, keeping them
out of sight beneath his coat.

Moments later, they were in Rautavaara's car, once more

driving through the forest. The road was no longer so winding; its long shallow curves were leading uphill. The snow had
stopped and somewhere beyond the tree line the winter sun
had broken through. Particles of ice, small as dust motes,
sparkled in the pellucid air.

They had not gone far before Erich remarked, "Back
there, after you got off the phone, you called him 'Uncle
Janne' . . ."

"Oh no, he really isn't my uncle, but that's what I've called
him since I was a small boy. My father was a childhood friend
of his; they grew up together in Hämeenlinna. The name
'Jean,' by the way, comes from an uncle of his who was a
sailor. He traveled the world and eventually he got tired of
having to tell everyone he met where Finland was, so he
chose to present himself as French, under the name 'Jean.' "

"I suppose he got more girls that way," said Erich, impulsively using some "soldierly" banter to ingratiate himself with
the major. Instantly, he wished he had said nothing. Even if
Rautavaara did not think the remark out of line, his responding smile was thin and quickly gone.

"That may have been part of it. From what he said to me,
though, it was even simpler. Sibelius simply liked the sound of
'Jean'—it was more continental, more elevated in tone, yet it
really wasn't such a distortion of his own given name. He
could have the cachet that went with the name, and yet still
feel himself genuine, uncompromised. Both feelings are
important to him, even if they are sometimes hard to reconcile. Anyhow, as far as the outside world goes, 'Jean Sibelius'
it is—but family members still call him Janne."

"And what should I call him?"

Rautavaara ruminated for a second and then said something which revealed that he was not unaware of how privileged his position was, *vis-à-vis* the composer; a little
something to remind this German pilgrim of the relative difference in their status. "Well, the state pension checks are
made out to 'Professor J. Sibelius,' but I think 'Maestro'
would please him."

"I won't have any trouble with that."

Erich fell silent, for he did not want to risk alienating this man. He tried to distract himself by focusing on the shadowy forest that rolled by, close against the edges of the road, the snow-dusted upper branches creamy and bright, everything below them still, blue, and dusky.

Rautavaara filled in the silence with reminiscence: "My father used to go with Uncle Janne on hunting and fishing trips into the wilderness. They collected everything from butterflies to mushrooms, as boys will do. My father used to tell me about those days, long before Sibelius was famous, before he had even entered the music academy in Helsinki. He used to say, 'Sibelius sober was like the rest of us drunk.' "

Erich laughed nervously. "How did he mean that?"

"Oh, just that Uncle Janne's imagination was extravagant. When they went into the forest together, he used to insist that he could actually see nymphs and witches, goblins and trolls. Once, he claimed that he even got a glimpse of the great forest god Tapio himself. The strange thing about Uncle Janne, my father always insisted, is that he continued to see those things even after he had grown up. For all I know, he may still think he can see them."

The trees thinned suddenly at the top of a rising curve and the car emerged onto a circular plateau that had been cleared as a crude parking lot. Nervously, Erich got out, like a man sleepwalking, and stared. Gravel made from crushed Karelian granite was strewn loosely; where the snowfall had not covered it, it showed like chips of rust. Lofty pines, nearly limbless for the first ten meters of their trunks, shaded the parking area, and behind them stood the lodge. Its walls were made entirely from logs, so that it seemed to have assembled itself from its own surroundings. Slabs of snow-covered granite led to a front porch and a massive wooden door with brass trim. Through the first-floor windows, lamplight showed the color of horn. A second story rose to peaked angles beneath a steeply gabled roof covered with green tiles and pierced by three chimneys of dark red stone. "Captain?"

When he did not respond at once, Rautavaara shook him. Coming back, Erich realized he was still standing with one hand on the car door handle. He closed the door quietly; to slam it would have been as unseemly as dropping a plate on the floor at dinner.

"Go have a look around, Captain. Through the trees over there, there is a splendid view out over the lake. I'll go see if I can find Uncle Janne. He likes to greet every guest personally on the front steps of Järvenpää—no reason why he should want to do otherwise here."

Rautavaara crunched away over snow-covered gravel, leaving Erich alone. Erich watched him enter by the front door and strained to get a glimpse of the lodge's interior. A quick sight of wood inside wood, and the door closed. Before Erich turned away, he spotted a woman's face at one of the upstairs windows, a younger person than Erich presumed Madame Sibelius to be. Steam on the window glass lent a spectral, fluid quality to the features behind it, but Erich could discern a thin pale oval and a rippling hint of flaxen hair. Two fingers, long and gracefully articulated, swept moisture from the pane, and for just an instant, before her face withdrew into shadows, the woman seemed to peer down at him intently.

Erich started walking, entering an expanse of tall pines and thick stands of fir. He could not just remain standing passively by the car. He felt himself being drawn as though his body had turned into a dowsing rod. Was this feeling an illusion, he wondered, an aftereffect of the strain he had been under since the start of hostilities, or was it a real emanation from the forest? Perhaps the feeling was simply explained: the sense of being *in* this forest world, rather than merely observing it through a car window, seemed to have a tonic effect on his entire being, as though he were an instrument being sensitively tuned.

The lodge occupied the spur of a ridge and the thin, spotted shadows ahead indicated a rapid falling away of the trees. Beyond, he saw a light-filled space that seemed to beckon him out of the forest's gloom. When he stepped from the trees to the overlook, the sudden yawning of space made him dizzy.

What stretched before him was not one of the small bog-fringed lakes of the deep woods, but a huge expanse of water, mile after mile of it, out to and even beyond a horizon whose distance he could not even estimate. Ice lay like a crust of sugar over large sections of the surface and the open water reflected a color of dark lead. The horizon was a streak of lemon-white, the sun itself obscured by enormous arms of cloud, the rear guard of a retreating storm front.

Directly in front of him, blocking his view of the far side of the lake, was a large island. Its backbone appeared to rise, in places, a hundred meters higher than the narrow strip of grey beach directly in line with Erich's gaze. Peering at the island through squinted eyes, Erich could make out a little nub of a dock, jutting precariously from the ashy beach. The beach itself was fringed by groves of bare-limbed birches that looked as black and thin as strands of wire against the snow. In a wooded hollow back from the beach, he saw a log cabin, a wisp of smoke idling up from its roof.

Down the slope on his left, Erich could see a small, tree-girt cove. Where this bay entered the lake, on a gently sloping thumb of land, there stood a large sauna hut, its shape almost hidden by the mounds of split birch logs stacked against its walls. From two sides of the hut, docks extended into the little bay and into the lake itself. An open boat rubbed against the pilings. In the middle ground, between the ridge and the sauna, clusters of birches, looking as crisp and dark as ideograms written on vellum, gave character to the thinly wooded slopes.

Now, for the first time, Erich also noticed that there was a man standing down the slope from him, motionless, beside an ivory shaft of birch. The two of them might as well have been the only two human beings ever to people this landscape, so intense and automatic was the attraction that compelled Erich to step out from the cover of the trees and approach.

So: here his moment was. No illusion had drawn him away from the parking lot, but some strange connection with this time, this place, this meeting. And he had gone to find it himself; there was no major to introduce them, no intermediary needed to set this in motion.

In profile, there could be no doubt as to the old man's identity. Of all living composers, Jean Sibelius was perhaps the least likely to be passed unrecognized on the street. During the course of his studies, and his extensive concertgoing in several cities, Erich had seen many composers in person. One could pass Bartok or Schoenberg on the street and scarcely notice them: surprisingly pale and anonymous men, oddly bureaucratic-looking, like figures stepped from a Gogol story. Pfitzner looked like a doddering pensioner from the Franco-Prussian War; Richard Strauss resembled a Munich haberdasher; and Erich had seen more than one Russian waiter, never mind a doorman or two, who, with the proper wardrobe, could easily have passed for Igor Stravinsky. But the head of Sibelius, with its massive smoothness, its powerful nose and chiseled mouth, its lofty forehead scored by deep vertical furrows (one, it was said, for each of his seven published symphonies), looked as though it were waiting to be cast in bronze.

Roofing the profile, casting it into hard shadow against the ice-glare reflected from the lake, was a large flat-brimmed hat that seemed supported only by the ridges of the composer's eyebrows. The old man's figure was ramrod straight and surprisingly erect for a man in his mid-seventies, although the elegant cut of his fur-trimmed topcoat might have contributed to that impression. His right hand, gloved, gripped the curving top of a wooden cane, with which the composer seemed to have pierced the skin of the earth, so deeply was its tip driven into the crust of snow.

Movement broke the spell. The old man's hand, gloved in black kid, rose to his lips, carrying the stump of a large cigar. As he sipped the smoke with his thin sharp lips, without taking his eyes from the landscape, he spoke in a voice that was high, reedy, and firm.

"You must be the young German captain who is going to dine with us."

"Erich Ziegler, Maestro. I once had the honor of conducting one of your symphonies. This is a great privilege for me."

"And a damned unexpected one, I'm sure, given the circumstances and the location." The composer laughed shortly, not with an old man's ruminative chuckle, but with surprising heartiness and vigor.

"Still," Sibelius continued, "you don't come here as a musician today, and that's fine with me. I have come to prefer the company of soldiers and businessmen to the company of artists. Artists always talk about money; soldiers and businessmen, when they come to see me, prefer to talk about art. Come, Captain Ziegler, let's have ourselves something to eat, and afterwards, you can tell me something about yourself."

The feeling of unreality settled over Erich as he took a seat at the dining table, after having been introduced to Aino, the composer's wife, a handsome, quiet woman with white hair pulled back into a bun. Even in peacetime, the meal would have been excellent; given the sort of rations Erich had existed on since June, it seemed lavish. There was a large smoked salmon, a golden sauce made from chanterelle mushrooms, dark rye bread with real butter, steamed potatoes, coffee with cream, and fine crystal stems containing an ounce or so of fiery *aquavit*. Sibelius, Erich noticed, tossed his off almost as soon as he sat down, with no visible effect other than a sudden breath of color on his white cheeks.

Conversation was, at first, fairly stilted. Erich followed Rautavaara's lead and confined himself to noncommittal nodding and polite monosyllables until he had forked down enough crumbly, fragrant salmon to assuage the appetite that had seized him at the sight and smell of such a meal. Mistaking his silence for shyness, Aino smiled pleasantly at him and said: "It's so nice to have company again, Captain. Since we came here, it has been very quiet, not at all like it used to be at Järvenpää. We were only an hour's train ride from Helsinki, after all, and every day, it seemed, there would be a journalist or a colleague or a conductor, coming to ask questions. Always questions."

"I don't miss it, Ziegler," growled the composer, tapping nervously on the stem of his empty glass. Observing the gesture, Aino said: "I'll have one of the girls fill it, Janne, just once." She raised a tiny brass bell and waved it. Moments

later, a tall, somberly pretty woman of indeterminate age entered the room. She was dressed in loose peasant linens that
outlined her body only where the fabric clung to her hips.
Perhaps it was she who had observed Erich's arrival. But despite the fleeting duration of the glimpse he had obtained, he
was fairly certain that she was not. There was a resemblance,
however, which struck him as more than coincidental. The
woman paused for an instant to appraise Erich with cool grey
eyes before decanting another measure of liquor into the
composer's glass.

"Thank you, Anna-Liisa," said Aino.

As the woman's shapely bottom vanished into, presumably,
the kitchen, Sibelius mockingly raised his glass in salute to her
backside and muttered: "My humblest thanks, O daughter of
Tapio!"

"Janne, do not tease the girl, for heaven's sake. You might
hurt her feelings. We are very fortunate to have two such
conscientious servants out here in the wilderness. Who would
help us keep house if they should leave our service?"

"The army would provide," said Major Rautavaara.

"The army," said Aino, "has already provided quite
enough. I sometimes wonder whether your men are here to
keep the Russians out or to keep us in."

"Now Aunt, we've been over all that many times before.
Uncle Janne agreed to come here for his own safety and in
the best interests of the nation."

Sibelius snorted and washed down a forkful of potatoes. "I
agreed to come here in order to get away from that damned
parade of journalists. Erich here comes to us as a soldier, an
ally. If he'd come here as another time-beater, I'd have
thrown him through the ice." The old man laughed garru-
lously. Erich wondered if he were not already just a bit tipsy—
the *aquavit*, to judge from the two discreet sips he had taken,
was very high-octane.

The mood around the table was now that of an affectionately squabbling family. Since the modulation seemed to have
embraced him as well, Erich ventured a remark.

"Don't you miss the amenities of Helsinki, Maestro?"

Sibelius acknowledged Erich's tactful choice of address with a tip of his glass that caught a flash of light and a hooded half-wink from one eye. "Helsinki! The cleanest, most puritanical, most architecturally boring capital city in all of Europe!"

"Is that why you used to take the train into town every Friday morning and stay gone until Sunday night?" chided Aino.

Suddenly the composer looked frail again; old, and quite touchingly vulnerable. His combative mood vanished. He leaned over and patted his wife's hand with unfeigned tenderness.

"You know me too well, my dear."

"I've known you too long to be fooled. Most of the time."

The conversation inevitably turned to the war. Erich described his own mission in outline, portraying himself in terms of his official function—liaison officer without portfolio—and carefully steering away from any hint of his intelligence-gathering duties.

"Where in the Third Corps' area will you be stationed, Captain?" asked Rautavaara.

"I'll be staying with the Third Division."

"Ah. Their headquarters is not far from Suomussalmi, about three hours' drive from here. I'll have to meet you there some time and show you around the old battlefield—that's where we won our biggest victory during the Winter War."

"You won't be so far away, really, Captain Ziegler," said Aino. "You could come for another visit, if your duties permit."

"Oh, they'll permit," said Rautavaara with a trace of a sneer in his voice. "They'll permit because the front will stabilize soon, now that winter's here. The high command won't push far beyond the old border—just enough to reach the best defensive ground—and then they'll dig in. After that, they can start to bargain with the Russkies, or so they think."

"What's your appreciation of the strategic situation, Major?" asked Erich, thinking that his first dispatch to Klatt was about to be dictated.

"We should throw everything we have against Leningrad from the north and west, and simultaneously make an all-out effort to cut the Murmansk Railroad at the White Sea, all in conjunction with a German offensive from the south. Leningrad is the heart of the Communist state, the workers' own fortress. If it falls, Moscow will shake to its roots and the war will soon be lost to Stalin. Our goals, therefore, are too limited, Captain . . . in my opinion, of course."

"You would prefer Finland to go all out, then? Try to knock the Russians out of the war altogether?"

"With us as the hammer and the Germans as the anvil, it could be done. How else can we ensure the future survival of Finland?"

"Don't put our guest on the spot," said Sibelius. "Why should Herr Ziegler give a damn about the survival of Finland?"

"I care because I feel an affinity for this land. I think it was born in me when I first heard your Seventh Symphony."

Erich really had not meant for the remark to sound as charged with flattery as it had seemed. The response from around the table, however, was as though he had just delivered a perfectly delectable *bon mot*. The composer clapped his hands—"Well said!"—and toasted Erich with the remnant of his drink.

"Aino, perhaps Captain Ziegler would care to hear a bit of real Finnish music after lunch. Have Kylliki see to the tuning of her *kantele*. A few songs would go well with our liqueur."

While Aino did this, and the grey-eyed servant cleared the dishes, Sibelius ushered the men into comfortable leather chairs gathered in a pool of wintry light in front of a picture window. The sky was mostly clear now, filled with a glow the color of white grapes. The lake too had changed hues, and was now the color of wetted slate; the encroaching ice gleamed as though it had been painted on with molten diamonds. Sibelius opened a finely carved humidor and offered cigars to the other men. After a steady diet of rough, ursine native cigarettes, Erich found the cigar almost unbearably savory. Observing his look of bliss, Sibelius laughed dryly.

"The expression on your face is that of a man who truly appreciates a good cigar. I like you better and better, young captain."

"It's exquisite. Where on earth did you get such a thing in the middle of this war?"

"Vasquez, the Spanish ambassador in Helsinki, sends them to me. He gets them in diplomatic pouches, straight from Cuba. Sometimes, the greatest rewards of being famous are the small ones. Enjoy your smoke."

Erich did just that, ruminatively surveying the room while he did so, and while the now returned Aino served glasses of raspberry liqueur. The floor and walls of the house were of smoothly planed logs, finished to a warm reddish color; the ceiling was massively beamed. Most of one entire wall was taken up by a great fireplace-cum-stove faced with green tiles; periodically, Aino or the major would open its copper doors and thrust into its maw a foot-long cylinder of birch wood. The inside of the stove was cherry red and the heat radiating from it seemed sufficient to warm several rooms. On the other walls were framed paintings, including several of the composer, and a pair of large rya rugs hung like tapestries—abstract designs in warm umbers and earth tones. There was also an enormous wreath of dried flowers whose faded ribbon proclaimed greetings to Sibelius on his fiftieth birthday. Through an open door, Erich could see a smaller book-lined room containing a large radio-phonograph console, a case of record albums, and the ebony jut of a piano—the composer's studio?

Before Erich could ask, the door to the kitchen swung open and a girl walked diffidently in, carrying a triangular musical instrument with two straight sides and one curved one. He rose as she entered but the others did not; she was, to them, just a servant. Instantly, Erich knew she was the one who had watched him from the upstairs window. He understood now why that trivial incident had registered so clearly, for he must have sensed her unusual beauty even if he did not have time to bring it into focus. She was dressed, like the other servant, in plainspun peasant clothes, her head covered by a scarf that disguised the length of her hair, but could not hide its glory: What was visible formed a corona the color of winter sunlight, crowning a smooth white forehead. Her high cheeks were dusted with constellations of *café-au-lait* freckles and the shadows beneath them led gracefully to a striking mouth: a full lower lip surmounted by a thinner, more delicately sculpted upper lip, and both the color of crushed berries. She smiled slightly, with seeming embarrassment, when Erich rose, revealing white teeth and a suggestion, the barest hint, of a youthful overbite. The smile made her look as though she were just disengaging from a deep kiss. Erich found the configuration charming and quite sensual. The girl acknowledged his stance with a slight nod and a quick glance of open curiosity. Her eyes were a dark lavender, the color of scorched lilacs.

"Have you ever heard the music of our *kantele*?"

"No, Maestro, but I look forward to it."

"Kylliki is rather accomplished on the instrument. She says that her grandmother taught her, but I say she learned to play from the birch trees. Such music can only be learned from the forest. That's why the old rune-singers always accompanied themselves on the *kantele*—its music reinforced their spells enormously, made their magic more potent. Play, my dear, play something sad and Finnish for our young captain."

The composer repeated his question in Finnish and the girl, softly but not bashfully, responded with a remark that made Sibelius smile. Her voice reminded Erich of an alto flute.

"What did she say, Maestro?"

"She said that most *kantele* songs already are sad, and she's right—most of them are."

The girl rested the instrument's sounding box across her lap and strummed a tentative arpeggio on the strings, filling the room with a delicate silvery filigree of sound. The instrument looked like a zither and had a timbre rather like a dulcimer, yet even finer-drawn, more evanescent. The girl launched into a Karelian folk song laid out on a slow modal melody of grave melancholy, ending in a cascade of arpeggiated notes, rich with overtones, that seemed to swirl through the room like a gust of birch leaves. A lighter, more bantering song followed—Erich guessed it was a love ballad—and it danced with faerie lightness, the notes like grains of pollen swirling in sunlight. At the end of the ballad, Sibelius gestured to the girl and requested another song.

As the girl played, her fingers moving agilely across the strings, the notes seemed to spring up from beneath her fingertips; her face became grave and composed, an unmistakable mask of ritual. The music was more measured, less adorned, more incantatory; it seemed to Erich immeasurably old. Gradually the tempo quickened and the accents became more rhythmic than lyrical, and Erich was surprised at the way his own pulse accelerated. Although he could not understand a single word, he felt their power, and he thought that any runes sung to such music would be powerful ones, and surely would be heard by whatever atavistic spirits they were addressed to.

Listening to Kylliki play, Erich gradually reconnected with his oldest and deepest motive for listening to music: its unequaled power to conjure dreams. All his life, he reflected, at least until the day he'd been drafted, had been driven by such dreams; and as he came under the spell of the girl's sad silvery songs, he was swept back in time to a startling incident that had happened to him years before.

Perhaps it was the power of suggestion, but ever since his twilight encounter with the old man in the Alps, Erich had become obsessed with the life and achievements of the Dream King, Ludwig II. His points of reference, and his points of departure for all his deeper ramblings through the alpine region, were the many incredible storybook palaces, castles, and lodges built by Ludwig throughout the region.

Sometimes, when he was wandering alone in the deep recesses of a wooded valley, or beside a small, perfect lake high in the mountains, Erich fancied he could visualize Ludwig's nocturnal rides through the forest, in his gold sleigh, followed by his wraithlike attendants, their great sputtering torches dripping clots of fire into the snow. He also envisioned Ludwig in one of his jewel-encrusted castle grottoes, drifting languidly in a clockwork swan while Wagner, seated onshore at a grand piano, dressed in silk and surrounded by clouds of incense and opium, stoked the royal fantasies by playing, far into the night, arrangements of the music from *Lohengrin.*

Gradually, over the course of many summers of hiking and many winters of ski vacations, Erich had become familiar with every well-known site associated with Ludwig, and thanks to his incessant questioning of local inhabitants—some of whom, after his third or fourth obsessive visit, had come to think this young man slightly mad as well—quite a few places that were not listed in the guidebooks.

Among the hardest to find was the place that old man had mentioned, just before the blatting of Uncle Rudy's horn had shattered the spell: the Tatzelwurm Gorge. Erich had spent many days trying to discover its location, and had finally tracked it down by consulting a very old travel diary, a document dating from the eighteenth century, housed in a very small village museum. Once he got close, he found a few local inhabitants who would give him additional directions, but none who would serve as his guide. The place was too remote, too hard to reach, too dangerous for the inexperienced hiker. But, Erich assured them, he was very experienced.

They gave him directions and told him he was welcome to try his luck. Erich stayed for several days at the local inn, and found that, as usual, a display of generosity was the quickest way to loosen provincial tongues. In his sturdy little surveyor's notebook, he jotted down their tall stories, their legends, their endless supply of bad and sometimes bawdy dragon jokes.

It transpired, in fact, that Ludwig II had indeed visited the gorge, in company, it was said, with the great Wagner. A whole expedition had been laid on, complete with professional alpinists and a hundred porters to carry the luxurious fur-lined tents and down-filled sleeping couches, the champagne and five-star brandy, and the small hand-pumped organ that Wagner would play each night. The people of this village had seen them depart one bright summer morning and had seen them return one week later in haste, by night, their ragged progress lit by torches and the oaths of servants lashing the pack animals through the darkness. Several village folk had been roused from their sleep by the racket, and they peered from their windows at the procession as it went by, astonished to see the king, wrapped in furs, his eyes wild and terror-stricken by torchlight, and behind him, raving drunk and in a manic state, arms flying and hair disheveled, Wagner, who was heard to cry as he passed through the center of town: *"Der Drache liebt!"*—"The dragon lives!" And in the morning there was no trace of the king and his retinue save for the droppings of their horses and a few bits of fallen baggage, which the townspeople had gathered and stored reverently against the day when Ludwig might come back to claim them.

Now Erich had come to try to discover what the Dream King had seen that night. He prepared systematically: a Leica camera with extra-fast film, an arctic-quality sleeping bag, and a powerful Mannlicher hunting rifle from Uncle Rudy's gun cabinet. He had also brought a small block of hashish, purchased, without much trouble, in the artists' quarter of Munich.

He tried to assume a scientific attitude from the start, wanting to add a veneer of rationality to a venture that was essentially metaphysical. His reasoning began with music, naturally: from music and its effect upon him, he already knew that transcendent states of consciousness could be attained. He had begun to formulate his own theory, to envision another dimension, more vibrant and vivid, existing parallel to the "normal" one, yet ordinarily undetectable; the two worlds might touch sometimes when music or some other aesthetic ritual was the intermediary.

Perhaps the Tatzelwurm Gorge was a place where the skin that separated the two planes had worn thin, where one might, as it were, peek through and see what was in that other place.

Erich was secretly very pleased that his personal quest had such an illustrious royal precedent. If the villagers were to be believed, some occurrence had induced terror in King Ludwig's expedition, more than sixty years earlier. Ludwig's panic could be dismissed—he was by nature unstable and hopelessly prey to suggestion, which was how Wagner had gotten such influence over him in the first place. But Wagner's state of excitation could not be explained away so casually. Erich had studied Richard Wagner the man, and he knew that, for all the transcending power of Wagner's imagination, the man himself was hardheaded and eminently businesslike in most of his dealings—no campfire ghost, no bogeyman illusion, would have elicited genuine terror from flinty old Richard. Of course, there was always the possibility that the king and his court composer had dosed themselves with laudanum, but what of it? That was a time-honored way for poets and philosophers to cross the normally impermeable bounds of experience and enter into transcendental states, or so went Erich's reasoning when he purchased the block of hashish.

He used skis in the lower valleys, but had to leave them behind and advance on foot once he reached the three-thousand-meter level. He made steady progress—considering how fickle alpine weather could be in the spring, conditions were remarkably benign.

Following the advice of several local people, he backtracked one of the main rivers that flowed from the falls, tracing the arteries of the great gorge itself. Gradually the riverbed narrowed until he was climbing over thin-edged piles of scree only inches from the torrent. Walls of rock closed in overhead, and he spent the afternoon entirely in shadow, the sunlit sky visible only as a ribbon of blue above his head.

In the last moments of twilight, he reached the bottom of Tatzelwurm Gorge, and when he stepped around a promontory of granite and beheld the full extent of the place, he was stunned to immobility by its savage grandeur. With unimaginable force, the melted snows of winter were pouring from the peaks above, funneled through a space too small to contain their volume, so that the water did not fall so much as explode, shot into space and then sucked down by gravity. When Erich looked up, attempting to chart the course of the water with his eyes, he reeled. There was nothing serene about this waterfall: All was violence and discharge. The roar was deafening.

The gorge opened up into a confused system of pools, caves, ledges, and miniature canyons about a kilometer across at its widest. He could see few details in the shadows, so he concentrated on finding a campsite. There was a fairly level plateau thirty meters above one of the broader and more tranquil pools, with just enough space for his tent. Enough driftwood was scattered about for a dozen campfires, so he spent the remaining minutes of daylight collecting a pile of it and coaxing a small pilot fire from some shaved twigs, using a bit of lighter fluid to kindle the initial flame, then stacking driftwood around it to begin the process of drying.

He heated some canned stew for supper, smoked and enjoyed a cup of brandy, then unrolled his cocoon-like sleeping bag and enjoyed a peaceful night's rest. After daybreak, he explored, took pictures, even did some sketching, feeling very much like an explorer who has fulfilled a longtime dream, yet oddly surprised that, for all the Gustave Doré elements in the landscape, he had felt not a single goose bump, not for one moment felt the presence of something from what he now thought of as "the Other Side." He was a romantic young wanderer in as wild a spot as the Alps had to offer, but the most exciting thing he did was catch a trout for dinner.

Four days went by and Erich's supplies began to run out. So did his fishing luck, for he caught nothing else. Nor was there any game; aside from a few scrawny birds, the gorge seemed lifeless. The weather held good, and by any conventional standard of judgment, he was simply experiencing a very fine camping excursion. Tomorrow he would have to go back.

After supper he smoked half of the hashish and drank the rest of his brandy.

And promptly fell asleep.

When he woke, just on the far side of midnight according to his watch, he knew that he was no longer alone.

Above him, the moon seemed to be choking in thick tentacles of fog that writhed up from the gorge. Before he could recall that he had ingested a considerable quantity of drugs, he was startled by the acidity and vibrancy of the colors: moonlight like the phosphorescence of bones beneath the sea, the mist now particulate, so that he could perceive each molecular pattern of droplets, rainbowed from within, as well as the webbing of harmonic tension in the air that kept them suspended. Why, there was so much music here it was enough to drive the mind into overload: music of water and wind and light and rock, harmonies undetectable to the ordinary mind, wavelengths of light and color that had no earthly names.

He was absolutely awake now, and aware that he was the exact focus of the entire mighty gorge. The falling water eyed him like a vast transparent serpent, and in the pools where the water fell, the mist thickened suggestively, coiling and flexing, coming together.

A snake's head of mist lashed out and struck at his foot. He cried out and drew back, bringing his knees up and instinctively reaching for his rifle. Now the water laughed at him, mocking him. Where will you fire your bullets, my son? Into the falls or into the mist or into the rocks?

Now the hallucinations began to spin out of control, faster and more intense. So much light! So much sound!

The waterfall's roar had become a chorus, chanting pagan songs at the moon, and the mist around him had assumed a variety of half-recognizable Walpurgis shapes. Something was happening to the waterfall. It was changing. The portal he had so casually sought to unlock was in fact opening, and what was coming out was primal and horrible.

Here was the dragon all right, the terrible *Wurm*: the waterfall itself had assumed a scaly sinuous solidity, as though a serpent five hundred meters long were sliding down the mountain and surging forward to take him in its stupendous jaws.

There! Its red eyes! Its fangs! Oh Christ, the stench of its breath, the terrible crushing power of its coils!

The dragon's head subdivided now into a hydra's bouquet, a writhing nest of flared heads and flaming eyes. Screaming, Erich stood and raised the Mannlicher and fired until the magazine was empty, the reports painful to his ears. His mind laughed at his acts: You cannot wound mist with a bullet! The snakes' heads collapsed into an intricate knot of squirming water-flesh, as though the spirit that animated the water were debating what form to take next.

Now the mist resolved itself into muscles and organs and limbs of various sizes, as though trying out and discarding a thousand shapes. Finally, it rose above the rocks in the apparent form of a huge, ferocious bear with live coals for eyes and the stench of Hell's sulfurous pit for breath.

Beyond all reason now, the drug burning in his cells, his pupils wide as pennies, Erich fled blindly into the darkness, skinning his knees and elbows on the rocks, hearing the determined, hideously organic undulations of the shape pursuing him.

Once, he looked over his shoulder and saw that the entire gorge was now filled with a massive coil of scale-bright water-flesh, surging upward—miles in length, it seemed—spotted leprously with a hundred curdling, transforming visages of the Bear, each one with its hissing teeth bared and its volcanic eyes trained upward, gazing malevolently at Erich's pathetic attempt to escape that which he himself had summoned.

What might have happened next, Erich would speculate on for many years. What in fact did happen was solid contact between his head and an outcropping of granite that, in his panic-stricken flight, he did not see until the last second. He went down like a felled tree and when he woke the next morning, with a stupendous Wagnerian headache and a mouth as dry as alum, he discovered that he had been lying all night just inches away from a two-hundred-meter drop into the raging middle falls.

In the silence that followed the end of the girl's song, Erich felt himself curiously disembodied. Once, furtively, the girl looked at him, just as her fingers were rising, as palely graceful as those of a Balinese dancer, from the strings. Their eyes met, and he realized that they were both in another place—she from playing this music, and he from listening to it for the first time. In those eyes, now shifted in hue to a smoky amethyst, Erich beheld the same intensity he had felt within his own, on the night he conducted the Sibelius Seventh.

"Thank you, Kylliki," said Aino, dismissing the girl.

More liqueur was served. Without anything being said, both Aino and Rautavaara, although they remained seated in the room, seemed to recede from the conversation. The composer turned his attention fully to Erich, and the others seemed simply to withdraw, as though the elderly man had sent a telepathic signal to them. Perhaps he had; perhaps this was the way he ritualized his conversations. Perhaps this scene had been repeated a hundred times at Järvenpää, for visiting dignitaries and musicians and journalists. But not all of it, Erich found himself hoping; some moments of it seemed truly to be only for him.

"So: you conducted my Seventh. Not the easiest of the lot, I'm afraid. Its birth was difficult."

Erich expected the composer to continue, but he did not. Clearly, it was Erich's turn to speak, and, just as clearly, the logical progression of the conversation dictated that he say: Yes, Maestro, and *how* was it difficult? But that, Erich calculated, was a *journalist's* question, a supplicant's gambit, a boringly predictable way to secure something quotable. Erich wondered if he dared ratchet the conversation up a notch or two, so as to make it clear from the outset that he wished to be treated as a colleague, not a sycophant.

"I did more than conduct it, Maestro. I wrote a dissertation on its form."

"Ah! You're a brave man. The German critics don't think it has any."

Erich felt the quick heat of satisfaction at the composer's testiness, but beneath that, he detected a glow of genuine interest. He decided to press on.

"Oh, it does, I think, but it's not the kind of form they're

comfortable with or can easily understand. When I was preparing it for performance, I studied it first of all from the
viewpoint of sonata form, but it was like putting a corset on
a thin woman: you could do it, but it didn't really fit and it
wasn't really necessary. It was a symphony, yes, but only in the
sense that it was cast in symphonic proportions. I finally concluded that it was a rhapsody, a poem. So that is how I performed it, and that is the viewpoint from which I analyzed it."

While Erich was talking, Sibelius poured another glass of
liqueur for himself. Erich was surprised to note that the bottle
was now half-empty; while Erich had been daydreaming to
the *kantele* music, the old man had evidently been helping
himself liberally. Half a bottle of this liqueur, on top of the
aquavit he had consumed at lunch, was enough to inebriate a
man in the prime of life. Yet the composer held it well, be-
traying his intake only by the increased color on his cheeks
and the thickening of his German—a kind of phlegmy growl
had begun to roll with the "r's" and a trace of exaggeration
had crept into the letters beneath the umlauts.

"Damned close to the mark, Captain. Bravo to you. Did
you know that the original manuscript bears only the heading
Fantasia Sinfonica, not as a subtitle, but as the title proper—in
recognition of the very qualities you just spoke of. It does!
That is how I wanted to publish it. But I was not allowed to,
you know. I *had* to call it a symphony. They wanted one."

"Who is 'they,' Maestro?"

Sibelius gestured, spreading his arms, and grazing the liqueur bottle in the process, to encompass the unseen world of
his distant admirers.

"All of them wanted a symphony. The critics wanted a
chance to sharpen their claws on a new symphony. The conductors were squabbling for the first performance rights to a
new symphony. The record companies wanted to issue a new
symphony—not another tone poem. And so . . . I gave them
a seventh."

He drained his glass and refilled it, glancing at Erich's
glass to make sure it was not empty.

"Tell me, Ziegler, do they still perform my music in Germany?"

"Sometimes it is played, yes, but usually by visiting orchestras." Now Erich hesitated once more, if only for a few seconds. He did not want to sound boastful, but he did want Sibelius to know that here was a German conductor who had fought and won a small skirmish on behalf of his music. "I myself had to overcome some resistance when I conducted it. It's only a whim of musical fashion; it will change. The music is too strong not to win its rightful audience."

"But perhaps not in Germany, eh? Well, I'm glad you have the kidney to speak the truth, Ziegler. Of course, one does not always wish to hear it . . ."

There was now a gruffness in the voice, perhaps a moodiness brought on by drinking. Erich hurried on, wanting the conversation to become more comfortable and suddenly made insecure by the knowledge that there were unspoken rules of decorum to be obeyed in Sibelius's presence, protocols of which he knew nothing and which he might be able to circumvent by seizing control of the dialogue whenever he legitimately could. And a bit of national self-deprecation might go down well.

"I have a theory about that, Maestro."

"Do you, now? Let's have it."

"You know how we Germans are: dogmatic and overly structured in our cultural attitudes. We hold preconceived ideas: thus-and-so is the proper form for a symphony and nothing else will do! Academic careers are built on mastering the formulas, often at the expense of originality of thought and real feeling. On the other hand, the two nations that have embraced your art the most passionately are England and America, two countries that are not bound by calcified traditions in aesthetic matters. Their conductors, and their audiences, shop on the open market for music, and when they find something that speaks to them, they welcome it with open minds and hearts. The Germans don't have such open minds. And as for the rest of Europe, well, my God, the Italians don't care for anything but opera and never will—a nation of mu-

sical mountebanks. And the French remain hopeless xeno-
phobes, as they always have been. Look across the Channel,
Maestro, or look to the new world—your admirers there are
legion and what they choose to adopt, they care about passionately."

Sibelius smiled and drank, obviously mollified by Erich's
tact. Then he caught Erich off guard by asking: "And Strauss,
Ziegler, what of Richard Strauss? Does he still speak up for
my music?"

"I confess, Maestro, that I did not know he ever had."

A deep sigh went through the old man. He stared into the
bubbles in his glass and when he lifted his face, the blue eyes
had dulled, whether from tiredness or the effort of memory,
Erich could not tell.

Then, abruptly, to Erich: "I need a new champion in Germany."

Erich took a measured drink before responding. His answer, when he gave it, was not only the response he knew was
expected, it was the one he had prayed for a chance to give.

"I shall be your music's champion in Germany, Maestro. If
I survive this war, that is."

The old man's eyes glittered, full, and when he spoke his
voice held an odd timbral mixture of pride, affection, and self-
pity.

"We will help you do that. We'll make a place for you
here, and you must come here whenever you can. We are safe
here. The forest protects us."

"I'll come whenever my duties permit, Maestro."

Sibelius rose, ponderously and a bit unsteadily, and walked
to a bookcase inside his study. He returned with a full orchestral score, which he handed to Erich. "Here. If you responded
to the Seventh, which really is not a symphony, then you
should by all means become familiar with the Sixth, which is.
It and the Third are the least popular of the lot. I can understand about the Third, for I was never satisfied with it myself,
but in the case of the Sixth, I simply don't comprehend its
neglect. Take this score with you, and tell me what you think
when we meet again."

Erich thanked him, assuming that this was the end of his visit. This seemed an auspicious moment to bring up a subject that had been prodding his mind ever since the conversation had started.

"Maestro, what I should really like more than anything else is a peek at the Eighth Symphony. Just enough to get some idea of how it sounds. My curiosity is frankly enormous and I ..."

Sibelius dropped his hand stiffly. His eyes narrowed and grew cold, his lips compressed into a thin line. A faint tremor fluttered his cheeks.

"It is not finished. And questions like that are keeping me from finishing it."

He turned away, his shoulders hunched with rage, and stalked from the room. Somewhere in the depths of the house, a door slammed. Erich looked at the other two people in the room, seeking some explanation. The score in his hands felt as heavy as a tablet of stone. Aino came to him and laid a hand gently on his arm.

"He has had ... difficulties with the Eighth, Captain Ziegler. You must understand: the worldwide expectations for it are so great and so daunting, so many claims have been advanced for it by critics who have never heard a note of it. He agonizes over it, for fear that, when it is released, it will disappoint those who have made so much of it. It's become a kind of talisman for all those who have taken a look at all the fashionable musical styles and have said 'No, thank you.' The weight this has put on him is enormous, and tonight he was overstimulated."

An interesting euphemism for "drunk," Erich decided. His mood of intimacy with the composer was shattered, perhaps beyond repair. In spite of his ignorance, he felt boorish, betrayed by an adolescent eagerness—had not Rautavaara warned him? But this serendipitous meeting with Sibelius, coming as it did after so many weeks of combat, had not only reaffirmed the notion that Erich was destined to be something more than cannon fodder, it had fanned the embers of his ambition to a delicious, almost uncontrollable heat. Of course his enthusiasm had been too intense! What conductor in the world would not fight for the chance to lead the world premiere of Sibelius's Eighth, the most eagerly awaited and most speculated-about symphony of the last quarter century?

"It's getting late, Madame Sibelius. I think I should go. Please give my deepest apologies to your husband. Here is his score."

"No, you take it. He would wish it. I know him."

Erich and Rautavaara were donning their coats in the front hall when a telephone buzzed somewhere in the house. Rautavaara excused himself and went to answer it. He returned quickly, in a state of agitation.

"A message relayed here from a front-line observation post. Russian bombers just crossed the border, and if they stay on their present course, they'll fly directly overhead. I'm sure it's just a coincidence—they're probably on their way to raid the shipping at Oulu—but we can't take any chances; this house is highly inflammable. I've ordered everyone to take cover in the forest until they pass."

As he spoke, he hustled Erich outside into the thin afternoon light. The two servant girls, featureless in hastily donned cloaks, had stumbled from a rear entrance and could be seen huddling beneath a large spruce tree a hundred meters away.

"Where's Sibelius?" cried Erich.

"Aino will bring him out through the kitchen. Come on, head for those trees at the top of the ridge. I want to get a good view of them as they approach."

Aino and Sibelius, meanwhile, had appeared at the rear of the house. The composer was scowling furiously, waving his arms, and shouting in Finnish and in what sounded like Swedish as well.

"What's he saying?"

"He's cursing the Russians, very inventively, and in at least two languages. He has spunk for an old man, eh?"

The composer's ranting faded away as a faint hum spread over the sky. Erich could see them now, coming in high from the east: a V-shaped wedge of twin-engined Tupolev SB-2s.

His attention was quickly diverted from this spectacle by Aino's scream. He turned and saw that Sibelius, still cursing, had broken free of her arm and was running back into the house. Astonished, Erich saw the composer emerge, seconds later, brandishing an old Tsarist Mosin-Nagant rifle nearly as tall as he was.

"Christ, we'd better stop him!" Erich shouted as he sprinted from cover. Rautavaara followed, but slipped on the newly crusted snow and tumbled gracelessly. Erich reached the composer just as the first shot cracked out over the lake. For an instant he was stunned to immobility by the spectacle of the old man, red-faced and puffing angrily, wheezing out curse after curse, furiously working the rifle's bolt. A spent brass cartridge tumbled out, a tiny golden acrobat, and hissed as it struck the snow. A second shot shattered the afternoon's frozen calm. Sibelius was now so beside himself that he could not work the bolt properly—the spent round, bitten by the bolt-face, jammed against the fresh one trying to ride up from the magazine. A howl of fury tore from the old man's throat.

Erich stepped forward, gripped his shoulder, spun him around, and handed him his sidearm, butt first. As his fist closed on the checkered grip of the heavy Luger, a vulpine smile lit the composer's face.

"Use this, Maestro—it's cocked and ready to fire."

Holding the pistol stiff-armed in both hands, Jean Sibelius blasted seven 9-mm rounds into the sky in the general direction of the Soviet bombers, which flew on, regally undisturbed. The pistol shots' brutal crack rolled like thunder across the lake, and the sound waves blew snow loose from the nearest trees. At the last shot, the breech locked in the open position, the spent shell casings forming a necklace of steaming brass at the composer's feet. However ineffectual the volley had been as antiaircraft fire, delivering it appeared to have had a cathartic effect on the old man. Still grinning a half-crazed wolf's leer, he handed the smoking weapon back to Erich and cried: *"Lieber Gott! Wunderbar! Ausgezeichnet!"* Then, without another word, he stalked back into the house.

A moment later, as Rautavaara was holding the staff car

door open for Erich, he said: "That was good thinking, Captain. If he had, by some miracle, unjammed that weapon and actually hit one of those planes, what happened next might have gone down in the history books."

"He might have reached them with that rifle, but they were far beyond pistol range. Besides, I thought he would have more fun shooting it." And besides that, he realized, he had instinctively seen in that moment of confusion an opportunity for him to atone for his conversational *faux pas*, perhaps even to regain the old man's favor.

Just as they were about to drive off, Erich spotted Aino coming from the house. She carried an awkward stack of papers in her arms, which she thrust into the car when Erich rolled down the window.

"These are pocket scores to all the symphonies, and some other things as well. He wants you to take them with you and study them when you can."

"I couldn't take these from him."

"Please, Captain, he insists. It's his way of apologizing for that outburst this afternoon. You can return them later, when you have a chance to visit us again—a much longer visit, naturally; we have several guest rooms, but never any guests." She turned to Rautavaara. "Major, please arrange security clearance for Captain Ziegler, so that he can get past the guards even if you're not there to vouch for him."

As he entered Rautavaara's car, Erich felt a great sense of relief. Not only had he been forgiven, he had been formally invited back for a longer visit. And best of all, he thought as he hefted the stack of scores in his lap, he had been given a tangible sign that Sibelius, too, regarded their encounter as something more than happenstance.

Twilight was descending as they finally drove away, back into the forest. Aino went inside. Erich stared, his head painfully turned, until the lodge called Tapiola blended with the deepening shadows and seemed to merge with the forest itself.

Five

The first angry shots Erich heard when he and Eino finally reached the Third Division were delivered by weapons of such peculiar pattern that Erich insisted on stopping the car, approaching the three-gun battery, and observing its drill. The fire mission ended four rounds after they parked, at which time Erich was introduced to the lieutenant commanding the battery, who seemed happy to give Erich a tour of his singular weapons.

Erich's new role as an observer began the moment he set eyes on that artillery battery. Its anachronistic appearance might have meant more to a professional soldier, but Erich did know he had never seen weapons like these except in history books. They seemed almost Napoleonic: six-inch-caliber weapons cast in the form of a single long tube, the barrel itself uncluttered by such modern niceties as sights, recoil mechanisms, or range-finding gear.

Two-thirds of the way back from the muzzle, the barrel was surmounted by two U-shaped handles, where block and tackle could be attached for repairs, or for hoisting the barrel to another carriage. The breech block was little more than a crude metal plug. The gun carriage was wood, as were the wheels, and terminated in a one-piece iron trailer that tapered to a point five meters behind the breech. The wheels were nothing more than oversized wagon wheels, axles caked with fists of grease, whose rims had been modified with a series of flat iron plates to give a modicum of traction in mud or snow. To absorb recoil, the gunners used a system that looked, to Erich, like something from the late Middle Ages: the ends of the carrying trails were placed on the thin ends of enormous wooden wedges. When one of the cannon was fired, its brutal recoil drove the entire gun back until the angle of the wedge canceled out the backward push and more or less stabilized the weapon. The gunners would then surge forward, roll the pieces back into firing position with iron bars and brute strength, cram another shell into the smoking breech, then step away with their backs arched, ears covered, and mouths open against the blast wave. When Erich was observing this drill, he was surprised that a powder monkey did not run out with a smoldering stick, clamber up the trunnions, and apply fire to a touch hole; instead, a corporal with cotton in his ears stepped forth and tugged at a greasy lanyard, and the gun coughed, the explosion raw and hot-breathed and producing an enormous cloud of smoke. With each round fired, the guns slid massively up their wedges, plumes of smoke gushing from both ends.

"How do you hit anything with these antiques?" Erich asked the battery commander.

"Each gun is different," the man replied with a shrug. "I was trained by the man who commanded this battery during the Winter War and I've trained others to take over here should anything happen to me. It's a personal thing—you have to know the weapons intimately in order to get the most out of them. But what these pieces lack in accuracy and lethality, they make up for in psychological effect—those old shells have a much bigger flash and bang than the modern ones. Scares the hell out of the Russkies."

Proudly, the lieutenant helped Erich climb up the gun carriage of the nearest weapon, and there pointed out to him the worn but still defiant Tsarist eagle cast on the base of the barrel. According to the inscription beneath the emblem, this particular piece had been cast at the Tula arms factory in 1889.

After they left the battery, Erich and Eino spent two days trying to track down *Vanha Mikko*—"Old Mickey"—the armored train on which Eino was engineering officer and ranking noncom. The *Vanha Mikko* itself dated back to the Russian Revolution and had been liberated by Mannerheim's White forces from a roundhouse in Tampere. Eino had originally been detached to chauffeur Erich because the train could not go into action until Finnish-gauge track had been laid on the eastern side of the border. That had been accomplished during the last two weeks, but the train had been shunted back and forth so many times since becoming operational, as often on supply runs as on combat missions, that no one had a precise idea of where it was. It had been here, yesterday, supporting operations on the left wing; it had been somewhere else the day before, hauling ammunition and rations. Erich was struck by the fact that all the soldiers they spoke to referred to the train with affection. Not only did it serve as a floating reserve of firepower, able to add weight to attack or defense up and down the overextended divisional front, but its very appearance—snorting and roaring out of the forest like some slab-sided prehistoric monster—was always a morale booster.

So, without having planned it, Erich ended up getting a thorough tour of the Third Division's sector while Eino looked for his train. Erich studied everything that passed before his eyes, taking discreet notes in the back seat from time to time. If what he saw was typical, the Finnish Army was a functioning museum, a flea-market collection of hand-me-down equipment from warehouses all over Europe and America. That a force with such motley, out-of-date equipage should be able to function at all was remarkable; that it had been able to mount a successful offensive against the Red Army, along a front of more than five hundred kilometers, seemed almost fantastic.

On the second day of their odyssey, darkness began to settle at five in the afternoon. Light snow blurred the lines between road and landscape. According to Eino's last information, the armored train was ten kilometers to the north. Finding it in the dark would be chancy, dangerous, and not altogether necessary; clearly, the pace of fighting along this front had become lethargic—another night on the road would not matter. Eino found accommodations for them with a quartermaster platoon, conveniently close to a field kitchen.

Erich shared evening mess with the supply troops. Their commander, a stocky Bothnian lieutenant, spoke fair German. Erich noticed that the enlisted men treated their officer with extraordinary familiarity. He remarked this especially when, on two occasions, enlisted men entered the tent to ask for instructions from the lieutenant. He issued his orders casually, addressing both of the supplicants by their first names; at no time during these two exchanges was a salute given or taken by either party. When Erich asked Eino about this, Eino smiled, shrugged, rolled his eyes in mock exasperation: "Better get used to it, *Kapteeni.* Most of the men save that stuff for the parade ground, or when there's a general passing through. The closer they are to the front, the harder it is for Finnish soldiers to bend their elbows. I guess it's not like that in the German Army."

"No," said Erich, "it isn't. I'll try to get used to it, though."

The last hour before sleep was spent poring over maps spread on a plank table beneath kerosene lamps. Erich had a theory that if you really wanted to learn the specifics of a campaign in progress, you should talk to the men right behind the front lines. Officers in the rear were map-bound and made their decisions at a necessary remove from the fluidity, chaos, and violence of the front. The men who were actually in the lines were too preoccupied with survival and hence with immediate tactical problems—the machine gun pinning them down, the minefield they blundered into that wasn't supposed to be there—to correlate their short-range experience with the maps' big picture. Somewhere in between, one could usually obtain information that was fresh yet reasonably objective.

By the time the supply platoon had finished refighting the campaign on its maps, Erich had a clear idea of what had happened in this sector, a reasonably accurate understanding of current conditions, and the beginnings of a professional assessment of Finnish capabilities—everything he needed to write his first report to Klatt. He still did not know his own exact location, however—only that he was somewhere inside the twenty square kilometers defined by the fingertip of the Bothnian lieutenant, pressing against a set of map coordinates that showed trackless forests and a wild jumble of bogs, swamps, and lakes.

Between the boundary lines with the Karelian Army to the south, and with the German Thirty-six Corps to the north, the Finnish Third Corps—comprising the Third and Sixth Divisions, with a few packets of armor—was responsible for an enormous stretch of front: almost two hundred kilometers. On the Russian side of the border, there were few roads, none paved, and only a scattering of tiny, wretched Karelian villages, depressing and Dostoyevskian places of mud-rutted streets and bleak unpainted houses, walled in and towered over by the forest. Only two towns of any size—Kesten'ga in the north and Ukhta in the south, at the tip of Lake Kuyto—lay between the Finnish border and the curve of the Murmansk Railroad which brought it up against the shores of the White Sea. It was in this region that the Finns had achieved their maximum penetration into Soviet territory. Their lines now ran through Kesten'ga, encompassed half of big Lake Topozero, then gradually bent west again and passed through Ukhta, an average depth of seventy-five kilometers inside the USSR—almost half the distance between the border and the railroad's most vulnerable point.

Beginning their offensive in the last days of June, the Finns had advanced slowly, hampered nearly as much by the terrain as they were by Russian defensive actions, and having to build their supply lines as they went. A large-scale Finnish advance in this desolate region had taken the enemy by surprise, and not until October had Russian resistance stiffened, as reinforcements were fed into the line to screen the vital railway. By the end of November, the Finns had more or less reached the chain of rivers, ridges, and bogs that comprised Mannerheim's "stop-line": the best defensive positions available at this distance from the border—far enough inside Russia to provide defense in depth for Finland, deep enough to serve as a bargaining chip in any future negotiations, yet not so deep, and not seized so rapidly or violently, as to panic the Soviets into a major response. Except for localized operations to straighten out the lines or to gain a bit of ground for better observation, the Third Corps' front had been relatively quiet for a week, and it was the supply troops' opinion that things were going to stabilize pretty much where they were. Already, heavy construction material was starting to trickle in from Oulu, indicating that the high command would soon ordain a line of permanent fieldworks. In the morning, the supply officer managed to get enough radio time to track down the missing armored train. Its current fire mission accomplished and its magazines almost empty, it was steaming toward divisional headquarters, south of Lake Topozero; Eino could rendezvous with it there. Erich was agreeable; they had been in transit now for the better part of a week and it was time for him to get situated somewhere and begin composing his first report to Klatt. He was resolved to be scrupulous in his duties. He thought that if the Fatherland, in its wisdom, had chosen to assign him congenial duty on a stable sector of the front, he should certainly do his best to justify its decision.

"What sort of man is the division C.O.?" Erich asked, while they drove slowly along the outer edge of a horse-drawn supply column.

"Pajari is his name. He's a Winter War hero. His unit was outnumbered twenty to one when he took command, but he stopped the Russians cold and even threw them back to their starting place. They say he personally killed more than fifty Reds."

Erich was surprised to hear the admiration in Eino's voice. "I've never served under a real live hero before," he muttered, not entirely sure he was looking forward to the experience. Eino seemed to divine some of his thoughts.

"You'll find him tough but reasonable. He's done a good job of keeping the division together over a wide front, and he has a terrific instinct for knowing where the Russkies are. That's the important thing, Captain—you can move a lot of men through those trees without being seen, if you know how to do it."

"Do the Russians know how to do it?"

"Not yet, but you can bet they'll learn. After we kicked the shit out of them in December of thirty-nine, they learned plenty fast. When they came back at us again in February, they showed us how much they'd learned."

Pajari's headquarters dugout, *korsu* in Finnish, was a multi-roomed shelter as large as a cabin, hacked into the granite-flecked soil and roofed over with three meters of crisscrossed timbers and sandbags. A single-file entrance led down into it on the western side, but from every other angle, even at close range, the *korsu* resembled a mound of snow. Under the eaves of the log roof, a neat vestibule had been cleared just in front of the canvas sheets that closed the doorway; half a dozen Suomis stood there in a varnished wooden rack, their leather slings smeared with petroleum jelly against the cracking effects of the cold, tin cans carefully placed over their barrels to keep out the snow.

Inside, the air was close but not oppressive, indicating that some care had been taken to provide ventilation. The earthen floor was covered with duckboards that had recently been swept. Through an opening to the right, Erich glimpsed wooden bunks, tiered four deep from floor to ceiling. The main room contained radios, maps, a pair of clerks pecking out orders at trestle desks, a switchboard, and an efficient wooden stove which turned little yellow wedges of birchwood into great amounts of heat without giving off more than a hint of smoke. At the far end of the room, six-foot racks of smooth orange pine held skis, ski poles, white camouflage capes, and gauntlets of reindeer hide. Wooden crates stacked beneath contained extra drums of Suomi ammunition and potato-masher grenades.

Eino obviously knew the orderly who sat nearest the entrance; the man grinned as they entered, then, catching sight of Erich's uniform and rank, leaped smartly to his feet and saluted. Erich smiled to himself: evidently even in the Finnish Army, elbows bent more quickly in close proximity to high rank. A few minutes later, beside a plank table covered with maps of the Karelian wilderness, Erich shook hands with General Pajari.

Pajari had a face like chewed leather: sallow, pitted cheeks, eyes of pale blue-green surrounded by wrinkles like the pleats in a fan, a blunt, pocked, graceless nose, and sparse eyebrows the color of straw. The air around the general's head was cloudy with fumes from the black Russian cigarettes he smoked and his voice was a splintery three-packs-a-day croak. His handshake was brusque, as was his appraisal of Erich's papers. While he flipped through the documents, he motioned for Erich to sit, ignoring Eino, who stood uncomfortably at attention off to one side. Unbidden, an orderly brought Erich a mug of coffee. Then Pajari looked up and ordered everyone else out of the room, leaving only Erich and himself.

"Your papers are in order, Captain Ziegler, but then of course, one would expect them to be. I'll add my own signature to them—there—and now you can go anywhere you like and see whatever they sent you here to see."

"I beg the general's pardon?"

Pajari lit another cigarette. Only the frequency of his smoking betrayed any sign of nervous strain—his hands were as steady as the tree roots they resembled, their spatulate fingers groomed to the nails.

"Oh good God, Captain, let's you and I start this thing off honestly, shall we? You may be here as an ally, but you're also here to spy on us for your German masters, and I don't know whether to welcome you or have you shot. I really don't know how I feel about you Germans any longer."

"Perhaps then, sir, we'd better clarify things now, at the start, as you suggest."

Pajari swept his hand across the maps. "On the one hand, I suppose we ought to be grateful to you. By attacking Russia, you've given us a chance to get back the land Stalin took from us in 1940. Well, we've done that and more. We've achieved our objective for going to war. Now we're going to stop, dig in, and hope that things develop in our favor. But I wonder whether you Germans will allow us to do that. We've hitched a ride on the tiger's back—will it be possible to dismount now?"

"I'm afraid I don't follow the general's argument . . ."

"Don't you indeed? Then answer this, Captain: Where are *you* going to stop and dig in? How far will you try to go? How much of Russia is enough? If it's *Lebensraum* you're fighting for, you've already got enough for ten times the population of Germany. But if your objective is to destroy the Slavic race, then you're trying to do the impossible—not even Genghis Khan could manage that."

Erich had long entertained similar misgivings, but had been able to offset them by concentrating on the one objective he could wholeheartedly support.

"I don't think the war is about destroying the Slavic race, General. What about the destruction of Bolshevism?"

"That's a side issue. Tell me, Ziegler, have you read *Mein Kampf*?"

"Good Lord, General, I don't know anybody who's actually *read* the thing."

Pajari allowed himself a tiny smile.

"Well, I waded through it, and my conclusion is that your führer wages war the way other men have seizures of *grand mal*. To him, it is a biological imperative, a process which justifies itself. You see, Captain, because you Germans have no rational goals for this Russian campaign, you will inevitably become impatient with our own modest objectives, all of which we have already achieved. And I resent that, for it poses a mortal danger to my nation. On the other hand, we owe our achievements to the opportunity you provided for us on June twenty-first, so please try to understand my ambiguous feelings about you and what you represent."

Pajari thumped his fingers along the thick black line of the Murmansk Railroad, making a rippling, arpeggiated sound. It was absolutely quiet in the *korsu* now, except for the faint clicking of code from the radio.

"Even the Lord himself must have an Antichrist to strive against, otherwise how could he define his purposes? For Hitler, Stalin is the Antichrist. For him, this is not a war for political objectives, but a manifestation of mystical urges—a war that expresses, in Hitler's mind, the primal drives of racial blood. That is why, sooner or later, quite apart from its strategic value, Hitler will exert pressure on us to launch an offensive against the Murmansk Railroad ... somewhere up here, on the White Sea coast.

"Did you know, Ziegler, that we've been fighting the Russians on and off for five hundred years? Both of our countries know what's on the agenda by now: land, borders, territorial security—hell, it never changes. That's why we have tried to achieve this delicate balance with the Russians all along our part of the front. We've told them—actually come right out and *told* them—that we want nothing more than what we've taken already. We Finns have a relationship to History that is much less grandiose than you Germans perceive your own to be."

"Then what comes next for your army?"

"The tricky part. At this moment, things seem to be stabilizing; both sides have exchanged blows, now they can dig in, make themselves as comfortable as possible, and wait for negotiations to start. But if we went all out for the railroad, way up here in this wilderness, the Russians would react like a bear to the goad."

"But the Russians are stretched so thin, surely you'd have enough strength to deal with them."

"We're stretched thin too, Captain, and we don't have a million men in Siberia to call on for reserves. My division took a thousand casualties in the past eight weeks, and we're covering a front that's twice as wide as we're supposed to cover. If the Russians should make a serious effort against us, I cannot guarantee that we would be able to stop them. Most of our heavy artillery ammo has been fired off, and it will take weeks for adequate stocks to work their way up to us. You saw the condition of the roads in this region!"

Pajari had worked himself up righteously, his manner assuming a curious blend of pedantic lecturing and genuine anger—as though Erich, by popping up just when he did, had been deputized as a stand-in for the German General Staff. Now the general rummaged through a stack of message flimsies, selected one, then slapped it with his hand, inches from Erich's nose.

"Yesterday I received this order: 'Due to repeated enemy efforts to break the ring around Leningrad, imperative you create diversion by launching feint'—a *feint*, mind you!—'in direction of Louhki, signed Mannerheim.' That's a railhead on the edge of the White Sea, about fifty kilometers east of our farthest advance. A *gesture*, Captain, is what I'm ordered to make, to prove to the Germans that our hearts are in the right place, and to shut them up and get them off our backs. The only reason I'm obeying this order instead of resigning my commission is because I think I see what our high command is doing. If they make this gesture now, hit the railroad now, at the Germans' request, then later on this winter, when you try to pressure us into launching an all-out attack on Leningrad from the northwest, we'll be in a better position to say no."

Self-consciously remembering his instructions from Colonel Klatt, Erich ventured to ask: "How does Field Marshal Mannerheim feel about the Leningrad issue?"

"Ha! The old man would never order an assault on the city. He loves it too much. Don't forget: he was a member of the Tsarist court, and he knew St. Petersburg well. When he was a young hussar, he danced in its ballrooms. Do you think he wants to be remembered by history as the general whose troops used the art galleries of the Hermitage for latrines? I know the outside world thinks we're primitive people up here, but we're not barbarians!"

Pajari broke off into a spasm of coughs; when they subsided, he lit another Russian cigarette. Erich had recovered somewhat from the shock of Pajari's initial hostility. Whatever strains the man was under, he at least knew why he was fighting. If Klatt and his intelligence people wanted to know about the attitudes of the Finnish officer corps, he already had plenty to tell them. But hard on the heels of that thought came a more sobering one: Pajari was not far wrong about one thing, although until that moment, Erich had chosen not to regard himself as a spy. It was not possible that Pajari, seeing through him from the first moment—or perhaps even warned of his coming—had designed this lecture with the knowledge that some account of it would reach German ears.

"If I may ask, General, will you appeal the order to attack the railway?"

"I already have. The response was immediate and negative. But my division is in no shape to launch a major offensive, and if I ordered those men to charge for the White Sea, they would quite properly mutiny and put me in a straitjacket, provided they didn't shoot me first. So I am 'demonstrating' by sending in a single large ski patrol, thirty-five men, to make a quick dash for the line, lay some charges, then get back here as fast as they can. The damage they do won't be anything the Russians can't fix in a matter of hours, but at least that way I'll have fulfilled the letter of my orders."

"Can your men get through?"

"Oh yes. We did it several times during the Winter War, more for psychological reasons than anything else. Getting there won't be hard—the front is porous enough on both sides, since neither army has the strength to man continuous lines. But when we hit that track, we'll be sticking pins into a nerve; they'll know exactly where to look for us and they'll converge like a swarm of bees. My men left this morning before dawn. They'll be lucky if half of them make it back. I knew that when I asked for volunteers, and they knew it when they agreed to go."

Silence settled over the table. Pajari seemed lost in gloomy contemplation of the map before him. Erich felt that he had been dismissed. He rose and saluted.

"General, I respect your position and I understand the pressures on you. I give you my word that I'll not be a burden on you while I'm here, and I assure you that I am acting under only the most generalized instructions. I'm mostly supposed to assess weapons, tactical capabilities, that sort of thing."

Pajari smiled, his expression carrying a hint of sardonic warmth. "And attitudes?"

"Well, yes," admitted Erich, "of course that was mentioned too."

"Quite. Well, Captain, you are free to come and go as you like, see what you want to see, and ask questions of whomever you meet. It may well be that your presence here will prove useful to us as well as to your superiors."

"In some ways, General, you're fighting a strange war."

"Stranger than you know, Captain. Well, I appreciate your frankness with me, and I want you to know that as far as my men are concerned, you're simply a liaison officer from our powerful German ally—that's the story I'm putting out, anyway. You're free to make your own friends and enemies. We'll find quarters for you in one of the dugouts, or you can bunk down in that dinosaur of a train. A staff car is at your disposal unless and until I have need of it. You'd best stop in at the ordnance depot, pick up a Suomi, and familiarize yourself with it—if I need you to fight, I'll put you in the line just like any other able-bodied man. You can do that, can't you?"

"Do what, sir?"

"Fight."

There was a challenge in Pajari's eyes as well as his voice. Forcing himself to return the gaze steadily, Erich answered in measured tones: "I've been in the front lines outside Murmansk since July."

Pajari nodded slowly, gazing up and down Erich's stiff, self-conscious figure. Then in a sudden shift of character, he placed a burly paw on Erich's shoulder and said: "Take your driver and get something to eat in the officers' mess. Tell them you're my guests. The rest of it can wait until you've had some food. Just be sure to let me know where you decide to bed down—I want to know where to find you if I need to."

Six

Not far from Pajari's headquarters, an east-west line of track, hastily extended from the Finnish border, joined a north-south line the Soviets had constructed to supply their border troops. The latter track ran across the base of the Finnish salient, between Ukhta and Kesten'ga, until its proximity to Russian lines made it unusable. It was along this line that "Old Mickey" operated, rolling back and forth as needed, providing an added increment of firepower first in one place, then in another.

The *Vanha Mikko* showed up, as predicted, not long after Erich and Eino had finished their meal. The train came bellowing out of the forest in a dramatic surge of steam, its blunt steel-plated nose, streaked with whitewash and emblazoned with Walt Disney's ubiquitous mouse, suddenly looming through the center of a fluffy white cloud. The discharge from its stacks knocked great dollops of snow off the low-hanging branches, the helmeted antiaircraft crews in their armored cupolas ducking low and shouting unheard curses as the stuff rained over them. Troops near the railroad track responded enthusiastically as the train approached, cheering and hurling snowballs at the engine's snout.

There was a big steam locomotive at either end, a necessary redundancy of power required to move the train's immense extra weight. Both engines were completely skirted with steel plate around boilers, drive wheels, and cabs. The coal tenders too were plated and their tops had been roofed over and turned into gun platforms where three Maxim-pattern water-cooled weapons had been bolted together to form a flak battery. There were armored crew cars, a pair of armored boxcars for cargo and shells, and in the middle, an extra-long flatcar on which reposed the canvas-shrouded bulk of two German-made 150-mm cannon. Stabilizing platforms were folded up at the sides of the flatcar, with outriggers which could be dug in during firing. Here and there along the armored skirts, the steel had been indented by shrapnel strikes, and on the thick plating of one locomotive, a deep scooping dent surrounded by a compass rose of scorch marks showed where the train had taken a direct hit from a medium-sized Russian gun.

Erich was fascinated by the train: a big ugly toy, probably far more useful to the Finns as a morale booster than a weapon. Inside the crew cars, he found quarters that were cramped but warm. Each man had a bunk and a bit of personal space, bounded by pine-board partitions, which gave at least the illusion of privacy. There was a tiny galley, dominated by a profane but remarkably skillful cook, and a latrine that was kept warm by the proximity of steam lines beneath the train. To Erich, it looked like a fairly pleasant setup, and when the train's commander, a young ensign named Segerstam, offered him a vacant spot, Erich accepted.

Eino introduced him to the crew, then hurried off to attend to a hundred repairs, minor and otherwise, that had backed up while he was off chauffeuring their German guest. Erich discovered that most of the crew were working-class reservists, called up last May when renewed conflict seemed imminent—factory hands from Tampere and Hämeenlinna, longshoremen from Turku, civil servants from Helsinki, and scarcely a woodsman in the lot.

Erich was happily surprised at the number of them who could speak either German or English—a language which had been part of Erich's curriculum at the conservatory. It turned out that everyone in the *Vanha Mikko's* crew who had graduated from high school could converse, however rustily, in at least one foreign language. Even so, Erich prevailed upon Eino to be his primary teacher of Finnish. Their journey together, and the personal side trips each man had taken during its course, had created between them a closeness which was starting to become genuine friendship.

At first, he found the Finnish language impossibly difficult and bewildering, which did not surprise the Finns in the least. That he should even make the effort, however, seemed both to amuse and to flatter them, and eventually, as the sheer strangeness of the tongue faded, he made rapid progress.

Erich was almost as quick a study in languages as he was in music, and he had several strong motives for wanting to become proficient in Finnish. First of all, he wanted to do his job well and thus improve his chances of keeping it—hell, he even liked this army better than his own! Beyond that was his desire to impress Sibelius by being able, at their next meeting, to converse with him in his native tongue. Still deeper, but not so deep that he was not deliciously aware of it, was the recollection of that hauntingly beautiful girl, Kylliki. The sight and sound of her playing the *kantele* had become an almost Madonna-like icon in his memory. And she, unlike her master, could speak only Finnish.

Eino scoured the division for written material that would help Erich. The best things he came up with were a German-Finnish military dictionary published back in the 1920s, when numerous young Finnish officers had gone to Europe to further their technical educations, and—to Erich's delight—a side-by-side Finnish/German version of *Faust*. Goethe's direct, uncluttered, yet highly subtle use of language made a perfect vehicle for study.

As Erich lay in his bunk, smoking and studying by lamplight, he came to suspect that there was some truth in Eino's assertion that Finnish must at one time have been an Asiatic language. Its words tended to great length—like the Germans, the Finns seemed inordinately fond of compounds—

with a multitude of umlauts and double vowels. The grammar was fierce in its complexity, impenetrable, as even the Finns themselves admitted. All but barren of prepositions, Finnish made do instead with more than a dozen case endings—Erich never could remember the exact number—each of which changed the internal spelling of the root word, often drastically. For the purposes of military science, or technology of any kind, it seemed a baroque and cumbersome tongue.

On the other hand, in keeping with its mysterious and possibly Eastern origins, Finnish seemed to Erich to be extraordinarily rich in onomatopoeic nuances. In many instances, not only were the words themselves beautiful in sound, but they seemed uncannily expressive of the ontological qualities of what they described. The word for "tiny" was *pieni*, a little piccolo-toot of a word that seemed perfectly to evoke the wee-ness of something that could be held in the pinch of thumb and forefinger. The word for "warmth" was *kuumuus*, with long *u*'s, precisely the kind of gratified sighing sound a cold man might make as he stretched his palms toward a welcoming fire. "Brown" was *ruskea*, with a roll on the *r* and a purse-lipped breath on the *us*, imparting to the word a Novemberish quality.

Inevitably, as he made progress, the rougher elements of the soldiers' vocabulary were carefully drilled into him by his mentors. In this branch of linguistics, the complications of Finnish grammar permitted some extremely colorful and inventive swearing, as he found out one day when Ensign Segerstam poked his head in and brusquely ordered Eino to stop giving language lessons and go fix an electrical short the cook had just discovered in the galley. Eino waited until the officer had left, then made a universally understood hand gesture and snarled a toothy, two-syllable oath in Finnish.

"I need to learn those words, too," said Erich, grinning. "You can't serve in anybody's army without learning how to say 'fuck you!' at the proper moment."

"Indeed you can't, Captain, and that's the fucking truth!" replied Eino, clapping him on the shoulder.

So Eino taught him the word, as well as a great many

other usefully profane and scatological terms. And Erich, as his familiarity with Finnish increased, had fun playing with their possibilities. A simple interjection such as "Fuck you!", he discovered, could be modified by basic grammatical rules to form an exceedingly creative and tasty adjective that denoted having-the-qualities-of-one-who-habitually-fucks-himself.

Ensign Segerstam, the train's commander, seemed particularly eager to ingratiate himself with his German guest. The ensign was an intense, busy little man, pale as ivory, with long-fingered, blue-veined hands, their wrists as close to hairless as those of a preadolescent boy. His enthusiasms, too, seemed almost boyish. He spoke glowingly to Erich about the "historic partnership between the two great Nordic peoples" represented by Finno-German cobelligerency. After supper one evening, Segerstam invited Erich into his cubicle for coffee and proudly displayed a framed photo of Hitler. The young officer launched into a passionate and somewhat incoherent ideological tirade about *Lebensraum*, "racial destiny," and "the innate superiority of the Nordic type over the bestial Slav."

Politely drawing the man out, in accordance with his instructions to take the pulse of the Finnish officer caste, Erich soon learned that Segerstam was a proud member of something called the Karelian Brotherhood, a right-wing splinter group which, the ensign insisted, numbered in its ranks many prominent officers and scholars. Erich listened, fascinated and a bit nonplussed, while Segerstam outlined a fantastic scenario of growing political, military, and economic power—all quite hopelessly beyond the capacity of Finland's gross national product to sustain—which would culminate with Finland dominating not only the Scandinavian subcontinent but a sizable part of the Soviet Union as well. At the climax of his rhetorical flight, Segerstam reached into his locker and unfolded for Erich's edification a map, printed by the Karelian Brotherhood, showing a hypothetical "Greater Finland" which not only incorporated all the provinces of Karelia but stretched eastward as far as the Ural Mountains.

The next day, Erich took Eino aside and asked him point-blank if such extreme irredentist views enjoyed much currency in the army. Eino shook his head, smiling sadly, as Erich recounted the details of Segerstam's diatribe. "I know, *Kapteeni*; all of us have gotten the same lecture at one time or another. The ensign is brave enough, and not a stupid man, but he is obsessed. He was too young to see action in the Winter War—he was still in training when the armistice went into effect. His family were Karelians, and they lived in one of the provinces we had to cede to the Russians. Overnight, Segerstam's mother and father were forced to load all their belongings onto a sled and drive westward more than fifty kilometers. The winter that year had been unusually bitter; conditions remained harsh even by mid-March. A blizzard struck while the family was on the road. The ensign's mother froze to death, sitting upright on the sled. His father drove right through the storm without realizing she had died. When he discovered what had happened, his heart gave out. A Finnish patrol found them after the snow stopped falling. On the day Segerstam finished training, he learned not only that his home was now inside the Soviet Union, but also that both of his parents had died as a result of that fact. He will not rest, that one, until every square inch of Karelia is once more Finnish. And over the years, his obsession has grown to the point that he now wants far more than Finland ever had a legitimate claim to. There are others who feel as he does; but not many. A handful of crackpots, and some superannuated officers that Mannerheim put out to pasture years ago. Segerstam would be pathetic, if he didn't do a good job running the train. And after all, every man needs a private dream to get him through what's happening."

Erich felt his respect for Eino growing daily; when he had first met this rough-looking working-class man, he would never have expected the fellow even to think in terms of "private dreams," but now he realized how presumptuous, even haughty, that response had been. All men felt pain and loss, all men had hope and desire—therefore, all men had dreams, articulated or not.

Certainly his own dream was taking renewed shape, renewed vividness, from the stack of Sibelius scores that he burrowed into every night before sleeping. Each time he lifted one of the crisply printed Breitkopf and Härtel editions, he was acutely and pleasurably aware that they had come to him from the composer's own hand. He marveled as he turned the scores over under a light and saw upon their covers, front and back, rings left from coffee cups and brandy glasses, small brown ideograms branded by stray cigar ashes. The pages even smelled of the wood and smoke and woolliness of the composer's study.

He delved first into several of the tone poems, based, most of them, on the Finnish national epic, the *Kalevala*. When Erich asked Segerstam where he might obtain a copy, the ensign proudly produced not only a modern, annotated Finnish edition, but also a moldy German translation dating from 1907. By comparing the two, Erich greatly accelerated his study of Finnish, as well as his understanding of the cultural wellsprings that had fed Sibelius's art.

The *Kalevala* had not been written down until the 1830s, when a Finnish physician named Elias Lönnrot spent years crisscrossing not only the lands inside Finland's modern boundaries, but vast tracts as well of ancient Karelia, all the way up to Murmansk, collecting every scrap of oral material he could find. God alone knew how old many of these verses were—some of the tales could be cross-referenced to the fourteenth century, but the oral rune-chants themselves might well predate the time of the Mongols.

In fifty long, rambling cantos, totaling some twenty-three thousand lines, the epic told of the comings and goings of ancient Finnish heroes from the land of Kaleva, often striving against an older "northern" race in the land of Pohjola—possibly the inhabitants of Lapland, or even the ancient and undocumented forest tribes who had lived here before the Finns themselves wandered in from Central Asia. Despite the monotonous rhythms, obviously intended to help memorization in an age before there was such a thing as written Finnish, Erich found himself carried along by the characters. Men and women alike, they were a vital blend of the heroic and the all-too-human; they fought, cast spells, got drunk, plundered, plotted, wept, sang, and the men abducted wives and daughters with lusty regularity. Erich came to feel that, on the whole, it was at least as interesting a cast of characters as that found in the Germans' *Nibelungenlied.*

But it was in the *Kalevala*'s poetic references to nature that Erich found the closest kinship to the music of Sibelius. He was quite charmed by the opening invocation:

Then the Frost his songs recited,
And the rain its legends taught me;
Other songs the winds have wafted,
Or the ocean waves have drifted;
And their songs the birds have added,
And their magic spells the tree-tops.

He read and reread the passage, letting his mind drift. Like that ancient bard, he too felt on the verge of opening a box of treasures, a trove of legends and songs.

Once he had gone through the tone poems, Erich turned his attention to the symphonies, going through them in chronological order; a clear progression was evident, when all seven works were viewed as parts of a single *oeuvre.* There was much of Tchaikovsky in the First—so obviously the work of a young composer with much to say and in a hurry to say it all. The orchestration verged on the purple and there were more than a few moments of gawky, heavy-handed transition, but there was no mistaking the enormous talent and power contained in its blustery, unkempt rhetoric.

In the Second, with its majestic coda and highly original slow movement, Erich found much to admire, as well as a number of stylistic traits that spoke of greater confidence and maturity. The Third was clearly a transitional work, bridging the expansive and romantic gestures of the first pair and the leaner, more sinewy style of the later symphonies. Parts of it seemed self-consciously Brahmsian, but there was a lovely little *andantino* movement that made him think of a clear, cold brook meandering downstream to join an alpine river.

He was aware, from articles he had read years before, that the Fifth was the most popular of the later symphonies with Sibelius's ardent British and American admirers, but Erich saw in it a host of pitfalls for the conductor. The ending of the first movement, for example, seemed all but impossible to conduct or to play. When no one was about, he tried it, moving his arms and conjuring the orchestra in his mind. No doubt about it: the strings would tend to run away with it and get ahead of the slower instruments; the thing would fall apart. Yet how exhilarating if it *was* done right! He worked on gestures, formulated verbal instructions, made a mental note that this passage might require extra, section-by-section rehearsal time. And the symphony's stark chordal ending at first puzzled him, then irritated him, so that he finally flung the score aside and resolved to come back to it when he had digested this mass of music a little better.

Certainly, he concluded, the Fifth seemed a lesser work than either the Seventh, which he now studied with renewed appreciation of its originality, or the Sixth, which seemed, along with the Fourth, almost an invisible work in the composer's canon, so rarely was it performed or recorded. Yet from the first page, Erich felt that here was true enchantment: a shapely, cool reflection of the bittersweet Nordic spring, perhaps, and as chastely classical in its proportions as anything of Mozart's. Its delicacy, tenderness, and economy contrasted wonderfully with the growling and roaring of Sibelius's early orchestral style—Erich kept thinking of it, somehow, as almost Grecian. This, he decided, was the symphony he would conduct next, if and when such an opportunity came.

But the first time Erich read through the Fourth Symphony, he put it aside, disturbed, after just the first two movements. He returned to it only later, after he had become familiar with the rest. A palpable sense of desolation, almost of dread, came from its pages. Although a full orchestra was required, there were few *tutti* passages; instead, chamber-music groupings of instruments held colloquy across a gulf of black silence. There was not a single measure of warmth, pity, or compassion to be found in the entire score. Instrumental tones seemed to float across a plane of ice. At the end, there was nothing to please the crowd: the music just reached a kind of stasis, an equilibrium born of stoic acceptance or resignation. So totally unlike any other of the composer's symphonies was this bleak and wintry discourse, so stark and uncompromising was its style, that it must surely reflect a terrible inner despair, a sorrow beyond weeping.

Erich finally abandoned himself to the score, going over passages time and time again, until the oil sputtered in his lamp and the snores of the train's crew rattled the darkness around him. My God, he thought, an audience couldn't *begin* to get into the piece in less than five hearings! The music was as deep as death, and on its surface, about as appealing. This music could wrap itself around your soul like the coils of a serpent. If he programmed this, he had damned well better know what he was doing and had better not step on the podium with any thought of "bravos!" ringing out at the end. This was a symphony that would be followed by silence, not cheers. No wonder the bloody thing was never performed! What conductor would set himself up for that kind of reaction? *I* would, he thought. Just give me a chance, old man, and I'll show you what I can do with this music!

Seven

After the old train was resupplied and the dents in its armored skirt hammered flat, the crew had a few days of rest and light duty. Mail was delivered, the food got better, and truckloads of construction equipment were seen arriving at divisional headquarters. The tempo of the fighting was clearly slowing, on this front at least, and rumors began circulating of imminent furloughs.

Then the raiding party returned, what was left of it. As Pajari had predicted, the detachment had easily penetrated Russian lines and, after an undetected approach march lasting three days, had reached the main trunk of the Murmansk Railroad. Using the limited weight of explosives they had carried on their small supply sleds, the guerrillas managed to cut the line in four places, over a length of three kilometers—enough damage to cause the enemy great annoyance, but not enough to stop traffic along the line for more than a day or two.

To better elude the pursuit that was sure to follow, the Finns divided into two groups. One party, eighteen men, made it back to friendly lines with only a few wounded. The other group of seventeen was never seen again.

The local Russian commanders evidently interpreted these

minor incursions as a sign that the Finns were about to resume their offensive against the railroad. The specter of a major Finnish operation caused the enemy to advance his own timetable for a spoiling counterattack in the direction of Lake Topozero—a division-sized push designed to blunt, if possible forever, any new Finnish drive toward the White Sea.

The linchpin of the Soviet operation was a corduroy road surreptitiously built through the forest to within a few hundred meters of Finnish lines. Logs were laid tightly against one another, then covered with water. Within an hour the surface was frozen solid enough to bear the weight of tanks. The Russian planners were gambling that the numerous small lakes radiating from the western terminus of that road would be frozen hard enough by now to support at least the lighter-weight BT and T-26 tanks, while a dozen heavy KV vehicles, drawn from the Leningrad front's reserves, would plow straight ahead on the log road and punch a deep hole in the defenders' line. Masses of infantry would follow these armored spearheads, close behind the tanks. And an entire reinforced division—the Seventy-seventh Siberian—would therefore be thrown against a sector defended by a single Finnish battalion.

Extra batteries of artillery had been hauled forward to support the attack, and just after breakfast on the morning of November 27, Erich saw the curtain rise on this action. He had taken a mug of coffee up the ladder to the antiaircraft cupola on top of the crew car where he slept. The night seemed cut from black crystal and was dusted with the coldest-looking stars he had ever seen. From this position, he reckoned he should be able to see the sun rise over the forest. There was already a lemony wash in the eastern sky when he finished his coffee and ducked below with cupped hands to light a cigarette. Then he watched the light strengthen and the trees, rolling in endless pointed ranks to the horizon on either hand, go from inky black to ashen grey.

Then the sunrise was overwhelmed by another, closer cone of light, a drum-pounding flicker that rolled back and forth across the eastern horizon. Timpani beat through the resonating steel at Erich's feet and a far-off part of the forest began to shake and bleed smoke. It was the heaviest barrage he had seen since the first German attack on Murmansk, and it appeared to be landing north and slightly east of the train's position, up near the southern shore of Lake Topozero. Pajari had been right; the general knew his business. That railroad raid, trivial enough in itself, had provoked a response all out of proportion to the damage done.

In the crew's quarters below him, an alarm sounded. Steam was raised in the old locomotives' boilers as the *Vanha Mikko* shook to life. Erich was suddenly too excited to feel the cold and resolved that he would ride into battle up here, from a vantage point that would afford him a panoramic view of what was happening.

By full daylight, steam was up and orders had come through for the train: "Old Mickey" was to steam north and provide counter-battery fire for the local Finnish forces as needed.

Pounding at high speed through the wilderness, laying down a long white plume that glittered in the cracking-sharp air, the train took on a resemblance to a lean, straining warship cutting through a sea of white and dusky emerald. The train even flung out a bow wave of snow as it sliced through fresh drifts, its guns bristling black and deadly against the aluminum-colored sky of morning. To his surprise, Erich found himself enjoying this frigid ride hugely. Everything he had seen of war so far had been a slogging, degrading business; the only excitement he'd experienced had been the jangling of fear in his own nervous system. This morning, quite unexpectedly, war was showing him a remarkably poetic face.

Not until some time later was he able to learn exactly how the battle developed. The overture, in classic Russian style, had been a stupefying artillery and aerial bombardment, its effects multiplied because the Finns were off guard and had not had enough time to complete their field fortifications. Russian tanks fanned out from the hidden ice road according to plan, the lighter vehicles spreading north and south of that point, using the frozen lakes to probe for weak spots in the

Finnish line, while the heavy KV monsters growled straight ahead, a battering ram of steel. Antitank mines and satchel charges thrown by a handful of suicidally brave individuals accounted for a few of the KVs, but the most common Finnish antitank weapons—20-mm Lahti rifles and 37-mm Swedish Bofors guns—could do little more than chip paint off a KV's turret. True to the tactical doctrines perfected in the Winter War, the Finnish infantry just got out of the way and let the heavy tanks through, then concentrated on repelling the Soviet infantry units that followed.

For a while, the Finnish line held as platoon commanders and noncoms improvised a scrappy defense that mauled the first few waves of Russian infantry. Eventually, however, the lighter Russian armor slipped through on both flanks and began overrunning the wagon roads the Finns had been using to supply their units. Once they reached these crude but vital arteries, the Soviet tanks ranged north and south almost at will, shooting up supply vehicles, mortar batteries, command posts, and field hospitals. Confusion spread quickly, compounded by the fact that most of the unprotected Finnish telephone wires had been severed by the first bombardment.

By late afternoon, the Russians' own success had begun to work against them. The KV tanks never rejoined into a coherent formation, but simply roamed around until they ran out of gas or ammunition; the Finns organized tank-killer teams and took them out one by one. The lighter armor stayed in formation, but General Pajari's emergency call to Mannerheim resulted in a devastating low-level strike by Stukas from German bases in the far north. By nightfall, the Russians' forward progress had halted, and the Finns were regrouping and making plans for a counterattack. On the map at Pajari's headquarters, the enemy penetration resembled a long fat sausage just underneath the southern shore of Lake Topozero.

The *Vanha Mikko* remained on the other side of the Russian salient, firing until its ammunition bunkers were empty, then chugging back for more. Once it became clear that the Russian thrust had been contained, there were fewer calls for the train's support. Although it still remained on station, its crew was able to return to a fairly routine schedule. Segerstam found a heavily wooded area in which to park the train, beneath a snowy dome of tall arctic pines, and a few hours' work with camouflage nets and paint sufficed to make them invisible from the air.

When Erich woke the following morning, he was happily surprised to learn that Segerstam had allowed the crew to sleep an extra two hours. During the night, the region immediately around the train seemed to have become quite peaceful. Erich showered, dressed, then went to the mess car, where he found Eino and several other Finns gathered for breakfast. While they waited for food from the galley, they smoked, talked, and drank coffee; two men were diligently waxing their skis. The atmosphere could scarcely have been less warlike—Erich felt as though he had wandered into a small but exceedingly cozy ski lodge. He helped himself to a mug of coffee, laced with milk and sugar, sat down across from Eino, and lit the first, best cigarette of the day.

"Has the war stopped or something, Eino?"

"No such luck. But our part of it seems to have taken a recess today, for a fact."

Erich exhaled luxuriously. From the steam-obscured little galley, a private in an apron appeared, bearing a tray heaped with dark bread, cheese, and butter. Erich piled a stack of thin cheese slices over a thick foundation of butter and bit into it with relish, letting the hot sweet coffee swirl in his mouth until both butter and cheese melted.

Outside the steamy windows, beyond the clearing where Segerstam had chosen to park the train, the forest was dazzlingly white and clean, beneath a sky of pure blue-white. Erich felt more at peace with himself and his surroundings than he had since leaving civilian life. He actually felt more at home in this ungainly rolling fortress, in the company of these bluff but open-hearted new comrades, than he had ever felt in his own country's army.

"*Kapteeni* . . . ?"

Eino was leaning forward, touching his sleeve diffidently, trying to draw him back.

"Oh, yes, Eino? I was just noticing how beautiful the forest looks this morning. Daydreaming, I suppose. I thought I knew the woods pretty well, back home in Germany, but this is somehow very different."

"Well, if you'd like, we can go out and stretch our legs in the woods for a while. Segerstam said it was okay, as long as we didn't stray too far."

"I would enjoy that, Eino. Just as soon as I finish gorging myself here."

Eino coughed uneasily, as though he were about to say something presumptuous. Erich looked back at him with an open expression, curiosity piqued, inviting the sergeant to continue.

"And if the captain would like, I can show you a few pointers about our style of ski-warfare. Things that might come in handy. Actually, Ensign Segerstam ordered me to check you out, although I feel embarrassed putting it that way."

"I don't think Ensign Segerstam has anything to worry about. I grew up in the Bavarian Alps, after all, so I do know how to ski."

"Yes sir, of course. But, begging your pardon, most of what you know comes from alpine skiing, downhill runs at ski lodges and that sort of thing."

"Yes, that's true, but then, skiing is skiing, isn't it?"

No, it wasn't, as far as the Finnish Army was concerned. Preparing for a forest patrol, Erich learned, was a ritual of many steps. One dressed in layers, beginning with heavy woolen underwear, followed by two sweaters and three pairs of wool socks, over which it was just barely possible to draw a pair of boots lined with reindeer fur. Regulation Finnish Army winter field dress followed, dark grey woolen blouse and trousers, and over the entire ensemble went a long, light-weight snowcape, complete with cowl and drawstring.

"What about a helmet?" Erich asked as Eino finished fussing, like a solicitous mother, with the hang of the cape.

"Wear one if it makes you feel better—most of the Russians do. But most of our boys prefer a wool cap instead. A helmet's just so much cold, heavy iron weighing down on your head—it overbalances you when you're skiing and it cuts down on your hearing, which is as valuable in the forest as sight. Damned things won't stop a bullet anyway, just shrapnel, and if you're going to get in a firefight in the forest, it'll be suddenly, and at close range. And speaking of that, I rounded up one of these for you, and I want you to wear it whenever you go out into the forest."

He handed Erich a Lapp *puulka* knife, a murderous foot-long blade about the shape and heft of an American Bowie knife. Erich strapped it on with a shudder; like most soldiers, he recoiled from the very thought of hand-to-hand combat. Hanging from his side, the implement felt like a Roman short sword.

Observing his reaction, Eino smiled wryly. "Like I said, *Kapteeni*, if something happens in the forest, it happens fast and it happens close. You can pass a Russian patrol fifty meters away and never be aware of them, or you can turn around from taking a piss and find yourself looking right into their eyes. Fortunately, most of the time, you'll hear or smell the enemy long before you see him, out there in the deep woods."

Finally, Eino showed Erich how to field-strip his Suomi submachine gun, clean the petroleum-based lubricant from its moving parts and replace it with a thin film of alcohol and glycerine. This mixture, Eino assured him, would prevent the gun's mechanism from freezing. Remembering the trouble his men had had with their own weapons up in Lapland, Erich made a mental note to pass that tip along in his first dispatch to Klatt.

Surprisingly, there was nothing unconventional about the skis Erich was issued, other than the fact that when he bent to tighten the heel straps, he discovered that there weren't any.

"I know it'll take some getting used to, but our first rule of combat skiing is this: never fight on your skis if you can possibly avoid it."

"How did you learn so much about this stuff, Eino?" Erich asked his friend as they made their first tentative strokes away from the train and into the trees.

"I learned during the Winter War, of course, the same school most of us graduated from."

"No, I don't mean the tricks about dressing and weapons maintenance—I mean the way you ski! I did a lot of it in my spare time, and I even knew a few men who skied competitively, but look at you: you're a mechanic from a factory town and you ski just as naturally as they did."

"Well, I couldn't hope to match them on a downhill slalom or a ski jump—we don't have too many mountains in my part of Finland—but I've been skiing cross-country style since I was three. Mother and Father gave me these little stubby baby skis, about the size of barrel staves, and stood me up in them and gave me a push. I've been doing it ever since."

Eino checked Erich one more time, from head to foot, then nodded in the direction of the tree line. The two men began to move forward, their faces upturned to the generous flood of morning sunlight.

"One thing you have to remember, *Kapteeni*, is that for us Finns, winter is the single most important fact of life. Everything takes its color from that fact: our economy, our culture, our national psychology. On the one hand, it makes life harsh and demanding and makes us a dour, brooding lot. Too much darkness. It makes us sad and it ages our women before their time. On the other hand, we exult in mastering Winter, in wresting every little bit of civilized progress we can from it."

Just before they entered the trees, Eino halted again and removed Erich's Suomi from his shoulder. "First lesson: don't shoulder-sling your weapon. The barrel will snag on the branches. Here, stick your head through the sling. Let the gun ride at port, loosely, across your chest. That way, if something happens, you can just drop your ski poles and start shooting right away."

Eino continued talking as they entered the trees. "It's true that I grew up in Tampere, which is a grimy little industrial city right enough, but it's also true that the forest starts at the edge of town, and every weekend, every holiday, thousands of factory hands and their families are out in the snow, skiing, hiking, skating in the winter, camping and boating and orienteering in the summer. So despite the fact that I'm a 'city-bred' Finn, I've probably logged more hours on skis than some of your Bavarian athletes."

Erich dropped back a pace and studied the way Eino moved. For all his burliness and heavy clothing, the sergeant glided through the trees with a beautiful economy of motion, an almost feline grace.

As they left the train behind, with its steam-valve exhalations and machinery noises and the rough voices of its crew, the serpentine hiss of their skis grew louder until it was the only sound other than the healthy rhythm of their own breathing. Erich was warm under his layers of wool and reindeer fur, and the cold air burned his lungs with its purity. The quality of ambient sound changed dramatically. Every creaking branch, each falling clot of snow, each change of weight or direction conveyed by the sighing of their skis, took on a crystalline vividness, etched against a background of immense and lustrous silence.

They skied between the black glistening shafts of the tallest pines Erich had ever seen. The lower trunks were bare and straight and set together with a density and regularity of spacing that suggested pillars; the limbs did not begin to form a canopy for several meters above their heads and the interstices of their branches and needles were so cloaked with snow as to form a perfect lofty vault above the glazed silence of the forest floor. They skied through a vast white grotto. Diamond-bright particles of ice materialized in the pellucid air, as though the trees were gently breathing. When Erich looked up, several of them sparkled, drifting into his field of vision, and touched the surface of his eyes with the tiniest prick of sensation, as fine as the touch of a single eyelash. Far away, in the direction of the Russian salient, artillery fired, and the sound rolled to them with a long drawn-out hollowness, as though they were listening at the end of a long pipe.

Erich had stopped and was standing still, hands resting on

his ski poles, listening to the last echoes of the distant guns, gazing intently at the forest. Eino skied close and broke his reverie with a comradely thump on the shoulder.

"Hey, *Kapteeni*, what I'm going to say now may sound like bullshit and maybe it's impertinent of me, but I need to say it because it might save your life. Sometimes you can get into a state here in the forest that's like what happens to a deep-sea diver—a kind of dangerous rapture, you might say. It can be beautiful out here, spiritual even—but it's an environment that's basically alien to man, and it's neither as peaceful nor as benign as it looks. You have to try to become one with the forest, not merely be a spectator to it. If I had been a Russian ski-trooper just then, I could have slit your throat while you were contemplating the beauties of nature. Get deeper into it than that: appreciate the beauty of it, that's fine, but learn its savagery as well. The forest is no more sympathetic to human beings than the sea is. If you're not careful and let your mind wander, you can die just as fast out here as you can drifting in the ocean. I've seen it happen."

The first two times they went out, they stayed within a thousand meters of the train; fighting was still going on four or five kilometers north of their position, where Pajari's counterattacks were slowly containing the Russian thrust. Eino showed Erich some basic techniques of ski-fighting, drilling him hard, until he could kick off his skis, roll into a combat position, and then remount his skis, ready to move, in one minute or less.

"It's always better to shoot from the ground," Eino told him. "When you fire with your skis on, especially with an automatic weapon like the Suomi, the recoil can ruin your accuracy, maybe even knock you off balance."

"All right, that makes sense, but suppose you're caught in an ambush and you don't have time to do anything except react."

"In that case . . . just watch me; it's easier to show than to explain." Eino dropped into a tight hunkered-down position and jammed his skis into the snow at an uncomfortable but secure angle. "See? This way the skis act as a brace for you.

It's a strained position, but it provides reasonable accuracy at close range, which is what you'd encounter in an ambush situation. Got it?"

"I've got it, *Herr Professor,*" Erich laughed, helping Eino to his feet. "They should make you an instructor!"

Eino brushed excess snow from his knees and grinned back. "Fine with me. Beats the hell out of combat."

Next, Eino demonstrated, rather comically, the consequences of Newton's Third Law for anyone who attempted to pitch a grenade overhanded while on skis, then showed Erich a side-arm pitch out of a tight crouch that improved the accuracy by a factor of five. Using grenade-sized lumps of coal from the train, Erich practiced this technique a hundred times.

On the third day, they went farther than before, while Eino showed Erich techniques for skiing long distances, at a fast pace, with the minimum of fatigue. Erich's previous experience with cross-country skiing had been limited to short trips, for recreational purposes; doing it for extended periods required subtly different techniques and attitudes, which Eino strove to inculcate into his German pupil.

As Erich's expertise grew, so did his esteem for Eino Pekkanen. Although Eino continued conscientiously to observe the proper forms of military address, Erich had ceased to be conscious of any difference of rank between them. He laughed inwardly at the very notion of himself as a "superior officer" to the Finn. The pettiness of such matters seemed absurd, almost surreal in their irrelevance, here in the forest. What did not seem at all absurd, what had come to mean a great deal to him, was the fact that this outwardly gruff but inwardly thoughtful and sensitive Finn had become the first real friend Erich had made since donning a uniform.

The morning of that third day was particularly exhilarating. On such a morning, it seemed to Erich that, despite the military nature of the skills he was practicing, he was not involved in a war any longer. He was simply enjoying a weekend outing in the countryside with a good companion. Eino, too, seemed to exult in their freedom of movement, in the wild and uninhabited landscape around them, in the sheer physical joy of gliding smoothly through the trees, covering space with a calculated minimum of effort that left them pleasantly winded, but not really tired, by the time they stopped for lunch.

They shared coffee and bread. Eino seemed years younger, the lines around his eyes smoothed back into his flesh. This, to Erich, did not seem like a bad way to spend the rest of the war. As they lit cigarettes, after finishing the last of the coffee in Eino's thermos bottle, he said as much.

"I hope this is how we spend it," Eino said. "If the Russians understand that we mean them no more threat, maybe we'll be left alone. And if your people take Leningrad, it may all be over by next summer. If it is, *Kapteeni*, you must stay a while with me and get to see Finland in a more comfortable way. There are lakes I know, not an hour's drive from my flat, that have the best-tasting fish in the world swimming in them. I own a small sauna cabin on one of them—just a steam house and a room with a couple of bunks and a stove, but it's as peaceful as heaven there in the summer, when the sun never really sets. We could drink some *aquavit*, take six-hour saunas with some of the local milkmaids, catch our dinner and cook it right there over the coals."

"I'd like that, Eino. I'd like to know this country better."

"It suits you, *Kapteeni*, being in the forest. Some foreigners can't stand it; makes them feel claustrophobic. On you, I think, it has the opposite effect: it opens your soul."

Suddenly businesslike again, Eino buried his cigarette and remounted his skis. "Come now: one final lesson, and then you'll know everything this old soldier can teach you. You need to learn how to turn yourself into a mound of snow. That's why the snowcape is cut as full as it is, you see—if you get surprised by the enemy, and there's too many of them to handle, you can just go down a certain way and with any luck at all, they won't spot you."

Eino made it look easy. He kicked off his skis, rolled into the shadows, humped and wriggled under the snowcape for a moment, and when he was done, Erich—standing fifteen me-

ters away—would not have known he was there if he had not
seen the entire exercise. Then Erich tried it. And tried it
again. And again. For some reason, he found it harder to do
than anything he had yet attempted.

"You're following your instincts too much, sir. If you
know the enemy's close, your first impulse is to dive into the
thickest cover you see—that clump of underbrush you just
landed in, for instance. Trouble is, the natural look of things
gets disturbed too much that way. Anyone passing by is going
to be aware that something just doesn't look right, even if it's
only on a subconscious level. Dive into the underbrush, and
you'll disturb the natural look of the snow, maybe make some
greenery break through where there was only white before.
Now look around you calmly: see how there are dozens of little mounds of snow all around? No one knows what's under
them, and no one cares; but the forest is always full of them,
and one more won't even be noticed. And it's best to let some
distant object cover you while you shape yourself into a
mound—that stand of pines there would be good. Drop ten
meters behind it and cover yourself, and nobody will see you
except by accident. But if you dive into that underbrush at the
base of the trees, you'll ruck things up and a sharp-eyed Red
soldier might spot you."

For two hours, they practiced, and finally, as long as he
knew when the movement would have to be made, Erich
managed to do an acceptable job. How he would do if he had
to react spontaneously to real danger he did not know, and
Eino, plainly, hoped he would not have to find out any time
soon.

"You just need practice, sir, that's all. Tomorrow, if the
train's still there, we'll come out again and do it until it becomes natural to you. If it's any comfort, it took me a long
time to get it right myself."

To celebrate the end of a fairly grueling training session,
they decided to spend their last half hour in the forest just
playing. They found a long level stretch of lightly wooded
land, leading to a small frozen lake, and raced to the far side
of it. Exhausted but exhilarated, Erich finished first, by about

fifteen meters. He turned to tease Eino about the difference
in their ages, and realized with a sudden chill that Eino had
not fallen behind; he had simply stopped, at the edge of the
lake, and was staring fixedly past Erich's left shoulder. Wordlessly, he made a motion with his hand that could only mean
"take cover"; then he rolled to the uneven terrain along the
shoreline, where scattered outcroppings of rock had created
numerous snow mounds, and vanished into the landscape.

Erich's already thudding heart lurched like an out-of-control
truck as he pivoted clumsily on his skis. Ahead, the trees
thickened and the regularity of their spacing was violated now
by a rippling of shadows, a flurry as of giant doves beating
their wings. Men on skis. Coming this way. A patrol. They
wore helmets beneath their snowcapes.

At that moment, it seemed as though everything Erich
had learned had deserted him. He was alone in a terrible wilderness, greatly outnumbered, already too close to the enemy
to run, and he felt as naked and vulnerable as a child. He had
only seconds to make a move, and even as he instinctively
dove for the thickest underbrush he saw, he could almost hear
Eino chiding him: "No, *Kapteeni*, not there. You are a poor
student, my German friend."

But having reached his inadequate hiding place, he had no
time to change position. He covered himself with his
snowcape, leaving a thin slit for observation, and thumbed the
safety catch on his Suomi.

It was really not fair that this should be happening. If he
had been able to practice another day, he would have become
comfortable with Eino's sudden-camouflage technique. If they
had gone back to the train instead of racing one another like
teenagers. If Eino had been in the lead . . . If Erich had really
been listening, instead of daydreaming about the pleasures of
cross-country skiing in peacetime.

It was not peacetime. They were not on a picnic. They
were soldiers in a combat zone, and they had forgotten that
the enemy, too, had experienced ski troops; that the enemy,
too, conducted long-range patrols in the forest. Erich could
hear Eino's voice, only a few days ago, saying: *You can move a*

*lot of men through those trees without being seen, if you know how
to do it.*

These Russians obviously knew how to do it. There were
six of them. They skied smoothly, with an economy of motion. One of them carried a Tokarev semiautomatic rifle, the
others had long thin Mosins draped around their chests, each
rifle topped with a long needle bayonet. If they suspected the
presence of two foes, they gave no sign.

In fact, their next action gave Erich some cause to hope
that all might yet be well. The man with the Tokarev slid out
of line, curving toward the lakeshore where Erich lay beneath
his snowcape, trying hard to master the trembling that had
begun to pulse in his calves and hands. The man muttered
something in Russian, in a stage whisper, and was answered
by growls and low derisive laughter from his comrades. The
other five slowed as if to wait for the man with the Tokarev,
then indicated that they would ski ahead and he could catch
up with them.

Huffing beneath his cowled helmet, the lone Russian now
skied directly toward the clump of underbrush where Erich
lay with his teeth gritted. As he approached, he hiked up the
hem of his snowcape. As instinctively as Erich had dived into
the spot where he lay, so too did this stranger, this enemy,
show an instinctive and damnably human preference for urinating behind at least a symbolic screen of cover, rather than
out in the open snow.

The Russian paused so close that his knees and thighs
filled Erich's vision. So far the man gave no sign of alarm, but
Erich could not tell for sure—to raise his eyes and observe the
man's face would be to generate movement that the Russian
could not possibly fail to observe at this distance.

This comrade had a bladderful, all right. And as something hot, wet, urgent, and spiced with fragrances began landing on Erich's shoulder, sending burning rivulets snaking
through the chinks in his many layers of clothing, Erich had
time to do an impromptu chemical analysis of the man's recent diet: whiffs of fish, an acrid undertone of onions, a slight
bitter char as of disease or medication and—was it really

possible to obtain such detailed information under these circumstances?—a passing reference to several cups of strong tea. The urinating man made a satisfied sound and shook himself free of the final drops.

Erich felt the instant when the Russian realized he was there—an electrical charge passing between the two men could not have proclaimed the discovery with more certainty. At that exact moment, his thoughts slowed to ponderous deliberation by a flood of adrenaline, time dilated for Erich. If he rose now, while the man was stupefied with surprise, and killed him with the *puulka* knife before he could sound the alarm, while his companions were still skiing in the opposite direction, the whole business could be finished in silence and escape would become possible.

Erich moved his hand from the trigger guard of the Suomi to the handle of the knife. He told himself, ordered himself that it must be now and it must be without hesitation or mercy. Eino's words echoed mockingly in his head: *When something happens in the forest, it happens at close range.*

The order went forth from his brain: *Now, soldier!* But revulsion and terror had paralyzed his hand, mutinied against his will. His face turned upward and he beheld the red-faced Russian staring down at him, his mouth open in an oddly prissy *moue* of disbelief.

Erich's lunge, when it came in the next second, was an awkward and compromised spasm, not the purposeful thrust of a hardened warrior. He lashed out with the big knife and succeeded only in ripping the sleeve of the Russian's cape. The Russian stumbled, ill-balanced on his skis, and Erich realized that he could still kill him, but not in time now to prevent the man from crying out.

Enraged with himself more than the enemy before him, Erich came up fast, tried to make a killing swipe with the knife, and succeeded only in tangling his snowcape in the branches and brambles he had been hiding behind.

The Russian fumbled with his Tokarev, the muzzle swinging toward Erich with deadly inevitability. There was triumph in his eyes: he had pissed on this man and now he was going

to kill him as well. He opened his mouth and started to bellow like a bull.

Then Eino's guantleted hand smothered lips, nose, and
jaw. The Russian snorted through his nose like a horse, eyes
rolling back toward his shoulder. The blade of Eino's *puulka*
slid in beneath the Russian's helmet strap and penetrated half
the length of the blade, pinning the man's jaws together, nail-
ing both his scream and his tongue to the roof of his mouth.

The man toppled forward, a steaming fountain of blood
bubbling between his lips, and pinned Erich to the ground.
Erich felt his own knife blade slide redundantly into the man's
stomach. As he fought to rise again, he saw the other five
Russians, skis off, running clumsily through the snowdrifts.
Realizing that further stealth was pointless, Eino whirled to
face them, firing his Suomi from the hip. Against the stillness
of the forest, the abrupt hammering of the gun was obscenely
loud.

There was not much distance between Eino and the five
charging men, but he had time enough to catch two of them
with a single loud burst, the Suomi's big 9-mm slugs burning
pepper-black holes in their snowsuits. Then there was no
more time or shooting room and Eino was transfixed where
he knelt by three needle bayonets, one of which pierced his
hip, one his stomach, and one his groin. The man who had
stuck Eino in the hip twisted his blade free, scooped up Eino's
Suomi as a trophy, advanced another few meters, and con-
temptuously brought his rifle butt down on Erich's skull.

When Erich opened his eyes, the eyeballs seemed to be
floating in slow concentric waves of pain. The snow beneath
his face was red, and his blood left curious marks, like Chinese ideograms, in the snow as he floated above it, anchored
to consciousness only by the pain that filled his skull. Angry
voices croaked above him in Russian. He understood, then,
that he had been knocked out and captured and was being
dragged, head down, toward enemy lines. Through the red
film over his eyes, he glimpsed upside-down trees. Erich was
alone; Eino had been left to die of his wounds, perhaps because his captors were in such a hurry to get away with their

prisoner. They must have known the train was not too far away—and there was nothing gentle about the way they were hauling him.

He tried to pull free, but his arms and legs were made of dough and all he received for his effort was a kick in the ribs from one of the men who was dragging him. The effort did loosen his captors' hold, however, so that Erich's forehead fell and began digging a furrow in the snow. He tried opening and shutting his eyes, but the nausea, from pain and from the vertigo imparted by his upside-down position, only grew worse. Suddenly his head was being dragged through a drift, a mound. His vision whited out; wet snow clogged his nostrils and filled his mouth. He tried to spit it out, but they were taking him into the deeper forest now and the drifts were higher; the snow filled his mouth and nose faster than he could spit it out. He gagged on blood and snow. He realized that he was going to drown.

Then Eino, his snowcape bright with freezing blood, lunged out of the forest, a *puulka* knife in each hand. Howling a berserker's cry, he plunged one blade deep between the shoulders of the man on Erich's left side. Erich felt himself falling free and as he did so, rolled to his right, unbalancing the man on that side. Eino went down with his last strength, grappling hand to hand with the third Russian. Spitting red cottony mouthfuls of snow, Erich scooped up one of the fallen Suomis, jammed the muzzle into the armpit of the man he had knocked over, and squeezed the trigger. The submachine gun protested the long burst by jamming on about the twentieth round, but not before it had blown off everything above the Russian's collarbone.

"Eino! God damn it, Eino!" Erich cried, struggling to a kneeling position, using the useless weapon as a crutch. Eino was dead, his blood pumping out in a cloud of red steam, his right fist still locked around the hilt of the knife he had driven into the last Russian's chest with his final measure of strength.

Erich felt a dark constriction closing around his heart like a fist of black ice. He had made the mistake of forgetting that he was still at war, and by the consequences of that lapse,

Eino had taught him one final, terrible lesson. The magnitude and suddenness of loss was beyond comprehension, and Erich's grief beyond containment. Crying now as his childhood self had sobbed at the sight of his bleeding father, Erich reached despairingly for Eino's throat, hoping to find some whisper of life still throbbing there, but he fainted before his hand could tell him that there was none.

Segerstam had dispatched a strong patrol racing into the forest at the sound of the first shots. They brought Erich in and patched him up as best they could. A proper doctor's treatment would have to wait until the train went back to replenish its ammunition and food.

Erich came to late that afternoon, groggy with morphine and nauseated by guilt. He spoke to no one and refused all food. After a while, the Finns respected his silence and left him alone to brood, although they kept him anchored to reality by means of small kindnesses and contacts—a cup of coffee, cigarettes, a diffident touch on the shoulder.

But he was far away from them. He remained stupefied by the suddenness with which the terror had come boiling out of the forest, white death, white shadows, white steel, splashed with red.

Night fell again and someone thoughtfully pulled the blackout curtain across the window beside Erich's bunk. A little while later, someone else sat down with him, propped him up on his bunk and tried to spoon some soup into his mouth, but most of it dribbled unheeded down his chin and soon the man gave up and left.

Neither darkness nor lamplight brought any measure of peace. When the train had grown quiet around him, Erich took out his shaving mirror and stared for a long time at his own gaunt, bandaged face, trying with the sheer intensity of his stare to put out the ravaged-looking eyes of the man he saw reflected there, a man whom he now despised.

My friend Eino Pekkanen is dead, and he died because of me. Because of my clumsiness and hesitation. And I am still alive only because a mild-tempered locomotive repairman from some grimy little factory town found enough strength in the last seconds of his life to sink his teeth into the throat of the enemy who would and perhaps should have killed me.

At eleven o'clock, Segerstam came in, bearing two more morphine tablets and a mug of *aquavit* and gave the still silent Erich a direct order to consume both. As the morphine daze spread its muzzy, gently throbbing wings around him, Erich idly lifted up the score of Sibelius's Fourth and thumbed through it.

Yes, he understood it better now. Yes, he had visited those desolate reaches where its tones floated and held colloquy.

I could give the greatest performance this score has ever had, if I had an orchestra here at this moment.

As the drugs overtook him and he finally began to sink into sleep, he conjured in his mind's eye a surreal and bitterly funny vision of such an orchestra, an ensemble of Lapps and lumberjacks, clad in furs and skins—tuning up in a big frosty semicircle around the train—and he fell asleep conducting them.

In the morning, he woke up deaf. A dull, roaring tintinnabulation filled his head. When he finally tried to stand up, impelled by hunger and the need to empty his bladder, he took three steps toward the galley, then fainted.

Eight

Erich heard the bear long before he saw it. Heard its paws crunching the snow. Heard the roar of its breath. Heard it ripping through the branches, stamping on the saplings.

Snow was rising as Erich tried to force his way through the forest. It was welling up from inside the earth, oozing up between the matted roots of trees, pouring forth like some purulent fluid being discharged from a cavernous subterranean abscess. He noticed this phenomenon because of the steadily increasing pressure on his legs as he half-ran, half-stumbled.

When he had first noticed it, the upwelling snow had brushed against his ankles, his shins, but now he was forced to push his knees, too, through its deadening heaviness. Snow filled his boots, curled its hard white knuckles between his toes. His leg muscles felt as though they had been replaced by wet sand, his veins by copper tubing; from the knees down, he had become a man of lead.

Behind, he heard the bear's coarse breathing, and the brittle crack of fracturing limbs as it came. A fresh wave of snow, creamy as white molasses, crested his knees and began to curl around the lower slopes of his thighs. He tried to shout, but his voice crystallized in the air, a thin cloud of filigreed silver which shattered and cascaded into the snow, glittering on its surface like mica dust, leaving behind in the air a faint hum of unseen faerie bells.

The snow surged higher, a cold demanding hand that enveloped his testicles and pulled at his pistol belt. All he could do now was thrash about in place as the snow corseted his waist. He could no longer feel his feet, but he could smell them beginning to blacken. He wished he could simply detach them and leave them for the bear, while the rest of him— torso, head, and arms—swung apelike to freedom through the branches of the high, mute pines. Unable to move forward, he turned and faced the sound of the bear, drawing his Luger and pointing it with both hands.

Cracking the trees as it came, the bear hove into sight. Such a bear could have gone against a mastodon. Fifteen meters high it stood, and between its barrel-thick arms it could have embraced a stand of full-grown trees and still have room to squeeze a man. Its snout, tipped with a black leather knob the size of a pail, shot locomotive jets of steam. Its fur was a dirty, clotted white, matted into spikes as though it had been rubbed down with grease. Its eyes were the decayed green of old, bitter ice. Spotting Erich, it stopped, and the curtains of flesh that concealed its mouth retracted. Long ribbons of drool tumbled from between the marlin spikes of its teeth and, striking the supercooled air, froze into steaming cables.

His hands now as heavy as his feet, Erich raised the Luger and steadied the front blade sight on the hammering kettledrum of the beast's heart. He suddenly wished for a clip of silver bullets, then began to giggle at the hoary monster-movie conceit. At the sound of his laughter, the bear's eyes darkened with rage and it lumbered forward in slow motion, as though time itself were congealing.

Other movement impinged on the corners of Erich's vision. Off to his right side, standing effortlessly on top of the snow, was a slender young woman, her skin the color of breath on pearl. She was looking directly at Erich with eyes the color of sooty amethysts. Draped loosely around her was a robe that seemed made from woven snow-crystals, clothing her in a shimmer of palest light. Now Erich recognized her as a transformed Kylliki, the servant girl from Tapiola. But she was no servant now: in bearing, in raiment, in glory, she seemed a creature from legend, a dryad queen perhaps. He tried to say her name, but his tongue had turned to ice.

She gestured to Erich, a wing of white-gold hair sliding over one cheek. She pointed first to him, then to a copse of birch trees behind her. *I cannot move*, Erich tried to say, waving his pistol toward the bear. *I cannot move and the bear means to kill me.*

She reached toward him with both hands, the robe of snow sliding over girlishly sharp-tipped breasts. Erich tried to move in her direction, charged now by a surprising urgency of simple desire almost as keen as his fear. His feet gained purchase in the snow, which seemed to part before him as he moved. Beckoning him onward, the woman retreated until she passed into the stand of birches. Erich staggered after her.

Once inside the birches, Erich felt protected, as though surrounded by a wall of impenetrable shadow. The quality of light changed from the bone-bleak pallor of the snowscape to something warm, secretive, enveloping. The bear lurched past them, face-twisted in fury, enraged by the sudden disappearance of its prey. It continued to bellow as it vanished into the deep woods, but the only sound that reached Erich's ears was dull and distant—a bass drum struck by wads of cotton. Erich's hand suddenly burned as though splashed by a drop of acid, for as the bear had thundered past, a globule of its saliva had landed on Erich's arm.

He turned toward the girl and discovered that she was no longer there. In the place where she had been standing, there was only another birch tree, the maculations of its bark exquisitely patterned. Hesitantly, with all the gentleness he had had no use for since the war had claimed him, Erich reached out and stroked the tree. Its bark was still warm, and as he rested his burned hand against it, he felt both longing and sadness.

"God *damn* it, Ziegler, I'm sorry!"

A hand was batting at his lap. A remote discomfort, a burning, registered somewhere in his awareness. Erich opened his eyes and saw Rautavaara's large red hand brushing awkwardly at a cinder on the back of Erich's wrist. The car was full of smoke and the dashboard ashtray clogged with the butts of Rautavaara's brand.

"Do forgive me, Ziegler," the major continued, "but I rolled down the window for a minute and the wind blew the ashes back inside. I hope it didn't burn you too badly."

Erich rose to a straight-backed position. The sensations in his joints told him he had been asleep for some time. The flicker of pain on the back of his hand seemed trivial. He deprecated it with a wave.

"It's nothing, really. About time I woke up. It wouldn't do to arrive half-asleep, in case my host is watching. How far have we got to go?"

"Not far now. The turnoff's just a few kilometers ahead."

Erich lit one of his own cigarettes and wondered whether the sensation of well-being he had awakened to was real or was an aftereffect of his dream, a vapor that would burn off quickly under the thin white sunlight of reality. As several kilometers of road passed beneath the staff car and the unmarked, all-but-invisible turnoff to Tapiola was reached and taken, Erich realized that the feeling, though somewhat attenuated, was real enough.

Rautavaara had found Erich on the morning of December 23. Erich had been sprawled on his bunk, smoking. He was bleary and unshaven. In his mind, a phonograph record rotated without stop. Its grooves were covered with blood and the needle kept sticking in the same place, replaying over and over again the sound of Eino, shrieking like a gutted horse as the bayonets penetrated him.

Erich's boots were resting on a pile of Sibelius scores. Rautavaara, crisp in field-grey uniform, polished badges, gleaming straps and boots, pulled himself to attention at the foot of Erich's bunk.

"Captain Ziegler, you look like shit."

Erich focused on Rautavaara for the first time, startled at this massive figure's sudden appearance. Rautavaara made him conscious of the fact that he was in this place as an official representative of the Wehrmacht, not as a vagrant. Acutely aware of his own bodily funk, Erich rose to a sitting position and forced himself to salute.

"Better. Come on, man, let's go get some coffee and then get you cleaned up. I can't take you to Tapiola looking like an unmade bed."

"Am I going to Tapiola?"

"Not until you pass inspection, soldier."

Exuding a beefy heartiness that Erich found barely tolerable, Rautavaara led him to the battalion commissary. After he had poured two cups of coffee into Erich and evidently judged him to be in a more receptive frame of mind, Rautavaara drew from his tunic pocket a folded square of heavy, linen-textured paper and handed it to Erich. He unfolded the document and read:

> My Dear Captain—
> Janne has asked me to write you on his behalf, requesting that you join us for Christmas, for such a period of time as your duties permit. I add my own invitation to his. Major Rautavaara will make the arrangement.
> Warmest regards, Aino S.

Erich felt suddenly cleansed: he had been summoned, after all.

"*That* perked you up, I see!" said Rautavaara, with a surprisingly boyish grin. The grin faded as he continued: "I've already spoken to Segerstam about it and he thinks it would do you a lot of good to go. He filled me in about what happened to you and your friend . . . ach, what was his name?"

"Eino," replied Erich in a dreamy tone. "I wonder why he invited me back so soon."

Rautavaara was momentarily confused by Erich's switch from proper name to pronoun, but then he saw that Erich was once again reading the invitation from Sibelius.

"Two reasons, I suppose. Number one: he's lonely out

there and feels cut off from the outside world, especially the musical world, and until you came along, he had no one to talk shop with. Number two: he likes you. One thing you must remember about Uncle Janne is that he's old enough and famous enough to afford the luxury of being contradictory and eccentric, if he chooses. He'll rave at you about how much he despised having to talk to all those journalists and musical pilgrims when he was living in state at Järvenpää, but the truth is that he thrived on it; it filled up his days and kept him occupied. He misses it."

"I would have thought his composing kept him busy enough."

Rautavaara studied Erich's expression for a moment before replying. "Captain, if Sibelius has written any music at all in the past fifteen years, he has certainly managed to hide that fact from both his colleagues and his family."

"But the Eighth Symphony, surely . . ."

"Oh, that. Sometimes I've seen him thumbing through a stack of manuscript pages that looks symphony-sized, but I'm not a musician, and I know better than to ask him point-blank questions about such matters."

"So do I, now, if you'll remember," muttered Erich, his face reddening at the recollection.

"Well there, you see? You committed the worst *faux pas* a guest could commit on your very first visit with him, yet he still liked you well enough to invite you back. You can hardly doubt the sincerity of the invitation."

Erich slept through most of the drive. When he awoke, he felt deeply refreshed, although he did recall that his dreams had been preternaturally troubled and vivid. He could not remember them in detail, as the car began its slow, winding ascent to the ridgetop where Sibelius's lodge brooded above the lake; there had been some kind of great beast, though, and a young woman, and some dim shadow of their presence lingered in his conscious mind. Now that he was fully awake and able to look back on the recent past from some distance, he was surprised to find that the experience in the forest had left a deeper scar on him than anything that had happened during all his weeks of combat duty in the far north. It was not only the death of his friend and his own part in it; it was also the eerie and bloodthirsty intimacy of the fight, as though both parties had met in the forest not as trained modern soldiers fighting for political objectives, but as two groups of barbarians, driven by atavistic hate, intent only on savaging one another.

Snow lay in knee-deep hillocks all around the parking area in front of the lodge. Smoke rose from the chimneys, and the windows were steamed. Logically, Erich had no right to feel the sensation of homecoming that swept over him as the car crunched to a halt.

"Major, I'll be along in a minute . . . I'd like to walk over there and see the view of the lake, now that it's frozen."

Rautavaara gave a suit-yourself shrug and trudged toward the front door. Erich found several paths leading from house to lake, and selected one that looked as though it would put him close to the vantage point from which he had obtained his first view. His intuition was right: the scene in full winter was much more beautiful than it had been when the winter was beginning, with the ice just dirtying the contours of the islands. Two-thirds of the sky was a creamy low-hung grey, fine-grained and even in tone. Far out toward the west, even though the sun itself remained hidden, ivory-yellow light bathed the frozen lake, obliterating the horizon and turning the thick surface ice into molten slag. Erich peered at that stupendous radiance until his eyes ached from the glare and the myriad scattering of islands started to swim in the brightness, fuzzily moving like great basking whales. Closer, he saw that the picturesque island directly across from the dock and the sauna cabin was now connected to the mainland by a clearly visible path to the beach at the foot of the ridge. Smoke rose from the little cabin nested on the island; whoever lived there had trudged back and forth enough times to wear a distinct groove in the lake's crust. In summer, he supposed, there would have to be a boat. Summer here would be short but intensely beautiful. He would like to see summer in this place, would like to get in a boat and see what lay beyond the island, and the islands beyond that.

"It is lovely, is it not?"

Erich turned, startled by Sibelius's voice. The composer was striding briskly toward him, with an erectness that belied his seventy-six years, jauntily poking holes in the snow with his walking stick. He wore an elegant, fur-trimmed topcoat and a broad-brimmed, fur-banded hat.

Seeing the old man, Erich felt several emotions: gratitude; pride; a touch, still, of awe, and a shadow of wariness. In their mutual attraction, in their complementary but lopsided needs, the two men seemed to be circling each other, searching not so much for advantage as for some elusive point of equipoise.

Sibelius clapped him vigorously on the shoulder, his eyes merry. Rautavaara was right: the old fellow was hungry— visibly, touchingly so—for contact with the outside world. After this demonstrative gesture of welcome, Sibelius nudged Erich into a leftward turn and thrust out his cane toward the lake.

"My old friend, Gallén-Kallela, the painter, tried for many seasons, when he was a young man, to capture that landscape, but he finally gave up in frustration. Then he turned to painting mythological subjects from the *Kalevala* and became rich and famous for it. Gallén-Kallela was an exceptional man— normally, we are not a nation that produces great painters. That kind of landscape is one reason why. You just can't paint it in the winter—the colors are too monotonous. And when you try to paint it in the other seasons, it just doesn't come out right on the canvas. Gallén-Kallela used to complain that all of his perspectives ended up in the sky, instead of out there on the horizon."

"Nevertheless," said Erich, "if I were a painter, I don't think I'd give up. The challenge would be to capture in paint what you have captured in tone."

The flattery implicit in that remark—more heavy-handed when spoken than Erich had intended—seemed to please the composer greatly; he went on ruminating in a tone of voice not entirely free of smugness.

"Yes, oh yes, Gallén-Kallela used to be jealous of me in that regard. He would get a few brandies into his system, then curse me for being able to delineate in music the very things he found so impervious to his own art. What he did not know, although after a while he must have suspected, was that when I worked on my own *Kalevala* pieces, the images that were going through my mind were always suggested by figures and scenes that he had painted. Now, Captain, let's go inside and I'll make you properly welcome. The afternoon meal is finished, I'm afraid, but if you're hungry, I'll have one of the girls prepare something for you in the kitchen."

"Thank you, Maestro, but I'm not hungry."

"In that case, we can proceed directly to my study and the bottle of exceptional brandy I've been saving to share with you."

Brandy? Had the man actually said "brandy" that had been "saved for him"? At that moment, Erich did not care if Sibelius had a whole cellar full of brandy, for it seemed clear that the composer was as keen to make him comfortable as Erich was to make his host feel appreciated. Their exchange was a formal set of bows, like the opening of a courtly gavotte.

The composer ushered Erich into the paneled room he had glimpsed on his previous visit. Erich looked around as Sibelius closed the door behind them: a piano displaying a Mozart sonata above its keyboard, a floor-to-ceiling bookcase lined with scores, several plump chairs, a cabinet full of record albums, and an expensive radio-Victrola console. Sibelius pointed to a chair; Erich sat. The composer then opened a humidor and passed it to Erich. The scent of fine cigars came to Erich with such intensity, such a redolence of the culture he had hungered for in his prewar existence, that he experienced an actual shudder of pleasure.

"What a marvelous aroma! One associates it with so much, so much that belongs to the past and not to the war."

Sibelius trimmed a cigar for himself and lit Erich's. The composer, too, sighed with pleasure as he drew on the smoke. "You're right—I can never light one of these without feeling a powerful nostalgia. When I was a child, in Hämeenlinna, my father used to smoke fine cigars such as these. He was a good man, a surgeon, and he provided a happy environment for me to grow in. Later, when I inherited his possessions—many years after those childhood associations had faded—there was a redolence of cigar smoke clinging to them: books, papers, clothes, everything. And when I first encountered it, I experienced a delicious lurch in time, as though, for just a moment, I could again savor the sensations of happiness that one associates with childhood. Now, when I smoke a good cigar, the aroma instantly soothes that part of me which longs to return to the child's state of grace. Cells deep within me are made happy by this little act, no matter where I am or what my external circumstances might be."

"Given the external circumstances I've been living in, sir, and given the remoteness of where we are, it seems an incredible luxury to sit here enjoying such a cigar."

"Add some brandy to the recipe and things will look even better," laughed Sibelius. He decanted two snifters' worth and handed one to Erich. The blend of cigar aroma and brandy bouquet was excruciatingly fine.

Sibelius sat in a chair facing the study's one small window, an elaborate affair of double panes and divided shutters, capable of letting in several gradations of light or air. The old man sipped his brandy, noisily sucked in a petulant drop that hung on his thin lips, gazed thoughtfully at his small rectangular view of the lake.

"You know, Captain, I am not a primitive, despite all the purple prose that has been gushed about the 'barbaric' qualities in my early music. I was born into and raised according to the standards of the middle class of my time. Therefore, I like comfort. It comes naturally to me, and I confess to a certain pleasure in flaunting it here, in the depths of the forest, where by all rights it ought not to be."

Indeed, at that moment, to Erich, the composer seemed to be presenting a profile of studied, calculated elegance. His suit was clean, impeccably creased, and tailored to minimize the angularity of an old man's bony frame; the shirt appeared to be of the softest weave, the tie was crisply knotted, the craggy head turned just so, in a pose that seemed designed to illuminate the cheek and throw the nose, brow, and chin into dramatic relief. Assumed by a man who lacked Sibelius's innate dignity, the same pose would have seemed ridiculously affected. Then, suddenly, the composer's expression grew cross, his gestures fussy and demanding.

"Damn it, Ziegler, do you feel a draft?"

"No, Maestro; I'm quite comfortable."

"I'm not. I distinctly feel a draft. I think it's that window, as usual."

Erich made a motion to rise. Sibelius gestured him back into his seat with an imperious wave.

"You sit still. I'll summon one of the girls to take care of it. That's what one has servants for." Sibelius leaned over toward the piano keyboard and pressed a small button mounted beneath it. Somewhere in the depths of the house, a bell toned softly.

As though she had been waiting just beyond the door for this cue, the girl Kylliki entered, her plainspun skirt whispering against long thighs. Her hair was piled in a thick, massy bun. It would be quite long when unbound, Erich speculated, and would form golden wings around her pale, bone-valleyed shoulders. She vouchsafed Erich a single coolly appraising glance, which passed over his skin in a chill violet tingle, and as she did so, the faintest wash of color illuminated the vellum of her cheeks from within. Although Sibelius remained seated, Erich rose, hoping for a formal introduction. Sibelius did not oblige. In a cranky voice, almost whining, he gestured at the window.

"There is a draft, Kylliki, coming through that damned window. Fix it, will you?"

"Is it a real draft, this time, Maestro, or a ghost of a draft?" replied the girl, in a tone of delicate and affectionate insubordination. Her voice was as Erich remembered it from his first visit: musical, bell-like, soft, yet not servile. How long had she worked for the family that she could address the composer so?

Kylliki moved across to the window and stood with her back shielding it from the composer's gaze. She reached up and fussed with a pair of latches at the top. Erich once more admired the length, the tapering grace, of her hands, and he was seized with a desire to hear her play the *kantele* again. The windowpanes rattled as she patted them and poked them; clearly she was going through the motions, humoring the old man. Finished, the girl stood back, crossed her hands demurely in front of her lap, and smiled at the composer. Her teeth were bright and Erich was attracted once again to the slightly swollen quality of her lips, as though she had only just finished a meal of tart but succulent berries.

With every fresh moment he spent in her vicinity, Erich became more and more intrigued by the details of this young woman: the slender valley formed by her collarbone, the fine-grained whiteness of her throat, the long downy shadow on the nape of her neck where hair blended imperceptibly with skin. She was, he decided, the most natural beauty he had ever met. He found it impossible to separate the erotic element of his attraction from the powerful but generalized sense of well-being she conveyed.

"There. Is that better?"

"I suppose it is. But that draft made it cold in here. Put some more wood on the stove, will you?"

The girl did so, pivoting on sleek rounded hips. Erich could not escape the feeling that he had seen her more recently than his first visit to the lodge. Then it came to him: of course! There had been a dream, in the car. There had been a girl like this in that dream . . . and a bear.

As she exited, Kylliki directed a soft wing-beat of a smile toward Erich, acknowledging both his presence and his interest.

The room grew uncomfortably warm. Sibelius either did not notice or pretended not to, for he neither mentioned the heat nor made any motion, by means of loosening his tie or removing his jacket, to ameliorate its effects. Cigar smoke hung heavily in the air. Erich accepted the offer of another brandy, then rose to pour it, taking the composer's glass as well.

"While you're up there, Captain, take a look at that cablegram on top of the piano—it arrived just this morning. You may find it of interest, since it's from one of your famous colleagues."

Erich crackled open the flimsy yellow sheet. It was a long and costly cable from Serge Koussevitzky, director of the Boston Symphony Orchestra. He cited a transitional passage in the last movement of the Fifth Symphony and requested the composer's permission to take that passage at a tempo considerably slower than the markings in the score. The reason given: a slower tempo permitted a more powerful articulation of the work's coda. Erich was surprised to feel a shock of recognition: when he himself had studied the Fifth, he had mulled over the same passage, thinking that its potential effect was lessened if the score markings were taken literally.

"How will you reply to this?"

"I've already drafted a reply on the back."

Erich turned the cable over. A spidery hand had written there, in pencil: "Dear colleague: Of course you must take that passage as you *feel* it, otherwise it would sound wrong no matter what the tempo. I know that, with you, my works are in good hands. Sibelius."

"Of course, that's what a conductor of Koussevitzky's temperament would have done anyway," continued Sibelius, "but it was uncommonly decent of him to ask me first."

"I don't suppose that happens often."

"No, and it probably shouldn't. Composers do not often make good conductors, especially of their own works—just as playwrights should never direct their own dramas."

"Is Koussevitzky a good interpreter of your works?"

"Generally speaking, yes, to judge from the recordings I've been sent. A shade too febrile, sometimes, if anything—which is why I'm glad to see him moving in the direction of a more expansive view of the Fifth." The old man's voice grew sly, teasing: "Tell me, Ziegler, how would you conduct that part?"

Erich's confidence returned in a bracing rush. He had spent several hours in his bunk on the armored train, score in hand, mentally rehearsing an orchestra in precisely that part of the work.

"Based on my initial exposure to the score, and without having lived with it as Dr. Koussevitzky has, I think I would take that passage slower than indicated, yes. On the other hand, instead of slowing down at the very end, just before those six final chords, I would press on, I think, in tempo, to keep the momentum building all the way through the ending. Many conductors would want to slow down too much, and that would permit some dead air to come between the chords. They are very enigmatic, Maestro, those final chords. How well they work depends on how well every note in the score has been presented up to that point. But if one has solved the tempo relationships and spaced the chords just right, so that they seem to be utterly without ambiguity, then I think the meaning of the ending will become clear to any intelligent listener."

Eyebrows arched, Sibelius peered intently over his brandy. Erich was standing, pacing, animated, the warrior's reserve sloughed entirely from him now, the long-dormant artist risen again within his breast. Quietly, the composer spoke again, urging: "And what *is* the meaning of the ending of the Fifth?"

" 'Here is my music. Take it or leave it.' "

"Bravo, Ziegler!" whispered the old man. "Bravo! And this from a man who has never even heard a recording of the piece. I am impressed. You have found a significant 'program' in one of the works that all the critics insist has no program."

"On the contrary, Maestro, I believe that all of your music has a program. It's just that no one but you will ever know what some of those programs are."

Sibelius gestured for more brandy. After two glasses, the old man seemed to be feeling some effects. "Music is not a telegram, and I do not go in for detailed analyses of 'inner meanings.' My music is like a butterfly—if you poke at it and touch it too hard, you bruise it. Perhaps the butterfly can still move through the air, but the creature is no longer as fair as it was."

Erich decided to risk giving offense. "With all respect, Maestro, that sounds like a stock answer you memorized in order to get out of having to discuss such matters seriously with journalists and pedants. I am neither."

Emotion flushed across the old man's papery cheeks, and a flinty glare hardened the color of his eyes. After three long beats of silence, he said: "Very well, then, how about this one instead: My music dwelt in the deepest caves of the forest. I had to go into darkness for it, but there it was, like dragon's gold, all covered with frost."

"Much better!" Erich lifted his glass in salute. A thin, grudging smile cut across the composer's face. For a moment, they had crossed swords, and had drawn back with new respect.

"But not accurate as far as the later works go, say from the Third Symphony on. The early pieces, the ones based on mythology and folklore, I *quested* for them, Ziegler, yes indeed— into the caves I went, sword in hand, like some brave and randy Lemminkäinen. No Finnish composer had done that before, so the treasures were there, just waiting to be grabbed and have the dust shaken off them. But the later works, ah, that was a different process altogether . . . for them, I had to sit still and listen."

Erich waited for a further explanation. When there was none, when Sibelius merely dropped his hooded eyes and smacked his lips wetly, with an undisguisedly tipsy appreciation, at the brandy fuming in his glass, Erich felt a sudden flash of irritation. He was being baited; harmlessly, perhaps, and surely without any real malice, but the old man was just waiting for him to prod. Somewhere, there was a prepared, set-piece answer, possibly containing truth but surely wrapped in glibness, and the composer was just waiting for a chance to deliver it.

Erich could now understand what the many press interviews at Järvenpää must have been like, with the interviewer being ushered into the Presence, list of pertinent questions clutched in hand, hoping for something oracular enough to throw his own byline into relief below the name of the world-famous composer. It was a game the composer had played for decades, and Erich was beginning to realize how masterfully, on the occasions when it suited his mood, Sibelius had toyed with his interviewers and supplicants. Drop the questions into a slot and in a moment's time, receive a prepackaged answer, aphoristic and succinct, all neatly wrapped, guaranteed sanitary, digestible, and suitable for framing.

Erich phrased his own gambit carefully: "Do you mean that the process became more passive after a certain point?"

Sibelius waved his cigar in reply; the motion spun a tiny meteor of ash off to one side. "Active, passive, all relative, like harmony and dissonance! You can become very Buddhistic about it, if you like: instead of fighting actively for a thing, you just sit quietly and let it come to you. It's all one process, although maybe with different stages. And it really doesn't bear close examination. It's like ice crystals—you get in close enough to really see them and your very breath first alters the shape, then destroys them."

That was, Erich had to admit, an eminently quotable homily, one which used a portion of truth to perhaps obscure a larger truth; of that, he was sure. It had been, no doubt, a long time since the old man had had the chance to deliver one of these statements. What was it Rautavaara had said in the car? *He'll rave to you about how he hated always having to talk to journalists, but the truth is that he thrived on it. And he misses it.*

Having delivered himself of several warehoused remarks, Sibelius seemed to relax. His tone became more conversational, less facile. "I had a long argument about those processes once, with Gustav Mahler. He came to Finland, you know, in 1907—or was it 1908? somewhere in there—to conduct the Helsinki orchestra. It was a fine concert; there was Wagner on the program, which he always conducted superbly. Afterwards, he and Robert Kajanus and I went out for drinks. Mind you, I had only written two symphonies at that time, while he already had seven or eight to his credit. Naturally, I wanted to hear what he had to say about his work.

But he asked me first, so I told him that, for me, a symphony was completely personal in scope, severe in logic, ineffably private, and constructed from a tissue of inner connections. Mahler listened politely, then said: 'No, my dear young man, no! A symphony is not a private world—a symphony must *embrace* the world, must reach out to press everything to its heart.' "

"He was right, Maestro, but then, of course, so were you. Look at it this way: if you were a Viennese Jew in 1907, trying to find your way and earn your living in an anti-Semitic milieu, it would be natural for you to stretch your arms wide, to embrace as much of the world as you could. You would draw strength and resolve from doing so. But here, in the forest, what difference is there between trying to describe one square kilometer of it and trying to describe it all?"

The composer grew quiet. The silence attenuated until Erich became uncomfortably aware of remote and peripheral noises: dishes being placed on the dining table in the next room, a door closing upstairs, the creak of the very wood the house was made from. In the act, seemingly, of contemplating Erich's remark, Sibelius had visibly become remote. His frame sagged against the armrests of his chair, the cigar clutched in one white, talon-thin hand, unheeded. It was more than simply an old man's drift into inattention—he actually seemed to have drawn apart from things, as though the animating part of his mind had levitated to another place and had become instantly and utterly absorbed by what he had found there. Erich felt alone. He also felt the need to reach out, at least with words, and re-anchor the composer to the present reality of this room.

"I have been meaning to thank you, Maestro, for loaning me all of those scores. I've studied them with the greatest interest. I have them in Major Rautavaara's car, if you'd like for me to get them ..."

"What I would like," Sibelius said in a strong voice, "is for you to keep them. I have a wall-case full of them. In the future, Ziegler, I shall need good interpreters. Koussevitzky, Beecham, Stokowski, they won't live forever. I shall certainly need good interpreters in Germany, where they have been in short supply since World War One. Tell me, which of the symphonies did you like best?"

Almost too quickly for Erich to follow the process, Sibelius had swept him from the relative obscurity of his past and the limbo of his present and elevated him—for conversational purposes at least—to the ranks of podium titans. Very well, then: if Sibelius favored him by lumping him with Stokowski and Beecham, he would act, for the moment, as if he belonged there.

"It may surprise you, Maestro."

"Then again, it may not," replied Sibelius, with a touch of testiness. "I am quite familiar with the strengths and weaknesses of each of them."

"Very well then: the Sixth. It is as transparent, and as classical in scope, as Mozart, and yet it hints of so much, adumbrates whole landscapes. When I read through it for the first time, I thought: this must be what spring is like when it wakens in the forest . . . as it might be seen through a child's eyes, all pure and golden. Yet, it may very well be the least Nordic of your works—there's an almost Grecian shapeliness of line to it."

"The Sixth is perhaps the least-performed of the lot, and surely the worst-performed. Probably because, as you say, conductors look for something 'Nordic' in it which isn't there. You've chosen wisely. Your sensitivity has not been utterly brutalized by your present occupation, Captain. And which of them was your least favorite?"

"Of the major works, I can't yet say," Erich replied as tactfully as he could. The brandy—his second, and Sibelius poured them generously—was loosening his tongue; he had dared the old man's displeasure once before and was perhaps about to do it again. "But I am puzzled by the shorter pieces that you included in that pile of scores . . . salon music, almost, some of them."

"Which pieces do you refer to, Captain?"

"Oh, they all have such similar titles, it's hard to single

them out . . . things like *Scène Romantique* or *Moment de Valse* or *Chant du Soir* or *Romance Charactéristique. . .*"

"Aside from there being too many *tiques*, what is wrong with them, in your opinion?"

"It's not that there's anything 'wrong' with them, Maestro. They are not *bad;* they're not even vulgar. Just . . . bland. Compared to your other works, they seem almost faceless."

"And I've written dozens of them, Ziegler, dozens. They litter my path through life. And not one of them has done what I wanted it to do."

"I don't understand."

"Back in 1903, my brother-in-law, Armas Järnefelt, wrote a play entitled *Kuolema—'Death'*—and asked me to write some incidental music for it. I dashed off some numbers, including a dark little waltz which was used in a scene in which the hero watches a loved one give up the ghost. I was fighting a hang-over the morning I wrote it, and I regarded it as just a little bird-dropping of a piece. Nevertheless, my Finnish publisher gave me two hundred marks for it. I pocketed the money gratefully, thinking I had been overpaid for once. Then, as soon as my back was turned, the bastard sold it to Breitkopf and Härtel, who decided to issue it under the name *Valse Triste*, in everything from a solo piano arrangement to an or-chestration for military band! Inexplicably, it became a best-seller. It made stupendous amounts of money for Breitkopf and Härtel, but not a penny for me, because I had sold away the reprint rights, and with them all the royalties. Still, it made me famous; what price can you put on that?"

"That depends on how much you value it. A lot, I should think, when you were younger."

"Yes. Not so much now. I can laugh at it all now. But for years, it rankled. And for years I tried to repeat that single, freak success by cranking out potboiler after potboiler, but not one of them ever caught the public's fancy the way *Valse Triste* succeeded in doing. That kind of lightning simply does not strike twice in one lifetime. It reached the point where I could not even stand to hear the damned piece on the radio."

"You puzzle me, Maestro. You can speak harshly of your

own work, yet when asked about it directly, you can be very disingenuous."

"One great advantage of being in my position, Ziegler, is that you can to a certain extent filter out what reaches your heart. Like all men, I must confront unpleasant truths, but I prefer to confront them in an environment where I can control their effects and measure out their dosage. Surely, if a man lives long enough, and does enough good work, he has earned the right to do that."

"If he can, sir; if it is given to any man to be able to do that."

"It's been given to me," said Sibelius, pulling himself erect in a gesture of swelling, self-mocking bravado, "because I had it written into the contract of my government pension!"

Enormously pleased with his own *bon mot*, the composer coughed on cigar smoke while he chortled, pounding the arm of his chair with a bird's-claw fist. Erich had a momentary spasm of panic: one of the world's greatest living composers was about to choke to death in his presence. He rose to be of assistance, but Sibelius waved him down and managed to clear his own breathing, by means of wet, syrupy coughs that reminded Ziegler again of just how old the man was. As breath wheezed back into the composer, the door of the study opened and Aino's round, pleasant face appeared. She greeted Erich warmly and announced that dinner would shortly be served.

As Sibelius rose, straightened his coat, and replaced the top of the brandy decanter, he began to chuckle in a low, wicked tone. As he put his hand on Erich's shoulder to usher him out, he gestured with the other hand at the record cabinets, heavy with shellac incarnations of his own works.

"I have had the last laugh on Mahler, though! All of my symphonies have been recorded—see, there they are!—and only two of his! Who can afford to record his? You'd need a wheelbarrow just to carry the damned records home from the store!"

After dinner, Erich and Sibelius talked music. Not the sources of music, not the metaphysics that connect the composer with whatever his sources of inspiration might be—they had covered enough of that ground during the afternoon—but the mundane, professional considerations of performance, the "nuts and bloody bolts," as the composer referred to them at one point. Together, they pored over the scores of several symphonies. There was brandy again, and Sibelius helped himself liberally, but the full stomach he had acquired at dinner cushioned the alcohol's impact. He was direct, unambiguous, and professional, speaking the while as one colleague to another.

As the two men discussed harmonies, key relationships, tempo changes, and the arcana of orchestration techniques, a sense of wonder stole through Erich. His career, which had not even reached the stage of being referred to by the critics as "promising," had been slashed in half by the war; it had been two years since he had lifted a baton in front of an orchestra, yet here he was, intimately discussing some of the most-played works of the century with their composer. Even the magisterial Koussevitzky had to stand in line and send a telegram to communicate with the remote Sibelius, while he, Erich Ziegler, was drinking brandy from the same bottle, going over a score of the Fourth Symphony whose marginal notations were in the composer's own hand.

"Here, Maestro," Erich said, finger jabbing at the last movement of the score, "in the percussion, the printed score said *Glocken*, but is that actually 'bells' or is it an abbreviation for 'glockenspiel'? The effect of the tone color here would be very different, depending on which instrument was used."

Sibelius bent closer and peered at the marking, shaking his head as though the mere sight was disagreeable. "Ach! I get telegrams about that three or four times a year. Stokowski, when he was recording the piece in Philadelphia, asked me about it. I told him what I told Koussevitzky: do as you please . . . which in Stokowski's case is probably what he would have done anyway."

"Well . . . which is it?"

"I wrote *Glocken*, damn it, and I meant *Glocken*—only, to tell you the truth, Erich, I've never heard a set of bells that really conveyed the sound I was looking for. Perhaps I should have done what Wagner did for *Parsifal*—commission a campanologist to design a set specifically for this symphony."

"What kind of sonority did you have in mind, then?"

Sibelius went to the window, peered into the night. A pale refulgence from the snow outside bathed one side of his face. As he moved his head, the auroral light touched his eyes with a ghostly pallor.

"Put your coat on, and I'll try to demonstrate the sound I had in mind."

Their feet crunched on ice, the only discernible sound as they followed a trail across the crest of the ridge. The sky was a low vault of curdled cream. Behind the clouds, the borealic lights were going wild; across the grey glaze of snow, their shadows flickered with crepuscular vitality. Trees hung in frozen stasis, thickly coated with white wax. The weirdly diffused light painted the lake with a marmoreal yellow-grey sheen. Far distant, between two black clots of fir-draped islands, the clouds had parted and the aurora reflected directly in the surface of the ice. At this distance, it looked like a silent vortex of yellow-green fire, a rippling, coruscating whirlpool. Fantasies flickered in Erich's mind: if a man took a boat, rigged to sail upon the ice, and steered into the silent pulsing heart of that glow, would he rise to the stars or sink into the puddled light? And either way, what would he find?

At several points along their path, Erich held the composer's elbow, for the way was down now, into the deeper forest at the northern end of the lake. Just before the trees rose all around them, Erich glimpsed a tiny beacon of light out on the lake—a lamp in the window of the cabin on the island? Inside, in that glowing warmth, would be Kylliki. Perhaps naked. At that moment, he remembered that he had imagined her naked, or at least scantily clad, in his dream. What would her little snowball breasts look like by firelight? Branches smothered with snow rose to block the cabin's light, like crenelations in a wall, and the image from his dream lost its vividness. The more he tried to recall it, the dimmer it became.

They halted beneath a towering vault of firs, thickly layered with snow. Sibelius lit a cigar.

"What I had in mind, Erich, was a sound I heard here, many years ago, when I was still a young man. I've heard it many times since, although never with the same clarity and presence as there was on that first occasion. It's the sound of ice-bells. The sound of long stalactites of ice, hanging down like tubular chimes, being rubbed together by the wind. The sound is always faint, but if you could amplify it, then *that* would be the timbre I want in the Fourth!"

"Maestro, there is no wind."

"In the forest, there is always wind somewhere. The forest is indivisible. Here, or in the far north, or across the border in Soviet Karelia, it's all one immense being. It lives. And it is structured the way any organism is structured, with cells and ganglia and systems that regulate the rhythms of its life. And there are certain places, just as in the human body, where you can take its pulse more clearly. This spot we're standing on is one."

The old man was shivering. In his pale and fragile fist, the cigar-glow wobbled in nervous circles.

"I tell you a secret, Erich: the forest has emotions too, but they are vast and unknowable and it is foolish to scrutinize them with human perceptions, human anticipations. If its essence ever truly penetrated our consciousness, our brains would burst from the sheer alienness of it. It is beautiful, yes. Magnificent. But also horrible."

A silence as pure and ringing as a diamond shell surrounded them; they stood beneath a crystal bell, bathed in the sepulchral light from irradiated clouds of ice vapor.

"There! Off to the north, on the far side of the lake! I hear the wind! Oh, I hear the wind! Listen, Erich, listen! There are my *Glocken*, my bells of ice!"

At first, Erich could detect nothing. Then, as the composer's words died into silence, he thought that he detected—on the very threshold of perception—a silvery vibration. But even as he tried to focus on the sound, it was gone.

"I'm sorry, Maestro. For a second, there, I thought I might have heard something, but it's gone."

Sibelius sighed and crushed his cigar underfoot. "Yes, it is gone now. Some things are very hard for me to touch now, things that used to come to me, flood through me, unbidden."

Pivoting on the end of his walking stick, Sibelius began to retrace their steps through the forest. At a clearing, he paused and pointed at a black monolith of rock thrust above the ice at the lake's edge. "Walk in the forest as often as you can, Erich, and learn to listen to what it tells you. Then you'll understand why I am able to treat the orchestra as I do. That rock over there, for instance—a bass clarinet."

"And the aurora's light, Maestro?" asked Erich gently, his hand on the old man's arm.

"I'm still trying to put that sound on paper. Even now. Even now."

By the time they reemerged from the tree line, the light in the cabin window was gone. Thinning clouds permitted great swatches of auroral light to play across the sheeted lake, so that the landscape itself seemed to pulse in an elaborate but elusive rhythmic pattern. Erich felt that if he stood there long enough, over the course of many winters, he would learn to read that pattern, to hear its music.

"It's true, of course, that I composed well enough in cities, because when I was in a city, the memory of the forest was especially keen. I used to enjoy the proximity of many people, and in a way, I still do—but there are trees out here that have been my friends since childhood, that have grown old with me. When I die, it is they who will mourn me the most deeply."

"Please don't be morbid, Maestro. The trees could not love you more than the people who have been touched by your music."

But Sibelius no longer seemed to hear him. Either that, or he was simply too worn out to play one final hand of verbal cards.

"No. The trees. The trees . . ."

Erich thought for a second that the composer was about

to pass out, but Sibelius rallied. He raised his head and spoke with a passion.

"A tourist who comes to Finland, Ziegler, sees only the picturesque monotony of the forest. You need to witness the seasons pass over it, see the white tableaux of winter and the glory of the midnight sun and the wild conflagrations of autumn; you must learn to watch long and quietly. If you do, you may be able to learn some of its mysteries—some, but not all. It never yields all of its secrets."

"Not even to you?"

"No. Only some. Long, long ago. Enough to drive me on in search of more. And always remember, Ziegler, that knowing more is not a guarantee of being able to say more."

In silence, they returned to Tapiola.

Nine

The next morning, Christmas Eve day, Erich joined the Sibelius household for a light smorgasbord lunch, after which Sibelius—in one of those sudden changes of mood which Erich was learning to anticipate and not take personally— chose to closet himself in his study. Twice, as conversation in the family room subsided, Erich heard teasing, shimmering chord progressions from the study piano, unidentifiable but haunting. Then silence.

"Is he working on something?" Erich asked Aino.

"Perhaps. I think probably he is just playing with old ideas, as he does from time to time. It's best that we remain quiet in the house, though, for he does not care for noises when music is on his mind. In the old days, when he composed regularly, it was my job to keep the daughters quiet. Now I must only keep myself quiet, and at my age that is not so hard to do." Her voice had fallen to a conspiratorial level. From a coffee table made from a slab of polished birch, she lifted a stack of carefully folded newspapers, proffered them to Erich. "These are from Helsinki, only a week old. If you would care to find out what is happening in the rest of the world . . ." Erich took the newspapers; he could read enough Finnish now to get the gist of newspaper prose, while headlines, maps, and photo captions gave no trouble at all. "The rest of the world," Aino had said, as if it were something abstract as well as geographically distant. After a few moments of scanning front pages, Erich found "the rest of the world" crowding uncomfortably into his mind. Rumors of German setbacks on the Eastern Front had been percolating through Finnish lines for a week; here was confirmation. The Helsinki newspapers took their stories from the Swedish teletypes, which meant that they were relatively free of censorship with regard to every front except the one Erich was serving on.

At the end of the first week of December, according to the arrow-crowded maps on the front pages of a succession of editions of the *Helsingin Sanomat*, the Red Army had unleashed a thunderbolt against the worn-out German divisions stalled in front of Moscow. The panzer spearheads, within sight of the capital's suburbs, had not only been checked, but ripped open and sent reeling. Watching those arrows move, in a time-lapse progression from one front page to the next, Erich had to wonder if they depicted the high tide of German military success. He reread the dispatches and restudied the maps, striving this time to view matters from a professional soldier's point of view. Any way you looked at it, the fastest way to bring this war to a victorious conclusion was to decapitate the Soviet state by capturing either Moscow or Leningrad. There was no need to take both—if one fell, the other would be mortally vulnerable. One city or the other—surely the Wehrmacht could have taken, *should* have taken, one city before the onset of full winter.

And yet—these uncensored newspapers confirmed what Major Rautavaara had told him—the führer had chosen to starve Leningrad into submission and had taken most of his powerful panzer divisions away and sent them to the Ukraine, where they could not be used against either city! Erich could see no logic to this development. Perhaps he would, in time, when he had developed his military expertise beyond its current fledgling level. There had to *be* some hidden logic, some grand strategic design; the consequences of defeat, at the hands of a now-enraged and vindictive Joseph Stalin, were unthinkable.

Kitchen odors stole softly into the room, seducing him away from the newspapers. Erich sensed two figures standing behind his right shoulder, close to the wing of his chair.

"Everything's washed up from the meal, Madame Sibelius. Kylliki and I would like to take the afternoon off, to finish our personal Christmas preparations. We'll come back before first light tomorrow, to start preparing the feast."

"Just make sure the stuffing for the cabbage is ready, Anna-Liisa. It's ever so much better if the ingredients have had time to blend. Then, of course, you may take the rest of the day off."

Erich turned slightly. Both young women had their backs to him. Before they could reenter the kitchen, he heard himself saying, while rising: "I'm going to go for a walk, Madame Sibelius. I'm too full from the meal—not used to such food."

Erich went out the front door, while, presumably, the two servant girls were finishing their tasks in the kitchen. Then he paced up and down along the fringe of the forest, cutting at right angles across the start of the paths that led down to the lake. It was after three o'clock and dusk would be thick in an hour. No snow had fallen for two days, but the sky was swollen with it, the clouds low, and the mid-distances of the lake faded in and out of sight as dingy fogs brushed across them.

The two young women appeared soon, wrapped in cloaks and low hoods, like monks trudging on some vespertine errand. They were talking volubly in heavily inflected Finnish, too low and fast for Erich to catch a word. They almost ran into him before they raised their eyes. As they stood side by side, their kinship was unmistakable: Anna-Liisa seemed older by some years, her features longer and more weathered, her grey eyes more appraising than friendly.

"Good afternoon, Captain."

"Ah, yes. Hello, ladies. I felt the need for a walk, after that fine meal you prepared for us. Before it gets too dark and gloomy. Perhaps you'd care to join me for a while?"

"We have matters of our own to attend to, Captain Ziegler, thank you just the same. Come along, Kylliki."

"I think perhaps I will join the captain, sister. You may go ahead without me—I'll be home before it gets too dark, I promise."

"Please do," replied the older sister coolly. With no other sign to Erich, she walked stiffly onto the path and vanished into the white-draped branches.

"Did you have any particular path in mind, Captain?"

"I hardly know these grounds as well as you do. With the snow this deep, it wouldn't do to go wandering off blindly into the woods."

"Indeed it wouldn't. There are hidden gullies and sinkholes that you can drop into before you know it. A bit to our right, though, there's a nice path that leads to the northern end of the lake."

Together they entered the trees, tunneling through silence. Intermittently, through clearings, Erich glimpsed the lake and its strewing of islets being slowly engulfed in a yellow-grey fog. There would be snow soon.

"I'm glad to see this path in daylight."

"You were here before, at night?"

"Yes. Last night, in fact. Sibelius led me down here. He wanted me to hear a sound that the ice makes in the wind, at a certain place down near the shore. I didn't hear it, I'm afraid ... at least I don't think I did."

"And you'd both had a bit to drink, I dare say."

"Yes, but he'd had more—maybe that's why he could hear the sound and I couldn't."

"Oh, you could have, too, if you were standing in the right spot. I'll take you there now, if you like. In the wintertime especially, sound travels strangely along the ridges here. There is a place deep in the forest where a rockslide caused the trees to fall almost perpendicular to the ground. When winter comes, the weight of the ice causes their branches to hang down like chimes, and if you stand in just the right place, you can hear a very strange sound when the wind moves over them. Probably the Master was a bit unsure of his navigation last night. As I said, the sound carries very strangely."

"I thought I heard *something*, though, just for an instant."

"You may have heard the forest-bells." Her mouth was coy, her teeth sugar white.

"And what are those?"

"From fairy stories and legends. It is said that if a traveler hears faint, far, silvery bells within the forest, it means that the spirits who serve the god Tapio are near at hand."

"And I suppose that the volume and clarity of the bells is directly proportional to the amount of brandy one has consumed," laughed Erich, delighted that conversation with her was so easy to sustain.

"Oh, don't take our legends too lightly, Captain. There is still power in them, in a certain sense. Great poetry came from them, and Gallén-Kallela's paintings, and of course the Master's music."

She turned and looked at him playfully, her pale dusting of freckles, in the wan and watery light, like fragments of crushed roses on lavender vellum. Her mouth gave off a sweet, kitcheny fragrance.

"Besides, we Finns used to have a reputation for being great magicians. In the Middle Ages, the kings of Norway passed laws forbidding their subjects from traveling to Finnmark to consult the shamans there. Even in the *Kalevala*, our heroes are not just fur-clad barbarians hacking their way through ranks of foemen."

"You're very well-read, Kylliki."

"What I know did not come from books, Captain. I was taught the runes even before I was able to play a note on the *kantele*. Every boy or girl in my family had his or her favorite characters from the poems. Somehow, I always fancied the heroes and heroines who were skilled in magic. They overcame with spells and charms more often than they did with swords and muscles."

"What sort of charms? I'd like to know, in case I ever need such a weapon."

"I was taught that the greatest shamans were those who

knew the secrets of the *origins* of things. The hero Lemminkäinen overcame the Frost God because he understood the
origins of the Cold, and only by understanding that could he
summon the words which would hold the ice at bay."

"How does one gain such wisdom?"

"The chief formula is to retrace, by means of runes and
incantations, the manner in which something came into being. That's how you can achieve power over that thing. You
see, every object, every being, was endowed with an inner
spirit, which the ancient Finns called *haltija*. The most potent
runes, the most frequently encountered spells in the *Kalevala*,
were those that enabled you to trace back to the origin of the
thing over which you wished to have power. Only that way
could its secrets be learned; only thus could a thing be subju-
gated and its spirit, its *haltija*, be taken into the fabric of your
own being, become part of your own magic."

"Magic was in everyone?"

"And everything. My ancestors were almost as pantheistic
as the ancient Chinese. Of course, the amount of it varied
from being to being and place to place."

"Tell me something, Kylliki ... The first time I visited
this place, you played some things on the *kantele*. Do you
remember?"

The girl's cheeks colored in a way that Erich found de-
lightful. "I remember your first visit, Captain."

"So tell me: were you singing from the runes then?"

"No. A ballad about the forest, and a love song, if I remember rightly. It takes special training to sing the runes—
not just the verses of the *Kalevala*, mind you, but the runes
that made up the *Kalevala*, hundreds of years ago. If you are
really interested, perhaps I can arrange for you to hear a real
rune-singer. There are not many of them left now. And they
are old. The time is coming when there will be no one left
who can do it."

"I would like that very much."

"Good. Perhaps on your next visit."

"You sound very confident that there will be a next visit."

"Oh, there will be. The Master likes you."

"I like him too."

"He also wants something from you, I think. He wants a champion in Germany, for after the war. Famous men championed his music there, he says, just before and after the First War, but they no longer do."

"After this war too, there will be a new crop of famous men. Sibelius will find his champions."

"Are you to be one of them, then?"

"If I gain enough insights from him, perhaps I can be, yes."

He took her hand. She flinched, a barely detectable semi-quaver of hesitation, then curled her fingers snugly around his own. Erich could feel time blurring around him once more, the future telescoping into the present. He could visualize Kylliki in a stunning evening gown, something emerald and elegantly simple, himself in conductor's tails, and the two of them sweeping side by side into the glittering concert hall.

"Captain?"

"Yes?"

"You're hurting my hand. Just a little."

Red-faced and startled by how deeply he had gone into reverie, he broke contact with her as though he had touched fire.

Kylliki shook her head teasingly. "*Now* you're hurting my feelings instead! Here, let me."

She slid her hand gently back into his and they resumed their walk. They emerged on the shore of the lake. A bank of murk was thickening slowly on the far side of the island where the sisters lived. It hid the landscape beyond the island's high ridgeline.

"I've never gotten a glimpse of the far side of the lake, the part of it that lies beyond the island where you live. Always either the island blocks it, or the mist and snow cover it, like now."

"It's just . . . more of the same. That's all the Finnish landscape is, really—more of the same."

"Yet, I don't find it monotonous. It's beautiful, even in its severity. Even the snow and ice. Look at it—a whole land-scape of glazed sugar!"

"Not so sweet when it starts to melt. Not so fresh and pure-looking by the end of March, when the rest of the world is starting to enjoy spring and we're still freezing. I think, Captain, that snow and ice have always had a far greater appeal for those who do not have to live with them six months out of the year."

She had stopped at a point where birches grew aslant a frozen bog, a brittle morass of crushed brush and tangles. The lake gleamed dully between the trees' mottled shafts. She reached back with one gloved hand and rested it on his arm, halting him. She was listening tensely. He remembered deep snow clogging his steps, furrowing on either side of his hips, slowing him down . . . a dreadful and furious beast clattering through the trees behind him . . . the dimmest gong-stroke of memory to begin with, the *déjà vu* sensation faded even as he tried to bring it more sharply into focus. Kylliki's head turned slowly and she threw back her cowl in order to listen more intently. The cold turned her ears coral-pink and the waxen light turned the yellow of her hair into silver. She became as motionless as the birches that surrounded her. The trees seemed to be her sisters. A strange, slow thrill woke at the base of Erich's spine.

"Now, just now, you can hear it. Listen."

Erich bent his head close to hers, conscious of the warmth that came from her, the scent of her hair. He willed his own breathing into silence. From deep in the forest, magnified by some freak distortion of acoustics, came a tingling, resonant murmur of bells. Erich had expected something delicate and elfin, but the actual sound was grindingly cold and, for all its faintness, inhuman, inimical to humanity, a sound made in and by a landscape where no living man dwelt or ever would. Images, swollen and Daliesque, came unbidden to Erich's mind: the dried and shriveled husks of souls, thin leathery gourds emptied of all human warmth, rattling in an arctic wind . . . a great and solitary tree, festooned with ice-encrusted bones—femurs and tibias, mallets of ice playing arpeggios on the glockenspiel of a sternum ... entire spinal cords, hung like frozen segmented worms and rubbed obscenely together by the wind. It was the vision of a drugged Lapp shaman: a fetish-tree, a macabre and charnal windchime, a ghastly Yggdrasil.

A sudden brutal wind clapped Erich's face, making him aware that his forehead and cheeks were dimpled with freezing beads of sweat. The images shattered, brittle as glass, and melted back into whatever subconscious cave they had come from. He took a deep, desperate surge of air into his lungs, as though, without being aware of it, he had actually ceased to breathe. Kylliki's brow, close to his and firm-set with concern and with a curious expression of readiness, was paper-white, and her violet eyes swam huge and deep as whirlpools in the pale lake of her face.

"Captain? Captain, are you all right?"

"I heard ... something. Like chimes, maybe. But was it ice rubbing on tree branches, Kylliki, or was it those other bells you told me about?"

"I think that when there is a weather front moving across the lake, the sound here is even stranger than usual. I also think, Captain, that no man who did not identify with the forest could have heard those things half so well, whatever they were."

"But it wasn't just auditory. I saw things."

"That is the way of it. Come, walk me back to the cabin before it gets too dark."

Large fuzzy snowflakes began to trickle from the sulfurbrindled belt of cloud that hung over the tops of the tallest trees. Kylliki made no effort to replace her hood and the snowflakes hung, unmelting, in the primrose twists of her hair, weaving a fragile garland about her face. They stepped into a sudden night-heralding wind as they began to cross the frozen lake; fistfuls of snow struck their mouths and eyes, peppered their tongues with ice as they spoke.

"How long have you lived here?"

Her laugh was incongruously musical. "We have always

been here, my family. We have been what you might call care-takers for this land, for many generations."

"Your sister, Anna-Liisa, does not seem to approve of me."

"It is the duty of older sisters to look stern and reproach-ful. She is older and far more serious-minded than I. She is protective of me, and perhaps a little bit jealous of your inter-est in me."

"Am I showing so much interest in you?" said Erich ab-ruptly, irritated at himself yet disturbed by how much her answer suddenly meant to him.

"Why, Captain, I believe you are."

"Does that displease you?"

"I think perhaps it is part of my duty to let you be inter-ested."

Erich was not sure how to reply to that cryptic remark, so he said nothing. A large snowflake landed on his nose; he reached to brush it with his hand and as he did so, she blocked the motion with her own, leaned forward, quick as a bird, and pecked the snowflake with her mouth. When her head drew back, he watched the crystal dissolve against the plump flesh of her lower lip. Before he could reach for her, as he surely would have in another instant, she had turned and started walking again, determinedly, toward her island.

They followed Anna-Liisa's footprints to the boulder-strewn beach. This close, Erich could see an upturned boat, a plank dock, a veritable rampart of firewood stacked beneath a roof of woven fir branches. Amber light showed through the cabin windows. A dim shadow passed, solidified momentarily, as the sister within paused to peer out at the approaching fig-ures. Conscious of that disapproving witness, Erich rather awkwardly took Kylliki's hand as they approached the door.

"Don't you and your sister ever get lonely, living by your-selves out here on this island?"

"We were born into the forest, Captain. Loneliness does not enter into it. If I had been born in a city and then forced to move here, perhaps I would know such a feeling. But I can-not, being a part of this myself."

He would have kissed her then, and properly, but she saw

it coming and gave the tiniest shake of her head, while simultaneously squeezing his hand affectionately enough to acknowledge the intimacy that had charged the air between them for a moment out on the ice. Erich turned to go.

"Oh, Captain?"

"Yes?"

"I'm glad you were able to hear the forest-bells."

"Is that what they truly were?"

"It pleases me to think so."

"Then it pleases me very much to think that we heard them together."

Veiled by drifting webs of snow, camouflaged by the perfect whiteness of her skin, she seemed insubstantial, a creature of shadows and filigree. Yet she returned his frankly appraising stare with eyes that seemed to contain a hard, fine heat.

Just before he broke eye contact with her, the thought occurred to Erich that innocence, under the right set of circumstances, might possibly be as challenging and full of peril as sin.

Ten

"*Hyvää Joulupäivä, Herra Major*—Merry Christmas, Major!"

"*Hyvää Joulupäivä, Joulupukki*—Merry Christmas, Santa Claus!" replied Rautavaara with a casual flip of a salute. "*Onko sauna kuumi*—Is the sauna hot?"

"*Erinomaisesti kuuma, Herra Major*—Exceedingly hot, Major!"

"*Hyvää on*—Good show!"

Erich mentally translated this exchange, through a fog of alcohol and cigar fumes, while the corporal of the guard, his chin spottily draped with strands of the mossy *Joulupukki* beard he had worn during the Father Christmas act of the Sibelius household's daylong feast, finished preparing the steam bath. Behind the corporal, himself reeling with good cheer, the door of the sauna all but trembled against the pressure of the steam building within.

Erich had developed a taste for saunas during his weeks in the line with the Third Division; even at the front, the Finns simply could not do without their traditional steam baths. The sauna made them the cleanest and possibly the sanest troops in the world: a soldier could go into a sauna tense as a violin string, muscles sobbing with fatigue, repulsed by the reek of his own body, but within ten minutes it became physiologically impossible to stay angry, tense, or dirty. Where the body led so inexorably, the mind had to follow. A good long sauna—Erich had seen this happen once or twice—could even wash away the first and foulest layer of grief.

He needed a sauna now, not because he was tense, but because he was both stuffed and drunk. Christmas Day had come brightly. Snowfall had been heavy during the night, but by full daylight, 10 A.M., it was clear. The sun hung like a knob of spotlit ivory above the ice-cream surface of the lake, and the massed reflection from the outside filled the wood-paneled lodge with light.

The two servant girls had been at work since dawn, and by the time Erich was roused from sleep, the house was filled with delectable smells. The plank dining table was covered with fine linen and arrayed with glass and silver, with bowls and platters and tureens. There were borscht, blinis, cheeses, fresh butter, green pea soup, boiled potatoes, sausages in great fleshy mounds, cabbage rolls stuffed with ground meat and rice, and *kalakulko*—small seasoned fish baked inside rounds of rye bread—and coffee, milk, and pale green bottles of *aquavit* to lubricate the toasts and the singing.

After the meal, the two sisters came in from the kitchen and the Christmas ceremonies began. A corporal from Rautavaara's security squad had appeared, decked out in the fur coat, wide leather belt, and scraggly beard of *Joulupukki*, the traditional Finnish Father Christmas. He dragged behind him a mail sack full of Christmas telegrams from music lovers around the world, forwarded to the composer's official Järvenpää address, including an eloquent and heartfelt message from Sir Thomas Beecham, which had had to be spirited into the country in a diplomatic pouch from Stockholm, due to the fact that a *pro forma* state of war existed between Finland and Great Britain.

Gifts were exchanged. Erich wished that he had something for Kylliki, but on reflection decided that it might have been improper to make such a gesture in front of the family. He had, however, remembered to bring a token for Sibelius: the latest issue of a prominent German music journal, forwarded to him from his Uncle Rudolf, on the cover of which was displayed the laudatory headline, "Sibelius: A Great Ally's Music Reappraised." The old man had grabbed the journal eagerly and had kept sneaking looks at it all through the rest of the afternoon.

For his part, Sibelius handed Erich a long thin package wrapped in plain manila paper. Inside was a beautifully crafted baton, balanced as finely as a dueling sword, the tapering handle inlaid with a runic pattern executed in mother-of-pearl. Erich was about to protest, but was cut off by a wave of the composer's hand. "That is the baton I used the last time I conducted, at a birthday concert in Helsinki four or five years ago. May you make good music with it, my young friend."

Surprised by the gesture, Erich felt a rush of real affection for the old man. By giving pieces of his legend, Sibelius was giving Erich the raw materials to fashion his own: "wartime service in Finland ... chance meeting with the great composer ... friendship developed ... entrusted to his young *protégé* the world premiere of the great Eighth Symphony ... Maestro Ziegler will conduct tonight with an inscribed baton given to him by Sibelius on Christmas Day, 1941 ... Maestro Ziegler is accompanied by his beautiful Finnish wife ..."

Sibelius seemed to know what was rushing through Erich's mind; the intimacy of his gaze was piercing, almost relentless, so that Erich finally averted his eyes. As he did so, his eyes met those of Kylliki, which were lustrous and dark against the snow-flare brightness that filled the room. She was resplendent in an umber dress trimmed with green, her freshly brushed hair glowing in the light. After the gifts were opened, Kylliki brought out her *kantele* and played, while the others in turn joined hands and sang holiday songs. Erich noticed that despite the amount of drinking going on—even Aino had drained a glass or two—neither of the sisters touched alcohol. Yet they grew flushed and spirited as the others did, so that even Anna-Liisa seemed for the moment less stern than regal.

In an ancient ritual of Finnish hospitality, each person was expected to clasp hands with every other person during at least one of the many songs, without regard to ordinary partnering or sex. Toward the end of the singing, Erich had found himself partnered with Anna-Liisa. He was drunk enough by then to feel no compunction about grasping her hands in a frankly admiring way; he had nothing to hide from this chilly but queenly woman, including his intentions toward her sister—and he was not really sure what those were yet. Anna-Liisa returned his grip firmly, giving him stare for stare, yet she seemed to be regarding him as though he were running for political office, not as a man who had all but declared his desire for her younger sister. Her gaze was not hostile, merely appraising, but the probe of her grey eyes made him uneasy, for there was something as intimate and searching there as the heat in her sister's gaze; only less furtive, less enticing, and much less like the gaze of a shy but randy young animal.

Erich was just as glad when the singing stopped and the motion was raised that the corporal be sent to prepare a sauna for the menfolk, for beneath the bulge of his belly, another swelling had made a ghostly appearance. A hint of an erection, maddeningly unspecific as to which woman it was focused on, had unwittingly come to him while he was holding the older sister's hands, yet staring, as openly as he could without rudeness, at the slender white arms and small high rising bosom of the younger woman.

Now Erich stood, wobbling and clutching a full bottle of *aquavit*, behind Rautavaara, at the entrance to the sauna hut. There was no sign of Sibelius, who had been noncommittal about the sauna and who in any case had put away a heroic quantity of alcohol himself. Erich was content that he and the major would be sharing the sauna alone. The fearsome temperatures, the lurching shock to the circulatory system of cold water striking lividly hot flesh, would scarcely have been healthy for a man of the composer's age, and Erich knew—if he knew any single thing absolutely at that moment—that he was in no condition to cope with the possibility that one of the world's greatest composers might keel over dead at his feet.

Rautavaara dismissed the corporal, then called him back long enough to tell him that the guards could use the sauna

later that night, two at a time, if they wished. "Be alert!"
Rautavaara mockingly cautioned as the soldier staggered away.
"It would be just like Ivan to drop parachutists on us on
Christmas Day!" The corporal guffawed and slapped his thigh
at that one, then lurched off into the trees without bothering
to salute.

The sauna consisted of two rooms: the actual steam room
and an antechamber which was used for dressing and socializing. Smooth wooden benches lined one side of this outer
room, flanked by buckets filled with fresh-cut birch twigs
bound together in loose, fascia-like bunches. Clothes pegs
protruded from the wall nearest the entrance. Both men carefully deposited their bottles of liquor on the table and began
to strip.

Rautavaara without his uniform looked rather as Erich had
expected: smooth and ruddy, with pectorals as hard and glossy
as upturned bowls, a massive but solid belly, thick muscular
shanks dusted with sparse bronze curls. The major retrieved
their bottles, handed one to Erich, then opened the door to
the steam room proper. At first contact with the superheated
air, Rautavaara's chest blossomed in sudden runnels of sweat.
Erich was dizzied by the heat until his internal thermostat adjusted to the change. He breathed vaporous fire, felt his pores
yawn open and his food-numbed muscles start to loosen.
Mother-naked, red as newborns, feet flapping on the wet polished floor planks, the two men padded into the steam room.

The clock-shaped thermometer on the wall read 105 degrees Fahrenheit, and climbing. The heat smote Erich in
waves, glazing his skin with a thick runny film. He had the
sensation that deep, forgotten layers of dirt were being routed
from his pores and flushing themselves, in elaborate estuaries
of sweat, down to the floor and out through the drainage
channels. Rautavaara whooped coarsely and thumped his
chest, relishing the heat. He leaned over, his ass cheeks beet-
red and as symmetrical as moons, grabbed a ladle full of cold
water and languidly dashed it over the red-hot stones. With
an angry hiss, a detonation of fresh steam billowed around
them. Erich felt another orgasmic flush of sweat, followed by

a marrow-deep sensation that was perfectly balanced between pleasure and pain. He took a swallow of *aquavit* and, as he had half-expected, it too seemed to spread through his skin; there was no sensation to tell him when, or if, it reached his gut. Saunas, his Finnish comrades had informed him, were good places for serious social drinking. First, you reached the precise degree of inebriation you wanted, then you went into the steam and sweated out some of the booze. With practice, it was possible to maintain a perfect state of drunkenness almost indefinitely. Erich had heard tall tales about sauna parties that lasted for days, and at the moment, he believed them.

The two men seated themselves at opposite ends of a three-tiered bench that filled one wall of the steam room. The bottles were passed, beaded and hot, through the steam.

"Did you know, Erich, that there are more than five hundred words and phrases in Finnish which signify various degrees of inebriation?"

"And six hundred, I'll wager, that signify various degrees of being roasted . . ."

"It's true, we drink a lot. It's all the darkness, all that cold. We drink because we feel lonely, yet loneliness is also what we seek—for us, it makes civilization palatable. A lawyer in Helsinki, what does he do on the weekend? Has a few drinks to warm his belly, then goes skiing all by himself."

Rautavaara rose from the sauna bench—bantam-proud, clean, ruddy, virile—and pounded his chest as though he were the embodiment of his people. "The world may think we're also cold-natured, but we know the truth about ourselves: we're repressed by our environment and inside we are furiously emotional and highly strung. When we turn violent, it's explosive and sudden. We prefer ax-murders to subtle poisoning, and we try to cure the violence in ourselves with violent drink. I warn you, Erich: sober, there is no more loyal friend in the world than a Finn; drunk—drunk past a certain point, anyway—there is no one who will turn on you more savagely and with less warning."

"I'll remember that, Major."

"You don't have to worry about *me*, of course," laughed

Rautavaara, with irony heavy in his voice, "for I am a comrade and a true friend of Germany! I give you Germany!"
They passed the bottle again. It was all true—Erich felt himself leveling out on a plane of drunkenness that seemed both
agreeable and indefinitely sustainable. Certainly, he would
drink to Germany! He *believed* in Germany, and in what Germany stood for. Or maybe, what Germany *had* stood for. He
rather hoped Rautavaara would stop short of proposing a
toast to Hitler.

"Tell me, Major, what do you like best about Germany?"

"Your sense of historical identity. We don't have it. We're
one of the orphans of European history . . . even our language
is a freak. For us, everything before the twelfth century is pre-
history. Christ, we don't even know where we *came* from . . .
southern Russia? Central Asia? Mongolia? Hungary? There
are some Ural-Altaic dialects that have similarities to old
Finnish, so who knows, perhaps some of those Siberians who
are fighting outside Moscow right now are descended from
the same ancestors as I am!"

Rautavaara drank, apparently toasting his Siberian cousins.

"All we know is that about two thousand years ago, some
nomads came from somewhere and settled down in this part
of the world, God alone knows why . . . I would have headed
south, myself. They were centuries behind the rest of
Scandinavia, which was a couple of centuries behind the rest
of Europe, and about the only indigenous resource they're on
record as having was a talent for magic. No social or political
coherence at all—you can see that in the *Kalevala*, for God's
sake: a collection of stories about rustic anarchists wandering
from farm to farm casting spells on one another and tumbling
each other's wives and daughters . . .

"To give the devil his due, it was the Swedes who taught
us political cohesion, much as we came to resent them. Believe me, Ziegler, if you must be ruled by another nation, try
to arrange for it to be the Swedes!"

Suddenly, Rautavaara gave a wild whoop and charged
from the steam room, yelling for Erich to follow him. Trailing huge clouds of white vapor, the major flung open the

front door and dived into a snowbank, his red glistening body
striking the mound with an audible hiss. The incongruity of
the sight held Erich for an instant: the big, powerful, erubes-
cent major rolling like a puppy, his scarlet flesh pouring
steam, his teeth bared, growling with pleasure. Rautavaara
heaved himself up, puffing, and hurled a snowball at Erich.
"Come on, my valiant German comrade! We'll make a real
Finn out of you yet!"

Erich bolted from the stifling heat of the sauna hut, hit
the steps in a diver's stride, and belly-flopped into the snow.
He heard the snow spit when he touched it, felt it vaporize
against his scalding skin with an intense and nearly sexual sensation, as though tiny jets of fire were simultaneously spurting
from and into his flesh. The feeling transcended cold, was
downright Nietzschean—if his heart did not burst from the
initial contact, surely it would be stronger for the experience.
He yelled, not from pleasure so much as from the sheer wild-
ness of feeling. For a zany, scrambling moment, he and
Rautavaara pelted one another with snowballs. Then the major leaped to his feet—his blunt club of a penis swinging like
a scarlet sausage—crying: "Back inside! Back inside!"

Once they had reentered the hut, Rautavaara said: "If I really wanted to be a traditionalist about it, I'd have the corporal chop a big hole in the ice at the end of the dock, so we
could jump into the lake water."

Erich was ready to suppose that the major was not joking.
He guzzled a long pull of liquor and ladled more water onto
the stones, hugging the fresh steam to his body as layers of
vibratory sensation washed over his skin and through his
muscles. Rautavaara gave him a stubby cigarette, a *Klubbi*
mounted in a long cardboard tube, the only kind of smoke
that would survive this moisture.

"So, Ziegler, what do you think of Uncle Janne?"

"I think he's a great composer."

"So I ask you again: what do you think of Uncle Janne?"

"Well, all right then . . . His conversation is full of contra-
dictions and surprises and little parentheses that somehow
never get closed. It's hard to know what is a serious utterance

and what just comes bubbling up to his tongue, like fizz in champagne. He's a cynical idealist, and a cosmopolitan mystic. He thrives on isolation, yet he's obsessed with what the outside world thinks of him and his music. And he drinks too fucking much for a man his age."

"But all you are saying is that he is, after all, a man. Like you and me."

"No. Not like you and me. He is Sibelius."

"I *thought* I heard my name . . ."

Wrapped in nothing but a towel, the composer was standing in the doorway of the steam room: a spindle-shanked, bald, slightly potbellied old man, with knobby feet and twig-thin ankles. This astonishing sight filled Erich with an unreasoning dread. He did not want the towel to drop; he was not ready for that intimate a glimpse of the composer's humanity. Sibelius padded in, delicately, and groaned as he sat down.

"I need to sweat out some of that damned food. And some of the liquor. My capacity is not what it used to be. The major's father could tell you, Captain, that once upon a time, I could drink every one of my friends under the table and still go home and write good music."

"Indeed, Uncle Janne, my father used to tell me tall stories. One of his favorites was about the time you and Kajanus and Gallén-Kallela started drinking at four in the afternoon. Kajanus had to leave at seven, because he had a concert to conduct at eight. He returned at ten-thirty in the evening, to the same table, and you only looked up and said: 'You certainly took your time in the men's room.' "

"I believe my exact words were: 'That must have been the longest piss in the history of western civilization,' but no matter." The composer's arm, bone wrapped loosely with brittle white skin, went past Erich's nose and grabbed the water dipper.

"More steam, Erich! More steam! Learn to breathe it; it'll make a Finn out of you!"

The composer's eyes turned to Erich's, sharp and calculating, hardly the eyes of a man far gone in drink.

"I'm grateful to you for your gift. According to what it

says in that journal, my prediction was accurate—they are starting to perform my music again in Germany. There's even some sort of Sibelius *Gesellschaft* being formed in Berlin, though I gather it's being sponsored by that little toad, Goebbels. I guess they need *something*, now that they can't perform Mendelssohn any more. Odd to think of one's music being mobilized as a tool of war."

"Oh, I don't know, Uncle—before they announced mobilization last spring, the state radio played *Finlandia*. It's a very militant piece of music. Perhaps you should write a *Finlandia* for this war."

"Or perhaps," said Erich with drunken presumption, "perhaps you feel about *Finlandia* the same way you feel about *Valse Triste* . . ."

Sibelius's voice became grating, quarrelsome; his gaze flashed out at the other men, raking them, his face now red and raw. "I do not! I know what the goddamned intelligentsia critics like to say! I know how all the sophisticates and all the Stravinskyites and all the *Boulangerie* sneer at the piece! I can recite all their snotty little remarks! A warhorse! A tub-thumper! Franz Liszt rides again on a reindeer! You listen to me: *Finlandia* was written for a historical tableau—it had to share the stage with a locomotive, for God's sake! Subtlety was not called for, nor was there time for it! We were Russian vassals then, and I was a young man burning up with patriotism, caught up in the act of flouting the Tsar's authority. God, it was intoxicating! It was so *pure* then, like nothing else has ever been since! And I wrote just exactly what the occasion demanded of me. Hey, Ziegler, do you think it's easy to write really good crowd-pleasers? Do you? The margin between what really works, what is truly suitable, and what is merely vulgar and meretricious, is not so wide as you might think!"

Fuming now, the old man angrily ladled water onto the hissing, spitting stones, until the walls glistened and rivered, until Eric's breath became hot and leathery in his chest. Now, from beneath his towel, Sibelius produced a bundle of birch twigs and brandished them.

"I need to have my circulation increased!"

Rautavaara, a look of displeasure and embarrassment twisting his features, reached through the opaque cloud and grabbed for the twigs. Sibelius furiously jerked them away.

"I want Ziegler to do it, damn you!"

His eyes grey chips of stone, the composer handed the bundle to Erich. The bouquet burned his hand, prickled as though the stems were lined with thorns. Sibelius leaned forward, exposing the wet red parchment of his thin shoulders. The towel slipped low on his hips; the knobs of his hips and the withered cleft of his buttocks ran with sweat. With revolting surgical clarity, Erich was able to see dirt trembling within the beads of several fat drops, rolling down the channel between the old man's nether cheeks.

"I've never done this before . . ." stammered Erich. "I don't know how hard to . . ."

"Lay on, man! Make me lobster red and don't stop until the air smells of crushed birch!"

Sibelius tilted his head and one fierce glittering eagle's eye drilled into Erich's. The old man looked like an eroded gargoyle now, perched on the rim of some private ledge. It made Erich furious to realize that he was being baited, tested somehow by being enlisted in this ludicrous parody of sadomasochism. He struck tentatively at the old man's shoulder blades, a jerky motion, the blow's force oblique and indecisive, as though he were swatting at an insect and not really wanting to crush it, just to drive it away.

"Harder."

The twigs slapped wetly, a curdled blotch appeared on flesh. Erich was afraid his hand would go lame.

"Again!"

He struck, this time an angry whack that left a scarlet arabesque.

"Better! Again! Harder still!"

He lashed at the old man's spine, shoulders, and hips until the twigs frayed and pulped and the dried leaves released their keen sour-sweet perfume into the heavy air. The composer's back was a galled vermillion, matted with bits of leaf and wood pulp. The flopping twigs fell from Erich's numbed fingers. With a sound between a sigh and a groan, Sibelius reached for the water dipper and raised it above his torso.

Then he turned and, just before he poured the water over his head, he favored Erich with a sardonic, thin-lipped smile and said: "You did well. If there is one quality I despise above all others, it is frailty."

Eleven

Erich returned to the front on the morning of December 28, feeling absurdly like a commuter as he stepped from Rautavaara's staff car. The major had been full of effusive *bonhomie* during the return drive, but Erich—his mind still focused on the memory of his last encounter with Sibelius, his emotions still warmed by the memory of his walk in the snow with Kylliki—had been withdrawn and untalkative. For the last two hours of the drive, the car had seemed unbearably stuffy and rank with smoke. As Erich thanked Rautavaara with a heartiness he did not really feel, he was grateful for the lungfuls of clear cold air that welcomed him back to Third Division headquarters.

Pajari had moved his command post to an area just behind the cordon the Finns had thrown around the Russian breakthrough salient south of Lake Topozero. It was a large bunker scooped into the side of a low wooded ridge. The motor road ended in a rutted turnaround fifty meters from the bunker, but a supply trail continued through the forest in the general direction of the front. A Bofors antitank gun covered this level ground, its shield and barrel swathed in white bunting. A Finnish corporal sat behind the piece, shaving, squinting into a shard of mirror wedged into the breechblock. There was movement all around: men and horses, transport sledges loaded with food and ammunition, wire parties laying line, medical teams erecting first-aid posts deep under the trees. Erich knew his assumptions were correct. The Finns, having contained the enemy push, were now planning to eliminate the salient altogether. There was no sign of "Old Mickey," but amid the general mutter of distant cannon fire, Erich thought he could detect the familiar sound of its main battery.

The bunker's interior was crowded, smoky, and overheated. Erich began instantly to perspire. The Finns, few of whom bothered to glance at him when he entered, were wrapped in layers of snowsuit camouflage and looked not unlike *habitués* at a spa. Pajari was bent over an oil lamp, lighting a cigarette. As he looked up, coughing, he gestured at Erich and growled in German: "So glad you could make it back before the termination of hostilities, Captain."

Erich cracked his arm in a parade-ground salute and took a seat at the rear of the tent, near the plywood tables where the wireless operators, burdened with old-fashioned headsets that had mouthpieces like buffalo horns, muttered their arcane codes and fussed with the pancake-sized dials of their antiquated field sets.

Pajari returned to the acetate-covered maps pinned to the wall, speaking too rapidly in Finnish for Erich to catch everything. The map made it clear that things had developed rather predictably. The Seventy-seventh Siberian Motorized Division lay in the configuration of a sausage three kilometers long, dug in along the corduroy road it had used to force its passage through Finnish lines. At the easternmost end of the salient, the Russian perimeter bulged north to include a few square kilometers of low forested ridges on the shore of Lake Topozero. By occupying some rocky islets out in the lake, the Finns had effectively sealed off that icy plain from being used either for escape or resupply. Small blue arrows showed where Finnish detachments were dug in around the enemy pocket.

In his exposition of plans, Pajari sprinkled his remarks with the word *motti*, a term new to Erich which seemed to mean "pocket" or "enclave," and he kept admonishing his men to apply *"motti* tactics" with the same zeal they had shown during the *Talvisota,* the Winter War. The officers smoked, took notes, marked their own maps, asked occasional questions. It was all very businesslike.

When the conference was over, Pajari motioned for Erich to join him over coffee. Although the general's gruff manner had not changed, his sallies at Erich were less barbed than they had been before the fight near the armored train—more in the manner of a ritual accepted by both men.

"I want you to stick close to this operation. It's going to be a classic application of *motti* tactics, just like we used them in 1939 and haven't had a chance to do yet in this conflict; a chance to see the Finnish Army doing what it does best. The land dictates our tactics, Captain—we use skis where you Germans would use tanks."

"I take it the word *motti* can be translated as 'pocket'?"

"It's come to mean that, but the word originally meant a pile of logs, held in place by stakes, ready to be sawed into firewood. That's what we do when we have them tied to a road: we use the forest for mobility, we cut their column into smaller and smaller pieces, seal off the pieces from one another, then let the cold do its work, along with our snipers." Pajari patted the lozenge shape of the Russian salient. "Inside that perimeter are about seven thousand enemy soldiers. My division is already stretched too thin for the ground it has to occupy, so I cannot simply wheel my whole front around and crush them; in fact, I can only spare something like two thousand men for the job. And yet, before the new year is very far along, we'll have eliminated them. Then we can dig our trenches and start waiting out the rest of the war and I can start sending some of these poor bastards home on furlough."

Pajari refilled their coffee mugs; the two men smoked. "Writers like to prate about 'the art of war,' but that's an empty cliché. There's precious little call for artistry in what one normally does with a division of infantry, and most battles call for the hand of a mechanic, not an artist—you deploy the machine, crank it up, and hope it runs properly. But *this* battle, by God, these tactics, they require something special: finesse, timing, a sense of balance, and superbly trained men. The movements on both sides of that road will be a ballet of ski tracks. Success or failure of an engagement will be measured by whether or not a twenty-man ski patrol is in the right place at the right time. This may well be the last *motti* campaign of the Finnish Army. When the Russians finally can spare the men to pay serious attention to this front, there will be nothing subtle about it. It will be a locomotive running into a brick wall."

"But surely, Leningrad will fall before the spring," said Erich, more tentatively than he had intended.

"Leningrad will bleed, and it will starve almost to death, but I do not think it will fall. Your armies, Captain, have laid siege to the iron cradle of the Revolution itself. What we do here, in the woods, hundreds of miles to the north, hasn't even a ghostly relationship to *that* struggle. So: come with me and see the Finnish Army at its best—this may be your only chance to do so."

Pajari glanced at his watch, barked some orders to staff members in the dark recesses of the bunker, then invited Erich to join him on a tour of inspection. Outside, the sudden frosty light was painful, the onslaught of cold intense. Some distance from Pajari's bunker, a returning ski patrol was herding five Russian prisoners into the shelter of a lean-to roofed with branches, which had, until that morning, been used as a stable. The ground was still strewn with petrified heaps of horse dung. A warm aftersmell of the animals mingled with the perfume of cut branches. Curious Finns gathered around the knot of prisoners. Pajari changed course and joined the crowd, Erich following.

Up close, the Russians were poor-looking specimens, their cheeks gaunt and their eyes exophthalmic and jaundiced. They were wrapped in shapeless greatcoats the color of poor-grade tobacco, their feet stuffed inside ill-fitting jackboots which had been insulated with rags and papers to such a degree that each man appeared to be suffering from elephantiasis. On the prisoners' skulls were Tartar caps, pointed at the top, with two dangling earflaps, stiffened by the cold, which stuck out like the wing span of a nun's wimple.

A Finnish private stepped close to the prisoners, bearing a bucket full of potatoes. He poured them onto the ground before the captives. As one man, the Russians dived at the ground, clutching at the rolling objects, pulling them from the piles of manure and eating them with crazed enthusiasm, filth and all.

Pajari strode up to the nearest prisoner, a hollow-cheeked man with skin like grey leather, and addressed him in serviceable Russian. The man answered in a papery whisper. Erich, eavesdropping behind Pajari's right shoulder, could hear little.

"He's a farmer from one of the western districts of Siberia," Pajari translated. "He has a wife and three children. His officers told him their unit was advancing on Helsinki. On Helsinki!"

The group around the prisoners was joined now by a Swedish journalist, his blue overcoat emblazoned with correspondent's identification, his shoulders weighted with a musette bag full of camera equipment. While Pajari interrogated the Siberian further, the journalist carefully unwrapped his camera and inserted a flashbulb. When he raised the camera to his face, Erich and several onlookers automatically stepped aside to give him a clear shot of Pajari and the prisoner.

Then the Russian looked up and saw the big press camera being pointed at him. His body went rigid and his mouth went slack, revealing through cracked lips a white worm of a tongue, coated still with bits of potato. The man's legs gave way and he fell forward, crashing into the startled Pajari. As the prisoner raised his head, the Swede flashed his picture. When the bulb blazed, the Siberian let out a wail of fear and fell to the forest floor. He gathered himself into a fetal knot, kicking and scrabbling amid frozen clods of dung. There was an embarrassed silence among the watching Finns.

Pajari knelt and raised the prisoner's face toward the camera, telling him repeatedly, in the soothing tone a parent uses on a frightened child, that the Swede had only taken his picture, nothing more. When the man seemed incapable of understanding what that term meant, Pajari reached into his own pocket and took out a leather billfold, opening it to a snapshot of a petite blonde woman and two school-aged children. He pointed to the photo and then to the camera. The Swede reversed the instrument and held it out so that the terrified prisoner could look through the viewfinder. Slowly, the realization came to the man that he was not going to be shot. A tremulous smile began to work its way across his lips; then it shattered and his face was twisted by sobs. He grasped at Pajari's leg, beating his head against the ground and weeping. Pajari carefully disengaged his foot, gestured angrily at the bystanders, watched as the prisoner was hoisted to his feet by several hands. Roughly, he pressed a packet of cigarettes into the Siberian's hand; the man only wept with renewed emotion. Pajari walked on, leaving the prisoner, still shaking and whimpering, staring blankly at the cigarettes in his hand.

"That man has not eaten in three days; he hasn't been warm for two weeks; and inside his heart, he knows he'll never see his family again, because even if he's repatriated, the NKVD will probably shoot him. Now you see how I can move against seven thousand men with two thousand."

"The troops we fought outside Murmansk hadn't been fed for days either, but they fought like mad dogs."

"God damn it, I only said we could do it! I didn't say it would be easy!"

Yet in the early stages of the battle, Pajari's fluid, elegant tactics almost made it look easy. The Russians held the road, the Finns held the forest—the advantage of mobility lay entirely with the Finns. For the past week, Pajari's engineers had been constructing a network of corduroy ice roads up to and around the front end of the enemy salient. By using these, Pajari could skillfully shuffle his handful of field guns from position to position. They would unlimber, fire a few galling salvos, then pack up and vanish into the wilderness so quickly that the Russians seldom had time to react effectively. Instead, they wasted thousands of rounds firing into terrain that was no longer occupied.

Predesignated assembly areas were staked out in sheltered

spots, just behind the reach of Russian patrols. To support the road-cutting operation, mortars and heavy machine guns were moved into position in boat-shaped sledges that could be nosed through the forest as a canoe was steered through white water. Aid stations, ammo dumps, telephone lines, all were carefully sited well in advance. Then the assault teams moved up.

Erich lay with Pajari on top of a brush-covered ridge five hundred meters from the road, rolled over on one shoulder, scanning the forest behind them with cloth-wrapped binoculars. In a gully between them and an 81-mm mortar battery, a fifty-man shock detachment was skiing into position. Erich admired the stealth and efficiency with which the heavily burdened men managed to negotiate the rough terrain. They moved with only a whisper of sound, shrouded in white, weapons draped loosely over their chests so that both elbows could pump freely. At a signal from their commanding officer, the skiers halted and swiftly kicked free of their skis. They also stripped off their heavy equipment—packs, canteens, rations, extra ammunition—and piled it up for later retrieval. The first assault wave would go in light and fast, the men wearing only lightweight snowcapes, armed with close-range weapons: Lugers, Suomis, grenades, and satchel charges.

Erich experienced a moment of painful nostalgia when he watched the ski troops make their preparations. What Eino had tried to show him individually, he now saw practiced *en masse*, and Pajari's imagery had been on the mark: it was not unlike watching a great troupe of dancers limbering up before taking on some barbaric and wildly demanding Stravinskian score.

I will become as good as these men, even if I can never be exactly *like* them. I promise you, Eino: no other Finn will ever die because I am slow or stupid or lacking in forest sense. Watch me, Eino. See how I learn!

Erich swiveled on one sore hip—they had been lying here for an hour while Pajari ticked off items from his checklist and spent long patient moments examining every visible inch of Russian lines—and refocused on his own fragmentary view

of the road. Pajari had chosen to sever the head from the enemy salient, attacking the spot just before it bulged out
through the woods toward the lake. The only clearly visible
part of the Russian defenses was a ring of tanks, their outlines
rounded and made strange by a foot of new snow, drawn up
in front of the infantry's positions in classic "wagon train"
fashion. The Russian infantry, Erich knew, would be dug in
deep behind and under those tanks.

Now skiless, the assault team worked its way around the
elevation where Erich and Pajari lay. In a matter of seconds,
it had blended invisibly into the snowy waste between the
trees. At hundred-meter intervals, a second and third wave of
attackers now took position. Pajari whispered something into
the field telephone tucked beneath his forearm. The forest
held its breath.

Erich flinched when the mortars coughed, from a point
that seemed to be directly behind his own buttocks. All
around them, from a crescent of gun pits hacked into the forest floor, came a steady "wonk-wonk-wonk!" of projectiles being spat from tubes. Then the road directly in front of him
burst into flurries of snow clods; shells striking the muffled
tanks produced sour, gong-like crashes. For ninety seconds
the mortars pounded a single fifty-meter-wide section of road,
chewing up everything that occupied that ground. From a
dozen heavily camouflaged positions near the road, heavy machine guns squirted long streams of tracers into that same
constricted zone, beating the snow, buffeting the vehicles and
log-walled dugouts. For precisely ninety seconds, that one
strip of road was at the narrow end of a funnel of fire.
Through binoculars, it looked as though a whirlwind laced
with meteors danced above the road, dipping down repeatedly
to suck up gobbets of snow, planking, metal, and bits of stone-
hard horseflesh from places where the enemy had fortified his
foxholes with the same material he had already been reduced
to eating.

Then, abruptly and with surgical precision, the sup-
pressing fires were shifted to the left and right of that initial
target zone, lining an invisible corridor with walls of fire. At

that instant the assault team suddenly erupted from the depths of the trees—wraiths, white on white, fluttering and flapping like fierce ivory birds—making straight for the road. They were on the defenders before the Russians could recover from the bombardment.

Erich saw the first Finns actually break through to the other side of the road, spraying both sides of the road cut with their submachine guns, tossing grenades into foxholes, thrusting satchel charges under the tanks. The point of impact, where the attack crashed into the wagon train of dug-in vehicles, seemed to boil with smoke, flashes, and movement, as though an anthill had been kicked. The next wave of Finns to reach the tanks, without benefit of such momentum, were greeted by desperate resistance. Erich saw a Red officer leap from the flaming turret of his BT tank on to the back of a snowsuited Finn, beating on the man with what appeared to be a large socket wrench. As the Finn went down, the hood of his snowsuit flowering scarlet, the Russian clinging to his back was in turn all but decapitated by a blow from another Finn's entrenching tool. Men swarmed over the vehicles now, grappling furiously, using sheath knives and pistols and rifle butts. Then the third and final wave of the attack arrived, coolly entering the fray and taking careful aim, methodically shooting every Russian who had come out to fight, systematically lobbing grenades or pushing explosive packs into the foxholes and bunkers on either side of the original smoldering breach.

Quickly, before the Russians could counterattack to seal that breach, Pajari ordered up reinforcements, a full company this time, to widen the cut and seal off its flanks. An engineer platoon moved up with them and began fortifying the ends of the road cut. Working back and forth along the road, the Finns forced apart the shattered ends of the Russian line until they had created a corridor two hundred meters wide, barricaded on both flanks. Now fresh ski units would move at will from one side of the road to the other, between the two shrunken Russian pockets. Pajari's men had cut their opponents into two completely surrounded *mottis*, and it had taken them, by Erich's watch, forty-three minutes to do it.

For the next three days, the Finns tightened the screws on the smaller *motti*, shelling it, nibbling at it hole by hole, paralyzing all movement within its perimeter. With total freedom of movement now, the Finns could coordinate three or four swift, slicing attacks simultaneously, making it impossible for the sluggish and increasingly hungry defenders to make efficient use of the formidable amount of firepower still at their disposal. By the end of the third day, the gap between the two Russian positions was so strongly fortified that their isolation, in a tactical sense, was complete.

In all his previous duty with the Finns, Erich had observed them engaged in more or less conventional fighting. Now, however, Erich found himself caught up in something quite different. Now the Finns were fighting their own kind of battle, a kind of super-ambush, their tactics honed to the perfection of art. Movement, weapons deployment, vectors of force, timing, all seemed to grow organically from the forest itself. Indeed, it occurred to Erich that *motti* tactics were as valid a manifestation of the forest *milieu* as the music of Sibelius.

Unattached to any unit, Erich roamed from place to place, seeking to grasp the totality of this battle, to absorb its rhythms as he would have done when studying a new and challenging score. After ten days of watching Pajari's men dance their murderous sarabands in the snow, he felt that he had been transported into a state of accelerated clarity, that he possessed new dimensions of awareness.

Danger's proximity only seemed to intoxicate him, his fear subsumed by a new thunder in his blood. Despite the fact that in all the time since he had donned a uniform, he had never had so much to live for, he felt—felt it as an exquisite, almost tactile, paradox—more immune from death as he moved closer and closer to it. He felt himself surrounded by a diamond-white, diamond-hard nimbus that would deflect shrapnel and change the course of bullets. Eventually, a hyperkinetic faith grew in him that he had been vouchsafed, through his friendship with Sibelius, the protection of Tapio, the forest god.

He had entered fully into the warriors' communion of the forest. It was an experience as mystical in its intensity, as deep in its ramifications, as any he had ever known from music. It was, for a time at least, as though he had been able to step back into the wide-open, freshly minted perceptions of his youth, when he had been driven to make his pilgrimages into the Alps.

What ghosts will come to me beside these frozen lakes? What dragon's gorge will they direct me to?

This time, wherever it is, I will not run from the dragon, but will look into his eye before I stab it out with my bayonet.

In particular, it occurred to him that the Finns' tactics approached not only the level of art, but also the quality of an atavistic tribal drama. However exaggerated by ideology and distorted by meretricious cant the racial theories of the Nazis might be, it seemed to Erich that there was an element of truth, truth about the blood, buried beneath them, far more subtle and powerful than all the propaganda clichés. He beheld not just two modern armies locked in struggle over political goals, but a conflict between the tribal souls of ancient Finnmark and Mother Russia. In its mood of blood-black tribal savagery, he could as easily have been witnessing a struggle between the Mongols of the Golden Horde and the fur-clad tribes of the forest, and in their arsenals might have been found not only howitzers and machine guns, but also the tom-toms and rattle-fetishes of Altaic shamans and the dark rune-chants of the wizards of Finnmark.

The Finns' intimacy with the forest gave them a deadly effectiveness. Time and time again, Erich found himself caught suddenly in the middle of ski detachments, platoon- or even company-sized units, that had seemingly materialized out of vapor. One second, nothing was visible but the trees, weighted down with their accumulations of snow, and the next, a river of white-clad warriors would flow past him, leaving hardly any greater trace of their passing than fish leave on water.

From the ring of dugouts they had established at varying distances from the encircled *mottis*, the Finns maintained sensible round-the-clock activity: two hours in the lines, two hours in sheltered warmth, two hours back on patrol, then a longer rest period for a full meal and sleep. After an especially arduous period of duty, Pajari rewarded hardworking platoons with a pass to the front-line saunas—back near the artillery batteries, and the one luxury the Finnish Army could not do without, even on a battlefield.

By contrast, from the third day on, the encircled Russian positions gave off a palpable funk. The Russians never ventured into the forest deeply enough to disturb the Finns' activities or spoil their attacks, and when they did sally from their wagon trains, they did so not with stealth but in slow lumbering groups of fifty to one hundred men, bunched together in claustrophobic discomfort. It was not hard to spot them, track them, and engage them from hidden positions.

Within their ring of armored vehicles, the Russians' style of bivouac was part of their own undoing. Whereas the Finns relied on small sledge-mounted stoves to provide hot food for a single platoon at a time, the Russians had come into the forest equipped only with heavy, cumbersome field kitchens. One by one, as their locations were given away by their tall stovepipes and plumes of smoke, Pajari's men knocked them out with pinpoint mortar strikes. With the destruction of their only source of hot food, a pall of cold settled over the *mottis*. The temperature hovered at twenty below zero.

Campfires became the Russians' only source of warmth, and they continued to build them even though the men who flocked to them, stenciled clearly by the flames against a backdrop of grey-white gloom, made splendid targets for the Finnish snipers who waited in distant treetops, peering through the telescopic sights clamped to their deadly accurate Mosin rifles.

Scourged by mortar fire, unable to venture into the forest or to make contact with friendly lines, deprived of hot food, unable to care properly for their wounded, tortured by the knowledge that a fire's momentary warmth could bring instant death, the Russians grew apathetic, hunkered down in their holes, and slowly froze. The noose tightened hourly.

Twelve

By the end of the week, the smaller *motti* had been reduced to a quiescent pocket only half its original size. The Finns harassed it and kept it tightly invested, but they no longer wasted men or bullets in direct attacks. All enemy patrol activity from that pocket had ceased forty-eight hours ago; Pajari was convinced that cold and hunger could finish the job.

He turned his full attention to the larger *motti*—an altogether tougher proposition not only because it contained much larger Russian forces, but also because it was well supplied with artillery, including two batteries of medium howitzers in defilade positions behind the lakeside ridges that formed the core of the pocket's natural defenses. Nor were the troops in the big *motti* yet suffering as acutely as their comrades in the western pocket. Intelligence reports indicated hundreds of horses inside the perimeter, and the broken nature of the terrain, in contrast to that of the road-bound *motti*, allowed the surrounded soldiers to cook their horsemeat without undue risk. Moreover, the Red Air Force was making an effort to reinforce the trapped unit by air—both ammunition and men had been dropped into the pocket from low-flying Ilyushin DB-3s, obsolete medium bombers converted into transports. Pajari had sent out a priority call for antiaircraft weapons, which had not until now been needed in this sector. While waiting for them to arrive, he fine-tuned the encirclement of the large *motti*, launching a series of quick, powerful attacks against isolated Russian strong points, operations in which the Finns' mobility allowed him to mass superior forces at any one point on the enemy perimeter.

During this period of limited action, Erich began attaching himself to Finnish ski patrols. His skill in camouflage, cross-country skiing, and what the Finns called "forest sense" had grown to the extent that Pajari no longer bothered to keep track of him, tacitly acknowledging that Erich could take care of himself.

It was on one such reconnaissance patrol, in the company of six ski-troopers with whom Erich had already shared coffee and porridge, that he saw the skull poles.

The patrol had spent a painstaking hour covering two hundred meters in the morning twilight, hoping to conceal themselves, before daylight arrived at 1000 hours, on a seemingly undefended little knoll that promised to offer a view into the heart of the large *motti*. Once there, the Finns hoped to spot the howitzer batteries whose presence had made the reduction of this pocket so problematical. Erich had rather enjoyed the crawl; he had learned how to move in the snow without attracting attention, how to take advantage of the shifting dappled shadow thrown by overhanging accumulations of it. Indeed, he had become fascinated by the shapes created by those thick pillowy accretions of snow that weighed down the trees, turning them into spires, caverns, long shadowy arcades, glittering arches of stardust.

When he finally lifted his binoculars and focused them on Russian lines, he saw only a brush-choked gully obstructed at one end with what appeared to be a mound of snow-covered firewood. As his eyes searched the subtler features of the landscape, details revealed themselves. He detected a white tarpaulin draped over the entrance to a large bunker. An odd location, it seemed, for a command post. He glanced to his right; the Finn beside him had already marked that location on his map with the word *kentasairala*—"field hospital." Erich understood then that what he had taken to be firewood was in fact a pile of frozen amputated limbs.

Now he started to detect other well-hidden Russian positions, including two all-but-invisible bunkers which appeared to be embrasured for heavy wheeled Maxim guns, as well as aiming stakes for a mortar battery, cleverly arranged to look like fallen branches. No, this seemingly undefended approach was in reality a baited trap, a preplotted killing ground into which the Russians hoped to lure their besiegers.

Rising beyond the hospital entrance was a bare, sullen ridge, ribbed with outcroppings of rusty granite, its scattered trees flayed bare by shell splinters. Erich was certain that the far side of that ridge would be heavily entrenched; the lake itself began only a hundred meters farther east, making that ridge the *motti*'s last inner redoubt.

Arranged on the ridge's outer face, spaced at intervals of three or four meters, like a macabre *cheval-de-frise*, were long poles embedded in the earth, held aloft in the forks of cleft tree branches. On the end of each pole was the sharp ivory rind of a horse's skull, and just behind the skulls long raw strips of hide stirred sluggishly in the wind. At the sight of those sinister, enigmatic totems with their grisly streamers, Erich felt a profound thrill of recognition. Had he not sensed the primordial essence of this battle? Had he not been seeking just such a confirmation? On his map, the Finnish scout next to Erich marked the ridge with a couple of question marks.

I can tell you what they are, comrade, but you would probably not believe me: they are the emblems of an ancient magic carried here from Siberia, where men still gnaw the bones of mammoths that were frozen before the gods of Babylon rose from the desert; a force now revitalized by the forest and deployed as a weapon by those desperate, frozen, trapped men on the other side of the ridge.

I will come here again. There is something here for me.

Erich followed the patrol through its debriefing, curious to see what Pajari's intelligence officer would make of this information. That individual turned out to be a Swedish-Finn man named Ostermann, who dwelt in a small dugout at the center of a bank of pipe smoke, behind a table strewn with maps, aerial photos, and boxes full of stained, rumpled enemy documents, some of them obviously combed from latrines. When one of Erich's companions expressed disgust at the unmistakable redolence emanating from the papers, Ostermann coolly replied: "We get some of our best information from their outhouses, Corporal; you'd be surprised what people will wipe their asses with."

Ostermann listened attentively to the patrol's report, sucking wetly on his pipe and flicking down quick little notes on a newsprint pad. When the report was finished, he clasped his hands behind his head, leaned back, and assumed a droning, professorial tone. Intelligence officers, Erich concluded, were much the same in every army.

"Well, that fits, although it is a bit extreme. You see, gentlemen, our opponent, the Seventy-seventh Siberian Motorized Division, is not a cohesive unit. It's an *ad hoc* formation assembled from the leftovers of a half-dozen military districts in central and western Siberia. In spite of all the equipment it brought into the woods, it's really a second-rate outfit. As you can imagine, Stalin feeds his best units into the fronts around Moscow and Leningrad; for a sideshow like this, he'll throw in any old trash that's lying idle in the replacement depots. If those units happen to be made up of restive Asian minorities, and if those politically questionable units happen to be exterminated even as they contribute to the defense of the Motherland, well, so much the better from the Kremlin's point of view—Stalin gets double value from using them up. One battalion inside the big *motti* is made up of Ostyaks from the Altai Mountains, a tribe that strongly resisted collectivization during the twenties. Some of the more backward villages in that region still cling to the ancient shamanist religious practices—another fact not likely to endear them to the Kremlin.

"Those skull poles you saw serve two purposes: as offerings to the spirits of the forest, and as warnings to their tribal enemies—in this case, ourselves. The presence of those poles means that there is a powerful shaman somewhere inside that *motti*. Better be careful, boys; I understand they can throw a curse at long ranges!"

Unimpressed, the Finn next to Erich muttered: "I'll shove some fucking magic into his belly!" and tapped the hilt of his *puulka* knife.

"According to the things we now know," the intelligence officer continued without missing a beat, "it's possible Stalin ordered their attack here for the purpose not only of blunting possible Finnish operations against the Murmansk Railroad, but also just to get rid of—perhaps 'use up' would be the better term—a unit composed of what he regards as politically unreliable elements. He ties us down, protects the railroad, and cleans house of some riffraff at the same time. In fact, some of the reinforcements that have been parachuted in are Karelians, also politically suspect. They'll have the effect of prolonging resistance, of course, but the primary reason all of those men have been sent into the forest is simply to die."

Erich left the dugout feeling drugged. As at Tapiola, the forest had presented him with a mystery and seemed to challenge him to be brave enough to quest for its meaning. He knew he had no business venturing to that part of the battlefield alone, but he was determined to see those skull poles again. In his overstimulated mind, that first glimpse of them had assumed visionary importance, exerted a pull that was irresistible.

He went out alone the following day at first light, seeking another approach to the *motti* that might offer him a glimpse of the shaman's bastion at the core of its defenses. Close to the lake was a thick stand of arctic pine separated from the Russian earthworks by a delta of frozen marsh. Since the open terrain between the trees and the enemy was covered by several machine-gun nests, the Finns did not occupy this ground in the daytime, but merely garrisoned it with nocturnal listening posts, trip-wires in case the defenders should attempt a breakout along the lakeshore.

Erich had it in mind to climb one of the trees—from the top, he reasoned, there should be at least a partial view into the *motti*'s interior. He arrived just as daylight came. It would be a clear icy morning and under the trees were lagoons of crisp shadow; the air, not yet touched by direct sunlight, was blue and oddly febrile, evoking in him a mood both tense and delicate.

Erich moved into this grove as a man might move into deep water; removing his skis, centering the weight of his Suomi just below his heart, he waded slowly through tidal pools of silver-blue shadow, drawn as though upon the currents of some powerful and mysterious inspiration. He was halfway through the grove when something disturbed the silence. He froze, in a small clearing in the center of the trees, like a startled animal. First came the drone of planes, then the rapid stuttering drumbeats of flak. Pajari had received his Bofors guns during the night, and these now opened a brisk and accurate fire against the three Ilyushins that had come in low, out of the morning sun. Black cotton puffs stained the sky around the planes, rocking their formation long before they reached their drop zones. One of the transports, its crew startled by the unexpectedly heavy fire, dropped its parachute load of supplies too soon—Erich could see by the canopies' drift that the bundles would land on the far side of a *motti*, on the lake, where they would be retrieved by the Finns or used by them as bait to lure an enemy foraging party into their sights.

The leading plane in the V-formation caught a Bofors round in its starboard engine and shuddered out of line, dropping low, unwinding a long pennant of smoke from the faltering motor; gnat-swarms of tracers from the lighter flak guns rose to meet it and the fuselage winked fire from a dozen strikes. Erich observed this miniature drama with growing apprehension, uneasily certain that he was involved as more than a witness. Indeed, the stricken bomber leveled out over the part of the *motti* just beyond Erich's grove, opened its bomb-bay doors, and discharged six parachutists.

One floated immediately into a shell burst, and when the shredded parachute drifted out of the smoke, its harness contained only a torso, a bright red lozenge in the fresh sunlight, a hock of beef drifting to earth. The other five parachutists succeeded in getting under the heavy flak and were soon too low and close to the trees for machine guns to reach them. In a diamond formation the five canopies fell, slow and bizarrely picturesque, like huge exotic spores, on a gradual slant away from the *motti* and toward the clearing where Erich stood, transfixed in an iris of pale blue light. Only when the drifting men were close enough for Erich to read their faces did he realize that they were consciously steering right for the spot where he stood: the one landing place in view which offered them a chance of survival. He was not especially worried because, snowsuited against a white background and utterly immobile as he was, they could not possibly see him. Then he saw that a thin wedge of sunlight had penetrated the screen of treetrunks and fallen across his position; from above, from the point of view of the descending men, his shadow must have been as dramatic and stark as the blade of a sundial.

Then the sleeve and hem of his snowsuit fluttered with such force that he was jerked sideways by the impact. Glancing down, he saw that three bullet holes had magically appeared in the fabric. Snow gushed in his face as other shots threw white fountains into the air, glittering like mica in the capricious sunlight.

Bursting from the ensorcellment that had nailed him in one spot for an almost fatal length of time, Erich threw himself wildly to one side, rolling, seeking to free his Suomi as he twisted and thrashed, followed by violent geysers of snow. He spotted a large fallen tree, executed a messy swan dive over it, and came up behind it with the submachine gun braced against a forked branch.

The parachutist closest to him was frantically trying to change magazines. Erich killed him with an economical burst, the man's white tunic fluttering as though a flock of birds were trying to escape from within. Instantly, Erich shifted fire to the next closest man, still ten meters in the air, desperately trying to swing his harness around so he could shoot at Erich. Even as bullets from the third and fourth men were ripping the bark of his tree, Erich put several 9-mm rounds into the second man, who twisted grotesquely in his shroud lines as he went limp, the canopy collapsing over him like an immense white jellyfish. Erich had plenty of time to kill the third and fourth men—they were higher in the air and he could aim and fire with calculation and stability, while they were still dangling helplessly.

At first, Erich could not find the fifth man, until the hammering echo of his Suomi had faded from his ears and the screams led his eyes to what, at first glance, appeared to be a large scarlet bird flapping in the lower branches of a tall pine. Erich approached this apparition slowly, in wonder.

The fifth man had come down far short of the clearing and had impaled himself on a limb. The end of the branch protruded from the front of his snowsuit like a spike, adorned on the end with a glistening loop of intestine. The impalement was dead-center: the branch had entered his body through the bowels and exited just below the rib cage. Heaving in agony, the man had spread his arms and legs in perfect symmetry, like Da Vinci's man-within-a-circle; his mouth was open to the blue-white sky, and his exertions caused cascades of tree snow to tumble over his face. For a moment Erich could do nothing but study this ghastly crucifixion; of all the kinds of death he had seen since the war's beginning, this seemed the most outrageous.

Then he swung the Suomi up and sighted on the dangling man, but the firing pin clicked on an empty magazine. Sighing, Erich lowered the weapon and fumbled with the catch on his holster. A terrible awareness came into the parachutist's bulging eyes; animated by lightning bolts of pain, he too groped for his sidearm and for a moment, pivoting on nothing more than the apex of his own sternum, he hung there, banging wildly at Erich with a Tokarev automatic, splattering the snow all around Erich's feet. Locked in a contest, compelled to accept the wager this dying man was making, Erich forced himself, for reasons he was never afterward terribly clear about, to stand there until the man had exhausted every round in his pistol. Then Erich calmly raised his Luger and shot him in the heart.

As he lowered the pistol, he realized that other eyes were watching him. Deep in the forest shadows, motionless, stood a vision from a half-forgotten dream that suddenly leaped, in full detail, to the surface of Erich's mind, causing him to cry out in alarm. He was looking at the bear that had chased him through his dream. Its fur was dirty ivory, its muzzle long, its claws like scimitars. Unnerved, Erich screamed and turned to run. The snow seemed to become deeper, thicker, like clotted cream, seemed to press heavily against his shins and knees, threatening to crest against his thighs, to bring him down. As he staggered toward his skis, he inserted a full drum into the Suomi. Now he had enough firepower to take care of ten bears.

At the skis, Erich turned to make his stand, sure that the bear was only meters behind him, its eyes like coals and its fangs streaming mucus.

Still motionless, however, its eyes hidden beneath the cowl of fur, the apparition simply regarded him from the deep blue shadows under the pines. He saw now that it was a man, tall and thin, obsidian eyes glittering in their hooded darkness, clad in the skin of a bear. The animal's flayed paws were strapped to the man's arms and hands, and in those hands Erich saw a wand, a fetish stick covered with rattles, charms, and feathers. An ice-water shock flooded his bowels. He could not move. Dimly behind him, he heard the sliding whisper of a Finnish ski patrol, attracted no doubt by the descending parachutes, and just before they arrived in the clearing, the shaman raised his stick and gestured once at Erich. To Erich's ears came the sound of cold, distant bells. Then the bear-figure was gone, blotted into the shadows as though it had been a phantom all along.

General Pajari, when he got a full report of Erich's single-handed massacre of the parachutists, was impressed. He began to treat the German with a curious, almost gentle, diffidence, as though wishing to put a respectful psychic distance between himself and a man who, according to the reports of slaughter that had reached him from the ski patrol's leader,

was clearly capable of entering the classic state of the berserker.

Erich did not, however, feel berserk; was in fact quite
calm. And when Pajari's operations against the *motti* suddenly
ran into a buzz saw of resistance, yielding Pajari more casualties in forty-eight hours than he had suffered in the previous
ten days, Erich understood quite clearly that this was the shaman's doing; that the skull poles were not merely the crazed
gesture of trapped and desperate men, but the outward symbol of something very real that had filled the hearts of the defenders and stiffened their resolve. Methodically, Erich
followed the logic of the situation to the point where the old
myths always seemed to lead: to the origin.

And what, Erich asked himself, was the origin of the enemy's newfound spirit of defiance? Erich thought he understood, even if Pajari did not. The bear-man, the wild Altaic
shaman, there was the origin!

By tapping the deepest, most primitive element of the defenders' consciousness, the shaman had galvanized them into
renewed effort. Even the educated men within that perimeter
would have felt it, understood it in their blood, if not their
intellects—even as Erich had come to understand it in his.

Oh yes—this was no conventional twentieth-century battlefield. This was the primordial forest. An arena outside
time, beyond even the fevers of ideology, the puling oscilla-
tions of politics. To break the Russians' resistance, Erich resolved to seek out its origin and strike at the root of its magic.

Pajari asked no questions, but only regarded Erich with
wrinkled blond eyebrows when the latter, two days after the
sudden increase of enemy resistance, came into his dugout
and requested a bolt-action Mosin rifle with a telescopic sight
and a pack of field rations similar to those used by long-range
Finnish patrols.

On two successive nights, Erich managed to penetrate
Russian lines, only to find himself too exposed, when light
trickled into the forest, to remain there. While he looked for
a perfect spot, he kept to himself, hiding from friendly patrols
as well as the enemy, trying to expunge from his mind and his

emotions everything except what the forest could tell him. When a Finnish patrol passed ten meters away without seeing him, he knew he had achieved a state of identification with his environment commensurate with the task he had set for himself.

Eino would have been proud of me that time, he thought, and when the memory of Eino brought no remorse, no flicker of old pain, he felt confirmed.

So that proves I am all right from the outside. Now tell me, Eino, how do I reach that state on the inside, without becoming too crazy to do what I have come here to do?

Become as the snow, the forest seemed to reply. Although Erich knew this conclave was being held in the chambers of his own mind, he nevertheless felt himself raw and open, utterly attuned to any possible emanation from his environment. Yes, he was whispering silently, mentally, to himself, but where were the words coming from?

Make yourself into a field as receptive as new-fallen snow is receptive, for whatever touches it, for whatever you wish to draw upon that snow.

He gradually converted his mind into a blank sheet of grey-white paper—fine, linen-textured paper—on which he mentally drew a single image: a hieroglyph of the bear-man. The shaman no longer roamed free in the snowy depths of the forest; some part of him had now been inscribed on the surface of Erich's will.

On his third approach, Erich's clean-swept mind allowed him to find the perfect spot to take his shot at the shaman. He scooped a tunnel for his body in the lee of the mound of frozen limbs outside the Russian field hospital. Hard as iron, their original shape all but obliterated by the snow, these arms and legs were nothing more than cordwood to him now; the cold took away all putrefaction, all trace of blood and mangled tissue, all the stench and fluids and glittering softness he had previously associated with battlefield injuries. These appendages lay inert, peaceful, as though their owners, having grown tired of carrying them around, had simply discarded them one day. Several times during the night, an orderly—a small, bent man who sniffled and muttered to himself in some obscure and birdlike Asian dialect—crawled out of the hospital dugout with a canvas sack and emptied the contents onto the far end of the pile. Erich could have extended the barrel of his Mosin and pricked the man's shins with it. Most of the newly cut limbs were already half-frozen; those that were not—a passing carnality on the air—froze to the texture of oak as soon as they were poured from the sack.

When he paused to consider his accomplishment, he was amazed. Such was the state of mind he had achieved that he could now encamp within a heap of amputated limbs and feel no revulsion at all; on the contrary, he felt only a fierce pride in having found the perfect place of concealment. In coming this far, he had liberated himself from a lifetime of conditioned responses—shed them as an animal might shed unnecessary fur in the summer—and had become, finally, a true creature of the forest.

At the moment Erich wriggled into his hideout, with enough of a firing slit—between what appeared to be a femur and a couple of forearms—to bring a shot against most of the skull poles and the ridgeline behind them, he felt a moment of exhilaration that almost made him giggle. He was in the heart of the enemy's camp—indeed, no living soldier had ever mingled more intimately with his enemies than he did now—in the one place that no Russian soldier was likely to spend much time contemplating. Sooner or later, the shaman would emerge to check his totems, to take some arcane reading of conditions, to sniff the air, burn an offering, take a pee, bless the troops ... whatever ... and when he did, Erich meant to slay him.

Hours passed; daylight came; Erich remained where he was. He took a few bites of rations before dawn, otherwise nothing. He was no longer hungry; he felt no thirst; he doubted he would ever need to sleep again. He was a quivering wand, a dowsing rod, a fern, a squirrel, a wolf; rooted in the forest, his mind emptied of the rubbish it had accumulated over two decades of well-fed middle-class European upbringing, he was both the perfect receptor and the perfect instrument.

If I could see my mind, it would be a smooth and glacial surface where the wind blows spirals of fine dry powder, snow as fine as talcum, fine as the dust of time-ground bones, fine as the music in a poet's heart. If my body seems numb, that is because everything that I am and have willed myself to become occupies a small, dense space behind the trigger of this rifle, which grows from me like the branch of a fir tree.

Columns of air, columns of wood, columns of air. Gradually, as the darkness gave way to a thick, soupy gloom and the tree spires began to define space in their serried way, music began to float above the plain he had made of his mind.

And this, he thought, must have been how Sibelius emptied his mind, gave it over to the forest, so that the music could come in.

Be welcome, music! Be my companion in this deep and somber vigil.

What Erich heard was, fittingly, the cold and remote Fourth Symphony, its dark horizontal lines blowing like ribbons of vapor across the fells of his heart. Meticulously, measure by measure, lying behind his sniper rifle, Erich conducted the greatest performance of his life, a re-creation of the symphony so vividly etched, so fine-grained in the fitting together of its inner relationships, so perfect in its ringing sonority, that he wished fleetingly that he could have recorded it straight from his head, and played it back later for the composer. "Yes," the old fellow would say, smiling around his cigar and throwing back a gulp of his beloved brandy, "yes, by God, Ziegler, you're *inside* the music now! And where did you get those bells? They're like stalactites of ice being struck with a mallet of bone! What desolate perfection! Bravo, Maestro Ziegler, Bravo!"

Maestro Ziegler . . .

Yes.

Riding the swell of celli and double basses, a second white skull appeared beside the one he had been sighting on. Then gone. The music quickly faded and Erich became a lightning rod again. He beheld the landscape with preternatural clarity, saw the gathering light of morning, the heaviness of the sky, knew that snow was imminent, and knew that Pajari would attack soon, for these conditions would give the Finns good cover. Already, clouds of snow-streaked gloom were drifting through the treetops. Fat, isolated flakes, the size of small biscuits, fell to earth.

He listened. He could hear them strike the ground. Each one.

The shaman knew he was there. The ridgetop was disturbed by the shape of his cowl as he sought a glimpse of the landscape beyond his own trenches. It was as though he could smell Erich, out there somewhere. Erich felt it going through the air between them. But the place he had chosen for concealment would distort and mask his spoor, he knew—a wolf could have walked past without smelling him where he lay. The shaman was perturbed. Erich represented something he was not prepared for, something that sought him out on his own terms. Wizard though he was, clad though he might be in a ceremonial skin that could have been a thousand years old, he was still a man, whose personal, perhaps even professional, curiosity, was piqued by the strange emanations reaching him from the wilderness. He therefore could not resist raising his head for a quick hard look at the gully below the ridge.

His pale leathery face, the black lacquered beads of eyes embedded in webs of creases, shadowed beneath the dried snout of the dead bear, filled the lines of the telescopic sight. Erich would do him the honor of not shooting him in the face—he lowered the sights to the base of the shaman's throat. He waited until he fancied he could detect the soft fluttering of the carotid artery.

Look at me, wizard.

The shaman's eyes shifted as the thought went out from Erich, bore straight through the telescope into Erich's own, an electric current of awareness arcing between the two men. At the touch of it, Erich squeezed off his shot. The shaman's head whipped back from the bullet's impact and vanished behind the crest of the ridge.

About thirty seconds later—a measureless interval to Erich—Pajari's mortar barrage struck across the face of the ridge and shattered the skull poles, tossing bones into the air. Erich ducked low as the ground around him erupted in columns of dirty snow and the clean air turned bitter with cordite and char. He lay with his cheek against the rifle stock, and finished conducting the symphony in his mind.

And why not? He had accomplished a fabulous thing: he had struck at the origin of the enemy's defiance and pierced it, perhaps mortally. Erich had no doubt that Pajari's attack would succeed, and so he had all the time he needed to finish his performance. He no longer had any awareness of temperature as such, nor of time. Having entered so deeply into his present state, he had no wish to leave it just yet.

Pajari had chosen this sector of the enemy perimeter for his breakthrough attack. He figured that a single deep penetration of their pocket, rather than a gradual pecking away, would yield the quickest results. He had zeroed in all of his mortars, all of his field artillery, on this one sector, and to give added punch to the assault, he had ordered four of his Bofors antiaircraft guns laboriously wheeled into point-blank range, their barrels depressed to the horizontal. These rapid-fire weapons now smothered the Russians' outer positions with a hailstorm of fire, chewing up log bunkers, vehicles, and foxholes alike. After a ten-minute bombardment, fifteen hundred assault troops went in, sweeping past Erich's hiding place and pouring into the pulverized, smoking earthworks of the *motti*.

Thereafter, it was close and bloody work. Many isolated groups of Siberians resisted savagely, coming up like wraiths with knives and pistols and grenades, and the Finns had to wrest them out of each hole, each dug-in tank turret, one by one. But the heart had gone out of the defense now, and when Pajari committed his reserve companies to finish the attack, they were able to do so in a single rush that carried them to the lake itself. Resistance fragmented into scattered holdout pockets, neither large nor numerous; large numbers of the defenders simply bolted for the lake, running blindly through the snow. Dense formations of men flowed out on to the ice where, nakedly outlined against its smooth pale surface, they were cut down in windrows by Finnish machine guns emplaced on the offshore islets.

When Erich finished the Fourth Symphony, he continued to lie in his hidden nest of calm, coolly observing the flow of battle around him, while his mind moved on to the sunnier Sixth, then to some of the tone poems. Not until the concert was complete, several hours later, did he wriggle from beneath his sheltering mound of flesh. His lower legs were numb now, but he could still move them in a hesitant shuffle. Using the sniper rifle as a crutch, he toured the inside of the fallen *motti*. Finns skied past him; occasional gunfire in the distance indicated that mopping up still continued, but here in the *motti*'s heart, silence reigned.

From the westernmost tip of the smaller *motti* to the highwater mark on Lake Topozero where the fleeing mass of defenders had been scythed by machine guns lay the bodies of almost six thousand Russian soldiers: scattered along the road, dug in along the ridges, were the pocked and blackened shells of thirty-six tanks and dozens of trucks, tractors, and hulking prime-movers—squat, canvas-covered, like shrouded catafalques.

Russian dead lay everywhere, twisted and lonely and losing their form as soft fat snowflakes drifted down upon them. Their faces were ivory, their eyelashes bleached with rime. The snow was littered with papers, equipment, weapons, snapshots, letters, knuckles of half-gnawed black bread, ropes, empty shoes, eyeglasses, harnesses, and the butchered corpses of horses, their exposed flesh woody and grey from the cold. Erich absorbed a hundred vignettes of horror, soaking them into his mind in the same receptive, finely tuned way in which he had received all the other data the forest had given him since he had tried to become one with it.

He passed a shallow foxhole where three Russians had taken cover from sniper fire. Pinned down too tightly to restore their circulation by movement, the men had frozen to death, untouched by a single bullet. Near the road, he found a Siberian and a Finn who had slain one another in hand-to-hand combat; the cold had stiffened their entwined bodies into a Goyaesque embrace. Not far away, he came upon a Russian signalman who had become entangled in his own telephone wire when he had come under fire. The man had tried to run, been hit, and had fallen into a snarl of unspooled wire. There he froze, a macabre Laocoön, struck down by the cold as fatally as if by a second bullet, arm outstretched, still pulling at the wire wrapped around his legs and hips, an expression of utter vexation engraved on his waxen face.

Everywhere Erich looked, he saw men flash-frozen by the cold in bizarre and lifelike poses, stone-stiff corpses with arms raised, legs uplifted in mid-stride, mouths twisted in conversation or command, as though hundreds of soldiers had simultaneously turned and stared into the Hydra's eye. Soldiers embedded in ice, like prehistoric warriors hacked from the Pleistocene permafrost of Siberia itself, they had attained at least a seasonal respite from corruption.

Snow had begun to fall more heavily by the time Erich finally reached the lake. Dusk was near. Already, flares were kissing the low and swollen clouds, bathing the ice in a sickly, flickering light while the Finns finished their work. Erich's feet had lost all feeling now, but he, in turn, had temporarily lost all concern for them. He limped, enraptured, among the heaps of the ice-dead, down long levees of corpses, piled, in places, to his waist. He examined them in the dwindling light, fascinated.

Even death was different here. In his earlier battles, he had known it a matter of glistening fluids and stink and flies and maggots and the smell of decay.

But death here in the wintered forest was not a business of fluids but of crystals. Dusted gently with snow, given a kind of benediction by the sky, the dead he wandered among had a purity that gave them dignity. Little blood or mangled flesh was visible beneath the snow; horror was muted, rounded, leached of color, rendered obscure. The sprawled bodies were not the distorted, pulpy, misshapen blasphemies he had seen

in the summer. They had not gone down howling and flopping in muck, but had fallen in precise, chiseled postures,
forming as they died statues of themselves.

Out on the lake, in the last dying light, Erich found a
squad of dead men staring up at him from beneath the ice.
Howitzer shells had shattered the surface here, cleaning off all
the old snow and seasoned ice, breaking through to the un-
imaginably cold waters below, and dumping these men to a
quick and relatively painless death. A thin layer of new ice had
started to form over them almost immediately, and between
the dust of new-fallen snowdrift, Erich could study their pale,
stunned faces beneath the transparent floor on which he
stood. Dark currents nudged the corpses. A dead sergeant
turned slowly beneath Erich's left foot, one arm curved out as
though waving to Erich to follow him; then, as the man was
sucked deeper by the current, his open, inquisitive eyes dwindled to points and then vanished into the darkness deep beneath the ice. Bubbles, like a broken strand of pearls, wobbled
up from his descending nostrils and rolled like blobs of mer-
cury on the underside of the ice.

Flarelight bathed Erich in a wash of lime. Lazily he raised
his head. Heavy weather was rolling over the lake, toward
him, and the snowfall was increasing. He knew, in some distant part of his mind, that he needed to return and seek medical attention for his legs, but the consideration seemed
hugely remote and without urgency.

Just before the twilight's fog obscured the far reaches of
the lake, Erich beheld the shaman in his ancient bearskin,
standing alone on the verge of a great wing of shadow blowing over the ice. The man was slumped, dragging his body
with great care as though against a tide of pain. A bandage at
his throat showed where Erich's bullet had torn through. In
his hand—Erich could barely make it out—was his fetish
stick, and dangling from his cartridge belt was a small gourd
drum.

As Erich felt consciousness draining from his brain into
his wooden and immobilized feet, there came to him the low,
slow, methodical pounding of that drum. With great effort

Erich shook his head and tried to clear his sight, unsure of the reality of what he was seeing. The man rapped angrily with his fetish-stick, as though batting at snowflakes, and Erich heard a ripple of far, cold bells. When he looked again, the figure of the shaman had vanished into a dark, swirling vortex of fog and snow, leaving only the faint receding heartbeat of the drum.

Suddenly Erich wanted to call out to the man, as desirous now of saving him as he previously had been of taking his life. What secrets he could learn from that man! But as his cracked lips strove to form the first words he had spoken in many hours, the snowflakes around him changed into bright points of fire, their color shading from gold to crimson as he fell, senseless, onto the ice. He lay there, separated from the embrace of the drifting dead by a few centimeters of frozen water, until a Finnish patrol found him, an hour after nightfall.

Thirteen

The Finnish Army's medical corps knew a great deal about how to treat frostbite. That hard-won skill kept Erich not only alive, but much more intact than he would have predicted. When he had swum to the top of his delirium in the aid station where the ski patrol had brought him, it had been just in time to see an orderly cut the boot from his right foot. When the man got to the sock, pinching it with a forceps and loosening the matted cloth with the tip of his scalpel, Erich had watched with resigned detachment, knowing that if his foot was as far gone as he suspected, there would be no pain. There wasn't; the orderly tugged a spiral of sock from his foot like a man unwinding a turban, revealing flesh the color of slate and toes that looked as though they had been dipped in tar. That foot is gone, he thought, and then passed out before the orderly could get to the left one.

Yet when he came to, in a convalescent ward in a hospital in Ilomantsi, he was pleasantly surprised to find that he had, in fact, lost just a portion of his right foot—two and a half toes, to be exact—and only a single toe from his left. The swelling and discoloration were severe, however, and he remained under treatment for those symptoms long after the amputations themselves had started to heal.

A week ago there had been a flurry of interest in him when a bouquet of flowers arrived bearing the greeting card of "Professor J. Sibelius," and Erich had spent an embarrassed but proud afternoon explaining to curious inquirers that, yes, it was *that* J. Sibelius; a friend of the family, he claimed, from musical sojourns in Germany during the Weimar years. To lie about it seemed best, for he could not otherwise define his ambiguous relationship with the family at Tapiola, and even to try would be to compromise both his own situation and Sibelius's security.

But now, nearing the end of his convalescence, on the next-to-last day of February, Erich was bored. There was nothing left for him to read in the hospital's meager library that was not in either Finnish or Swedish. The kind, bovine ward nurse had rejected his advances as she routinely rejected those of the fourteen other men in his part of the building. He supposed the Finnish doctors would discharge him soon; meanwhile, he countered the boredom with apathy—the hospital was warm, the food passable, and the fighting, according to all reports, had bogged down to position warfare all the way from the Arctic to the outskirts of Leningrad.

On that particular day, Erich was once again contemplating the absurd appearance of his left foot. The only toe the doctors had been unable to save was, strangely, the middle one, which had been snipped off at the base. Now that the bandage was off, and the flap of skin healing pinkly across the socket, the foot presented him with a strange and humorous aspect. Whenever he grew really bored, Erich simply placed his leg outside the blankets and spent some time wiggling the deformed foot, lining up objects through the pink-skinned indentation so ridiculously poised between the two pairs of surviving digits. When other inmates of the ward saw him doing this, some of them looked away, embarrassed for him. Erich did not think his behavior was *that* eccentric—the foot really was silly-looking—and responded to this discourtesy by swinging his leg like a rifle barrel, sighting through his toes on the face of the onlooker, waving jauntily, and making bang-bang noises.

On this occasion, he swung his feet toward the ward's front entrance, hoping to put his sights on the nurse's ample hips as she bent to change the plumbing of a man who bristled with tubes. Instead, the cup of space between his toes was suddenly filled with the florid, hearty features of Major Rautavaara.

Erich extended his foot in greeting as another man might hold out his hand. Rautavaara countered by reaching over to a vase of flowers, removing one, and wedging it in place between Erich's toes. Both men laughed. Erich kicked his foot with a flourish and the flower spun away. The ward nurse glowered at them as though they were misbehaving children.

Pointing to the visible foot, Rautavaara said: "Not a bad job on this one. How's the other one—the one you conduct with?"

"I'll never hold a baton with it again, I'm afraid."

Erich was really laughing now, and it felt good. Rautavaara brought with him his usual reassuring sense of comradeship, his woolly, vital smell; a hint of the outdoors.

"They were going to discharge you tomorrow, you know."

"To where?"

Rautavaara scanned a sheet of paper in his hand. "Back to active duty, I'm afraid; you've got to lose more than a few toes to get sent home, the way things are going now. But never mind—you've got forty-eight hours' leeway, so why not come for a drive with me and see something you can tell your grandchildren about?"

"And what might that be?"

"Leningrad dying."

Erich tried, without success, to read the emotions behind Rautavaara's words. Then, suddenly feeling as though he were waking from a long, pointless sleep, he sat up and gestured toward a locker by his bed.

"My clothes are in there, Major. If you'll hand them to me, I'll only be a moment."

They spent the night in Sortavala, on the western edge of Lake Ladoga. The lake was a desert of ridged and crinkled ice, swept by ferocious winds. A hundred kilometers to the east, German patrols lived on that ice, in conditions of polar desolation, and struck by night at the Soviet truck convoys that tried to bring supplies across the open ice into beleaguered, starving Leningrad.

The next day they skirted the western shores of Ladoga and drove south toward Viipuri, the only major seaport on the Gulf of Finland, annexed by the Russians in 1940, retaken by the Finns in the late summer of 1941. The twice fought-over city was largely uninhabited now. Filthy and dispirited gangs of Russian prisoners—as many as fifty men, guarded by pairs of bored-looking Finnish riflemen—worked to clear the rubble from the city's main avenues, moving the loose brick and plaster and glass into big piles along the curbs, where other groups of prisoners transferred it to wheelbarrows and carted it away. The main streets were mostly passable, so Rautavaara had little trouble navigating toward the harbor and parking on a cobbled plaza in front of the hulking stone castle that was Viipuri's landmark.

Rautavaara's expression was troubled; had been since they arrived in the city. "We have a few hours," he said hesitantly, "so long as we arrive at the front in time to find a billet for the night. I'd like to show you some of the city . . . what's left of it. We could begin with the castle—the view from the top is splendid. If you think you can make the climb, that is."

"Let's find out."

Viipuri's citadel was not a sprawl of gothic battlements, or a gilt-and-gingerbread Wagnerian daydream on the pattern of Neuschwanstein; it was instead a blunt, massive, utilitarian symbol of the turbulent era of Swedish imperialism. It had been a major chess piece in the protracted, epochal struggles between Charles XII and Peter the Great. It was businesslike and unelaborate: looming outer walls of extraordinary thickness, embrasured for cannon, dominated by a single octagonal tower capped by a pointed helmet of green copper. Together with coastal batteries on the approaches to Viipuri harbor, it had been sited to command this part of the Gulf of Finland and it had been built to withstand the heaviest bombardment. Charles's engineers had known what they were about: two and a half centuries later, modern artillery shells had done little more than chip the masonry.

Inside the great octagonal keep, the stones were as cold and ringing as iron. Their footsteps were metallic and the echo of their passage hung like old dust in the thin, sharp air. Erich's feet began to hurt halfway up, but the discomfort was dull and he could manage it. Once, near the top, his balance became unsure and Rautavaara had to steady him with a stout forearm. Both men were winded by the time they reached the final steps. Each face of the towers' eight sides had been pierced for a single huge cannon, and through those embrasures piped a bitter wind. They sheltered from it and cupped hands to light cigarettes. Rautavaara pointed: "The best view is from the south side, over there."

When he looked, Erich forgot how uncomfortable the climb had been. They could see from the waterfront—an untidy sprawl of blackened roofless warehouses and charred docks—all the way to the Baltic Sea's horizon. In between, in an enormous spreading V-shape, lay the whole of the Gulf of Finland—an ash-blue plain mottled with the silver of naked ice and the drifting mirage vapors of fresh wind-borne snow. Black, granite-humped islands dotted the gulf in profusion. Closer to land, like the carapaces of huge dead beetles, the hulls and superstructures of a dozen sunken vessels protruded from the ice at strange and whimsical angles. Nothing moved out there but the wind. On either side of the frozen gulf, the rough and jumbled coastline of Finland receded far away. The Baltic itself seemed to have no clear horizon—smooth, snow-heavy clouds glowered over dun-colored ice, and beyond that lay a disorienting emptiness, as though not Europe but an end-of-the-world void loomed out there beyond the rocky shoals and derelict ships.

The two men could lean out of a single embrasure with room to spare. Using his cigarette as a pointer, Rautavaara indicated certain parts of the landscape as he talked: "See that big island in the middle of the gulf? I was there during the last week of the Winter War. The Russians had pushed us out of the Mannerheim Line, then they pushed us out of the sec-

ondary line, and finally they pushed us all the way back to
Viipuri, and we turned there to make our last stand, hoping
the Allies would land in Norway in time to save us."

Rautavaara laughed bitterly and flipped his cigarette into
space.

"I was in command of a scratch battalion of coast defense
troops—boys just out of boot camp, old men who hadn't held
a rifle since the Civil War, walking wounded . . . hell, we were
so desperate by then that we were issuing weapons to con-
victs. One of my platoons was made up entirely of pimps,
pickpockets, and burglars; they fought like crocodiles."

The major paused for a moment, gathering his self-
control. Erich was surprised and moved by the honest sign of
emotion.

"On our island, we were screening a shore battery of six-
inch guns. They fired time-fused rounds that exploded ten
meters above the Russians' heads, like shotgun blasts. Can
you conceive of it, Ziegler? They went down like wheat before a threshing machine, leaving huge red smears on the ice,
yet they kept on coming, climbing over their own dead. We
threw them back a dozen times. Held them for two days. At
night, I sent patrols out with power saws to cut moats in the
ice, but six hours later, it was refrozen solid enough to bear
the weight of tanks. During the last assaults, we fired our six-
inch shells with no fuses at all—they burst a second after leaving the barrels, only fifty meters from our own trenches.

"We thought they were going to overrun us by the end of
the third day. They had used their own dead to build barricades closer and closer to us, and we had run out of shells for
the shore battery. We could hear tank engines, lots of them,
but we had nothing left to fight them with except hand grenades and a few Molotov cocktails. But I had been given a
code word, one that was to be used only when our situation
was hopeless and not until then. Fortunately, we still had a
phone line open to the mainland. I waited until we could hear
the Red infantry shouting '*Uuu-rah!*', working themselves up
for the final assault. I picked up the telephone handset and
spoke the word I had been given. A voice on the other end

asked for the coordinates of the enemy force. Then the line went dead. I thought that was the end for me."

Rautavaara pointed to the west, to a long wooded peninsula at the farthest reach of sight.

"Out there, miles away, was a battery of twelve-inch coast defense rifles. They had no antipersonnel shells, of course, only these great monstrous projectiles designed to penetrate the deck armor of battleships. They didn't even explode. They just rained down like enormous wrecking balls and shattered the ice like so much glass, opening huge crevasses. The tanks' weight tilted the ice slabs so that the vehicles slid, very ponderously, into the water. And the soldiers who had clustered behind them to make their attack, they were spilled into the gulf. They were weighted down with packs, helmets, ammunition, grenades . . . most of them sank in seconds. A moment later, the tanks fell on top of the ones who were still struggling. Perhaps the eeriest thing about it was the sounds: the hammer-cracks of the shells hitting the ice, the roar of the tanks as the drivers tried to race their engines and escape, then the screams of all those men falling into the water. The bombardment lasted just three minutes, but when it was over, a square kilometer of ice had been turned into soup, and an entire Russian battalion, along with sixteen tanks, had vanished before our eyes.

"We were pulled out a few hours later. We had been outflanked closer in toward shore, and we were supposed to help mount a counterattack on the outskirts of Viipuri itself. But the next day, the war ended. Just as well . . . none of us could have lasted more than another day or two."

As they descended, Erich felt the density of history gathered in the cold air above the gulf, crowded with event and pageantry, adumbrated by Rautavaara's remarks. A bulwark city, perched between Russia and the west, gateway to the Karelian Isthmus, how many times had Viipuri been fought over in the centuries since Peter the Great had first sunk pilings into the swamps of the Neva delta and proclaimed the founding of St. Petersburg? Empires had ebbed and flowed around this citadel like the Baltic Sea itself. And still it continued, still the soldiers drowned in those black and pitiless waters.

Russian resistance had collapsed swiftly in late August, when the Finns—for once in their history enjoying numerical superiority over the Soviet rear-guard detachments left to delay them—swept into what had once been Finland's "second city" and reclaimed it. The harbor district had suffered extensive demolitions, but the damage to the old city itself seemed curiously arbitrary and haphazard. As Rautavaara drove slowly through the pitted streets, Erich studied long blocks of severe, functional Swedish architecture, enlivened here and there by older, Tsarist-era buildings that carried in their cornices and decorative motifs a faded hint of the gingerbread style of old Novgorod.

In a relatively undamaged block near what was formerly the university campus, Rautavaara stopped the car outside a terraced building that offered what must have been, in peacetime, a fine view of the waterfront. Dangling from one hinge, perforated by bullet holes, was a wooden plaque on which Erich could discern a prognathic cartoon of Peter the Great, executed in flaking paint, above the name "The Bronze Horseman."

Erich followed Rautavaara into the smashed interior. Not a chair, bottle, or glass remained intact—everything had been reduced to heaps of dirty, glittering splinters. The interior smelled of rotting wood, overlaid with a faint trace of smoke. Rautavaara stood silently for a moment in the center of the room, a veil of private sadness drawn across his eyes. Erich cleared his throat discreetly against the smell and stayed close to the entrance.

"You cannot imagine, Ziegler, what a fine city this used to be! It was our Paris, our Vienna, our Heidelberg. The cafés were full of students, poets, artists, demented old anarchists hiding out from the Cheka, dreamy aristocrats who sighed away their lives staring off toward the St. Petersburg they would never know again, longing for a city that had already been transformed beyond anything they could have endured.

"I wrote plays, myself, when I lived here—can you believe

that? I had some vague notion of becoming the Finnish Strindberg. Our days were slow and full of interesting people, here in this city. And in the summer, no one slept—we stayed up around the clock under glowing skies that never grew dark. We sailed in the gulf and had picnics on the islands. We carried on crazy conversations with cubist poets and Cheka agents—sometimes, with cubist poets who *were* Cheka agents! And I would sit and drink at a table on the terrace of the Bronze Horseman, undressing the daughters of duchesses with my eyes and writing hyperthyroid dramas crammed with meaningful symbolism. Had the Winter War not taken place, I might be here still. Ah, who ever knows?"

Erich listened intently as this unexpected window opened on Rautavaara's heart. He would not have guessed that such memories dwelt within the man. Not really sure how to respond, but feeling that the growing silence required some contribution, he quietly said: "You would have liked it in Munich, where I grew up. It too was a city with such a character—we used to boast that it was the Paris of Germany."

For a split second, anger flared in the major's eyes. "Yes, yes, but when this goddamned war is over, Munich will still be there, and Paris too. But even if we manage to keep control of Viipuri, its past is gone forever. All that's left is what you see."

Rautavaara suddenly laughed. The sound came from his throat like an order being barked at a subordinate—perhaps at an unruly younger soldier within himself.

"I also stopped here to take a piss, my friend. I suggest you do the same—we still have a long ride before we reach the front."

The ride turned out to be longer than Rautavaara had estimated. There were only a handful of roads through the Karelian Isthmus and the main one out of Viipuri was clogged with military traffic. Still, the three hours it took them to cross the isthmus seemed short enough compared to the hundred days it had taken the Red Army to batter that same distance. Just as the last light was draining from the sky, they entered a region of such lunar desolation that its very appearance made Erich uneasy. On either side of the road, the once-dense forest had been utterly stripped away. Acres of land bore the fading indentations of thousands of overlapping shell craters, their outlines made clearer by the snow than they would have been in another season. There was scarcely a touch of green to be seen, as far as Erich could see into the gloom; just straight, bare, shell-flayed trunks. A hundred meters from the road, Erich saw a pair of massive concrete blockhouses that looked as though they had been pounded into the earth by titanic hammers. In the center of this man-made desert, they drove slowly past a cairn of stones marked by a Finnish flag.

"*Vanha raja,*" growled Rautavaara as they drove by, "the old border. When the Reds broke through here in 1940, they hit this sector with four hundred shells a minute for forty-eight hours without pause. Some of the men in our bunkers went mad from the concussion alone."

Erich was exhausted, and his feet ached abominably, by the time they reached a checkpoint at the eastern end of the isthmus. A sentry with a hooded flashlight stepped forward to inspect their papers. When Rautavaara rolled down the window, Erich heard ponderous, regularly spaced detonations that reminded him of a bass drum.

"Those sound big. Ours or theirs?"

"Those are the big sixteen-inch coastal guns over on Kronstadt. They shell the road every night. But they always do it in the same place, so it doesn't bother us much."

"Are we that close to Leningrad?" Erich was astonished—the great naval base at Kronstadt was in the city's backyard.

Rautavaara laughed, this time a little grimly. "I promised you a sight you could tell your grandchildren about. Trust me to provide it."

As they breakfasted on porridge and coffee the following morning, in a command dugout that had been dynamited into the rocky Karelian soil back in September, Erich learned that they were just east of the old Tsarist resort of Alexandrovka, eleven miles from the limits of Leningrad proper. They would be going into the easternmost point of Finnish lines: a granite ridge, where the Finns maintained a strong observation post, two hundred meters beyond the main line of trenches. The position was dangerously exposed; the only time it could be reinforced or supplied was at night—which meant a time-consuming crawl, inch by inch, following a guidance tape the engineers had rigged along the safest route. The distance between the main line and the outpost was exposed to Soviet observation from two directions. Mortar rounds fell on it every night, at unpredictable intervals, and machine guns swept it with long-range interdiction fire. Sometimes, the guide tape was cut—two weeks ago, an entire squad had taken a wrong turn and wandered into an enemy minefield. Since then the outpost's garrison had been relieved, whenever possible, during daylight periods of fog or heavy snowfall. And there was fog, this close to the sea, almost every morning.

Erich followed Rautavaara, at the tail end of a supply party laden with containers of hot food. Ears strained for the rush of an incoming shell, they crab-walked through a white void that got brighter as they went. They heard, at some distance, woodpecker taps of machine-gun fire, but nothing came close to them as they negotiated the exposed defile and reached the lee of the outpost. Rautavaara led Erich through a maze of trenches and strong points, like something out of World War I, and settled him, finally, behind a massive pair of Zeiss spotting glasses that filled the observation slit of a bunker perched atop the ridge's highest elevation. Beyond lay only a thick nacreous fog.

"How long before we can get a look?" Rautavaara asked a noncom who was cleaning his Suomi nearby.

The man shrugged. "You may not get a look, Major, with the soup as thick as it is today. Maybe a quick one, around ten o'clock, just after the sun gets above the tree line. It usually thins out about that time, for a while anyhow."

For the next fifteen minutes, Erich strained into the eye-cups of the big binoculars. After a time, he experienced the dislocating sensation of floating within the fog, so downy and cloudlike did it appear through the glasses. He stopped looking and smoked for a while. When he resumed looking, half-heartedly, already resigned to frustration, he gasped: "Oh my God, there it *is*!"

As though a curtain had parted, he beheld Leningrad spread before him like a stage-flat panorama carved from chalk. The leap his eyesight made, from the vague middle ground of the fog to the deep clear focus of the distant city, made him momentarily dizzy. There was something waxen and unnatural about the view; it had the clarity, and also the strangeness, of something viewed underwater. In a sweeping vista, foreshortened and somewhat flattened by the glasses' optics, blurred now and again by passing scraps of mist, the workers' fortress—object of the greatest siege in modern history—lay open to Erich's astonished gaze.

For all Hitler's prattling about the Ukraine, anyone with the most rudimentary understanding of the dynamics that had created and sustained the Soviet state could see that Leningrad was the heart of the Russian cause. *In extremis*, the Russians could burn Moscow again, and only be out so much furniture and bad architecture—but they would never burn Leningrad, never abandon it, for that would be like putting a torch to the Revolution itself.

Since September, the city had been surrounded, locked in a vise. Shelled and bombed daily from three sides, supplied only by the fickle and inefficient "ice road" across Lake Ladoga, Peter the Great's city was enduring a winter more terrible than any European city had known since the Hundred Years' War. Horror stories about conditions in the city had been circulating through Finnish ranks for weeks. It was said that rats and dogs, cats and birds, even the animals in the zoo, had all been eaten by Christmas. In that still, dark, silent city, men made soup from book bindings, attempted to congeal edible fats from mixtures of hair oil and sawdust, conjured jelly from boiled wallpaper paste, boiled tree bark to make broth. Deserters spoke in whispers about a black market in human flesh. Piece by piece, the city died: two thousand people a day from starvation, from alimentary dystrophy, from scurvy and dropsy and fatigue and despair and cold and now—it was rumored—from typhus. German siege guns rained shells on the city's heart while squadrons of Stukas and Heinkels unloaded their bombs from above. There was no end to the city's torment by man or the elements. Nor would spring bring much relief—the cold would fade, but so too would the city's only lifeline, the fragile ice road across Ladoga.

Yet Leningrad endured. Erich's breath was stopped by the sense of historical enormity that came to him with the sight of the city, as though he were witnessing the working out of some vast and implacable curse.

When he recovered his mental balance somewhat, Erich studied the view more dispassionately, seeking the details that would give points of reference, on a human scale, to the Olympian dimensions of the scene. He beheld a grey-white wall of glass and concrete, the compacted urban shoulder of the metropolis, pierced at intervals by spires and cupolas; he beheld the smokestacks and factory chimneys of a great industrial city frozen in its tracks: serrated roofs of assembly-line plants, bleak rectilinear blocks of housing, hulking motionless derricks—the whole foreshortened by the glasses into an almost abstract array of hard monochrome shapes. Details emerged as he strained his eyes: a factory wall, ripped open by bombs, revealing an enormous steam hammer poised over a black pile of rubble—a gigantic fist whose blows had been halted by some mysterious edict. To the right of that, a black tangle of fallen pylons and ruptured fuel tanks marked a devastated power plant. In the background, a gigantic sable column of smoke, circled by tiny dots of bombers, marked the pyre of the great Putilov Steel Works, once the pride of the workers' unions.

Erich shifted the glasses to the left and refocused. Now the River Neva delta became visible, the wooded islands where the elite of St. Petersburg had once gathered to stroll beneath the glacé skies of summer's White Nights, where Pushkin and Repin and Dostoyevski had argued and schemed and flirted, brooded and dreamed. Far beyond, in the depths of the city, he could discern, from an inference of shadows,

Admiralty Square and the Winter Palace, womb of the Revolution. In the dugout around him, others were focusing on the city with binoculars. No one said much. Even for the Finns who were used to the sight, it was enough to stop casual conversation.

Then quite suddenly, just as the noncom had predicted, the fog blew in again, almost obscuring the city, rendering it as spectral, and Erich's memory of it as seemingly mythical, as a vision conjured by a Tartar magician in an opera by Mussorgsky.

Fourteen

Spring came late and strong to the Third Corps front. One mid-April morning, in sunlight that seemed thicker and more nourishing than it had the day before, the branches began to drip. Twenty-four hours later, they were shedding snow in wet, fist-sized chunks. In every direction, in myriad tiny channels beneath the matted forest floor, faint whispers of running water could be heard. After a few days, fresh splashes of green outnumbered the remaining pockets of snow. As the snow receded, the smell of the forgotten dead—those who had been buried beneath the drifts, corruption arrested by the cold— began to sweeten the air over no-man's-land. Local truces were arranged so that burial parties from both sides could comb the forests and retrieve the bodies before they were too far gone. No one questioned the need for the task, no one wanted a comrade's remains to go unburied, but it was gruesome and squalid labor, and it depressed the men who did it.

Erich had drawn for his billet a deep, comfortable pine-finished blockhouse, and he had been content there, except for the boredom, until the stink started filtering in through the ventilators. After living with the odor for four days, Erich was glad to learn that he had been granted two weeks' leave. That was not enough time to go home to Germany, given the uncertainties of transportation between Finland and the Reich, but Erich did not mind. Germany had, for the time being, become a distant abstraction to him. Using codes and procedures given him by Rautavaara, Erich put through an inquiry to Tapiola.

Two days later the reply came back: "My dear Ziegler: Regret prior commitments have me in Helsinki when you arrive. Aino will keep you well fed until I return. Stay as long as you can or want to." The message was signed "S."

Since the front was so quiescent, Erich had no trouble requisitioning a staff car from Pajari's motor pool. He did have trouble, however, navigating the primitive roads—many of them new, unmapped military construction—that led from the frontier to Tapiola. It was several hours after dark before he found the correct turnoff. Madame Sibelius welcomed him, took him to the kitchen and fed him, and all but tucked him in for the night. He was disappointed that he had arrived too late to catch a glimpse of Kylliki; he inquired casually about the servants, and was informed that they had retired to their island an hour before his arrival.

Erich slept late the next morning, and felt obliged to spend the hours immediately after breakfast in polite conversation with Aino. But he listened intently, even as they were speaking, to the sounds made by the servant girls in other parts of the house, and on those occasions when he heard the lilt of Kylliki's voice, he felt something loosen inside his chest. A light meal was served, promptly at noon, but to his disappointment, the tray was carried by the older sister, Anna-Liisa, who favored him with a chilly smile and a barely civil nod as she placed the coffeepot within reach.

After the meal, Aino retired for a nap. Erich drank his coffee, finished scanning some week-old Helsinki newspapers, and began to feel anxious. The house was still now; a clock ticked in a distant room. The faint domestic noises that had earlier emanated from the kitchen, pantry, and laundry had ceased. Where were the two women? Was Kylliki avoiding him? Had the strangely sudden intimacy on the last night of his previous visit been imaginary? Had the older sister, for reasons of her own, somehow poisoned the younger woman's attitude toward him? He helped himself to one of Sibelius's cigars—the humidor stood open, as though by invitation—and strode outside into clarion light.

From the top of the ridge, fully half the view was of water: the lake stretched to the horizon like a dazzling inland sea, stippled with islets that had been nothing but snowy humps the last time he'd seem them, and were now outlined in bright, feathery green. The water was a chill azure and the sky above it a fine-grained blue-white skin painted with clouds. The vast ridge-pleated sweep of the forest, off to his right, was now itself a green and undulant sea. On one distant ridge, a strong wind he could not yet feel bent the trees play-fully, tossing their spires, ruffling them. A red squirrel leaped, chittering, over his head. The breeze was a rich broth of ver-dant smells, grainy with a lavishness of sunlight. The forest had exploded into life again, and he had never seen anything so redolent of the power of seasonal rebirth; it was torrential against his senses, a raw, wild tide.

Below him, a hundred meters down-slope, there was a wink of color and movement. Knee-deep in a froth of ferns and wildflowers, scrutinizing the forest floor with great care, was Anna-Liisa. Erich extinguished his cigar, arranged his fea-tures into what he hoped was a friendly expression, and walked cautiously toward her. Clumps of heather brushed his boots, releasing a cool and mossy fragrance.

"Hello, Captain." At first she did not look up, and when she did, she had to shield her eyes from the blaze of the sky. In full sunlight, she appeared older than she looked indoors: a fine web of lines fanned out from the corners of her eyes and he saw the deeper lines around her mouth that could have come from sadness or from too many winters. He sensed something about her that hinted of old pain, as though she had been betrayed once, long ago, so bitterly that the experi-ence had colored all her relationships from that moment on. In her seasoned way, she was still an attractive woman, but there was something unapproachable about her—a nun-like, shielded quality—that arrested any sort of erotic speculation.

Erich wondered if it might not perhaps be more politic to leave her alone, but he needed to find out if her guardedness was directed at himself personally, or was simply her attitude toward all strangers, or for that matter, all men. That information would be helpful to him when he laid siege—as he fully intended to do—to her beautiful younger sister.

Half-hidden by the ferns at her feet was a small wicker basket. Bits of vegetation filled it halfway to the rim.

"I see you're gathering herbs for the kitchen . . . what grows around here that's suitable?"

"Well, the blueberries aren't altogether ripe yet, but they'll do for a pie if I add more sugar than usual. As for the rest—crowberries, lichens, and liverwort. Not too palatable, I'm afraid, but good for poultices and stomachaches."

She rose and straightened her dress, brushing off bits of leaf and lichen—a maiden from an Arthur Rackham drawing, he thought.

"Won't you come and walk with me for a time, Captain? There has not been a lovelier day this spring."

They descended the long slope toward the lake, through blue-green heather that washed over their ankles like surf. Wildflowers nodded as they passed, adding their spice to the piney smell of the trees.

"You were hoping to encounter my sister rather than myself, Captain," said Anna-Liisa, matter-of-factly.

Erich replied with more tact than he thought the statement warranted. "Any man would count himself fortunate to escort a woman such as you on a day like this."

When Anna-Liisa laughed, there was genuine mirth in her voice, something he had not heard there previously. "Oh, come now, Captain, I don't need a mirror to know how my beauty compares to that of my sister, although it is gallant of you to say such a thing. I am of course older than Kylliki, perhaps a good deal older than my appearance would suggest. And you have reason to be wary of me, for I have felt very protective of her until now . . . where you are concerned."

"I'm not certain I understand . . ."

"I haven't exactly been warm toward the possibility that you and she might become interested in one another."

"Is she . . . interested?"

"Look to her for that answer, Captain, not to her older sister. I don't know exactly what passed between you during your previous visit here, but to my eyes the symptoms were unmistakable . . . At that time, I would have interposed myself between the two of you like a wall. Now, however, I am not so sure. Now my instinct tells me that whatever happens between you, should happen. Is meant to happen."

She halted and turned. They stood in a glade of slender pines, their feet submerged in fern-lace and hair-fine grasses. An almost tropical richness of light poured through the high branches, sparkling in her eyes, freckling her high cheeks with a damascened fretwork of shadow. Erich could see that she must have been a formidable woman when she was younger; even now, with every wrinkle clearly scribed, floodlit, she possessed a banked, cooled accumulation of erotic power that made him uneasy in her presence. She touched his sleeve, her fingers weightless along the top of his wrist.

"Something has happened to you during the war, Captain. Something happened to you in the forest. Something *of* the forest . . ."

These words, so unexpected and so unerring, brought memories boiling to the forefront of Erich's mind, and in the sudden pounding of his own pulse, he heard an echo of the shaman's drum.

"Before, the other times when you were here, you were a stranger to the forest. You clearly did not belong here. Yet, just as clearly, there was something inside you that was open to this world. Why else would the Master have responded to you as he did? And now, I think, perhaps the color of something has changed in your soul."

White! He had never suspected how terrible the beauty of white could be until he had seen, beneath the skin of ice, the white and staring dead man, trailing pearlstrands from his puzzled mouth, floating past Erich's feet, waving—or was it beckoning?—as he passed from shadow into darkness, as though Erich's own shadow had detached itself and swum away into the depths.

"Something has happened to you in the forest that has stripped away several layers of your heart and left you open, now, in a way you could never have been before. You see and hear and feel more intensely. Before, you only walked through the forest—now you're beginning to learn how to listen to it, how to see it as it truly is. All wisdom must have a beginning, an origin, even if that beginning comes in a ritual of death. There is no place more beautiful than the forest, yet there is no place more empty of pity. It is possible, Captain, that I judged you too hastily. It is possible that you, too, belong here."

Fat, stately clouds passed over their heads, trailing shadows across the forest; the pine canopy shivered with streamers of darkness. When the sunlight momentarily cut off, the air grew chilly; Erich felt his arms stipple with gooseflesh. Anna-Liisa crossed to a lichen-covered outcropping of granite and sat down; the moss crinkled like cellophane as she patted a place for Erich beside her. From here they could see nothing but a sea of treetops, stirred by the wind.

Anna-Liisa had taken Erich beyond surprise, into a sense of confirmation, almost of relief. He knew beyond any doubt what the true nature of his experience had been, that day when he went to kill the shaman. There were few people, however, in whom he might confide that knowledge. Certainly not General Pajari or any of the other down-to-earth soldiers he had served with in the *motti* battles. He had thought to describe it all to Sibelius, certain of his understanding, or at least his lack of cynical rejection. But now here was Kylliki's older sister—a woman who had hitherto treated him with indifference, if not disdain—suddenly confirming that, yes, he had entered willingly into a visionary state and had come back profoundly altered.

"It looks chaotic, doesn't it?" Anna-Liisa continued, sweeping her hand toward the landscape. "But you and I know—both of us know it now—that it is all exquisitely balanced and orderly and you cannot tell its rhythms from looking at any one aspect any more than you can diagnose a man's state of health by looking at a few strands of his hair."

Erich was startled when she took his hand and turned to look him fully in the eyes.

"I know the forest better than you can ever hope to know it, Captain. Believe that. And I tell you that the existence of love, in the forest, is not always easy or welcomed—it is an extraordinary and fairly rare phenomenon. Here, it can be an unstable element, volatile as flame, a catalyst for storms. Love cannot work itself out here as it can in the cities or the villages. And no one knows that better than the Master."

"Sibelius?"

"He was a young man, about twenty. The year, I think, was 1885. He had come to the lodge—"

"Here? To Tapiola?"

"—Yes, but it had another name then—came here to spend the summer. You see, his father wanted very much for him to become a lawyer; he was even, if you can believe it, enrolled in legal classes at the university in Helsinki. He had already sketched out a string quartet or two, and he was powerfully drawn to music, but he had not yet rebelled against his parents' wishes. When he arrived here, he was nearing the cusp of that decision. His father engaged the lodge for the summer, to give the boy a place to go and weigh his options, free from pressure. Sibelius, however, came prepared for a two-month-long party, complete with half a dozen drinking friends from the university. Tell me, Captain, have you ever seen a photo of him when he was young?"

"I don't think so."

"Oh, he looked different then. He had a huge shock of wheat-colored hair that was always falling over his forehead. His eyes were very blue, very penetrating when he was inspired, but very misty and remote when he was daydreaming. He had a good mouth and a fine, virile mustache. He dressed well, too, even then. How handsome he was!

"Not long after he took up residence, he met a local girl. A girl who had been born to the forest, and who knew nothing but the forest's ways. To her, he seemed like something

from a dream, a knight come riding in from another world.
But she sensed in him the same openness to the forest that I
now sense in you, and it was in the forest, close to here, in
fact, in one of these glades, on a bed of ferns and moss, that
she gave him her heart. For all that summer, they were lovers,
quite gloriously, and eventually she showed him the places in
the forest where the music dwells. With her at his side, he
wandered freely in places where people ordinarily . . . just *do
not go*. It is hard to explain it more concretely than that, and
perhaps wrong even to try. But Sibelius found his center that
summer, his heart's own core and cause, and by the end of
that time, he knew what his path would be; he had found the
origins of his music, and he had set firmly out on his path.
From that time on, he never looked back."

"And the girl?"

"She stayed in the forest, of course, where she was meant
to be—the only place where she could be. He promised to return every summer, to renew their love within the forest. And
for two or three summers he did. Then his music began to be
performed, and suddenly he had a career instead of a calling.
Years went by and he did not return. Not in time to save their
love."

Erich's mind was sprinting to follow all this. Was she
speaking of her own grandmother? It was possible, given
Sibelius's age. If so, what resentment and bitterness Anna-
Liisa must have absorbed at that woman's side, to be able to
recount this tale, more than a half century later, with such im-
mediacy of feeling.

"You heard this story from that woman herself, did you?
How many years ago?"

Anna-Liisa chose to look away. "My people have lived in
this part of the forest for a long, long time, Captain."

When it became obvious that she would say no more, he
asked: "Why are you telling me this?"

"I must go away for a while. Kylliki will be here by herself, and once her household duties are complete, she can
come and go as she likes. My sister is young, Captain, as
young as that other woman was when she met the Master, and

like that other, she has never been beyond the forest. To her, you are exotic, romantic, a knight from a far place. She is convinced that there is something more than mere coincidence to your coming here, and in that, she may be right. You are still young too, and your dreams have not yet been drowned in blood, only enriched by it. If something is destined to happen between the two of you, I cannot stop it. But I beg of you not to love her just because she is available, just because you are both in the forest together, under these singular circumstances. Kylliki belongs here. Perhaps, with certain limitations, you do too. If it is inevitable that you be lovers, then it is beyond my stopping, and my reservations, even my disapproval, would be irrelevant."

She was some older sister, this one! thought Erich. That she had sensed his interest in Kylliki was not surprising—he rather suspected everyone in the house was aware of it. But he resented the extravagant conclusions Anna-Liisa was drawing from what was, so far, only a simple but powerful case of physical attraction, not to mention the fantastic assumption she had woven in which he and Kylliki took prescribed roles in the reenactment of some old family tragedy. Erich was damned if he would play Tristan to Anna-Liisa's familial version of Isolde. He certainly had no intention of playacting the young Sibelius and abandoning his forest princess to her provincial fate.

What could this woman's motives be? he wondered, his confusion now tinged with resentment, even rebellion. An aging, unwedded woman's bitterness, most likely, at the prospect that Erich might one day claim the young dryad for his own, taking her away to a life of glamour, travel, and fame, leaving Older Sister alone here in the woods, not an eligible man in sight and none likely to come along in time to avert the spinsterhood she feared so desperately.

Anna-Liisa went on, calmly, reasonably: "I only want you to understand that there would be . . . terms . . . to such a union. The Master, being who he was, knew that and understood it—even now, although it is gall to his heart, he understands."

"Perhaps he does; I'm afraid that I do not."

"He came into the forest looking for music. She showed him where to find it. Then he went forth into his own world and took with him the seeds of his art, but in so doing, he violated his pact with her, and with the forest itself. Does not all great art involve a pact, Captain? The limitations of one's craft, the spacing and proportion of successes, rewards, and failures, maybe all of these are determined by the time, the place, and the circumstances under which the bargain was struck. The hidden, the ultimate price, that of course differs from heart to heart, but be forewarned, Captain Ziegler, that there always is a price. The Master's price is his silence. There is music in his heart still, struggling there to be born, and it burns him like acid, but he no longer has the power to bring it out of the forest."

As she spoke, her features became so grave that Erich grew uncomfortable. It suited him to have the subject of his relationship to Kylliki associated with more positive emotions. He tried to recapture the lighter mood with which their conversation had begun.

"You speak of a 'pact' as though you were Mephistopheles himself. Dear lady, if Faust had been fortunate enough to have your sister as his companion, he would have bargained more happily."

"Perhaps not if, after a certain time, he could never touch her again, or if the insights she had helped to waken in him continued to live and cry out for expression, yet he could never give them voice, not ever again."

"And why not? Because of some bargain made with the forest muses? I'm sorry, but there are surely other, much more practical reasons why Sibelius has stopped composing. His prodigious consumption of alcohol, for instance."

"Think as you like, Captain. I felt compelled to speak to you, because I have seen the looks exchanged between you and my sister, and I have felt the charge in the air between you. There is great beauty here for you, Captain Ziegler, but it does not come without its price. Do not let the war change you too much more, Captain, for there are perils in other places besides the battlefield." She stood up and stirred the herbs in her basket with long white fingers.

"Well, I have said my piece, Captain, and so farewell."

She leaned forward and brushed her lips across his forehead, where the skin was again warm from the sun. Erich remained sitting on the rock, his face to the light, for the time required to finish his cigarette. When he stood up, it was with every intention of finding Anna-Liisa and asking further questions of her; such as the present whereabouts of her younger sister, whom he was now hungry to see, and for whom he felt an almost adolescent flood of desire. But even though Anna-Liisa had left him only a few moments before, he found no trace of her except for the slowly rising flowers her feet had trod, and when he called her name only the wind replied.

Fifteen

Sibelius had reappeared by the time Erich sat down for dinner. The composer was in a testy mood and spoke little. When Kylliki entered to serve the meal, Erich managed to exchange glances with her, but held his tongue. There was no predicting how his host might react to the knowledge that his German guest was romantically interested in one of the servants. He might be amused, he might be offended—Erich suspected that the reaction would depend on the composer's mood, or, just as likely, the time of day or the weather.

He had hoped to spend some time with the girl after the meal, or at the very least, after the two elderly people had retired for the night, but Sibelius forestalled him by ringing for Kylliki during the final coffee and peremptorily ordering her to prepare a sauna so that he could "wash off the smells of the capital." He insisted that Erich accompany him in the steam ritual, and Erich, trying hard to repress his impatience, complied.

This time the birch twigs remained in their wooden bucket, much to Erich's relief. Once he had soaked up enough steam to relax from the fatigues of his trip, Sibelius became garrulous. He had missed Erich's company, he said; and lots of newspaper clippings had come in, since Christmas, concerning performances of his music in the Reich. He asked about conditions at the front, about Erich's stay in the hospital, then spent a few minutes bent over in contemplation of the pink stumps where three of Erich's toes used to be. Erich, by that time, had steamed out most of his irritation, and after all, he could not afford to be impatient with the old man. Too much depends on his favor, Erich reminded himself as he shifted to avoid a hot nail head in the bench.

"What business took you to Helsinki, Maestro?" Erich asked when the composer had finished inspecting his toes.

"Some hack in the Defense Ministry has made band arrangements of some of my orchestral marches and *pièces d'occasion*. For the troops, you know. They were unveiled at a ceremony honoring this year's crop of cadets at the military academy. I think they were surprised when I accepted their invitation. Truth is, I longed for a taste of the city again, wanted to be feted a bit. It's a perquisite that goes along with having a state pension."

"That must have been wonderful for you, being able to devote all your time to composing, not having to lecture or endorse products, the way I'm told famous musicians must do in America."

"Oh, there were friends, struggling young men with talent, some of them in no small measure, who never spoke to me again after that pension came through. The government was honoring me as a figurehead, Ziegler, as much for the extra-musical value of my compositions as for the music itself. Remember: up until the 1890s, nobody really knew what it meant to *be* a Finn. We knew we were not Swedes, even those of the upper class who spoke Swedish, and God knows we never thought of ourselves as Russian; by default, we were something other. My music came along at just the right time to help define what that something was. The forest gave me the music, I gave the music to Finland, and Finland gave me a lifelong pension. Rack my conscience though I can, I've never found anything suspect or compromising about that arrangement."

Sibelius leaned over and hurled a ladleful of water onto

the sauna stones. Erich gasped as the fresh wave of heat smote his breast. After a lifetime of this, he thought, the old man must have heart muscles like an athlete.

"Were the band arrangements any good?"

"They were noisy and effective, which amounts to the same thing given their function. The fresh young lieutenants marched well to them, I thought. They'll also be used on the radio to sell war bonds and whip up patriotic resolve, which seems to be flagging now that the Germans are stalled. Well, the state has been paying my bills for decades, so I don't mind if they tart up some of my lesser pieces and use them for movie music."

Erich glanced sideways at Sibelius, whose massive bald head now gleamed with sweat. Did any disciple of Beethoven, he wondered, ever have such intimacy with his master?

"A lot of composers would adopt a loftier attitude, you know. They wouldn't want to give their art away for such mundane purposes."

"Well, of course, I might feel differently if they were using one of my symphonies, but what they were using was, I'm afraid, every bit as mundane as the purposes they were putting it to. It costs me nothing to give such music away, and to tell you the truth, I derive a certain pleasure from it. Being able to give is one of the marks of a true aristocrat. I give back to people a certain awareness of nature and nation—the same nation that fathered both the bankers and the lumberjacks. To produce precious works that can only be understood by a handful of colleagues who share an insider's set of attitudes—people who are, so to speak, *in on the secret*—that, I think, is reprehensible."

"Like Schoenberg?"

"No, no, not like him. He has integrity. God help him, he even believes in the historical logic of what he's doing. Look, when you've painted yourself into that kind of corner, you'd bloody well better believe it's for a good reason! Of course, ultimately, he will fail, because so much of the music he has produced will always sound ugly to most people—not just difficult, but actually repulsive. And those who follow him, like all ideologues who embrace the ideas of a better man, will do infinite mischief to the art of music before they finish their turn on the stage. No, Ziegler, I was referring more to Stravinsky and all the other *Boulangerie ...*"

Emboldened by their intimacy, Erich said: "I once read an interview in which Madame Boulanger was asked about your music. All she said in reply was: 'Ah, Sibelius! Poor, poor, Sibelius—a tragic case!' "

Erich laughed; the composer did not. Instead, he hurled the ladle across the room with such force that the handle snapped.

"What a disagreeable old hag! Her and her salon full of pansies! Dogmatic as only a French intellectual can be! Sometimes I think Hitler had a point about the goddamned French—they don't deserve the civilization they are heirs to!"

Erich stared at Sibelius with frank amazement—he had not seen the old man so worked up since the day he had tried to shoot down the Russian bombers.

"I suppose they can't forgive you for writing emotional music, just as they've never been able to forgive Tchaikovsky; even we Germans play him better."

The composer's ire was not yet spent. He began toweling himself, snapping belligerently at Erich, looking for all the world, from the neck up, like an angry old tortoise. Erich hoped this foul temper would not be turned toward him, for he would not know how to deal with it.

"And I am damned tired of being compared to Tchaikovsky! Not that he's a colleague to be ashamed of, but his symphonies delineate the *soft* parts of human nature. Mine have in them the sinew and the flint!"

Erich could only nod, reinforcing what sounded suspiciously like the sort of clichéd blurb one might find on a record album. Still, if Sibelius wanted to talk like his own press agent, Erich would be glad to humor him.

Back in the anteroom, dressed, the heat slowly dissipating, they opened a bottle of brandy and lit cigars. Sibelius, clothed now and with his temper settled, once more became the *grand seigneur.*

"I realize, of course, that my output has been uneven. I trust that, with the help of sympathetic interpreters such as yourself, the future will judge me by my best work, not by marches written for officer cadets. Come on, it's still early; let's finish this bottle back in my study."

A few moments later, back at the lodge, leaning forward to stack a pair of shellac discs on the spindle of his Victrola, Sibelius said: "We've discussed the symphonies at some length, but here is a work I did not give you the score to, one that you probably have not heard. I'd like for you to listen to it now, here, with me, following the score. Indulge an old man's whim."

From a cabinet, the composer withdrew an inch-thick manuscript and handed it to Erich. It was the holograph original, complete with corrections and pasted-over measures. This was the first time Erich had seen an original score from Sibelius's own hand, and he was intrigued by the spidery neatness of the writing—a whole universe removed from the tortured birth-pangs visible on a page of Beethoven's drafts. At the head of the first page was the title: *Tapiola, Op. 112*, and beneath that, the composer's own preface:

> *Wide-spread they stand, the Northland's dusky forests,*
> *Ancient, foreboding, brooding savage dreams,*
> *Within them dwells the forest's mighty God,*
> *And wood-sprites in the gloom weave magic secrets.*

Erich drew on his cigar and placed his index finger on the first bar of the score as the stylus dug into the lead-in grooves of the first record. There was a gruff, almost snarling rap on the timpani followed by a gnomic three-bar statement in the strings—in and of itself, hardly worth being called a theme. Then the development began to unfold, like leaves opening to the sun. Each phrase, for the work's remaining 631 bars, seemed to grow organically from the phrase that preceded it, and to foreshadow inevitably the phrases that would follow.

There was a clear analogy for Erich in this music. He felt at the beginning as though he were standing at the edge of the great forest, still in a clearing, about to go into the trees. Then the music took him to the shadows that marked the start of the forest world, and then led him deeper and deeper inside, to places where the colors were more vivid and the shadows a great deal darker than they were outside. For a time, the music's mood was relaxed, even intimate, as though a camera were focusing on close-ups—cells pulsing through the veins of a leaf, dust motes dancing in a shaft of light— then gradually pulling back to reveal the true breadth of the forest in all its immensity. The tone poem's climax was a ferocious windstorm, depicted by intricately divided strings: the music grew dark and frowning, unseen currents seemed to blow, in torment, through the room itself. Erich had never listened to a piece of music more saturated with atavistic awe, to the extent, almost, of terror.

As his mind filled in the orchestration—the strings *divisi* sawing furiously, sending up a whirlwind of sound, and the trombones, like a striding titan, stamping out the rhythm of the approaching climax—Erich remembered those moments of hallucinatory immersion he had experienced during his duel with the shaman.

Oh yes, just let me conduct this and I'll whip up a storm that will chill the listeners' blood! He leered almost savagely as he followed the music into and through its chilling climax.

He knew he had just been exposed to an unqualified masterpiece. There was not a wasted or superfluous note in the entire twenty-minute piece. As perfectly as Debussy had evoked the sea in *La Mer*, just so had Sibelius re-created the essence of his chosen subject, inextricably blending elements of tension and repose, so that his thematic transformations mirrored every mood of the forest, from tranquility to savagery. If the man had never written another note of music, this piece alone would have given him immortality. It was not a crowd-pleaser, this tone poem; perhaps only those who had actually seen the great forest could understand how truly it conjured up its subject—and surely, only another musician, and a sympathetic one at that, could fully understand how brilliant, eccentric, and solitary were the formal means by which the composer had accomplished his purpose.

As the music ended, Erich reached for more brandy. When he spoke, there was no flattery in his voice or in his thoughts, but only profound admiration and an awareness of the privilege that had just been granted him.

"Maestro, you've created a masterpiece from ... from *nothing*! From a few threadbare measures that don't even deserve to be called a motif. From air, from dew, from a few particles of sunlight and raindrops! Your transformation of that thematic germ is unbelievable. If you played it on the piano for anyone, anyone at all, they would say that it is utterly insignificant and nothing whatever can be done with it. How is it that you were able to do this? Where did this concept of transformation come from?"

Sibelius waved a hand, smiling; clearly the music had had the effect on Erich that he had wanted. There was something touching and disingenuous about his hunger for approval.

"Don't approach it like a vivisectionist. It isn't so complicated. Mystical, perhaps, but not complicated. I just took long walks in the forest, deep within it, losing myself in it. The ideas came to me not so much as phrases, and not as themes, but as motes, germs, cells, animalcules; that explains their terseness. As for the method, the techniques of their transformation, that was suggested by the forest itself. From micro- to macroscopic. The infinite reflected in a raindrop, an entire universe shimmering, suspended, in the sunlight. And for every one of those musical 'germs' that were capable of sustaining development, there were fifty, a hundred, which could not. Those, I recycled into that overstuffed collection of potboilers that you once described as 'faceless.' Still, I gave them my name and my blessing and sent them out to let people make of them what they would. Once in a while, however, the forest would give me the cell of an idea such as the one you just heard. Not often. One simply does not get such ideas often, from whatever source."

Sibelius shifted, groped for a cigar: a brandy-fumed, thick-tongued old man by now. Erich gave him a light.

"Do you know the old children's game called 'word-making'? You have these tiles with letters on them and each child takes a certain number of tiles and tries to make as many words as he can with them. Just so with music, in my experience. Some spiritual force—call it God, if that makes you comfortable—throws at you a handful of letters and says: 'Here, fellow, make of these what you can,' and most of the time you can only make 'cat' or 'dog' . . . But now and then, ah, now and then you can make a poem! And when that happens . . . If that happens, ever again . . ."

Erich leaned forward, alarmed; a look of concentrated agony had passed across the composer's face, as though his heart had faltered. His lips compressed into a bloodless line and he fell silent. Unattended, his cigar went out. The air in the room seemed close and heavy with some kind of unresolved, perhaps unresolvable, tension. Gently, Erich took the glass from the old man's brittle fingers.

"I'm going to take you to your room now, Maestro. It's gotten very late, and after such music, words are superfluous. I will always remember that I heard that music first at your side."

Sibelius rose stiffly to his feet, with a faint popping of joints, and took Erich's hand.

"You will conduct it, Ziegler, won't you? There would be no one better for that music. Most people see the forest and they are either bored by its monotony or frightened by the face of its vastness. But you have gone deep into it, and you can go deeper still."

"Of course I will conduct it. As soon as the war is over."

"Yes. The war."

At the door to his bedroom, Sibelius turned and impulsively embraced Erich. The old man's head was immense and heavy. Then he raised his face, stood back with both hands on Erich's shoulders, and said in a clear, thin voice: "I became who I am because of where and when I was born, Ziegler, and because of something that happened to me when I was a young man, here in this forest, at Tapiola. If I had been born twenty years later or earlier, or in another country, or if I had not gone into the forest, I would have ended up being, oh, Grieg, maybe, or Glazunov, or somebody . . . Instead, I found myself cast as the indomitable Sibelius. I've grown accustomed to playing that role—it afforded me a perfect reason to shroud myself in the silence which everybody thinks is part and parcel of my art. At first, that silence was a comfort, for I believed that I could break out of it whenever I really chose to. Only now, it has taken root too deeply. Silence is all there is for me now."

Back in his own room, finishing the last of the brandy, Erich turned to the back of one of the published symphonic scores, to the appended pages where the publisher had listed, by opus number, all of the orchestral works by Sibelius that had been issued.

Tapiola was listed as Opus 112. Below that entry, the page was blank.

Sixteen

The next morning, while the composer was sleeping late,
Erich went straight to the kitchen. Kylliki turned from the big
wood-fired stove, a wooden spoon in her hand and a dab of
porridge on her nose. She looked so totally the part of the
kitchen drudge that Erich could not help laughing. This
seemed to irritate her, however, for when he impulsively
reached for her hand, she whacked at it with the implement.

"Captain, please behave yourself!"

Erich stepped back, suddenly unsure of his position. He
had assumed, on the basis of his conversation with Anna-
Liisa, that Kylliki was as attracted to him as he was to her, but
at the moment the cast of her features seemed to be telling
him otherwise.

"I am sorry, Kylliki, but you look so lovely standing there
in the sunlight, with your nose covered in porridge . . . the
last time we were together, you ate a snowflake from my nose;
I merely thought to return the gesture by having breakfast
from yours."

He smiled brightly at her, basking in the way her presence
made him feel expansive, youthful.

As quickly as it had appeared, the bristling don't-you-dare
edge vanished from her eyes and she laughed.

"In this household, we eat from plates."

"Really? In my part of Germany we crouch in caves and gnaw on bones."

"I'm serious, Captain," she continued, in a not-quite-serious voice. "If Madame Sibelius should come in and find me bantering with you instead of doing my chores, she might sack me."

"And replace you with whom—a trained bear? I haven't noticed a lot of eligible employees in the neighborhood."

"She could send to Helsinki and get whomever she needed. I'm overworked as it is, what with my sister away."

"Oh?" Erich arched his eyebrows, all innocence and interest. She had certainly managed to work that information into the conversation quickly. "I suppose that means you'll have no free time to share a walk with me, then."

"A walk? To where?"

"Where? Well ... around the lakeshore, perhaps. Or a boat ride. This weather is so beautiful."

Kylliki gave the porridge a final stir, moved a hissing coffeepot onto a trivet to cool, pulled a wooden stool into the oblong of sunlight that streamed in from behind the sink, and sat down facing him. She tilted her head slightly, first to one side, then to the other, her lavender eyes darkening against the light, each gilt filament of her eyelashes glowing like a heated wire. She folded her hands around the wooden spoon, and as she did so, Erich noticed the way sunlight brushed the faint golden down on the back of her arm. Even that rather mundane glimpse quickened his desire for her.

"I cannot go walking with a man whose first name I don't even know."

"Erich. My name is Erich."

"I am playing with you a little, Erich. To see if you are still human enough, after all these months of soldiering, to enjoy being flirted with."

"I often thought about our last walk together during those weeks of soldiering. The memory, I think, helped me to get through it."

She held out her hand. It was warm from the sun, and light against his own.

"Forgive me, Erich. I was prepared to speak with you later, after breakfast, but you were too quick for me. In fact, I was going to ask you to join me for a walk at sunset, just after the evening meal. I'll be free then, and it will still be bright enough to find our way."

" 'Find our way'?"

"Why, yes. The last time we talked, you said you would be interested in visiting one of the rune-singers. There is one such person in this region, a woman who lives deep in the forest, and she has agreed to sing for you. We should go tonight, if possible."

"What excuse should I use with Sibelius?"

Again that flash of something in her eyes; Erich felt, more and more, that she was remarkably independent for a mere house servant. There was not, as far as he could see, one damned thing servile about her.

"You are a guest here, Captain, not a prisoner. If you wish to absent yourself after dinner, you may. If the Maestro is in a bad mood, he might even prefer it."

Remembering the previous night's brandy consumption, the old man's swings from anger to sentimental melancholy, Erich admitted that she had a point. He wondered, for the briefest moment, if she somehow knew about what had happened last night, or if she had simply hit the mark by chance.

"Where shall I meet you?"

"You know the high ridge on the island where I live? When the sun has fallen to the top of that ridge, meet me at the boat that's tied to a birch tree opposite the cabin. That's how I get to work each morning."

Sibelius, in fact, did not appear until noon. He ate sparingly, conversed gruffly, and retired almost immediately to his study, shutting the door behind him. Aino cleared a writing desk in the living room for Erich, who busied himself writing a report, for Klatt's intelligence people, about what he had seen during his trip with Rautavaara to the Karelian Isthmus: "Leningrad," he wrote, "is to all appearances a city of the dead. It seems white, hollow, ghastly in its pallor and devastation; no movement is visible in its streets. I must, however, emphasize that the Finns I spoke to, without a single exception, do not believe that the city will fall without a direct assault, something which their army has no intention of launching. Hitler's decision to forgo such an attack in favor of a protracted siege, and to shift his panzer divisions to the Ukraine rather than use them to take Moscow and Leningrad, is discussed quite openly as an irrational blunder which, in the opinion of most division- and regimental-level commanders, is likely to cost Germany the campaign, and possibly the war itself."

Promptly at six o'clock, Sibelius emerged from his study, looking preoccupied and growling for his supper. He was voluble and animated during the meal, discussing everything from wine to literature, as though he and Erich had just met for the first time, but as soon as he had taken coffee his mood seemed to change; he excused himself and retreated to the study once more.

"He acts as if he were working on something," mused Aino. "If so, I hope it will see the light of day."

"What do you mean?"

"He has torn up or burned many pages of score paper over the past fifteen years, Captain. I've never been permitted to hear a single note of what was on them. He abhors ridicule, and the public expects so much more of him now than they did when he was younger. At least Beethoven could write his last quartets without anyone speculating in the daily newspapers about what they might sound like when they were finished. Jean has read a hundred accounts of his 'next' symphony, some of them quite ridiculously detailed, and he's had impresarios and conductors bidding for the rights to the first performance, as though his art were something to be sold on an auction block. It has all had an effect on him, I'm afraid."

Erich wanted very much for Aino to speak further, since she was coming close to the quick of his own great desire, but a furtive glance told him the sun was declining, and he had a more immediate kind of desire on his mind. As soon as he could without being rude, he excused himself and went outside.

By the time Erich reached the boat, the sun was perched atop the island's trees. Kylliki was already sitting on the forward seat, leaning against an oar. He rowed them out from the reedy shoreline, out into the heavy, leaning light and then into the cool edge of the island's shadow. The lake water was still cold and he could feel its breath as they passed out of the sunlight.

Five minutes of rowing brought them to the island. When they were close, Kylliki leaped from the boat and made it fast to a rickety wooden dock. Across a small meadow stood the cabin where she and her sister lived. It looked like something from a storybook: Erich saw a wall of cut firewood left over from winter, a covered well, a sauna room built off to one side, screened by groves of birches, and the cabin itself, surprisingly large and multi-roomed. A short distance behind the cabin, the forest thickened once more and the ground angled up steeply. Taking his hand, she led him around the cabin and up a faint, mossy path through dark bowers of treegloom. Not far into the climb, Erich's foot slipped on a stand of wet, leprous mushrooms.

"Why don't we just take a boat and row around the island?"

"Because that is not the way; this is."

Erich had never before realized how necessary a full complement of toes was to good climbing stability. By the time they reached the ridge's summit, he was winded and there were wet stains on both knees of his trousers. As Kylliki tugged him to the top, he looked up and saw the sky glowing red-gold above the stenciled outlines of the topmost trees, as though a great molten furnace burned on the summit's other side. Then, with a surprisingly powerful pull, she drew him beside her and he recoiled as his face was thrust into the light; he was instantly and powerfully disoriented. The sun was low on the crested waves of the forest, blazing with painful brilliance from the wild jumble of lakes and bogs that stretched out before him. The myriad water surfaces danced with coruscating fires, as though the strike of light made the water tremble.

"Can't we sit here until the sun goes down a bit more?" he asked, a plaintive timbre—unbidden and unwelcome—creeping into his voice.

"We need the light. In the darkness you could get lost very easily, Erich. Come, give me your hand and I'll lead you. I know the way by heart."

He soon began to wonder how she, how anyone, could know the way "by heart." As she led him down through cross-hatched bands of coarse, ruddy light, his dizziness increased. He stumbled many times, and by the end of the descent, he was grasping her hand in a state of near-helplessness. When they once again stood on level ground, she unhesitatingly strode westward, straight into the sun. From every direction came the fiery glance of light from long, irregular bodies of water, as though they were negotiating a long and winding causeway, an isthmus. Had they been walking like this for a few minutes or for hours? Surely, the sun would go down soon and he would again be able to take stock of his surroundings and forgo the need to be led, like a child, by a young woman who was not much older than a child herself.

Suddenly, a curtain dropped over his tender eyes and the world regained some measure of focus and stability. Sweating, panting, he tugged hard at Kylliki's hand and pawed the air, unable to speak, signaling her to stop, to rest.

"We're nearly there," she said, insistently pulling him onward as though some deadline had to be met. Glancing over his shoulder, he was surprised that he could no longer see the ridge behind the cabin, even though it should have completely dominated the sky behind them. Instead, the sky was wide open and flocked with salmon-tinted clouds, as though the ridge had been pulled aside like a stage flat. Too many things were different, not as they should be. Where in God's name had she taken him?

As his balance returned and his breathing became more regular, he was able to observe their surroundings more clearly. They had left the serpentine causeway with its bewildering maze of waterways, and were now walking through an immense pine barren, the trees spaced with an almost disturbing regularity and the ground between them cleared of underbrush, as though it had been groomed.

With the sun gone, Erich had no reference point for the passage of time. He had not consulted his watch for hours and could not see it now, for Kylliki was leading him by his left hand and he had a strong fear of letting go, of losing contact.

An absurd fear, surely! He told himself that he was a trained man, trained by the best orienteers in Europe—the Finnish ski-troopers—and that there was no place he could go and not find his way back from.

Except perhaps this place, whispered the stillest part of his mind.

You do not know this place, although you have sensed its existence and many times you have stood upon its borders.

At the fading of the very last light, just as the pine-tops' outlines were being absorbed into the ink of the sky, Erich saw, a hundred meters ahead of them, a faint waxen light. In a few moments, they arrived in front of a small log hut. The light he had seen came from a small fireplace within, and had shown through the cracked door, rather than through the two windows, which were covered with woven curtains. Kylliki led him through the door; clearly, they were expected.

Inside, the firelight's illumination seemed to dwindle. Try as he might, Erich could see nothing of the interior except a radius of ten meters out from the hearth. Dimly, as the merest solidification of shadow, he thought he could discern the outlines of a spinning wheel, a trestle table, a wooden bucket, and what might have been a spindly chair. Erich was reminded, fleetingly, of the cabin where he and Eino had spent the night, his first night in the deep forest; this place had that same air of timelessness.

In front of the fireplace was a broad wooden bench, worn in the shape of two pairs of shallow crescents, as though generations of people had straddled the bench. The air was drowsy with birch smoke. In the darkness beside the chimney stood a very old woman.

"When she comes into the light, step forward and let her look at you."

If the cabin's interior looked like a setting for a tale from the Brothers Grimm, the crone who shuffled out to greet him looked like one of the main characters. Yet, Erich reminded himself, she was real. He had taken no hashish before venturing here; his only intoxication was with the girl, whose presence had the effect of rendering this experience utterly concrete, giving it a reality that was not to be questioned.

With great delicacy, the crone's hands traced the planes of Erich's face. Her fingers were as light and frail as hollow reeds and her touch, far from being repulsive, was disturbingly intimate and lingering. For an instant, if he had shut his eyes, Erich could have fantasized a lover's explorations.

"*Tervetula*," whispered the old woman. "Welcome." She inclined her face, much of it shadowed by a kerchief, toward Kylliki, and said: "*Olen sittä aivan varma.*"

" 'I am quite sure of it,' " Erich translated silently.

He would have turned to Kylliki with a question—quite sure of what?—but when he tried, the old woman's fingers, suddenly wiry and insistent, kept his face where it was. When her scrutiny was complete, she motioned toward the bench and muttered a few sentences in Finnish made incomprehensible by its swiftness and archaisms.

"You must sit on this end of the bench. She will sit on the other end, and you will grasp hands. I will be nearby, on that chair, playing the *kantele* while she chants. I'll try to translate as she goes along. She has asked me what legend you might like to hear, and I suggested that perhaps you would enjoy the story of how the hero Väinämöinen created a magic harp—it's one of the best musical tales in the *Kalevala*."

"That sounds fine," said Erich, straddling the bench. He waited until the rune-singer had sat down facing him, then extended his hands. She wrapped them with her own long fingers, remarkably firm and strong. Then she began to rock back and forth, crooning wordless strings of vowels that were anchored to a vague melodic line whose tonality was modal.

The slow, swaying rhythm got into Erich's arms and spread to his torso, kneading gently at his heart and, he discovered with some amazement, his loins; the polished birch wood cupped his buttocks warmly and rubbed silkily against his thighs as he swayed with the old woman in a parody of an embrace. From what seemed like a great misty distance, he heard the shimmering chords of Kylliki's instrument, swirling around his body like a silver fog. The air vibrated at his ears as though the shadows contained unseen tuning forks.

Now the old woman left off her crooning, having evidently established both the rhythm and the degree of concentration she was waiting for, and, in a voice like a marsh breeze, like a branch creaking in the grip of autumn's winds, she sang the runes of Väinämöinen and his harp:

> *I am prompted by my desires*
> *to sing the tale of Väinämöinen's harp,*
> *to those I meet in wayward places*
> *in the northland's lonely marches*
> *in this realm of dreary forests . . .*
>
> *These are lays I've drawn from ice-flows*
> *these are songs the wind has taught me,*
> *on my tongue their words are melting,*
> *words I've wrested from the ravens,*
> *verses whispered by the birch trees . . .*

Erich was no longer sure of who was singing. The crone's folded-paper voice and the light caress of Kylliki's tones had blended into one, as directionless as they were sourceless; the word-stream flowed within his head and all the forest seemed focused here in this dim firelit circle, as though myriad unseen eyes watched them from behind an incorporeal yet absolute demarcation of darkness.

> *Väinämöinen, old and steadfast,*
> *journeyed far into the northland,*
> *to the wooded realms of Tapio . . .*

Väinämöinen, aged hero,
found him there a weeping birch tree,
found a tree downcast and sighing,
asked the birch why it lamented . . .

Answer made the slender birch tree:
"Long and joyless all my days are,
here in the forest god's green world;
rooted am I here forever,
fearful am I of the snow's white coming . . .

Old hero, can you bring me succor?
Can you bring me music, laughter,
songs to melt the bitter snowdrifts?"

In the fireplace a knot of birchwood sputtered as it settled. The rune-singer's voice had blended with the *kantele*'s plaintive shimmer, its tones had entered his flesh, and the swaying rhythm had opened the gates of his mind, his blood, his manhood. Deep within the layers of this waking dream, some rational part of Erich's mind called out to him to turn back, ordered him not to surrender to this pagan dream, but another and now-dominant part of Erich dismissed that voice from his presence and gave him over to the experience that engulfed his soul.

Before him, the face of the crone rocked in and out of darkness as she swayed. Her hands, still firmly grasping him, now warmed by contact and by firelight, might as well have been those of a young and desirable woman—he felt as though the secrets of his heart were being read.

Then spake Väinämöinen, long-enduring hero:
"Weep no more, white-girdled princess;
by my skill will I transform thee,
and by my magic make thee over . . ."

From the sinews of the pine tree,
from its tall and graceful branches,

carved the hero out a harp-box;
from a sturdy oak, the pegs he whittled,
then fitted them with runes of power . . .

Then, through Tapio's great realm,
roamed the ancient hero widely,
seeking strings to fit upon his harp-board;
came the old one to a clearing,
where he found a maiden comely,
combing hair as gold as sunlight . . .

Spoke the hero, resolutely:
"Give me of thy hair, O Fair One,
give me hair to make my harp-strings,
for my songs of greatest power,
for my tones both fair and bitter."

Seven were the strands she gave him,
seven strands all soft and golden
gave she for the hero's music . . .

The *kantele's* rippling arpeggios darted through the air like a cloud of exquisitely enameled birds, like a graceful, glittering school of silver minnows, flash-lit by the sun inside the tube of a curling wave. No longer sure of where, or when, he was, it seemed to Erich that both he and the old woman had become gigantic, mythological creatures, titans teeter-tottering above a vast black star-pricked gulf, with the Earth itself as a fulcrum.

Erich no longer heard words as such, no longer dreamed images as such. He was enthralled by a full-blown hallucinatory fugue, in which gnarled old Väinämöinen had come to resemble Sibelius, and the birch-princess resembled Kylliki.

Väinämöinen remonstrated with the beautiful maiden: his harp had pegs for eight strings, yet she had donated hair only for seven.

The maiden's visage changed, undergoing a dreadful series of metamorphoses, changing from Kylliki into a fierce incarnation of Anna-Liisa, wrathful as a Valkyrie, with fire-shot eyes, and then both women merged into one again, a terrible witch-hag with limbs like knotted tree branches and teeth like a wild animal's.

> *Then spoke the maid, her voice like thunder:*
> *"I am no farmer's bitch to be so ordered!*
> *Know, old hero, I am Tapio's own daughter,*
> *Tuonetar am I, both proud and jealous,*
> *and only seven strings I'll give thee!"*

"The eighth string!" Erich cried aloud, his voice lost in a fire-roaring darkness.

But the forest god's daughter was unmoved, and the eighth harp string could be played only within the realm of Tapio, only for the pleasure of his gloomy daughters. And Väinämöinen wept because his finest songs could not be sung outside that realm, and never would their power and magic touch the lives of men, never would the bard's tongue be other than lame and partial.

> *Then the saddened hero played,*
> *until the clearing filled with maidens,*
> *slender maidens, shaped like birch trees,*
> *pretty girls with laughing voices,*
> *to mock the hero, old deceived one,*
> *and stir to coals his aging lust,*
> *to make him play his eight-stringed harp,*
> *that only plays within the forest . . .*
>
> *That only plays within the forest . . .*

A cold and gritty wind blew, ash-laden, from the fireplace, stripping the cowl from the rune-singer's head. Matted with leaves and twigs, long tangled sheaves of bronze-streaked hair blew free and wild, their ends snapping at Erich's eyes and lips like darting vipers. Below and all around the immense ebony holes where her eyes should have been, from the fan-shaped wrinkles to the long aristocratic nose to the once voluptuous, now shriveled, mouth, loomed a hideous caricature of Anna-Liisa. The teeter-totter board snapped like breaking bone, and Erich tumbled, with a groan, into an engulfing emptiness that roared past his ringing ears.

When he regained his senses, his boots were full of water. He was flopping about in a shallow bog, flailing his limbs like a disoriented and panicky animal. He had no idea where he was or how he had gotten there.

He lay on the edge of a moonlit tarn, surfaced with a liquescent muck that had the tense, sinister look of quicksand. Across the bog, watching him silently, steam rising from its mouth and moons burning in its eyes, was the bear.

He ran. Briars tore his hands and face, tree branches knouted him on his shoulders, forehead, and cheeks. It was as though the forest had come alive, animated by some spasm of anger or malevolence. He ran until he could run no more, and when he stopped, there was no sign of the cabin, the ridge from which they had originally descended, or Kylliki.

At length, he climbed another ridge; it was not—again, he was sure—the ridge from which he and Kylliki had descended, untold hours ago; he was no longer even sure if this realm in which he wandered was the same as the tree-covered land around Tapiola, although in some mysterious way it was contiguous with that other, that "real" forest.

Finally, he reached an overlook, and from that point he beheld an ocean of trees beneath a low albescent moon, framed at a great distance by a sullen range of hills that seemed outlined in phosphorescent purple-white, as though their backlit color shone through translucent bone. The stillness was brittle, as unnatural as the spacing and precision of the great pine barrens had been, as though a vast breath were being held in deference to his presence. Below the place where he stood, the moonlit trees curdled and surged violently, as the sea might boil when predators fed below its surface. Immense black shadows knotted and writhed beneath the trees. He knew he could never go forward; knew that if he ever got close enough to see the source of that violence, those shadows, not only his life but his soul would be imperiled. He did not belong here.

The way down was no easier than the way up, and his disorientation returned as soon as he left the ridgetop. He feared for his reason, even his life, although he knew that a dream, a hallucination induced by the runes, and the close, possibly even drugged, air inside the cabin might—no, *must!*—be the cause of his apparent situation. And yet, the evident reality of what he was experiencing made a dangerous mockery of his own presumption: he had presumed to know the forest well; had been foolish enough to think that it had accepted him, imparted some of its wisdom, maybe even its blessing. What a fool he had been. All he had seen and learned before this night was but pale, deceptive adumbration, was but the kindest, mildest mask of a realm whose true essence was implacable, alien, horrific.

Somewhere behind him, he heard the bear's thick, phlegm-clotted growl, heard the trees snap and splinter as it came. Then he felt the wind change direction and the sounds of the bear stopped as it lost the scent.

Erich turned away from the black river and faced the sudden warm, sweet, piney breeze that kissed the side of his throat. And as he did so, as he turned like a compass needle to the vector of that hopeful and nurturing scent, he heard them: a soft, liquid, rustle of distant bells.

He walked fifty meters down the riverbank and the sound faded. He retraced his steps and walked at a right angle to the river, and the sound grew subtly but clearly louder. He steered by it, veering a few degrees in one direction, then in another, so that the volume continued to grow. After a time—how long, he could never afterward guess—he realized that he was once more walking through what seemed like ordinary forest: thick, but not surrealistically jumbled, not bathed in sickly light, and not inhabited by things that could never be glimpsed by the sane, clean light of day. Familiar odors came back into the air; the edges of his perceptions softened and grew less preternaturally vivid.

Ahead, now, he could see a campfire, like a beacon, and as

soon as he fixed his course toward it, the chimerical bells faded into a whisper, then were gone. A few moments later, he saw Kylliki, her arms wide and welcoming, standing before the fire, calling to him. He ran toward her, his heart suddenly fierce.

"Erich! Erich, look at me!"

Her face wavered in firelight. He was hot all over. Blearily he beheld the red-hot coals of a sauna fire, wooden benches . . . homespun towels . . . a water bucket . . .

How did I get here? Where have I been?

Can she tell me? *Will* she, if she knows?

"Where am I?"

"In my sauna, near the cabin. Just as the last verses were being chanted, you had some kind of seizure, and you began to tremble and moan. Then you gave a kind of shriek and fell off the bench in a faint. My sister and I managed to bring you here."

Some seizure, Erich thought, looking around groggily. There was no sign of Anna-Liisa, who must have absented herself discreetly while he was still unconscious. Erich had not even known that Older Sister was back.

"The last thing I remember was the verse about how Tuonetar refused the eighth and final string of Väinämöinen's harp, so that he could make his finest music only in the forest, for the pleasure of Tapio's daughters."

She peered strangely at him. She was wrapped in a loose fur robe, rather like a monk's habit. Her eyes were dark and probing, and the firelight made her mouth look hot and sweet. Shadows danced languorously in the hollows of her cheeks and throat. She seemed all gold and lavender, and the pale dust of her freckles formed constellations which he longed to trace with his fingertips, his tongue.

"Then you must have fallen into some kind of trance even before you fell off the bench."

"What do you mean?"

"There are no such verses to that song. Väinämöinen strings his harp with the maiden's hair and when he plays all the birds and animals and tree sprites come out to listen. The poem ends with a long catalog of all the creatures and spirits he plays for, and then the princess who was imprisoned as a birch tree changes back into a woman and gives herself to the hero as his final reward. There is no mention at all of Tuonetar."

What had his mind done, then? Already, the visions were becoming nebulous, but he remembered Sibelius in them, and both sisters, their visages blending, melting into one, and a terrible hag emerging from that blend. What a mix-up he had made of dreams and reality!

Thinking about it made him dizzy. There was a warm herbal taste on his lips, and a nearly empty bowl beside his head.

"What's in that?" he said with just a trace of suspicion.

"Some herbs and broth my sister made. To calm your nerves."

Indeed, he was beginning to feel more than calm. Warmth and well-being spread throughout his limbs, as though he had just come from a masterful massage.

He thought that Kylliki was the most beautiful woman he had ever seen. He felt the edges of his desire soften, even as the desire itself bloomed through him. Where there had been only want, there was now, as well, a sense of need, a yearning for some kind of completion embodied in this young woman.

"Strange," he agreed, rising to one elbow so that he could see her better. "Strange to have a dream that begins when you are unconscious and continues after you have fallen to the floor, without missing a beat. Tell that old woman that she is a great singer of runes."

"I shall. And now I will tell you something new about saunas, my brave captain."

In his mind and heart, she replaced all other dreams. Something vulnerable had appeared in the welter of his feelings for her, something that flowed from a sweet new wound. All the borders of his emotions shifted, expanded, and what had been hitherto a pleasurable but calculated plan of seduction now became a desperate yearning.

She turned to face him, the fire at her side, and slipped

the robe from her shoulders. Beneath it, she wore no other clothing. Erich saw fire-shadows play along the convexities of long, down-dusted thighs, up to a convergence of amber that ended in a crown of woolly gold. Her eyes were pools of amethyst smoke. As he moved to embrace her, he realized that he too was naked.

"What you must learn about saunas," she crooned in a dusky voice, "is that they are very good for two things besides bathing. They are good for having babies in, and according to the stories women swap among themselves, they are propitious places for losing one's virginity."

A long time later, when they lay curled together in the fire-glow, love-slick limbs intertwined beneath the furs, Erich wondered, briefly and sleepily, as a kind of dozing abstraction, just how far away the rune-singer's hut actually had been—as opposed to how far he had perceived it to be—for the two sisters to carry him all the way back to the sauna hut on the island. He did not let this thought disturb him, however, for Kylliki had already proven to him, several times that night, that she, at least, was much stronger than she looked.

Seventeen

Adolf Hitler was, in person, considerably less imposing than he looked in the newsreels. In the moment of silence between his emergence from the Junkers trimotor and the opening crash of the honor guard band, the pale morning air thrummed with the whipping of flags. When the führer emerged, a thin, expectant smile on his wan face, the wind got under the hem of his coat so that it, too, rattled like a banner. As the German leader's foot hit the tarmac, Erich stiffened to attention while the honor guard cracked heels together behind him.

While waiting for the führer's scrutiny, Erich retraced the circumstances that had led him to this spot on the tarmac of the Helsinki airport. He felt as though a whirlwind had plucked him from the forest one morning, spun him through the sky, and deposited him on this spot two weeks later.

Erich had been occupied for most of May putting together a comprehensive report on the state of the supply and support elements on the Third Corps front; orders for him to undertake this study had been waiting for him upon his return to the somnolent Third Division sector. For two weeks he had driven around the rear areas, waving his documents and poking his head into depots, magazines, and motor pools. Boring though the work might be, he had forced himself into a state of diligence—now that the Finnish front had frozen into a positional stalemate, Erich was worried that he had become only marginally useful to those who had sent him here in the first place. What if someone decided he was no longer needed? A transfer would mean the end of his trips to Tapiola, and that prospect was unthinkable.

He had been inspecting a quartermaster facility in Kajaani, on the unit boundary between the Third Corps and the Karelian Army Group to the south, when orders arrived summoning him to the port of Oulu, on the Bothnian coast, for a high-level meeting with Klatt and several other intelligence officers attached to Dietl's Norwegian Command.

Erich's impression, on meeting Colonel Klatt face to face for the first time since their initial encounter on the Arctic Front, was that the intervening months must have been strenuous ones. There was much more grey in Klatt's hair, and his face had acquired a pastiness from being indoors, bathed in stale cigarette smoke, for weeks at a time. Nevertheless, the older officer's tone of camaraderie had not changed—he pumped Erich's hand vigorously, congratulating him on his success.

"What success, *Herr Oberst*?" asked Erich, while the two of them made their way into a stuffy, map-papered conference room.

"You really haven't heard yet? Well, I suppose the paperwork hasn't caught up with you, yet. You're being decorated, Captain—Iron Cross, Second Class."

"Whatever for?"

"Oh, for single-handedly wiping out a squad of Russian parachutists, if I remember correctly. Surely you would recall something like that . . ."

Klatt closed the door. Fussing with documents on the other side of the conference table was a thin, ramrod-straight colonel. Although their putative ranks were the same, it was instantly apparent that this person had authority over Klatt. His name was Schleicher, and he stated that he had come from Berlin to "coordinate" intelligence work on the northern fronts more closely with that of the strategic planning echelons in Berlin. More closely, his tone seemed to imply, than Klatt and his people had been doing. While Klatt had the appearance of a middle-class lawyer impersonating a Prussian officer in a community theater production, this tight-lipped Berliner was the real thing. He addressed Erich in a businesslike tone.

Erich sat on the same side of the table with Klatt, feeling absurdly as though both of them were schoolboys being lectured. Erich had objectified Klatt into an abstraction, an address to be written on document packets, and had long ago lost whatever feeling for the man he had gained from their one brief encounter. Fifteen minutes under the gaze of this rear-echelon martinet was enough to bring Erich into a state of profound sympathy with Klatt, who, after all—and however unconsciously—had proved himself Erich's benefactor. Schleicher was probably smarting from being sent to this god-forsaken sector, so far removed from the swirling nebulae of power in Berlin, and he would have found a hundred petty ways to take out his resentment on poor Klatt.

During introductions, Erich imagined he heard a touch of suppressed longing in Klatt's tone when he said: "Colonel Schleicher is here on temporary assignment. I'll let him explain it."

"On the third of June," Schleicher began, beaming his address mostly toward Erich, "Field Marshal Mannerheim celebrates his seventy-fifth birthday. The führer has decided to pay a visit to Helsinki, in order to congratulate his Nordic ally in person. He will also hold meetings with Mannerheim's staff and with our own personnel to coordinate activities on this front with the rest of the Wehrmacht's summer campaign—an offensive which will drive the final nails into the Red Army's coffin, Captain, I can promise you!"

Schleicher leered with bloodthirsty anticipation. As long as the bastard didn't have to do any nail-driving with his own well-manicured hands, Erich thought, he would be a cheer-leader for those who did. He was clearly the sort of officer who spoke glibly about "flinging" divisions hither and yon, as though they were quoits.

"One can only hope for our complete success, naturally, sir," said Erich, carefully filtering the contempt from his voice.

"Quite so, quite so. You'll hear the plans from the führer's own lips; it should prove inspirational. But as to your part in this historic event: there will be a ceremony on June second at the airport, during which either the führer or Mannerheim will decorate you and some other men. On the evening of June third, following a state banquet in honor of Mannerheim, there will be a gala concert which will feature both Finnish and German music. A Finnish conductor will lead the program's first half, and you have been selected to conduct the second half. That *is* what you did in civilian life, is it not?"

Yes, you pompous ass, it is. But this is not how I wanted my career to resume, not to be trotted out in my new Iron Cross like an organ-grinder's monkey, to perform in your propaganda circus!

"Yes, but . . . I don't know, sir. It's been several years since I stood before an orchestra, and I have no program worked up, and no rehearsal schedule . . ."

"That's been taken care of. You'll have three hours rehearsal time on June first and another three hours on the second; for an hour's worth of music, no more. Shouldn't be too difficult—I'm sure you'll pick up where you left off. It must be rather like riding a bicycle, eh? Once you learn how, you never really forget?"

Schleicher made a noise, a fart-like splutter that Erich assumed was laughter.

"Just imagine, Ziegler: it's your chance to conduct for the führer! That cannot help but be a boost to your career. Just tell me the name of the pieces you'll be conducting, and we'll make sure the orchestral parts are ready for you."

Inwardly, Erich sighed acceptance. What, really, did the circumstances matter? Music had been welling up inside him ever since his first meeting with Sibelius; impure though it was, here was a chance to unleash some of that artistic energy.

The more Erich thought about it, the less objectionable the prospect seemed. He had yearned for a chance to put some of his new insights to work, to find out if he had really gained the understanding he believed he had gained, or if he were only deluding himself. One thing was certain: the orchestra would know; and he could tell, five minutes into the rehearsal, whether they were truly convinced by him or simply going through the motions.

"I'm honored, *Herr Oberst*, of course. I'll submit the repertory to you later on, if I may. I'll also need to know what else has already been programmed."

"I have that here someplace. Ah, yes: the Haydn Variations of Brahms and the Violin Concerto of Sibelius. Choose whatever else you like, provided there's a German piece and a Finnish one. Oh, I must not forget to tell you that you'll also have to function as an intelligence operative on this same occasion. The day before the concert, there will be a full-scale strategy conference at Mannerheim's headquarters. The führer will discuss the coming campaign, there will be a general exchange of ideas between the two staffs, and then there will be a second conference later, during which General Dietl will address the führer concerning the contribution his Norwegian Command can make to the campaign as a whole. At some point, they'll ask you to make a brief report on the state of things in the Finnish Army, based on your personal observations. I assume you're prepared to make such a presentation, Ziegler, for I notice that your last formal report to Colonel Klatt was dated more than a month ago."

Erich tried to remember: of course, he had forwarded that pessimistic report to Klatt. But Klatt—one glance at the man confirmed it—had not thought it advisable to pass the document on to Schleicher. Was Schleicher fishing, then, or criticizing, or making an attempt at veiled sarcasm? His features gave no clue.

Erich patted his briefcase with feigned enthusiasm, smiling at Schleicher: "I have a new report, sir, that I was about to turn in, after a bit more work on the Finnish documents I use to support my data—it's a hard language to translate, you know. I'll work things into presentation form—say, ten to fifteen minutes?"

"Maximum. The führer admires concision."

Erich, Klatt, and Schleicher flew to Helsinki the following morning, accompanied by uniformed factotums who struggled with luggage, portfolios of plans, bundles of rolled-up maps. Erich's first impression of Helsinki, as he glimpsed it through the windows of the staff car that drove them into town from the airport, was of a bright, well-laid-out city of wide boulevards and clean-lined architecture. They were driven to the Hotel Torni, adjacent to the square in front of the famous railroad station. From his bedroom window, Erich could look right into the faces of the immense stone figures, each benignly holding a light-globe in both hands, that supported the roof of architect Aalto's heroic building—enigmatic figures whose stern and imperturbable faces gazed out over their city with hooded Buddha eyes.

The first official function was a reception at the Palace of Government, held in a cavernous room of polished red granite, its surfaces aswirl with reflections from chandeliers of Swedish crystal. The flagstones shimmered with the passing strokes of glossy boots. Here were technicians, diplomats, liaison officers, neutral-country observers, spies, Stockholm correspondents, and white-gloved uniformed orderlies bearing large silver trays of hors d'oeuvres. Hovering like butterflies on the edge of this leather-and-brass throng were the wives, mistresses, and girlfriends, decorated with corsages, gloved, curled, powdered, and bright with lipstick.

Erich's eyes kept returning to the lipstick. The two sisters at Tapiola neither wore, nor really needed, any makeup. It had been a year, in fact, since Erich had seen lipstick on anyone; the artificiality, the simple queerness of it, drew him with fetishistic intensity, as though he were observing something brought back by archaeologists from a remote and exotic culture.

After a half hour of champagne-sipping and canapénibbling, Erich thought he had spotted all the women in the room who were either unattached to begin with, or who could have been persuaded to detach themselves after a little courting. For a while he even exchanged banalities with the slightly equine but exceedingly buxom wife of a hard-drinking Swedish journalist who was more interested in lecturing the Portuguese attaché on Mediterranean strategy. Erich kept staring at the little white spades of her teeth as her thickly painted lips moved back and forth. After their second drink together, he knew he could have taken her off somewhere, after her husband had drunk himself into a stupor, and probably enjoyed her favors; he also knew that the experience was almost certain to be repellent.

Before he had slept with Kylliki, he would have indulged himself with this woman. But now he had that memory and he was reluctant to sully it. His erotic obsession with the forest girl had only grown by being fulfilled, but afterward, it had undergone a transformation, enlarged, absorbed more of his emotions than he had expected. However naturally gifted Kylliki had been in bed, it was her unearthly innocence, her formidable and unself-conscious purity, that had taken hold of him most deeply. The way she regarded him, as some kind of gallant knight who had ridden into the forest, bearing tales of a strange and glittering world she had never seen! Now his ambition was to show her that world; even more: to lay it at her feet.

He was ultimately relieved when an equerry rapped the floor at the main entrance and announced the arrival of Field Marshal Mannerheim, for this gave the Swedish journalist an excuse to reclaim his roving spouse.

Two days short of his seventy-fifth birthday, Baron Carl Gustaf Mannerheim—an aristocratic Swedish-Finnish who had risen high in the ranks of the Tsarist army, who had returned to Finland in 1918 to command the White counteroffensive, and who, called out of retirement, had brilliantly led his small army against the Red juggernaut during the Winter War—still looked every inch a soldier. There were rumors that he dyed his hair and maintained his erect posture by means of a corset, but up close, in the reception line, Erich decided these were probably exaggerations. The man's physical presence was formidable. His face was grave and a trifle jowly, but the field marshal's mustache did not droop, there was granite in the line of his jaw, and his eyes were clear and strong. When Erich's name was read from a list held by a pomaded adjutant, crisply poised the regulation two paces behind the *generalissimo*, Mannerheim stepped forward and searched Erich's face with the sort of gaze that strips a man to his skin. His handshake was gruff, his voice gravelly.

"Well, Captain, it seems I shall be decorating you tomorrow. I hope you bear up under the ceremonies as manfully as you bore up under the attack of the—what was it, Heinrichs?" Mannerheim angled his head inquiringly toward the staff officer in his wake.

"Soviet parachutists, sir. In Third Corps' sector, during the *motti* operations in December."

". . . as well as you handled the parachutists, then."

"I shall try my best, *Herr Feldmarschall.*"

"And so shall I, Captain. Good luck to you."

Salutes were exchanged. Erich clapped his heels and stepped back into the reception line; Mannerheim passed on to the next man. For an instant, during that last exchange, Erich had looked straight into the old warrior's eyes and thought he had seen some dark shadow of the weight of his responsibilities. His people had given the marshal an impossible charge: to recover the land taken by the Russians, but not to beat them so badly that the Russian bear was goaded into thoughts of revenge. What a tightrope the old man had to walk. He was being squeezed to death between implacable ice floes of historical circumstance, and his maneuvering room was dwindling with every passing month.

Erich got another glimpse of Mannerheim's character from a vignette he observed as the reception party was disbanding, an hour or so later. The room was noticeably less crowded—even the staggering Swedish correspondent and his top-heavy wife had left, after some urging from less inebriated countrymen—and Mannerheim was engaged in conversation with several German officers, including Schleicher. Klatt, who had poured a good deal of champagne into himself earlier on, was nowhere to be seen. Erich sidled close just as Schleicher, attempting to drive home a point to his host, began waving a large phallic cigar under Mannerheim's finely turned baronial nose. Erich saw a quick look of horror flash over the features of nearby Finnish adjutants. Schleicher, still carried on the tide of his discourse and not realizing that his was now the dominant voice in this part of the room, whipped out a lighter and touched flame to the tip of the big cylinder bobbling from the corner of his mouth. The end of the cigar detonated in a cloud of acrid fumes. Almost as an afterthought, Schleicher said: "I trust the field marshal does not mind if I smoke a cigar while we converse?"

In the silence which suddenly framed this remark, Mannerheim gazed back at Schleicher as though he were watching an insect on a dinner plate and replied: "I really don't know. No one has ever tried before."

Schleicher retained his composure until he left the building; then he snapped angrily at the driver who picked them up at the main entrance. Erich had not had a chance to inform Klatt of the exchange, although he had every intention of doing so, but Klatt was still so deep in his cups that he smiled blearily at everything and thus gave the impression that he was amused at Schleicher's discomfiture. The back seat of the staff car became a very tense place. Erich sought to break the mood by suggesting a good dinner.

"Dinner? Yes, why not, provided there is a decent place to eat in this provincial manure pile!" growled Schleicher, making sure the German-speaking Finnish driver heard every word.

"Permit me, Colonel." Erich leaned over to the driver's ear and said, in reasonably idiomatic Finnish: "I apologize for this overbearing asshole, driver; do you happen to know the way to Kemp's Restaurant?"

"Of course, Captain, we can be there in a matter of minutes. An excellent choice, if I may say so."

"What was that all about?" demanded Schleicher.

"I asked the driver to take us to a restaurant I've heard about—one that comes highly recommended by a Finnish friend who used to dine there often."

"Really? Anyone prominent?"

"A composer, sir. Fellow I met up in the lake district."

Kemp's, though it remained atmospheric and redolent of prewar elegance, was a culinary disappointment. The original menus—woven placards edged in gold, the size of place mats—had been covered with crudely mimeographed revisions, paper-clipped over the list of prewar selections. When Schleicher demanded an explanation from their waiter, the elderly gentleman merely shook his head sadly and replied: "Shortages, sir, shortages of everything. Even the bread is no longer complimentary, I'm afraid. It's the war, of course; all our continental sources are cut off from us."

The wine list remained surprisingly healthy, however, and after a pair of not altogether contemptible bottles had been brought to the table, Schleicher announced: "Did you know, gentlemen, that the Finns had to import one hundred fifty percent more grain from Germany this year than last? Not to mention beef and pork? Now they depend on us not only for their artillery, but also for their daily bread. And I tell you, we must get more from them in return for our generosity! If they don't want to move on Leningrad, then they should at least take out the Murmansk Railroad for us—there's a considerable flow of supplies coming into Russia through the arctic ports now, considerable. The convoys pay heavily, of course, but even one freighter can carry a squadron of fighter-bombers or a battalion of tanks."

"The Finns won't move against the railroad, that's certain. If they wouldn't do it last year, they certainly won't do it this year," said Klatt. "Our sources in Helsinki also tell me they've been warned by the Americans not to do it."

"Oh, fuck the Americans!" Schleicher growled, rather too loudly for Erich's taste. "The Americans are half a world away!"

"The point, Colonel, is that the very thought of a state of war existing between Finland and America is simply ludicrous to the vast majority of Finns. Relations between the two nations have always been extremely cordial, and Sibelius is very popular with American audiences," said Erich in a patient, lecturing tone. God, how he hoped this disagreeable man would depart as soon as Hitler and his entourage went back to Berlin! The strategy discussion, lubricated by a liberal supply of wine, continued throughout the course of the meal. Schleicher dominated the conversation more and more, making extravagant claims for the coming summer offensive against Russia and insisting that the chances of a Wehrmacht victory were greater than ever, despite the stupendous losses of men and equipment suffered during the previous winter. They would see, during the führer's briefing, the essence of strategic genius! Russia was doomed, and if Finland wanted any of the table scraps, she should make stronger efforts to support her faithful cobelligerent.

Schleicher bluntly asked Erich if the Finnish officer corps would turn against the Mannerheim-Ryti government if its policies became too pacifistic. Erich was surprised—could a *coup d'état* still be considered a serious contingency by the German high command?

"In a sense, Colonel, the question is moot. Without the Finnish Army itself, even the most rabidly right-wing officers could do nothing. They could shout and wave their swords until they turned blue in the face and they would be doing it all alone. Those men fought superbly to regain what they regard as Finnish soil—I know because I saw them fight—but they would not fight with anything like the same spirit to achieve the objectives you're talking about."

"But surely, the Fascist groups within the army, the Lapua Movement, the Karelian Brotherhood . . . surely they exert enough influence to shape Finnish policy in our favor."

"Colonel, I don't know who prepares your intelligence reports, but it's obvious they haven't read *mine*—the only admitted member of the Karelian Brotherhood I've met since coming to this country was a paltry second lieutenant who had the political sophistication of a twelve-year-old."

"But you admit that there are Fascist sympathizers among the officer caste?"

"There are Fascist sympathizers in *any* officer caste, in any army. But sympathizing with an attitude is not the same thing as committing to an ideology with all your heart and mind."

Tired of being contradicted and having only the meagerest supply of factual ammunition with which to reply, Schleicher abruptly changed the thrust of his remarks.

"Ziegler, whatever your personal misgivings, you must keep them to yourself. After the joint strategy conference, you will be admitted to a private, high-security briefing. You'll have about ten minutes to speak. I suggest you word your impressions so that the most optimistic color can be put on things—the führer did not come all this distance to hear depressing remarks."

"I thought perhaps he had come this distance to hear the truth."

"Oh for God's sake, Ziegler, tell the man what he wants to hear! A few generalities about Finno-German comradeship—Christ, you're a propagandist, you know what's suitable! Later on, in private, the generals will read your reports and fit them into the overall picture. I assure you that your expertise will not be wasted; what's needed on this occasion is your tact."

Erich had no intention of hectoring Adolf Hitler. The conversation with Schleicher faded, along with his hangover, when he reported, the following morning, to the University Concert Hall, to begin his first rehearsal with the Helsinki Philharmonic. The orchestra, by this stage of the war, was comprised entirely of elderly and middle-aged musicians, and its tone tended to a certain raggedness. Erich experienced a moment of real tension as he strode to the podium, flipped open the score on the music stand before him, and raised his baton. "*Guten Morgen, Maestro*," said the white-haired concertmaster, his tone carefully neutral; like every orchestra, they were waiting to see who would be the boss, and on what terms.

Erich smiled, nodded, casually removed his army tunic

and flung it across a nearby chair. Now he stood before them in a plain dark shirt, without rank or insignia or nationality.

"Hyvää päivä, Herrat," he began, in his best Finnish accent. *"Hauska tavata!"* Good morning, gentlemen; I am pleased to meet you.

The tactic worked better than he had hoped. He was later informed that he was the first foreign conductor ever to address the ensemble in their own language. After fifteen minutes of rehearsal, when his competence as well as his civility had been proven, the orchestra was his. Their playing became firmer, their tone more solid, their phrasing more expressive, their attacks more unanimous and full of bite.

For the concert, he had chosen *Till Eulenspiegel* by Richard Strauss, because it showed the playful and high-spirited face of German music, and the Sixth Symphony of Sibelius. He thought the works made a good pairing, each reflecting kindred qualities of the poetry and humanism that were perhaps the best part of both nationalities.

After ninety minutes' work, with all the preliminary outlines of the interpretations already jelled, Erich called a halt for lunch. A delegation of players, fronted by the orchestra's personnel manager, invited Erich to dine with them. Flattered—for such spontaneous gestures did not come often from hard-bitten orchestra professionals—Erich accepted, and was in the process of tucking in his tunic when he noticed a tall, whip-thin man with brilliantined hair regarding him from a seat in the fourth row. The man's eyes were intense, his mouth full and sardonic; the face would have been recognized by any musician in Germany as that of Hermann von Golzer, the new *Wunderkind* of the podium.

Since Erich's first encounter with him at Mannheim, von Golzer had risen from relative obscurity to fame. A couple of years before the war, when Furtwängler had resigned some of his posts to protest the Nazi ban on the music of Hindemith and Mendelssohn, there had suddenly been a great void in German concert life. Few other reputable conductors wanted to step into the vacancy left by the man who was generally regarded as the greatest of them all. But von Golzer, until that time a barely known provincial *répétiteur*, had materialized, heralded by a drumfire of publicity from Goebbels's propaganda office. He had seized the reins and, while nattily dressed in his Brownshirt uniform, had led the Bayreuth pit orchestra through what was, by all accounts, a brilliant performance of *Tristan und Isolde*. He was now Hitler's favorite maestro and he had conducted every good orchestra in the Reich, with the exception of the Berlin Philharmonic, where Furtwängler doggedly soldiered on, sustained by a bedrock belief that great art could counterbalance some of the excesses of the regime.

Von Golzer was crisply attired in a black and silver Nazi Party blouse. He had a pile of scores tucked beneath his arm. He advanced down the aisle with his hand outstretched in front of a wintry smile.

Astonished, Erich held out his own hand and mumbled: "Maestro . . . I am surprised to see you here . . . and, of course, honored to meet you."

"I'm merely here as a kind of cultural observer, Captain. I hope you do not mind that I sneaked into your rehearsal, and I hope you'll accept a colleague's compliments on your work. The Sibelius piece, I confess, I found somewhat pallid, but the Strauss had great vigor and splendid color. You have a very considerable talent."

But I don't have someone in Berlin greasing the way for me, thought Erich. Until he knew what von Golzer was doing here, he decided to at least be civil.

"A very rusty talent, Maestro, I'm afraid."

"Nonsense! I say, shall we go and have some lunch together? I'd love to fill you in on what's happening in the musical world back home."

Von Golzer had already thrown a comradely arm around Erich's shoulder and was leering at him with an excessive, mint-scented smile. Erich had rarely felt such an instant dislike for any man. This was an opportunistic young jackal; talented, yes—even those who despised him admitted his gifts—but utterly without scruples. He seemed the embodiment of a type Erich had observed too often in the concert world: a man so consumed by ambition that he was on the make, instantly, with every person he met.

"Thank you, Maestro, but I'm afraid I've already made other plans. Some other time, perhaps?"

Hats in hands, a cluster of orchestra players was standing beside the stage, obviously waiting for Erich to join them. Von Golzer glanced at them haughtily.

"Them? Surely they'll understand if you prefer to have lunch with a colleague."

"With all respect, Maestro, they are my colleagues too. At least for the duration of this engagement." Sensing von Golzer's irritation—the man was actually scowling like a rejected suitor—Erich hastily fabricated an extenuating motive: "Besides, I am under orders to establish good relations with this Finnish orchestra. Orders of the highest priority."

That was something von Golzer could understand. "Ah, yes, I see, I see! Duty always before pleasure, eh? Well, it's all for the war effort, of course, even our little stick-waving activities! Another time, then, surely. Pleasant meeting you, Ziegler, and best of luck with your concert!" He pressed Erich's hand with his dry one and strode away, a coiled, elegant watchspring of a man.

Despite the other man's cordial words, though, Erich felt that he had just made an enemy.

Now Erich stood with damp armpits under a blazing summer sun on the tarmac, smelling tar and petrol, rifle oil and leather polish, watching Adolf Hitler and Field Marshal Mannerheim pin medals on the row of men to his right. As they drew closer, he sucked in more air, his chest swelling. When the two leaders moved into his straight-ahead vision, Erich thought he detected a twinkle of friendly recognition in Mannerheim's eyes. Hitler reached up and draped the Iron Cross over Erich's neck, then made a few banal remarks of congratulation. The man had a sallow vegetarian's complexion and remarkably offensive breath, but his gaze was omnivorous and its very touch made Erich feel, in some vague, generic way, guilty. A damp, perfunctory handshake, and the ceremony was over.

It was an altogether different Hitler whom Erich saw later in the conference room. He entered swaggering, flanked at a respectful distance by the leathery, crew-cut Halder, the blunt-faced Jodl, and the dapper, mustached Keitel, each man toting full attaché cases and rolls of supplementary maps. The führer began his presentation in a calmly methodical manner, then worked gradually to a pitch of enthusiasm that captured the attention of even the most skeptical listeners in the room. With emphatic chops of his hands, he roamed back and forth across the large map of Russia, dismissing the winter's setbacks and stressing not the German, but the enormous Soviet losses. Equipment shortages had been made good by new shipments, he insisted; the panzer divisions were straining at the leash again, and the armor-ripe plains of the Ukraine beckoned—the Soviet Union's breadbasket was waiting to be plundered. Arrows appeared on the maps, showing Wehrmacht axes of advance that enclosed thousands of square miles of land, stabbing as deep as the Baku oil fields on the Caspian Sea, piercing the Caucasus Mountains, scooping out the entire Don basin, rolling over Rostov and Voronezh and the industrial city of Stalingrad, whose very name seemed to inspire Hitler's voice to a slithering portamento of hate. The offensive was not merely bold, it was visionary, and if its enormous pincers functioned according to plan, a million Russian soldiers would be trapped, probably annihilated. There were also, Hitler continued, beaming, dozens of new divisions of allied troops being committed to the campaign: Slovak, Romanian, Hungarian, Italian, and Spanish.

Erich heard one of the nearby Finnish staff officers snort quietly in derision as this list was read. Erich kept looking back to his map, a generalized version of the detailed one Hitler was using. The German offensive formed an immense tapering salient, with its point on Stalingrad, its right flank washing through the gorges of the Caucasus (did Hitler really believe that armored columns could sweep so easily through terrain where even Georgian ponies had to struggle?) and its left, to be manned by those same questionable satellite divisions, curling along the western bank of the Don. Any military cadet worth his bars could see that, with Moscow and its railroad nexus untaken, it would only be a matter of time until the Russians amassed a huge force opposite that very flank. The more Erich examined the map, with its fantastic sweeping arrows going through the perpendicular gorges of the Caucasus as though they were the Vienna Woods, the more he was filled with foreboding. On those open steppes around Rostov, the panzers would, to be sure, encircle and eliminate vast numbers of Russian troops at first—of that, he had no doubt. But what about later, when the autumn rains came and the tanks began to bog down and the partisans started blowing up the trains on that long, frail supply line back to the Reich?

After Hitler's dramatic summary, various staff officers, in turn, delivered a quick *précis* of a specialized nature: armor, air power, the naval situation in the Mediterranean, Baltic, and Black seas. Jodl concluded the session by outlining the role of the northern flank in all this: the Finns must, he said, give serious thought to renewing their actions against the Murmansk Railroad while increasing pressure on Leningrad from the northwest ... the usual litany. Mannerheim listened with a face carved from stone.

After three hours, the meeting ended. Following lunch, the Finnish and German delegations retired to separate areas to discuss among themselves. Erich accompanied Klatt and Schleicher into the conference room. First to speak was General Dietl, who summarized the operations and capabilities of his Norwegian Command. He then turned the rostrum over to Schleicher, who spoke at some length about the disproportionate number of Soviet troops being tied down in the far north, about the poor state of their morale and equipage, and, as though to hedge his bets, about the endless difficulties of just keeping an army fed and clothed in such terrain, never mind launching a major offensive. As for the state of their Finnish allies, well, for that report, Schleicher wanted to yield the podium to an intelligence operative who had lived closely with the Finns and whose recent Iron Cross had been won while actually fighting alongside them. With a slight flourish, he introduced Erich.

Though he was considerably more nervous than he had ever been when standing in front of an orchestra, Erich was outwardly controlled. He had no intention of flouting Schleicher's distasteful but realistic advice to soft-pedal the Finns' reluctance and growing disillusionment. He adopted an optimistic tone, one that took on a more positive coloration when he skirted difficult or unpleasant topics and resorted to ringing generalities; he did this whenever possible.

The admiration of the Finnish soldier for the Wehrmacht was strong, he insisted; the Finns had a clear political perception of their war goals, as did the führer; there was the strongest respect among the Finnish officer caste for their German counterparts. He also stated that, in order to withstand any serious Soviet attack, the Finns required more antitank guns, self-propelled artillery, and, in an emergency, the ability to call upon the Stukas and Heinkels based in Norway. Finally, he believed that the comradeship between the two great Nordic states was an inspiration to his Finnish colleagues, and he was proud to have represented the Reich in battle alongside such men as General Pajari. As he concluded with that last remark, Erich smiled to himself, wondering what that crusty, ill-tempered old soldier would make of the compliment.

There was a peculiar silence among the visiting German staff officers when Erich finished. No one said: "Thank you, Captain, that will be all." To fill the silence, Erich coughed. A prickle of nervous dread, a kind of doctor's-office uneasiness, worked its way through his abdomen.

"Are there any questions, gentlemen?" he finally stammered.

To his horror, Hitler raised his hand, like a schoolboy asking to be excused.

"*Mein Führer?*" Erich responded, making a gesture of deference. A fat bead of sweat crawled down his back like a caterpillar.

"Captain Ziegler, I have here a copy of a top-secret report, initialed by yourself, which contains the following statement: 'Hitler's decision . . . to shift his panzer divisions to the Ukraine rather than use them to take Moscow and Leningrad, is discussed quite openly as an irrational blunder which, in the opinion of most divisions and regimental-level commanders, is likely to cost Germany the campaign, and possibly the war itself.' Did you originate that report, Captain?"

Erich's legs began to tremble. Hitler's face was inscrutable, his eyes hard and glittering. Both Klatt and Schleicher looked stunned—Schleicher because he had not known such a report existed, and Klatt because its appearance in Hitler's hands meant disloyalty and spying within his own staff, the only others who would have had access to Erich's reports.

"*Mein Führer,* my orders were to report the thoughts of the Finnish soldiers I lived with. It is my impression that an opinion exists at OKW concerning Fascist sympathies within the Finnish officer caste which is highly exaggerated, and that decisions based on that delusion could hurt German-Finnish relations, and the war effort, far more than decisions based on the facts, however unpalatable they may be. What I wrote was not a personal opinion, but that of the men I lived and fought with. If I had glossed over those facts, I would have been derelict in my duty."

"And what *is* your personal opinion, Ziegler?"

"I have been serving, *mein Führer,* on a remote front some two thousand miles distant from the battlefields that have occupied your fullest attention. How could I presume to have enough knowledge to pass judgment on strategic decisions whose origin and consequences are so far away from my own area of experience?"

Erich knew he was starting to swim and that the water would get deeper and colder with each new question from Hitler. But the führer, much to Erich's relief, moved on, turning his attention entirely away and ranting at the room in general about how much pressure he could put on the Finns by denying them grain shipments as well as withholding heavy armaments and aircraft. "They'll realize sooner or later that this is not a separate war up here, gentlemen! And based on Ziegler's information, together with other impressions I've gotten from my own dealings with Mannerheim's people, I think it's time we started turning the screws!"

Erich remained standing throughout this diatribe, his entire body numb, sour crescents spreading under his arms. Would Hitler, like some ancient despot, slay the messenger who brought bad tidings? Why had he simply not waffled the wording of his report? Because he had come to trust Klatt? Or because he had become so involved in his personal situation, his intimacy with Sibelius and the doors it might open for his career? Or because he had become so distracted by the startling passion he felt for Kylliki that he had forgotten to protect himself?

Finally, Hitler noticed him again—or had he known, all along, that Erich was still there, drowning in funk?—and waved him impatiently to a seat: "Sit down, Captain Ziegler; you were only doing your duty."

When the conference broke up, following another tense hour of Hitlerian rhetoric, Schleicher stormed out of the room without a glance at Erich. Klatt offered him a cigarette, his own hands shaking, and said: "I'll find the son of a bitch who leaked that document, and I'll have his balls, I promise you."

"I feel as though mine have already been had," muttered Erich, disengaging himself. There was another birthday party for Mannerheim that evening, but Erich feigned illness and went instead to a quiet waterfront café, where he sipped *aquavit* and savored the midsummer twilight as it deepened over the harbor.

What now, Maestro? he asked himself. He had seen the "Führer Principle" at work, up close, and it had been a draining experience. If even he, barely trained as he was, could see the danger of Hitler's strategic plan, how much more must those field marshals and generals have seen it? And yet, not one of them had made an objection, not one had suggested any changes.

That in itself was frightening enough. That he, Erich Ziegler, had been publicly cited, by the führer himself, for a

top-secret report that went against Hitler's wishes—this
caused a worm of fear to gnaw at his bowels. Anyone looking
at his military record could see that his loyalty to Germany
was beyond question. But evidently, that loyalty was now
passé, was not enough; one had to transfer it, whole and without question, to the man who had taken it upon himself to be
the embodiment of Germany.

No, by God! Erich swore to himself. Germany was
Goethe and Beethoven and Heine and Kant and Bach and
Thomas Mann; that was the Germany whose values his father
had bred into him, and that was the Germany he had been
willing to protect as a soldier. But somehow, insidiously, that
Germany had been replaced, abrogated, by another, lesser,
corrupted thing that castigated its Furtwänglers and heaped
praise upon toadying sycophants like von Golzer.

Erich finished his second drink, and let his emotions roll
freely, determined not to leave this vantage point until he had
found some center of gravity again. Christ almighty, he had
come to Helsinki to conduct a fucking orchestra, not to give
a lecture in grand strategy to the German high command! His
position was ludicrous! Absurd! Kafkaesque!

Defiance began to emerge while the third drink went
down. Very well, he told himself, there may be consequences,
but then again, there may not be. Hitler has far more important things on his mind than Erich Ziegler's unpalatable report. Whatever happened next week or next month, he had an
orchestra to conduct tomorrow and a concert to give soon after.

By the time he had finished his third drink, he felt confident once more. Screw them, he thought. I'm a conductor,
not a politician. I'll go out there and conduct and do such a
great job of it that they'll have to leave me alone.

He permitted himself the luxury of a fourth drink, this
one sipped slowly, nurturing his far more optimistic mood. It
was all simple, really: he would just go on conducting, and everything would work out.

Before him, the harbor lay under a pearlescent sky. He
watched the gulls pirouette above the fish-market stalls, con-

templated the small white steamers bustling back and forth, taking couples out to the Suomenlinna fortress, where they could stroll beneath the lavender-white skies on broad, romantic ramparts. In his present mood, even the complexities of grand strategy became really very simple: the Red Air Force could have flattened all this without much opposition if it had been ordered to. But that strange, unspoken bargain between the two nations still held firm: the Finns had not shelled Leningrad, so the Russians had not bombed Helsinki. To Erich, that seemed a fair enough trade, and an irrefutable testament to Mannerheim's sagacity.

As soon as Erich stepped onto the podium the next morning for his final rehearsal with the Helsinki Philharmonic, everything became even clearer. By now the rapport between himself and the orchestra was solid. He felt confident of the results; which was just as well, given the fact that he would be conducting in the spotlight, for an occasion of state, and his efforts would be reviewed by German as well as Finnish critics. Just before the rehearsal began, the smiling old concertmaster handed him an envelope. Inside was a wire from Sibelius: "When you conduct the Sixth, think of the way the light comes through the pines on a spring morning and the way the cranes fly low over the lake at dusk. I will be listening on the wireless. All luck be with you. S."

When Erich gave the downbeat for *Till Eulenspiegel*, the music had a lilt and verve it had not possessed before. The performance was superior to anything he had yet coaxed from the ensemble—they were giving him their reserves of commitment, and the results were dramatic. After finishing the Strauss, he gave the men a cigarette break, then stepped down to discuss a matter of phrasing with the leader of the cello section.

As he was opening the score, he felt a tap on his shoulder. He turned. Von Golzer was standing there, a vulpine smile across his undertaker's face.

"Could I speak to you for a moment, Herr Ziegler?"

They walked toward the rear of the hall. Von Golzer held out a printer's proof of the evening's program; under his other arm, he carried a sheaf of scores whose titles Erich could not read.

"We have a small problem, Ziegler. The führer has decided that the selections on the program's second half are somewhat too low-key, in view of what he now knows about the state of Finnish morale."

If this was a reference to the report, Erich found it incredible that von Golzer, who of course had been excluded from that top-secret session, should already know of the incident. The confidence Erich had generated within himself at the café melted like sand. He was aghast at his own naïveté. There were forces at work here, it seemed, which could crush him without blinking an eye.

"I'm not sure I understand what you mean."

"This concert has become highly symbolic, more so than when we first talked. It will be broadcast over the Finnish radio net, and it will be recorded for rebroadcast later to the Reich. It is important, in the führer's view, that it be the most inspiring occasion possible."

"Maestro, you must have been here during that Strauss rehearsal—you heard that orchestra play! It will be as good a performance of that piece as you could want!"

And probably a damn sight better than you could achieve!

The oily condescension in von Golzer's reply made Erich's flesh crawl. "I know, Ziegler, I heard it, and they played very well for you—you're to be congratulated. It's just that the program itself has to be changed, by order of the führer."

"Changed to what?"

"To something more emblematic of the common purpose that unites these two nations. Now, here is a list of suitable selections, which I took the liberty of drawing up after learning of the führer's wishes. I think a couple of Wagner selections, perhaps the Rhine Journey and Funeral Music from *Götterdämmerung*, and then something a bit more patriotic by Sibelius—*Finlandia* would be nice, coupled perhaps with something overtly symbolic, say the *Karelia Suite*. Well, you get the idea. Here is the list."

Erich barely glanced at the titles before balling up the paper and throwing it at von Golzer's feet.

"Good God, man, I can't change that program now! We've no time for rehearsals, we'd have to get the parts from somewhere, and last but not least, no conductor in the world would tolerate this kind of interference with his programming—as you well know! This whole business is insane."

"This is on the direct orders of Hitler, Ziegler. I admit it's extraordinary, but then, a conductor should always be prepared to step in on short notice. At least, I have always been prepared to do so."

Erich stared at him open-mouthed.

"Are you telling me that if I refuse to go along with this farce, you will replace me?"

"It's nothing personal, my dear fellow. I'm a soldier too, and I have my orders. If you cannot, or will not, make these changes, then I'm afraid I'll have to step in and do it myself. For the sake of your career, you really should try to accommodate yourself to the situation."

"What about the sake of the music? Even if I wanted to play Wagner and *Finlandia*, there is no time to prepare them properly. What you're telling me is that I have a choice between not conducting at all, and conducting what amounts to a sight-reading that's bound to sound like shit!"

"If you're a good enough conductor, you can hold it together, man."

"I am at least a good enough conductor to tell you to go to hell and take this whole disgraceful idea with you!"

With that, Erich threw his baton into the auditorium and stormed out.

The torment was not over for Erich. The next morning, as an additional measure of punishment for his sins, he received a written order to attend the concert. He sat there in the darkness at the rear of the box, trembling and fighting back tears, his mind racing ahead of a horde of malign possibilities. His name appeared nowhere on the program, and von Golzer, waving his arms like a deranged windmill, conjured

Wagner performances both rough and blowsy, and a reading of *Finlandia* that underlined the score's blatancies in so vulgar a manner as to make the piece sound like trashy film music. Hitler smiled his distant elsewhere-smile throughout the entire concert, and as he left the box at the end, he patted Erich ambiguously on the arm.

Ten days later, Erich received orders transferring him to a combat unit on the Russian Front.

Eighteen

Erich was curled up in a fetal void. As long as he did not move, the cold could not get to him. He was encysted beneath the rime ice that covered his blanket. It had taken him an hour to find the right way to lie in order to maintain body heat and keep out some of the steppe wind. What followed from this fragile equilibrium was not really sleep, just a muzzy trance. He contemplated descending spirals of darkness, like steps going into a lightless cellar. He played no music in his mind, but concentrated rather on a static-like hum of white noise that would mask the unending moan of the wind. He wanted nothing more than to gain for himself the exact physical and mental shape of a chick inside an eggshell. If he could do that, he believed, then he could warp time, and it might flow over him without noticing him; the sun would come up and the frost would melt from the steppe and the battle would be fought and nobody would notice him, curled here beneath his blanket, his mind like a piece of slate.

"Time to get on with it, Captain." A hand on his hip, shaking. He heard the disturbed frost shiver on the surfaces around him.

Fuck the lieutenant. He was not going to move. The lieutenant was a hallucination. And Russia itself was a vaster hallucination. And the war on the Eastern Front was a dream by Nostrodamus, a mad canvas by Hieronymus Bosch: scuttling creatures with the bodies of T-34 tanks and the legs of giant crawfish, howitzers with faces like lamprey eels, enormous elongated jackboots with torsos and heads like praying mantises, overturned helmets stuffed with bouquets of screaming mouths, cracked Easter Fabergé eggs with burning onion-dome cathedrals inside; and the flames made music, made a Magic Fire Music all right, like feeding a grand piano into a buzz saw.

"Come on, Captain—it's almost light."

Again the hand on his hip, rolling him insistently. The lip of the blanket, which he had spent so long tucking into just the right places, came loose and a knife blade of cold air slit his ribs. The Bosch panorama fled, the tanks-with-legs scuttling back into flaming chasms, long pustulant tongues wagging from the muzzles of their guns. Angrily he slapped at the lieutenant's hand and sat up, a fine powder of frost spinning away from his legs and shoulders. His head came up for air; he felt as though a bucket of ice water had been tipped over his face. His shoulders, knees, and elbows ached like those of a rheumatic old man.

"Christ, it's almost as cold here as it was outside of Murmansk."

"It's the wind. It never stops, never gives you a chance. Here, sir, here's some breakfast to help you get going."

Lieutenant Tarsala helped Erich into a sitting position and thrust a half-full canteen into his tingling fingers. As he unscrewed the cap, Erich inhaled the raw vodka smell and braced his insides for the arrival of the first swallow. They called it "tractor fuel," and Erich would not have been surprised to learn that, in an emergency, the stuff would actually power a vehicle. There was an old peasant, in some nameless shithole of a village five kilometers west of here, wherever "here" actually was, who had distilled the beverage. When they'd first discovered it a week ago, the battalion medics had tested it and pronounced it free of poison, high in octane, and

extremely flammable. Much of the battalion had stayed more
or less drunk ever since.

Oily and granular, the vodka smote the cobwebs from
Erich's brain and brought him to full consciousness. At the
same time, the alcohol began to insulate his mind with a
clinging film, a second skin that would grow, with each swallow, until part of him could stay behind and remain unin-
volved in the wretched business that was about to start.

In the darkness off to his left, he heard Kivikoski tittering.
Someone cuffed him into silence.

In front of their position, to the east, the sky had begun to
turn rusty. The edge of the woods, half a kilometer distant,
had started to acquire definition—branches and treetrunks
crinkled starkly against the burnt orange, giving the impression that the sky was an old oil painting that had begun to
flake at the bottom. Not far away to his right, Erich could see
the long thin barrel of the Flakpanzer's weapon, a 37-mm automatic cannon tipped with the inverted cone of a flash-
suppressor. Somewhere off to the other side, still shrouded in
darkness, was a self-propelled gun, hull down in a wrinkle of
earth, its blunt 75-mm gun pointed at the woods. Behind the
line of infantry, mortars were emplaced, zeroed in on the
same patch of trees. The anvil was ready. Several kilometers
distant, on the far side of the trees, the hammer would be in
motion already: two other battalions, altogether about half of
what remained of the Viking Division, a so-called "free-will"
unit of the Waffen SS, comprised of volunteers from the various occupied nations of Northern Europe. In the middle,
somewhere in those trees, a unit of Soviet partisans would
desperately be trying to figure how to fight their way clear of
this trap. Erich did not think their chances were very good,
but he had to give them credit for making a long chase of it.

He was awake now. The vodka made his eyes swim hotly,
and the wind made them burn. In the open rolling plains between stands of forest, the steppe was as barren as a desert
and the wind seemed never to stop blowing. Hot and dusty in
the summer, damp and penetrating in the autumn, flaying in

the winter. It was between winter and autumn now, and the wind was implacable.

Too bad about the wind.

And too bad about the old man who had made the vodka. Erich thought about him every time he took a drink. He would think about him even more when the supply ran out.

There were other things Erich allowed himself to think about only when the vodka was in him. Chief among them was a private daily ritual of torment in which he tried to come to terms with what had happened to him. The precise machinations did not matter, only the fact that all his plans had come to ruin and all his convictions about a special destiny had been cruelly mocked. He had worked it out so carefully! He had staked out an exciting, fulfilling future for himself; he had even—in the context of his Finnish assignment—made himself over into a braver and more skillful soldier than all the coercive power of the Reich had been able to make of him. And he had found the woman he wanted to share the rest of his life with.

Like any romantic young man, Erich had enjoyed affairs and flirtations. The nature of his job—the glamour with which the public invested conductors in general, and fiery, handsome ones in particular—had afforded plenty of opportunities.

But never before had a woman complemented him so fully, fitted in so perfectly; never before had he been able to contemplate the physical and emotional quanta of a relationship with the same sense of awe he felt when studying a great musical score. Kylliki had become the embodiment of all that he found beautiful and sensual at Tapiola, even as Sibelius personified all that was vast and enigmatic. If he could have returned to postwar Europe with the score of the Eighth Symphony in his briefcase and Kylliki at his side, there was nothing he could not have accomplished. Nothing!

And now that was what he had left: nothing . . .

He had managed to arrange his affairs so that he could make a farewell visit to Tapiola before being shipped out. Kylliki had met him on the winding road to the lodge. How had she known he was coming? She knew, that was all. He had parked the car and followed her into a moss-floored, sun-scented bower, where she had, in a single fluid motion, removed her skirt and carried him down to the forest floor in a powerful and impetuous embrace. When he had entered her, it felt like opening a vein and taking in sunshine, her fierce yet lyrical smell blending with the crushed-petal scent of the wildflowers beneath their straining bodies.

She was all women: both demure and shameless, greedy for him and equally greedy for her own pleasure. She made love with an artless abandon that left him exhausted, yet radiantly vital. She made his flesh sing. He did not know exactly when he crossed from obsession to adoration; he simply looked at her after that first embrace in the forest and knew with absolute certainty that he would never find anyone to equal her, and that he wanted her with him always.

In the days that followed, they had met whenever possible, wherever possible: in the sauna, in the forest, in the laundry room, in the pantry, and once on the thwarts of a rowboat drifting on the lake beneath a blazing summer sky. Beyond basic decorum, they made no effort to hide their relationship from the other inhabitants of the lodge. Anna-Liisa, apparently resigned, tacitly gave her blessing and stayed out of their way. On Erich's last night, she even absented herself from the cabin on the island, and the two lovers enjoyed an entire night in a real bed—a night whose barest breath of memory Erich now carried clutched to his heart like a sacred relic. When he felt his will growing dim, his mind growing sick with disgust at what was often necessary in order to keep on living, he opened the lid of the mental reliquary where he kept the memory of that night, and for an instant he could almost smell her personal odor—as distinct and alive as the sharp cut of birchwood on the air of morning, when the lake was still beneath a fog—and for an eye-blink of time he would remember the heated taste of her mouth, the shiver of firelight on her hair.

The morning after that night, he had rowed her back to the mainland and escorted her to the kitchen door. Sibelius had been out on the ridge, basking in the sun like a proud old sea lion, and he had observed them with an inscrutable expression. The composer was friendly, but a bit reserved, as though the prospect of Erich's departure for the Russian Front filled him with emotions to which he refused to yield. Once or twice, he had suddenly gripped Erich's arm and stared into his face as though seeking there a confirmation of something. Words seemed to struggle toward the surface, only to be choked back with a rueful shake of the head. Finally the old man passed on, into his study, head down, a look of intense and almost painful concentration twisting his granitic features. The study door closed, and Sibelius did not emerge for hours.

On his last day, Erich found the composer standing at an overlook, trailing cigar smoke. Something about the way Sibelius was looking at him, over his right shoulder, caused Erich to draw close.

"Good morning, Maestro."

Sibelius blew smoke upon a long and gusty sigh. He turned to face Erich and placed both hands on his shoulders.

"The girl—she loves you?"

Erich had supposed that side of the equation to be obvious enough.

"I believe she does. I hope we haven't offended your hospitality, sir. It was nothing I could help, believe me. From the first moment I saw her, and heard her play the *kantele* . . ."

"Believe you?" The composer had laughed, a bitter and sardonic twist of sound, rusted at the edges. "Yes, my boy, I believe you. And no, there has been no offense given. It is not offensive when the wind blows leaves against my window or the storm blows open the front door. Such passion as you feel now can no more be stopped than the wind can be sent back to its origins. I remember how it was to be young and full of such heat, and to find such a woman in the forest. Oh, I remember."

For a moment, Erich bridled at the suggestion that he was somehow following the old man's youthful path. So what if Sibelius had found such a love and then been callow enough to desert the one who gave it? Erich would do the right thing, the logical thing, the honorable thing: he would take his love with him, out of the forest.

It seemed to Erich that the composer was about to embrace him—him, or what he might, at that moment, have represented to the old man's memory. Instead, his next words were distancing and enigmatic: "She has chosen to give herself to you, then. So be it. I thought, from the start, that there was something special about your spirit. Where you are going, they will try to kill that. Don't let them."

Sibelius seemed to hesitate before continuing. "I don't wish to insult your honor as a soldier, but I can see no reason, other than bureaucratic caprice or sheer vindictiveness, why you should be forced to serve as cannon fodder on the Russian Front. I've made preliminary inquiries to see if you can't be kept here, in Finland, but so far I've hit a stone wall, probably due to the delicate political situation—no one in Helsinki wants to irritate the German government just now. I want you to know that I won't stop trying, that I shall use all of my influence to get you back to Finland, but it will take time—I am only a celebrity, not a head of state."

"Thank you, Maestro. I had not wanted to ask."

Later that day, as Erich was walking, suitcase in hand, to the staff car that would carry him to the rail depot at Kajaani, he passed the open window of the composer's study and was halted in his tracks, as surely as if he had been struck a blow, by the sound of a few dozen bars of haltingly played music.

It was a melodic line as simple and flowing as anything in Schubert, growing from a simple arpeggiated chord. The motivic statement contained the seeds of much potential development and elaboration. Within it Erich sensed gentleness and relinquishment, and yet it was strong and clear-eyed. Even a composer of mere competence could have made something noble from it. Then, in a surprise turn, Sibelius fragmented it back into cells, like dust motes falling through sunlight, back into a glowing chromatic mist, a nacreous pollen swirl—yet still, through dabs of ghostly harmonization, the ghost-shape of the original melody remained discernible, on an almost subconscious level. What stunned Erich most was not the mastery of the passage, but its total unfamiliarity. He knew this came not from any of the published works he had studied, and knew it was too good to be from one of the composer's potboilers or bagatelles. It was a shard from a masterpiece.

Had he been vouchsafed a fragment from the Eighth? It thrilled him to think so. In any case, he had memorized the excerpt on the spot and had wrapped the memory around his heart. But in the months since then, his heart had become small and hard and not always easy to find.

He had sailed in convoy from Turku to Riga; from there, by rail, he had journeyed to Minsk, to Kiev, and eventually to the Viking Division's replacement depot at Cherkassy, on the Dnieper. There he was met by the Finnish battalion's C.O., a small tense man named Bergstrom who was half-tubercular from his addiction to Russian cigarettes and who was consumed by the flames of fanatical anti-Bolshevism. On his tunic he wore a decoration earned at the Battle of the Ebro, where he had fought as a volunteer with Franco's Fascist legions. Erich found the man a humorless and self-righteous ideologue, discerned within him something shriveled and bitter that made him a totally different type of Finn from the men Erich had fought with in the northern forests, even the hard-bitten ones like Pajari. Was it the portion of bile inherent in the man's political fanaticism, or the strain of seeing his life's goal—the crushing of Bolshevism—recede constantly in the distance, month after bloody month, that had made of him so exposed and quivering a nerve, or was it just the nature of the Russian Front itself?

Erich never really got an answer to that, for by now, for these men who had been fighting in the southern half of the USSR for nearly a year, everything was subsumed to the nature of the Eastern Front itself. In the forest, Erich had felt a personal involvement in the issues being fought over, had believed that his actions did matter in the larger scheme of things. And until he came to Russia, he had never seen an action larger than his division's attack on Murmansk; even the *motti* battles in December had been conducted on a comprehensible scale, so that to an experienced eye, it was easy to relate the events witnessed on the ground to the circles, arrows, and cryptograms on the headquarters maps. Not here. Attacks and counterattacks were like the summoning of tides; individuals were drops on a blotter, rain in an ocean; armies ebbed and flowed and men were grains of sand caught within their currents. Casualties for a battle were measured in tens of thousands; those for a large-scale offensive, in numbers so large that the mind could attach no reality to them. The nature of the fighting, too, was different from what he had witnessed in the forest. It was characterized by a kind of impersonal, across-the-board brutality that seeped into one's pores like the dust from the steppe. Survival became an end that justified any conceivable means. Brittle and morally empty as they might be, zealots such as Bergstrom were best suited for this kind of war; Erich had no doubt that, on the other side of the hill, the best battalion commissars in the Red Army were men just like Bergstrom.

Counting the latest batch of replacements Erich had arrived with, there were about one thousand Finns in the battalion. It was the only "closed" battalion in the Viking Division and it was so because Mannerheim had insisted on it. The other battalions in the division were made up of Dutch and Danish Fascists, Norwegian quislings, Flemish Belgians, and a small number of dour Swedes—adventurers, Jew-haters, anti-Communist zealots, turncoats with death sentences on their heads from their own underground forces, and a smattering of outright psychopaths who were here because this was where the killing was. Except for the Finnish battalion, all the division's officers were Germans in the Waffen SS; Erich, once again, was an anomaly.

Since going on active duty, Erich estimated that he had marched, ridden, and crawled over approximately three thousand kilometers of Soviet Russia. The chronology was jumbled in his mind now, a kaleidoscope of violent images torn free from any matrix of time and place. All he could remember, and that in no particular order, was a litany of place names flashed on his memory from road signs and maps: places he had helped to attack or defend; places he had seen taken and lost and retaken five times in a single week; places he had helped to burn: Voroshilovgrad, Rostov, Tikhoretsk, Krasnodar, and Maikop, deep in the Caucasus, where he had seen ten square miles of oil wells burning under an azure sky and where the most mechanized army in history had had to be supplied by pack trains of camels driven by bandoliered tribesmen.

Off to his left, Kivikoski gurgled and snickered. "Shut up, you crazy fucker!" someone hissed.

It was too bad about the old man who made the vodka. And about the people, whoever they were, on that train, and about the poor bastard whose skull Bergstrom had been curing when Erich first arrived.

Erich didn't see the skull at first; he had been introduced to Bergstrom at a field kitchen near the battalion's headquarters outside of Cherkassy. The officer had been stirring a bubbling caldron, telling ancient dirty jokes to several leathery, chain-smoking comrades standing nearby. In the middle of his welcoming speech, Bergstrom had excused himself and leaned over the pot with a bayonet in his hand.

"You're just in time for supper, Captain," he said, suddenly pushing the bayonet point deep under the surface. Then, grasping the hilt with both hands, he raised his arms and Erich saw that the bayonet's point was hooked into the eye socket of a human skull. It was the color of unwashed piano keys and there was a neat small-caliber bullet hole through the temple. The flesh had not totally boiled off yet, and crinkled strips of it, like half-cooked bacon, still adorned the cheeks and nose. The top of the skull had been neatly sawed off and the cranial cavity was empty.

Erich felt as though a door had slammed shut behind him, that he had entered a terrible and primitive *milieu* from which no man, however strong his will, could hope to escape undamaged.

Bergstrom waved the steaming object toward Erich and

chuckled mirthlessly: "Alas, poor Boris! I did for him myself, only yesterday."

"Tried to escape, he did!" cackled one of Bergstrom's platoon leaders, and the others joined in the laughter, as though the ghoulish spectacle were truly amusing. Erich was suddenly afraid that he, too, would eventually see the humor, and throughout his months on the Eastern Front, he came to fear that more than he feared death.

Now, in the half-light, the Flakpanzer's cannon coughed four times. With deceptive slowness, fat wobbling golf-ball tracers sailed over the steppe and crashed into the trees, spattering sparks and bisecting a small white birch on the edge of the woods. Things were stirring all around. Soon they would go in. Erich drank again and rested his cheek against the stock of the Bergmann submachine gun he'd been issued when he took over this platoon. His breath, he noticed, now smelled indigenously Russian. He lay there inhaling his own fumes, fully aware that he smelled like a drunk on a Moscow boulevard.

It was too bad about the man whose skull had been boiling in the pot, like a cannibal's supper. When the bones were clean, Bergstrom had a brass handle screwed to one side of the cheek and jaw, had the brain cavity lined with hammered aluminum, and had proudly started to consume his morning coffee from the resultant vessel.

And it was too bad about the people on that train. Bergstrom had driven Erich up to his platoon's bivouac. A military policeman had halted them at a railroad crossing a few kilometers from town. They found themselves in the middle of an immense wheatfield where the tank armies had clashed earlier that summer. The grain had been rutted by their treads, and the black carapaces of burned-out T-34s still littered the scorched stubble on either side of the road. The train they had halted for was very long and it moved slowly over rickety tracks. Erich lost count of the boxcars, each one surmounted by a cupola where a black-uniformed SS man stood cradling an automatic weapon. Many hands protruded between the slats of the boxcars, some feet, too, and one small broken purple-grey child's leg. Inside those dark and tightly packed cars, hot as ovens and smelling of shit and sickness even at this distance, hundreds of pairs of eyes were visible, as though the boxcars were crammed with rats. A few times Erich heard groans or lamentations from within, but for the most part, the train creaked across the steppe in silence.

"Prisoners?" asked Erich as the train dwindled in the hazy distance—thinking about the dangling child's leg, mere hours from gangrene by the appearance of it.

"Prisoners of war always walk, and they don't waste fancy-dress SS troopers to guard them. Must be a 'special train.' "

"What's special about those people?"

"Undesirable elements rounded up for deportation. Jews, gypsies, Ukrainian nationalists, intellectuals, queers, the odd Cossack or two . . . Special-action groups herd them together, stuff 'em into the trains, then ship them back to the Reich."

"What for, if they're so undesirable?"

"Forced labor, I imagine. Who gives a shit?"

As the train dwindled to a smoky dot on the western rim of the wheat, Erich wondered what sort of labor they would be fit to perform after traveling another thousand miles in those boxcars.

Now, from the center of the woods, firefight noises crackled sharply as the advancing German troops, the hammer, had their first skirmish with the trapped partisan band. A wildfire crackle erupted. There was a flicker of movement at the trees' edge. The MG-34 gunner on Erich's left fired a long burst; tracers caromed from the trees. The sun arrived, on schedule, a smoldering orange rind above steaming black earth. Any minute now, they would be ordered forward. Erich drank some more.

It was too bad about so many things. More than anything else, he felt bad about the old man who'd been left in charge of the vodka distillery that had once served all the big collective farms in this district. Not knowing what else to do—having been abandoned by the local Party officials without any coherent instructions—the old fellow had simply gone on making and storing vodka. He had no family, he had insisted

when Erich's battalion had moved into the area two weeks
ago, in response to reports of increased partisan activity, and
the German soldiers were welcome to his vodka, if they would
pay him for his trouble with a little food, some cigarettes, and
permission to keep a bit of the product for his own consumption. As it happened, the communal distillery was not far from
the verminous huts where Erich's platoon had been bivouacked, so Erich had been able to visit the old man often.
Vassily, his name had been.

And it was certainly too bad about Kivikoski, the stocky
longshoreman from Turku who had been going insane for
several weeks, but nobody felt sorry for the bugger anymore.
The actual process of his dementia had probably been going
on for much longer than that, but it had only surfaced recently, when Kivikoski had suddenly started to giggle while he
was helping to bandage a wounded man. He had started to
shake with laughter so badly that he'd dropped the dressing
into the mud beside the stretcher. The giggles continued over
the next several days, erupting always at inappropriate moments, so Bergstrom had little choice but to have the battalion doctor examine the man. Acute battle fatigue, the doctor
had diagnosed—transfer him out at the earliest opportunity,
and until then watch him closely.

But the papers authorizing Kivikoski's transfer had not
come through yet, and the battalion was short-handed because of the partisan flareup, and to give him his due,
Kivikoski usually settled down when the shooting began, at
least to the extent that he still pointed his rifle in the proper
direction. Therefore, he stayed, and so Erich, as his platoon
leader, found himself saddled with at least one man who had
actually crossed over the border they were all nudging up
against. But Kivikoski's deterioration had accelerated in recent
days: two days ago, when he had started giggling during a
supposedly silent approach to what was thought to be a partisan ambush, Erich had crammed his Luger into the man's
mouth, chipping his front teeth, and told him that if he ever
laughed again during a combat situation, he would kill him.
After that, Kivikoski only giggled when it was safe to do so;

and, with the innate cunning of the truly mad, he fixated his craziness on his wife's tit.

That had happened at about the time Erich learned that the old man who ran the distillery was named Vassily. Vassily had served in the First World War, against the Austrians at Lemberg, and he still spoke a smattering of German. He was a gnarled old fellow with bright blue eyes, a long Tolstoyan beard and an inexhaustible supply of good stories and coarse peasant jokes. Erich considered him the only truly sane man for miles around, and the only times Erich himself felt halfway sane were when he was drinking vodka and swapping lies with old Vassily.

For a while after the Viking Division arrived, the partisans vanished into the woods, or into the swamps, or into the soil itself, for all anyone could tell. Rail traffic had started to flow again without interruption. There was a period of quiet, and Erich, who hated antipartisan sweeps more than any other form of combat because of their inevitable brutality and because of the suffering they always brought to the already wretched civilian population, had been able to drink with Vassily quite a lot.

But the partisans announced their renewed presence one morning by cutting the throat of a motorcycle messenger, two kilometers down the road from Bergstrom's headquarters. Next, an ammo dump was blown up, then the railroad tracks were cut again, and then, in the space of a single night, all the division's telephone lines were severed.

It was really too bad that old Vassily had turned out to be the local partisan band's chief source of intelligence, some of it gleaned from a drunken and loquacious Erich Ziegler.

Vassily's bad luck was to be found out on the afternoon following the discovery of a wire-replacement party—five heavily armed men—who had been captured by the partisans, dragged to a remote barn several kilometers from the nearest Viking Division outposts, and grotesquely tortured to death. The men's mouths had been held open by sharpened sticks and they had been force-fed horse dung until they choked to death—except for the noncom in charge, who had been hung by his feet with his own communications wire, gut-shot, and left to die. By the time Erich and the others found him, the man's head had swollen to the size of a watermelon, the skin ballooned and black with accumulated blood. The worse part was that, even after hanging that way for five hours, he was still conscious. Bergstrom himself had given the *coup de grace.*

It so happened that the strung-up sergeant had owned a very fine pocket knife, its handle made from reindeer horn, with a Lapp rune engraved on the blade. And Erich caught Vassily whittling with that knife when he came to Vassily's hut in search of oblivion, just after helping to bury the dead wire party.

Erich had been outraged beyond reason at this discovery. He had found in Vassily's company a psychic oasis where he could for a few hours lose himself in the sort of earthily philosophical dialogues he had once enjoyed in Russian novels. Vassily had seemed the personification of that long-ago Russia, so much richer in its soul than the bleak grey Stalinist entity that had replaced it. Vassily had seemed an emissary from an old and noble culture, and in talking to him, Erich had been able to remember, for a while at least, that he too had once thought of himself as the paladin of another old and noble culture. When he learned that noble old Vassily had actually been responsible for the slaughter of the wire party, Erich felt not just a sense of personal betrayal, but a vast, irrational rage that both of their cultures had been befouled.

Vassily was even tougher than he looked, and so it took a good while to get out of him any useful information about the strength and location of the partisan band. But such information had finally been wrung from old Vassily after Bergstrom poured a pint of the old man's own vodka onto his withered old crotch and touched it off with a match. Erich had been sitting on one of Vassily's legs; he remembered the sound of the patella cracking even more than he remembered the old man's screams. That, and the smell that filled the room afterward.

Most of all Erich remembered how, for just one screaming moment of righteous vindication, he had enjoyed wreaking that agony on old Vassily. Afterward, he felt that a wound had been ripped open in his soul that nothing could ever close, a wound made at least in part by his own hand. He had gotten blind staggering drunk, after they cut off Vassily's charred balls and hung him, and cried for Kylliki to make him whole again.

Before he started going crazy, Kivikoski had boasted to everyone about how amorous and well-endowed his wife was. To prove it, or at least to add color to his tales of marathon marital bliss, he had produced a tobacco pouch she had given him as a going-away present. The pouch had been crafted from the softest, supplest hide, and it was an exact replica—so he swore—of her right breast, even down to the nipple. It opened and closed with a leather drawstring and held a generous supply of tobacco. When Kivikoski started going crazy, he began to fondle the object openly, squeezing and patting it, crooning to it. Sometime during the last week, however, as Kivikoski's contact with reality grew more nebulous, he had lost the tobacco pouch. More likely, someone who was tired of watching him slobber on it had stolen the thing—as more than one man had already threatened to do. When Kivikoski realized his talisman was gone, he wept and cursed and threatened, and finally became morose and mostly silent. He told everyone who would listen that the Russian partisans had stolen it in order to undermine his morale.

Now: there was firing in the woods. The guerrillas had been driven to the very edge of the forest, and the full extent of the trap was becoming clear to them. To break from the trees was simply to offer the Finns better targets, so they dug in and resolved to sell themselves as dearly as they might.

Bergstrom was determined to keep the price of this engagement low, however. The driving battalions on the other side of the encirclement halted and withdrew a hundred meters or so, while Bergstrom's mortars and guns flailed the woods methodically. Erich ordered his platoon's machine guns to hose tracers back and forth across their front. After a twenty-minute pounding, Bergstrom orchestrated a Wagnerian finale by directing a V of Stukas to drop their bombs straight into the smoke. This time, whole trees spiraled into the air, trailing fire. After the dive-bombers had departed, the only sound was the faint crackle of flames and a few shrieks from the wounded.

"All right, let's go clean it up!" Erich was on his feet; the Bergmann cradled in his arm felt as though it weighed a hundred pounds. Black mud sucked like glue on his boots. Peripherally, as he started forward in a tense waddle, Erich could see Lieutenant Torsala booting Kivikoski to his feet, pushing him in the direction of the woods. Kivikoski moved, but slowly, carefully inspecting the ground as he walked, mumbling to himself, searching for his tobacco pouch.

Erich walked toward the flames, a man traversing an endless tunnel, with no goal ahead of him except fire and the smell, already discernible, of roasting flesh.

The music. Where was that music?

If he concentrated on the music, it would help. It always had helped, even on the day he'd helped hang old Vassily from the rafters of his own distillery. If he focused on the music, he could get through this day too. He tried to summon the sounds—the noble, heart-clutching sounds—he had heard coming from the master's study, tried to replay them in his mind, to anchor himself, if only by one thin glowing filament, to a faith that *this* was not all there was left of European civilization. If he did not soon find those elusive bars of music, and position them in his mind like a lamp flickering in the darkness of a gutted cathedral, he would soon cease to function as a man. Or even to care.

He walked the entire distance to the trees in a state of growing desperation. He could not remember a single note of the music; not one chord. All that would come into focus, swollen and mocking, as though played by an oompah band at a beer festival, was the opening motif of Beethoven's Fifth. The other music was just . . . gone. He knew he would never be able to recover it.

By the time he reached the tree line, as sporadic bursts of

fire began to chatter on either side of him, he had fallen way behind the rest of the platoon, and he was quietly, uncontrollably, weeping. The wind turned his tears to iodine against the raw skin of his cheeks.

The music was gone.

He stepped over the lip of a smoking bomb crater ringed with pulped wood, then swerved, without conscious volition, to avoid placing his foot on a blackened human torso.

Hell, there was nothing for it but to keep on walking. All the way back to Finland.

But there were some peculiar screams off to the right, where his platoon had just winkled out three guerrillas, and he was dimly cognizant that one of the screams belonged to Kivikoski and the other scream belonged to a woman.

Drawn toward the noise, he saw the bent backs of several of his men as they struggled to hold Kivikoski, and in front of them, bucking mindlessly against the smoldering earth while two white-faced soldiers tried to restrain her, was a partisan woman whose blouse hung in strips. One of her breasts was visible: a great earthy fecundating balloon of a tit, enough to suckle an ox. Where the other breast should have been, there was a flowing, serrated, crimson hole. Kivikoski, now howling like a maimed dog, was squeezing the amputated globe in his left hand, a dripping bayonet still clutched in the other, despite the efforts of two strong men to pry it from his fingers; he had finally gotten his pouch back. Someone, mercifully, shot the woman just as Erich stepped up behind Kivikoski, whose helmet had been knocked off in the scuffle, and swung the butt of his submachine gun against the howling man's skull with all his strength. The stock shattered, as did Kivikoski's head, and as the shock of the blow sang back through his arms, Erich's eyes and mind regained focus, and he began to smile.

Torsala and another man tackled him and drove him to the ground, and Torsala made sure this was the end of things by driving a hard right hook into Erich's jaw. Erich didn't really feel it, for he was already losing consciousness.

Just before he struck the earth, the music came back to him, in all its radiance and strength and purity, and he had a soft, gentle smile on his lips when they carried him, out of the trees and onto the steppe.

Nineteen

He spent a long time in a strange place where there was darkness, although he was visited sometimes by the furtive, wavering ghosts who passed in and out of his peripheral vision at regular intervals. At first, he felt surrounded by an impermeable membrane; he had a mental image of himself crouched in a cave, nurturing those precious measures of music like a primitive feeding twigs into the fire that stood between himself and the terrors of the outside night. Now and again a hand's pressure could be felt through the membrane, or something sharp would slip in—a visiting splinter—then withdraw, often leaving in its wake a sudden numbness, deeper darkness, the recession of the music into silence. At those times he would slip back into the cave, as though flowing on a subterranean river, and he would dream of white and bulbous cavefish, their eyes blind as milk. He took care not to let himself be carried too far back into the cave, however, because he knew that somewhere in the cave's deepest pit the white bear hibernated, like a dragon carved from ice, the roof of its lair fanged with marmoreal stalactites. He knew that was how the bear's cave looked because sometimes a wind would rise from some hidden source, blow through the chamber where he crouched, and blow deeper, into the bear's tellurian cavern, and it rubbed across the stalactites there and made them moan with the same bell-like timbre he had heard so long ago, while standing at the edge of the forest with an old man in a fur-trimmed hat.

Eventually the darkness grew patchy, like dissipating fog. His first conscious thought was about consciousness itself: he understood now that he was slowly spiraling up from that dark place toward full awareness, and before he made an effort to accelerate the process, he made sure that the music was safely tucked in his memory so that he would not lose it, like a misplaced handkerchief, when he came back into the light. Having made certain that the notes were safe and their progressions memorized, he took a deep breath, opened his eyes, and saw a plump nurse with pursed lips and a doctor with wire-rimmed glasses. The doctor pushed a beam of light against his eyes. Erich felt his pupils dilate, creakily like a rusted camera iris, and he turned aside, pawing feebly at the light, as though brushing at a swarm of gnats.

"Well, Nurse," he heard the doctor say, "it looks like we've got him back. Can you hear me, Captain?"

Erich felt himself nod. He gathered saliva to lubricate a question, and was astonished at the awkwardness of his own tongue. How long had it been since he had last spoken? That seemed to be an urgent question, so he attempted to phrase it aloud; he only managed to sound the first two words: "How . . . long . . ."

The doctor patted his shoulder, consulted his chart, and replied: "They brought you here on November tenth, and today is February twenty-third."

"Here," he soon learned, was a psychiatric rehabilitation center in a Victorian-era former asylum facing a tiny park on the wintry banks of the Teltow Kanal in Berlin. Once he had made the decision to let the light in, he regained his faculties with what the doctors told him was exceptional rapidity. Lieutenant Torsala had covered for him: his official records contained nothing about the fact that he had gone berserk and bashed in the skull of one of his own men—officially, he had suffered a breakdown, complicated by catatonia, due to the accumulated stress of combat duty. Every doctor who had examined him confirmed that the catatonia was deep and genuine. In view of Erich's combat record and his Iron Cross, no suggestion was ever advanced of malingering or cowardice. If he continued to make progress at his present rate, the doctor assured him, he could be discharged from the rehabilitation facility by the end of March, after which formality he had a month's leave coming.

Scarcely a week after he returned to full consciousness, Erich was permitted to leave the hospital, provided he returned before lights-out. He walked aimlessly through the streets of the capital, observing more bomb damage than he had expected, discovering in the spirits of the Berliners the first stages of the gradual pall that would grip the city tightly by the end of the year, a mood that coalesced from the ersatz coffee that tasted of bitter additives, the bread-crumb sausages that went mealy against the tongue, the rationed electricity and fuel and toilet paper, the hectoring broadcasts from loudspeakers hung at busy intersections, the sudden blade of fear that pierced the crowds at the sound of air-raid sirens.

As for himself, he considered that his obligations to the state had been discharged in full. He had been spared, but he had dwelt for a time in the darkness of those who had not been. His sole concern now was to find his way back into the light, back to music, if possible back to Sibelius, and Kylliki, and the haunted landscape of Tapiola.

He wrote a long letter to Klatt, enclosing copies of his updated service record and asking to be reassigned to light duties on the Northern Front, advancing the rationale that he would be more valuable, even in his reserve status, in a place where he was already well connected and well versed in the local conditions. In the same mail, he dispatched a letter to Kylliki, care of Professor J. Sibelius, Järvenpää.

In his mind now, as he wrote to her, the scraps of music he had fought so hard to preserve became *her* music, and to think of those tones was to think of her strong, slender arms, the violet fire within her eyes, the clean fragrance of her mouth, the rumpled flax of her armpits, the sweet musk he had savored at the junction of her thighs.

"In Russia," he wrote to Kylliki, "I learned that Death is not an absolute thing, the same everywhere. That it has degrees of hideousness and pervasiveness through which no man can pass and not be changed, not, finally, take some elixir of death into himself, in order to achieve basic animal survival. I finally had seen so much death, slept with it and tasted it and washed myself in its discharges, that my mind shut down into a coma very much like death, as though my only escape was to tunnel deeper into it in the blind, larval hope of reaching something better on the far side of the darkness.

"When I recovered and reentered the light, I was back 'home,' in Europe, in Germany, but in a world utterly and forever changed from what I knew and loved and believed in as a young man. This nation, this entire continent, is undergoing an epochal convulsion, as though our entire culture has made a Faustian pact with the most hideous devils of its own imagination.

"At first, this was deeply depressing to me, but then I began thinking about tomorrow, about how hungry the souls of the survivors will be for great music, and about my own role in bringing it to them. That is when I resolved to write you. And now my spirits feel lighter, just from writing these words. Just from anticipating writing them! I am alive, and I have been blessed by knowing you, and Tapiola, and the Master's music.

"More than ever, I feel rededicated to my art. Strong enough, clear enough of mind, to pursue my ideals with a force of will I might never have achieved if all this had not happened to me. I will live and eventually triumph; this war will end, and the future will belong to me. And to you, if you will share it with me. The memory of you helped me stay alive; longing for you helped bring me back to consciousness. Princess of the forest, I love you, and I will come back to you soon, if I have to walk and swim to get there."

The doctors had warned Erich against inevitable bouts of depression and self-pity which, they promised, would recur in conjunction with his nightmares of the Russian Front. But Erich found himself able to handle those evil memories, able to reconcile them to the sweeter dreams of Tapiola. His spirits soared even higher after he mailed his letter. A new man, a new artist, seemed to be rising, strong and refined, from the compost of the culture he saw dying all around him. He felt within him the clarity, the vision, of a fire-tempered Parsifal, emerging, bright with purpose, from the ruins of a civilization devouring itself.

One morning in mid-March, as he was walking down the Charlottenburger Chaussee, he spied a public notice, freshly posted, advertising a concert by Furtwängler and the Berlin Philharmonic. In addition to a Beethoven overture and the Bruckner Ninth, the program featured the tone poem *En Saga* by Jean Sibelius. Erich obtained a ticket and signed out of the hospital on the night in question.

The concert's highlight was, predictably, the Bruckner symphony, which under Furtwängler's inspired baton was both monumental and radiant. As the last seraphic string chords of adagio died away, a beribboned deputy *Gauleiter* sitting next to Erich turned with a beatific smile and sighed: "What music! It helps you to understand what we're fighting for!" "Indeed," Erich replied, with a tight nod, wondering what possible connection existed between National Socialism and the naive Catholic mysticism of Anton Bruckner.

The Sibelius performance he found compelling, but not very idiomatic. Furtwängler indulged in his wonted love of deliberate tempos to such a degree that the music became almost static, its development proceeding at a glacial pace. Just when Erich was about to lose patience with it, he realized that Furtwängler was imperceptibly tightening the screws so that, suddenly, the music no longer sounded slow. Erich could detect the seeds of the climax quite early on, and was impressed by the way Furtwängler prepared the ground for it many bars in advance. When it came, it was invested with a sense of elemental power that had a flattening effect on the listener. Erich's own interpretation would have been different, he was sure—he would have invested the work's earlier pages with greater color, highlighted more details, imparted a *chiaroscuro* effect in places where Furtwängler had worked in gritty monochrome—but there was no denying the force of the other conductor's approach, and it at least indicated a serious study of Sibelius's work. Erich wondered what a conductor of Furtwängler's stature might give for the chance to conduct the world premiere of the Eighth Symphony, and at the conclusion of the concert, he resolved to go backstage and ask him.

Ten years had passed since Furtwängler had come backstage, in an act, surely, of *noblesse oblige*, to congratulate Erich on his modest triumph in Frankfurt; and the Bremen post that Furtwängler had helped him obtain, Erich had lost through his own immaturity. He had no idea what sort of response he would get when he presented a note to an usher at the entrance to the conductor's dressing room, but a few minutes later he was invited to come in. Furtwängler rose from his chair, a tall gangling figure with an immense scholarly dome of a forehead, piercing eyes under sad, heavy brows, and long pale hands.

"Ah, Ziegler. I do remember you from . . . Frankfurt, was it not? How kind of you to come hear my concert. From your decorations, it looks as though you've been in the thick of things at the front. I've lost half the best players in Berlin to the draft. I'm glad you still have a full complement of arms and legs—basic equipment for our profession. Tell me, then, are you home on leave?"

"I've been in hospital, Maestro. I've been placed on reserve status now; I think my days at the front are over."

"Good. You've obviously done your share, and someone must survive to carry the torch when all this horror has passed . . . as it must, eventually."

Good, thought Erich. At least we are of like minds in that regard.

"I don't wish to take up much of your time, sir, but I wanted very much to ask you a few professional questions. You see, I was stationed in Finland, on the Karelian Front, and quite by chance I found myself in the position of becoming a confidant of Sibelius. When I saw one of his works on your program tonight, I . . ."

"Come, Ziegler, not here. Let's go back to my flat and discuss this over brandy like civilized men. I'd be interested in hearing about your experiences."

Erich decided to be very selective in that regard.

As they left the taxi, in front of Furtwängler's flat on the Kurfürstendamm, Erich caught sight of two men in leather coats loitering half a block from the entrance. As he walked by them, Furtwängler muttered: "Bastards!"

"Who were they?" asked Erich as they rode up in the creaking elevator.

"Gestapo men. They are never far away. They're afraid I'll try to sneak out of the country."

"I beg your pardon, sir, but if you don't mind my asking, why didn't you leave earlier, before things got so bad?"

Furtwängler held the elevator door for Erich and fumbled with his keys. Up close, he seemed much older than Erich had remembered; there was a vast accumulation of weariness in his eyes, and his shoulders slumped.

"I believed that somebody had to stay and conduct great music, without the taint of ideology. Somebody who could remind the German people of all the good and noble things they had given to the world, before the madmen came to power. I believed that great art might serve to counterbalance an ideology. I was very naive."

"Surely you could still leave, if you planned it carefully. With all the contacts you have in high places, in the outside world—Switzerland, perhaps."

"Yes, of course, I could leave . . . alone. But what about the rest of my family? I have a friend in Goebbels's headquarters, a man who sometimes passes information that is useful. He has informed me that there is a standing arrest warrant, already filled out, for my mother, my sister, several other family members. It will go into effect as soon as the Gestapo learns I have disappeared. If it were not for that, I would go . . . I have done all I can here."

There was much beneath the surface of that statement.

Erich had heard rumors that Furtwängler had used his international connections liberally and bravely to assist Jewish musicians, the obscure as well as the famous, to flee the Reich and find employment in the orchestras of neutral or even hostile countries. To Himmler, these actions were treasonable enough to warrant the great conductor's arrest and detention; the Reichsführer was blocked, however, by his archrival Goebbels, who found Furtwängler and his orchestra useful propaganda tools. By taking a civilized stand, Furtwängler had immured himself, willy-nilly, within the machinations of the regime; the Nazi authorities would not let him go because he had defied them and made no secret of his contempt for them; and the Allies, if they should win, would never forgive him for staying in Germany.

Over brandy, Erich sketched the details of his encounters with Sibelius, then went to the piano and played, without identifying it, the fragment of music he had been carrying in his mind for so many months.

"That was extraordinarily beautiful and pregnant with possibility. If developed in an original manner, it could be the germ of a great work."

"I have good reason to believe that it is an excerpt from the Eighth Symphony of Sibelius."

"Then his place in the pantheon of great composers is guaranteed. I should very much like to hear the rest of it."

"So would I, but that's all I know. I don't know how much of it is finished, or even written down, I don't know if it's scored, or how many movements it has. Whatever shape it's in, the old man guards it fiercely. He will not tolerate direct questions about it, nor is he prepared to release it for public performance. He's become something of a recluse, sustained by his ego and a large amount of brandy, and he fears that the work would not live up to the expectations of all those who've been speculating about it for so long. And yet, I believe it was intentional that I should hear this fragment of it, and I believe it is possible that he has thought of entrusting the first performance to me." Erich realized the immodesty of that statement; ten years ago, he would have been too much in awe of

Furtwängler to have dared it. Now he knew better: no one who had reached this man's position of eminence could have done so without plenty of ambition and the ego to fuel it. We do not have to pretend sainthood to one another, he thought; in that, at least, we are on equal footing.

Furtwängler gazed at Erich with new interest. "In that case, young man, your future is assured. People have been writing about that piece for years, and any conductor you could name—Beecham, Stokowski, Mengelberg, even myself!—would stop at nothing to obtain the rights to that first performance. It would make front-page news all over the world, and the recording companies would be lined up outside your door the next morning, waving contracts and buckets full of money."

A half hour later, as Ziegler was rising to take his leave, he felt a bulge in his coat pocket, reminding him. He withdrew a pocket score of the Fourth Symphony and thrust it at Furtwängler, stammering as he did so: "Maestro, I do need your advice about one thing, quite specific. There's a place in this score which calls for the tubular bells . . . here"—Erich pointed at the *Glocken* part in the last movement—"but the composer actually had in mind something for which I've been unable to locate an exact instrumental equivalent, a particularly cold and desolate timbre. He demonstrated it to me once by taking me out into the forest and standing in a spot where it was possible to hear the wind blowing through pendants of ice. It had something of the timbre of a low wooden flute, yet it was more metallic, almost glassy in its overtones, and still somewhat percussive. As you see, I'm having a hard time describing it even now. What he seems precisely to have had in mind is an instrument which simply doesn't exist. I believe it would please him immensely if I could somehow commission such an instrument and present it to him. It would be a way to repay his kindness to me, and it would show how hard I've tried to understand what he was striving for."

"And, not so coincidentally, it would also demonstrate that you are indeed the right man to be entrusted with the world premiere of his Eighth Symphony . . ." The smile on the conductor's face was not unkind. He waved aside Erich's protestations.

"Herr Ziegler, I meant no insult. Your motives are no more mixed than any other man's might be. And I cannot imagine any composer who would not be flattered and touched by such an offering. But to create what amounts to an entirely new percussion instrument, one for which only a single orchestral part exists, that is a very expensive and delicate undertaking, and if you don't mind my saying so, a rather quixotic one."

"If I can find a firm, or an artisan, to create such a set of chimes, I'll not be concerned about expense—my family is well off and there are financial resources I can draw on. What I need from you, sir, is the name of that firm, or that craftsman; no man in Germany knows more about such matters than you."

Furtwängler took a notepad from beside his telephone and wrote an address on the topmost sheet.

"There is only one man in Berlin who could produce a set of bells to match your rather metaphysical description—the man who lives at this address: Solomon Hurwitz. Tell him that I have sent you, and he may let you in."

"But Maestro . . . isn't that a Jewish name?"

Furtwängler sighed. "Are you familiar with the special bells that Wagner had constructed for *Parsifal*?"

"Why, yes. I attended a performance at Bayreuth about fifteen years ago. The sound sent chills down my spine."

"Indeed. Well, old Hurwitz is one of the two or three men in all Germany who could recast those bells if anything should happen to the originals—a stray bomb, for instance, or a crashing aircraft. He is, so to speak, being kept in reserve in case his skills are ever needed—on direct orders from Goebbels. He lives in an old warehouse that contains his workshop and his collection of percussion instruments—many of them museum quality, I might add. He is the greatest campanologist in Europe—no man living knows more about bells and chimes and cymbals than he does. It's true that he lives under what amounts to house arrest—even his food is brought to him, I understand—but as long as Wagner's bells are considered a national treasure, he is probably safe enough. There are more exceptions made in these matters than the public can possibly imagine."

The address was on Köpenickerstrasse, in a run-down section of old factory buildings and warehouses about two kilometers east of the Chancellery. In a seedy vacant lot across the street stood a huge concrete flak tower mounting two 88-mm guns. The warehouse in question turned out to be a shuttered building whose blacked-out windows yielded no sign of habitation. Erich knocked hesitantly, waited in silence, then knocked again, more loudly. From within came a faint scrabbling, as though from mice. A pale, thin boy of eleven or twelve opened the door a crack. Erich felt chilled air rush out against his face—the building's own breath. Erich asked for Herr Hurwitz, carefully emphasizing that he had been sent by Maestro Furtwängler. The boy, cuffing miserably at a runny nose, glanced outside to make sure no one had followed Erich, then motioned him inside. As the boy scurried off into darkness, Erich stood alone in stale-smelling shadows, sensing around him the particular desolation of a deserted factory. After a few moments, a door in the far wall opened, outlined by a thin rectangle of light, and the boy leaned through, motioning for Erich to follow.

The room he entered might once have been the cutting room of a garment factory—smooth-worn tables were visible, and dusty wooden shelves, dimly outlined under banks of porcelain light fixtures, only two of which contained working bulbs. The room shimmered, however, with highlights that seemed to come from the surfaces of old coins: crescents and cylinders and moons of gold and silver, platinum, and bronze. Scattered randomly about this vast and shadowy chamber were all the metallic percussion instruments known to modern music: tubular bells, plate-bells, mushroom bells, bells of silver and iron, brass and steel; xylophones, glockenspiels, delicate suspended cymbals, platter-sized hand cymbals, exotic finger-cymbals, sleighbells, a dozen diameters of gong, and in a dusty corner all by itself, like something looted from a pagan throne room, a huge ceremonial tam-tam of coil-wound brass.

In other dim recesses of the room, beyond the ranks of instruments, Erich could see laboratory instruments, furnaces, forges, molds stacked up like blocks of cubist sculpture, files and mallets and hammers and quenching tubs, asbestos gloves and goggles, tongs and face shields and vats of sand. And in the center of this array, shadowed between the instruments and the workshop beyond, hunched and white-haired, wary yet as proud as an alchemist showing his laboratory to a king, stood Hurwitz, former percussionist of the Berlin Philharmonic Orchestra.

"My name is Erich Ziegler, and I was sent here by Maestro Furtwängler."

"So my grandson told me. If the Maestro sent you here, then you could not have come to arrest me. Unless, of course, he too has been arrested."

"He is well and free and sends his respects to you. As for myself, I have come to give you a commission, one for which I will pay you handsomely. I am a friend of the composer Jean Sibelius, and I want to present him with a special set of tubular chimes, to be used only in his Fourth Symphony."

Erich felt, momentarily, as though he were talking with a creature who was not quite real, who dwelt in an urban cavern, in a state somewhere between life and death. Somewhere inside, he felt pity for this man, who after all, would have been a valued colleague under prewar circumstances. But to feel pity for Hurwitz would have deflected him from his purpose, and he was fixed upon that purpose as the subtlest masterstroke of his plan for the future. Besides, he could do nothing to help this little man except pay him for the chance to exercise his skills. A fair enough exchange, Erich decided.

"I see. Just as the bells at Bayreuth are only used for *Parsifal*."

It seemed to Erich that the old Jew was smiling at the ironies that had spared him.

"Yes. The part as it stands now is sometimes played on the conventional bell set, sometimes on the glockenspiel, but the composer is not happy with either sound, and unfortunately there really is no alternative. The instrument he had in his mind simply does not exist."

"Show me the music. And tell me 'what he really had in mind.' "

Erich told the story of his walk in the forest, of the composer's explanation of the timbre he had wanted, of the cold and inhuman sound of the wind stroking the ice. He held the score open to the relevant pages. When he had finished, Hurwitz laughed quietly, without a trace of warmth, then recited, in mocking tones, a scrap of verse: " 'Pale tunes irresolute, and traceries of old sounds, blown from a rotted flute, mingle with the noise of cymbals rouged with rust . . .' "

"I beg your pardon?"

"Lines from an English poet named Enoch Soames. They describe, I think, the qualities you seek to incorporate into these bells. Something inimical to the very fact of human existence—a timbre that knows cold, and even death. Not a red and howling death, but a pale, white, silent death. A tone that floats in an emptiness of polished ice. Am I close?"

In answer, Erich pressed the score into the old man's hands. He shivered from the chill in this big, strange room.

"Can you make such an instrument for me, Hurwitz? Yes or no!"

"I can. It will not be easy, however, and it will take time. You see, any fool can learn to cast. The formulae are written down and if you follow them—three-fourths copper to one-fourth tin and so on—you obtain a decent enough, if rather ordinary, bell. But shades of timbral color, ah, those are a matter of instinct, insight, artistry. Like a master chef, one must know what additives to use: a dash of zinc, a pinch of silver, a *soupçon* of platinum. It will take some weeks to work out the exact recipe, make some experimental castings. And it will be costly."

Hurwitz named a large sum of money.

"That is indeed expensive, although not beyond my means. Which ingredient will cost so much?"

"None. That is the price of the bribes that will be necessary to smuggle my grandson into Switzerland."

"I was given to understand by Furtwängler that you were safe."

"For the moment perhaps. But now that the war is starting to go against them, the ideologues will grow more dogmatic, more vengeful. It is inevitable. I am an old man, and I have enjoyed a life full of music; what happens to me is of small consequence. But my grandson deserves something better than hiding in this dank hole, waiting for the door to be kicked in."

As if in counterpoint to Hurwitz's words, the air-raid sirens of Berlin began to wail. The emaciated boy started to whimper. He ran to the old man and clutched at his legs. Distantly, flak batteries began to hammer.

"Here's a down payment, in case you need to purchase anything right away. I'll bring the rest, in cash, when I return from leave. In four weeks, shall we say?"

"Very well. Oh, there is one thing I need even to start. Brass. Brass of a fairly high degree of metallurgical purity. For the actual chimes, only a few pounds of it, but for the experimental castings, who knows? As you can imagine, brass is not so easy to come by in these times."

"I'll do what I can," said Erich.

Outside, part of the city was already on fire. The Lancasters were concentrating their tonnage around Tempelhof Airport. Searchlight beams wove a blinding tartan on the clouds. Like flickering ghosts, the outlines of airplanes stood out in naked relief, then melted into vapor. The ground slammed into Erich's feet, bucking and humping as concentric blast rings rippled out from the center of the targeted area. Suddenly, the twin 88s on the flak tower across the street opened fire, shatteringly loud. Erich stood for a moment watching the golden shafts of the searchlights spin, trying to pin the aircraft against the night. The gun crews across the street were visible only as tiny scuttling figures, ridiculously top-heavy in their helmets, frantically pushing shells into their guns, then bending away from the recoiling tubes, hands over their ears.

From the tower's top, a canvas chute ran down the side of the column and opened above a pit dug at the base. Empty shell casings rolled down the chute and tumbled into the hole below, where they could be collected in the morning and recycled with new warheads. From where Erich stood, it looked as though the tower were excreting an endless series of glittering turds.

The magic of a thing, Kylliki had told him, came from its origins.

Like a sleepwalker, Erich crossed the street, oblivious to the tinny patter of shrapnel falling on the pavement. Wincing against the heat from the still-warm casings, he bent over the edge of the shell pit and scooped up all that he could carry in both arms. Tottering against the concussion waves that rolled through the ground as the bombing got closer, dimly aware of the rising shriek and thunder of the raiders passing directly overhead, Erich ran back to the entrance of Hurwitz's lair and banged loudly on the outer door. When the trembling child opened it, Erich dumped the cordite-reeking cylinders inside.

"Tell your grandfather that I have brought him brass."

Four weeks later, when Erich returned from Mannheim with an envelope full of cash, the door to the old factory was opened by a bespectacled young man in a civilian Party uniform.

"Where is the bell-maker?" Erich demanded.

"The old Jew? Gone, along with his snot-nosed brat."

"Gone where?"

"I'm sure I don't know, Captain. I was ordered to take over his laboratory and the instrument collection. I am a fully qualified campanologist and a loyal Party member. There is no reason why an old Yid should continue in this position when there are fully qualified Aryan Germans who can do the same work."

"Damn it, man, I'm sure you're fully qualified, but I had left a commission for Herr Hurwitz—a special set of tubular bells. Do you know what the status of that project might be?"

"Oh, you are Ziegler? Then come in—old Hurwitz left a package for you and a full set of instructions for his successor.

I'll have no trouble casting those bells for you, if that's what you're worried about—although some of the ingredients do seem a little odd to me. I can have the final castings done in a month, then send them to you through official channels. You are connected with the Philharmonic, I believe?"

"This project has the approval of both Maestro Furtwängler and the Ministry of Propaganda. When the instruments have been completed, please send them to the Helsinki Philharmonic, by the safest means possible, care of this address. I may be there to accept delivery, but if I am not, I will have made arrangements. The money in this envelope should cover all expenses as well as compensate you personally for your work."

"This is a most generous sum, Captain. Rest assured, the instruments will be cast exactly as you wish."

"Exactly as Hurwitz specified. Not the slightest deviation."

"Of course. Now, if you'll come this way, I'll find that packet he left for you."

The factory's interior was even more bleak and depressing in daylight than it had been by night. Many of the instruments had already been shrouded in dust sheets or packed in crates. Some would probably go back into service with various orchestras, but the most valuable ones, such as the antique cymbals or the great Burmese tam-tam, would probably end up as decorations in the parlor of some well-connected Party official.

Inside the packet was a small glass vial, stoppered with cork, containing a smoke-colored powder and a barely decipherable note addressed to Erich.

"I have used up two thousand marks to make sure that this gets to you. I believe the formula I worked out for your commission will produce the instrument you desire, provided my successor, whoever he is, follows my instructions to the letter. As the final step in the process, he should add the contents of the enclosed vial. What's in there is not absolutely necessary to the formula, but it would please me greatly if this request could be granted."

There was no signature. Erich studied the formula and tapped his finger near the bottom of the page. He turned the vial over and over in his hand, unstopped it, took a pinch of the contents on his finger, rubbed, then cautiously sniffed at the grey smear of powder.

"Here. Just before the final casting, while the mixture is still molten, you are to add the contents of this bottle."

"If that is your wish, Captain, although it seems rather whimsical. Is this some sort of secret ingredient the old Jew came up with?"

"No," said Erich, placing the small container in the man's outstretched palm, "it seems to be rather more ordinary than that. Unless I'm mistaken, it is only a handful of ashes."

Twenty

Stripped to the waist, trousers rolled to his knees, Erich waded into the lake; cool bottom mud oozed up between his remaining toes. Against the coppery glare of the day's heat, the water was as pleasant to the touch as its pale olive color was to the eye. At the other end of the seine net, Rautavaara, blowing and snorting like a ruddy-skinned water horse, waved a cigarette in the direction of a current he claimed to have felt under water. Erich shifted his stance so that the net's open throat lined up as Rautavaara indicated. Almost instantly he felt the underwater tug of fish running into the submerged cords. With a yowl of triumph, Rautavaara hoisted his end of the net. Erich followed suit, clumsily, and then the two men waded back to shore, the writhing sack dangling between their dripping torsos.

Their arrival was greeted with exclamations from Anna-Liisa and Kylliki, and with a burst of applause from Sibelius and his wife, who stood some distance away, supervising the efforts of two of Rautavaara's men, who were erecting a string of tepee-shaped woodpiles along the shoreline.

As Erich knelt with his load of wriggling *muikku*—small, tasty, sardine-like fish—Kylliki leaned over and kissed a drop of lakewater from his nose.

"That's it, girl! Kiss the fisherman, for he brings your dinner!" boomed Rautavaara.

"Not for another two hours, he doesn't," remonstrated Anna-Liisa, reaching into the seine net and skillfully nabbing a fish. Taking a short, curved blade, she deftly gutted it, scooped it clean, reached in for another. Kylliki, meanwhile, was adding salt, onion rings, and a fistful of herbs to a big iron pot simmering over a rock fireplace. The fish were dumped into the pot only moments dead; the lid clanged down after a few vigorous turns of the spoon. After two hours of simmering, the main course of "lake fish" would be ready: the contents of the pot would have turned into a rich, salty soup, ready to be eaten with wedges of buttered rye bread.

It was Midsummer's Eve. Later on, after midnight, the sun would dip briefly below the horizon, but it would never really get dark. In Tapiola, the holiday would be observed as though the war did not exist. A plume of fragrant smoke extended from the sauna hut far out into the lake, where the sun had turned the water to polished brass. Plates, linen, silver, and glassware stood arrayed in front of picnic baskets; on a trestle table at the foot of the dock, an old wind-up phonograph played a scratchy tango, its notes echoing over the water. The groove-worn sound of accordions, dipping and stretching in sensual tango time, seemed to Erich both sweet and plaintive, in keeping with the way the Finns sought to wrest from this day of maximum sunlight all the urgent gaiety they possibly could.

Kylliki placed a rough linen towel across his glittering shoulders. Rautavaara, radiating outdoorsy vigor, squatted nearby and offered Erich a cigarette. The two men smoked while the sun dried their hair and shoulders. Overhead, light poured through the birch leaves, turning them into lemon drops. A sharp, higher light jumped at them from the water, and where it touched the grasses at the shore, it turned even those mundane weeds into glowing fields of grain.

In a small meadow behind the sauna hut, between two stands of white-armed birches topped with rattling doubloons,

Jean Sibelius—eyes bright and a fresh cigar clamped in one hand—daintily led his wife in a dance.

Erich watched them as they moved with the stately delicacy of the old, retracing a pagan gesture as ancient as civilization itself. Because of the angle, it seemed that the silky white plume from the sauna chimney was unwinding from Sibelius's head—he had doffed his hat to Aino and the great bald skull gleamed like a pumpkin—and before the illusion was destroyed by movement, it was made even more picturesque by the appearance, seemingly from within the smoke itself but actually from behind it, of two majestic ivory cranes. They glided low over the lake as though smitten with their own reflections, then vanished into the vortex of light that blurred all details of the westward landscape.

Suddenly, Erich felt an almost physical lurch of dislocation: the contrasts were too much to assimilate in the time he had been given. He had thought all this was lost to him forever, had begun to regard his days at Tapiola almost as perfervid dreams heightened by stress. It should have been impossible to find a chamber in his heart where this place could be reconciled with the things he had seen (and done, he reminded himself; and done) in Russia. Only a day's drive from where he sat joyously in the sun was the Eastern Front. There was no denying its reality, or the reality of the contesting armies who manned that line, locked in vast convulsions of blood and destruction. While packing for his furlough to Munich, Erich had resolved that, while he would fight again to protect Finland and what he had found there, he would never go back to Russia, not even if it meant a firing squad. And yet a single, seemingly magical summons from this world had been enough to pluck him from the grasp of the immense and implacable horror of the Eastern Front and deposit him here.

He had been sitting, bored, in his Uncle Rudolf's living room in Munich, at the end of May, having days ago exhausted his reserves of familial small talk. He had finally gotten it across to his uncle that, if he were pushed any harder to talk about his "experiences in Russia," he would, and Rudolf would not care to hear much of it.

Conditions in his beloved Munich, both physical and psychological, were only marginally more cheerful than he had found them in grim, bomb-pounded Berlin. His friends from university days were scattered to the far corners of the Reich, and a few dreary afternoons drinking ersatz coffee with old professors had exhausted the recreational possibilities of that activity. The faces of people he had known all his life as prosperous and well fed now displayed a pinched, withdrawn, low-grade misery; and in the first week he was home, he had spent three nights huddled in a fetid, airless bomb shelter while the Wellingtons methodically pounded a number of second-rate industrial targets on the outskirts of town.

Klatt's telegram came with all the unexpected impact of divine intervention. Whatever power struggle there had been behind the scenes, the odious Schleicher seemed to have disappeared from the picture. Erich was to resume his former duties in Finland, within thirty days of receipt of the telegram. The request had been approved by "the highest Finnish authorities." Sibelius must have been as good as his word; his entreaties had filtered up from the highest civilian levels in Helsinki to Mannerheim's own staff, if not to the marshal himself. Trying to read between the lines, Erich wondered which masters he would be serving, then decided that it didn't really matter, as long as he was going back.

He went out that same afternoon and had his travel orders cut. It required nearly all of the allotted thirty days to make the trip back to Finland. Bomb damage added days to the rail trip from Mannheim to Danzig, where he waited another four days until his ship could fall in with a slow-moving Baltic convoy. He arrived in Turku harbor with only a few days' grace remaining, and he had arrived here, at Tapiola, quite late on the night before Midsummer's Eve. Too late to meet Kylliki. Rautavaara, not altogether surprised to see him, had bunked him for the night with the security troops.

Now that Erich was actually here, he felt considerable anxiety. Had he presumed too much in writing that letter to

Kylliki? What if her interest in him now was really no different from what his interest in her had been originally? What if she regarded him merely as an interesting and exotic lover, not the potential lifetime companion she had become in his imagination?

As he tossed restlessly in his bunk, assailed by the snores of Rautavaara's men, he was startled to discover that his heart could still be so vulnerable. He could not afford such a weakness, not with all that he had at stake now. He resolved to firm up his emotions, so that, whatever Kylliki's response, he might remain the master of his own destiny.

Of course he could live without her. He could convince himself that she was provincial, an impractical choice for the worldly career he envisioned. There were many equally beautiful women, and after he had enjoyed his fill of them, the memory of this wartime interlude would no doubt fade into nothing more than pleasant nostalgia, just another war story.

But in his newfound mood of cresting self-confidence, he did not want those other, hypothetical women. He wanted Kylliki, his dryad, Tapio's svelte daughter, the forest god's radiant handmaiden. He had journeyed deep into her forest world in search of her elusive spirit, and the thought of being able to bring her out of that primitive world, into the swirl and dazzle of the life he intended to lead, made him feel like a proud conquistador sailing back aboard a galleon, a chest of plundered gold heavy on his shoulder.

At dawn he had rowed out to the sisters' island, and he was waiting, in the boat, when they opened their cabin door and emerged, talking brightly in the fine-spun light of the summer morning. When Kylliki saw him, she stopped, her mouth rounded in mid-syllable. Then she ran to him—taller and even more graceful than he had remembered—and then his hands were thrusting into the shadows of her hair and his nostrils were drinking her scent in long, parched inhalations. The tips of her breasts grew hard beneath the homespun blouse she wore. She repeated his name over and over again.

He had not misread her heart after all. Her embrace wove

about him the very spell he had longed for during all those bitter, brutal months in Russia.

He rowed them to the mainland, took breakfast with them in the kitchen, tasted coffee on Kylliki's kiss. When Sibelius appeared, he embraced Erich warmly; Aino, too, gave him a motherly hug. Finally, there in the kitchen of Tapiola, he felt the embrace of true homecoming.

The day was given over to decorating the lodge and parts of the lakeshore for the evening's festivities. The doors were wreathed with boughs and bundles of meadow flowers. Erich helped Rautavaara and his men drag wood from the forest to the shore and stack it into six pyramids for the bonfires that would be kindled at midnight. Aino and the servants baked bread, boiled potatoes, sliced vegetables, and prepared the sauna hut for daylong occupancy. Sibelius supervised, his widest felt brimmed hat pulled over at a rakish angle, pointing out things to be done with the tip of his walking stick, sometimes puttering by himself amid the trees near the lake, glancing and reglancing at the sky, water, trees, the alabaster icons of cranes above the hot gold-green of the islands, as though reaffirming to himself a whole inventory of things. Observing all this to-ing and fro-ing, Anna-Liisa shook her head with a sad smile and said: "How he wishes he could have all the family here—the grandchildren, the nephews, some of his colleagues from the city. Midsummer was always one of his favorite times."

"I'll bet he did some courting on this night, when he was a young fellow," Erich remarked, settling the heavy water-filled kettle on the bed of stones the two women had constructed. Anna-Liisa's smile grew more distant and there were shadows in her eyes as she squinted up at Erich.

"Why yes, Captain, I believe he did."

"I'll tease him about it later."

"Please don't do that," Anna-Liisa said, more soberly yet. "The memories may be both sadder and much closer to the surface than his age would lead you to expect. Besides"—her voice, her expression, her bearing itself, changed from one sentence to the next—"Besides, no one can be held accountable for what happens on Midsummer's Eve, can he? Things happen that are not supposed to be able to happen, and things are visible that supposedly cannot be seen."

Was she teasing him, proffering some sort of riddle, or admonishing him in some indirect fashion? Erich decided to let the remark pass at face value. For him, the day was already magical, and he wanted nothing more than to surrender utterly to its spell.

By late afternoon, the preparations were complete. Two rowboats bobbed close to shore, their bows garlanded with leaves. The cooking pot gave off steam. Rautavaara and Erich went into the lake with the seine net. The lake fish went into the pot. The drinking began.

As reluctant as Erich was to leave Kylliki's side, he felt it only polite to spend as much time with Sibelius as the composer wished him to spend. Not long after the fish were caught, Sibelius indicated his desire for a boat ride on the lake. Erich and Rautavaara pulled one of the boats well up on to the bank, so that the composer did not have to remove his shoes to step inside, then Erich took the oars, Rautavaara shoved mightily, and the boat wobbled into open water. They drifted along meandering channels between dense stands of golden reeds. Sibelius remained silent for a while, studying every detail of the people and objects on the shoreline, as though seeing them for the first time. He had brought a small bottle of *aquavit* and a pair of glasses. When the boat reached a spot halfway between the mainland and the sisters' island, the composer handed Erich a measure of liquor and a fresh cigar.

"Were things as bad in Russia as I have heard?"

"Whatever you've heard, Maestro, they were worse."

"You didn't belong there. You belong here, with us, in the forest. I'm sorry it took so long to get you back, but I had to try higher and higher levels of authority before I could break through to anyone with either the power or the inclination to help. Your Finnish SS battalion, by the way, is being disbanded, or so the major tells me. Mannerheim has ordered its men back to Finland, fearing that he may soon have need of them. With the war going as badly as it is for the Germans, sooner or later the Reds will turn their serious attention to us, the enduring nuisance on their northern flank. When that time comes, we'll need every man. Perhaps if we resist stoutly enough, they'll stop short of overrunning the entire country. Well . . . one way or the other, the war will end. Curious, isn't it, that on this day we celebrate another, far older war."

"What war is that?"

"The one between light and darkness. Our pagan ancestors started the tradition of midsummer bonfires in order to help the sun to stay aloft longer, to delay the coming of winter—a bit of sympathetic magic, eh? In some countries, so I've read, they went a step further and threw humans into the fires for good measure. When the Christians came into power, that sort of thing stopped, of course; they kept the festival but they renamed it for Saint John. No matter: it's still shamelessly pagan at heart."

"You seem to be enjoying this even more than Christmas. Did you ever try to write some music to go along with it?"

"What, and try to beat Mendelssohn at what he did best?" The composer laughed. "No, I'm afraid he's already said the last word on the subject. Although, to tell you the truth, I did make some sketches one night, right here, when I was quite young. I kept them, they grew seasoned, as did I, and in time they reemerged. Care to venture a guess as to the venue of their ultimate flowering?"

"As I look around me at the moment, I am irresistibly reminded of the Sixth Symphony . . ."

"Correct! You win another drink." They touched cups. Water pattered in slow fat golden drops from the blades of Erich's oars. Mirrored clouds sailed the depths of the lake. Floating from the shore came opaline trills of music—Kylliki had begun to strum her *kantele*, this time in a gay and winsome tune, and Rautavaara and one of his corporals were singing lustily.

"It's funny, Ziegler, but we have no real pantheon of deities anywhere in our myths, only a sort of anarchic individualism—very Finnish. Sometimes it's hard to tell who's a divinity and who's just a randy roughneck out for a good time. Our gods and goddesses form no big, quarrelsome, humanized family, either, as was the case with the Greeks, the Romans, even the Norse. In our myths, all the characters' relationships are just as messy and ambiguous as they are in real life. The heroes and heroines are mosaics of human and elemental qualities—even the good characters show meanness and troublesome shortcomings, while the sinister characters sometimes exhibit decent, even gentle, behavior. Lemminkäinen, for instance, was indeed a poet, a scholar, and a magician; but he was also a rustic lout and an utterly indiscriminate cocksman.

"Tell me, Erich, do you believe that every aspect of nature has its own indwelling spirit, its *genius loci*?"

"Yes, I do, Maestro. How could it not be? Many years ago, in the Bavarian mountains, I learned that certain places have a special feeling of power to them, as though the skin that separates this world from other, grander or more mysterious worlds, becomes thin enough to see through—even if it's only for a moment, only a glimpse. I'm certainly not surprised to feel the same way here in the forest."

"In our myths," continued Sibelius, "it's as though all of life—human, animal, vegetable, all!—were caught up in a gigantic dance, the pattern of which is elegant and symmetrical in its vaster dimensions, but swirling, chaotic, atomistic in its details. The relative strengths and influences of men and nature may wax and wane, from one place and one circumstance to another, yet there's still a rough, shaggy harmony being played underneath it all. And it's all connected. Even Tuonela, the place we have instead of Hell, is not a domain of eternal punishments and howling torments; it's merely the lowest level of the forest's consciousness, a place of darkness and low despair. And I believe that I saw it once."

Erich leaned forward, for the composer's voice had dropped. The alcohol had evidently opened another door for him, and he was going through. Perhaps this was why he drank as he did.

"It was on such a night as this one promises to be. The

woman I had found in the forest led me to a strange and beautiful land that night, after we had pledged to one another by leaping together through the flames at midnight. Overwhelmed by it all, and more than a little bit drunk, I confess, I somehow became separated from her. I wandered off into the forest, alone and disoriented. I regained full awareness only when I came to the shores of a black river, where a cold and heavy wind blew from a land I could not see on the far shore, a wind that smelled of ashes and old bones. I became afraid, because I knew I was near a place of the dead, and I was a young, hot-blooded man, not a corpse. The only human who supposedly had been to Tuonela while still alive was old Lemminkäinen, after all. But just as I was giving way to panic, I heard the woman's voice, calling for me, and I followed it until, after what seemed a long time, I once more came within sight of the bonfires. I babbled to her that I had seen Tuonela, and instead of laughing at me for a drunkard, she touched my face with her long pale hands and told me that I had been allowed to see it because I, in my own way, would be a hero as great as Lemminkäinen. How my heart swelled within me, Erich! And in a way, she was right, because from that night on, there was a flood of music welling inside me."

Erich remembered his own hallucination after the runesinging, but thought better of mentioning it, for he could now see tears on the composer's cheeks. The old man's flesh seemed to go slack and jowly and the thin, peremptory mouth trembled.

"Do you really believe that something like that is going to happen to me?"

"I believe it is already happening." The old man's expression suddenly became fierce, penetrating. "Don't you?"

"Yes," Erich whispered, spellbound by the way Sibelius's eyes suddenly seemed liberated from age, so that his gaze, at least, became once again the proud, headstrong eagle's glance it had been in his youth.

"It has started for you the way it started for me! But you must not let it end as it ended for me! You must have enough faith to choose a different path and stay on it. Take your woman's hand tonight, Erich, and leap through the flames with her. If you do, she will love you well. If you can open yourself to that love, you will gain a rare kind of power from it. And when you go back to seek your fortune in the outside world, and you learn to use some of that power you brought from the forest world, find a way to keep the door open to this world; return to her periodically. All you have to do is to remember where the origins of your newfound art truly lie. Do not delude yourself with pride into thinking that they come entirely from within your own heart. If you do that, the door closes. And all the wishes of all the burning dead in Hell cannot force it open again."

There were shouts on the shore—the fish pot was ready. Erich began to row back. Reeds whispered along the boat's gunwales as it glided into open water where crescents of sunlight jostled in their path like scales of golden armor.

Erich tried to pace his drinking, hoping to stay even with Sibelius and somewhat behind Rautavaara, who seemed capable of achieving a desired plateau of inebriation and remaining there indefinitely. They sat in a semicircle on the grassy slopes near the shore, beneath canopies of birch, balancing on their laps bowls of hot, tangy broth, wedges of bread, long-stemmed glasses. There were linen napkins and silver, bottles of good wine, and a supply of *aquavit* that seemed as limitless as the lake itself. The summer sun seemed caught in a perpetual early dusk, and a great convergence of light—not merely generous, but profligate and wild—throbbed above the water. Erich had already learned how it was possible for people to worship trees; now as he tilted his head back and let a fat grainy tongue of sunlight lap at his pale chest, he understood how they could also worship Apollo and Ra, how they had sought, through propitiatory rites and sympathetic fires, to aid the sun, prolong its brief and glorious ascendancy, delay the moment of its decline.

Sitting on a stump, the fall of her skirt draping the alluring curve of her calf, Kylliki played until the tips of her fingers grew red, the *kantele* vibrating in her lap, her head thrown back into the light, sucking it in the way a leaf soaks up rain. She seemed carved from ivory and gold: violet eyes beneath prismatic lashes, coral lips caressing the long liquid vowels of her native tongue; her unbound hair, blown full and curved like a sail by the breeze, gave back the sun's own bounty. He wanted to burrow into that hair, to burn himself against the trapped sunlight, to soothe himself in the rivers of its shadows, to drink its tawny smell. He wanted to bury his face in the fleece beneath her long sweet arms, and he wanted those musical fingers to rowel his back. He wanted her beyond simple penetration or crude possession. A slow tidal heat had been building in him since the moment he learned that he would be with her once more. Now, at the conclusion of a song, she rubbed her fingers together, lifted her head, regarded him with wide lilac eyes, and motioned for him to sit beside her. He sidled over and leaned back against the warm columns of her legs. When she started to play again, the *kantele* notes reverberated in him as though his whole body were part of the instrument's sounding board. He drank some more and closed his eyes against the sunlight. Eventually, he supposed, he would just drift off as a swarm of atomistic notes into the light itself.

Time drowsed away. Sibelius napped for a while in a chair that Rautavaara's men brought down from the lodge, his head tilted forward and his hat brim forming a column of shadow across his shoulders. Aino told stories of their courtship, and of the exciting days when Sibelius's fame was coming into being, that heady and historic decade when he went from being a promising regional figure to being an international celebrity, and, for a time at least, the most popular living composer in the world. Rautavaara soaked up alcohol and performed his duties with such exaggerated courtliness that eventually he, too, had to laugh at himself. Anna-Liisa, no longer dour but as always a bit withdrawn and undemonstrative, sat slightly apart, braiding wildflowers in the lap of her dress, delicately sipping from time to time from a glass of wine. The sun's arrested motion seemed to have altered their very chemistry. The light-filled space they occupied—the lake, the lodge, the forest itself—all seemed now to be outside of time, adrift and

almost incorporeal. The day was infinite. At one point, a trifle
unsteadily, Erich, Rautavaara, and an enlisted man named
Salokorpi took a bottle to the dock in front of the sauna hut
and played cards. The loser—Erich, in this case—was tossed
into the lake. When he climbed out, he threw a shoulder
block into Rautavaara and tumbled him into the water, then
grabbed the enlisted man's leg and hurled him in for good
measure. Erich dived in on top of them. After wrestling and
ducking one another for a while, all three men climbed out
together, winded from exertion and laughter, dripping and
flecked with tiny bits of lily pad, like three schoolboys who
had played hooky and fallen into a creek.

Returning to the main picnic area, Erich shook himself
like a puppy and reoccupied his seat at Kylliki's feet. She
laughed and thrust her toes up under his buttocks, wiggling
them teasingly. Both the girlishness and the intimacy of the
gesture enflamed him. Would it ever grow dark enough for
them to sneak away?

Twilight finally emerged, suffusing the western sky with a
rich, soft glow that would remain constant until the sun reappeared several hours later. The lake turned the color of tem-
pering steel, the islands and their trees etched in hard black
lines against the rusting sky.

The day had been long for Sibelius, and Aino kept suggesting that perhaps he might be ready to retire. She herself
was weary by this time and making no effort to disguise it. By
the last hour before midnight, she was dozing in a chair in the
shadows behind her husband.

The back of Erich's head was cradled in the space between
Kylliki's knees. Her fingers had been gently kneading his neck
and the pressure of her legs against his back had grown stronger with the coming of twilight. Finally, as a sense of lethargy
was settling over the meadow, Rautavaara looked at his watch,
announced that it was five minutes until midnight, and thrust
a pair of torches into the embers of the cooking fire. Pine
resin sputtered and flames, spitting tarry blue meteors of
burning sap, shot up from the ends of the two boughs.

Laughing and staggering, Rautavaara went from pyramid to pyramid until all six were ablaze.

Sibelius seemed to get his second wind from the sight of the bonfires. Kylliki struck up a dance tune and the composer clapped his hands in time, even venturing to sing a few bars in a split-reed voice, stumbling over half-forgotten words. Toasts were drunk and wishes made. Noticing that his bottle was empty, Erich went to the table and claimed a half-full one. When he reached Kylliki's side again, she had put aside her instrument. She was instead listening to several of Rautavaara's men, who were singing what sounded like a student drinking song. Their voices blended well—there was a bass whose tone was as black as Chaliapin's—and their song floated bravely over the lake, riding on wings of fire.

Kylliki stood, dusted her skirt, took Erich's arm and said: "The best view of the fires is from the lake—that way you can see the reflections as well. Come into the boat with me."

Erich needed no urging. Soon, in a boat garlanded with flowers, they drifted on open water between the lodge and the sisters' island. In perfect symmetry, six fires burned on the land and six inverted cones of flame answered them in the water. Erich splashed with an oar and one of the reflected fires shattered into molten rings. Then he turned, rising to a half-crouch, scanned the distant reaches of the lake, out toward the dove-and-scarlet horizon.

"My God, how empty of people it is, yet there must be tens of thousands of bonfires burning all over Finland tonight. Is there no one at all, no farms, no villages, in that direction?"

She shrugged, smiled. "Not for a hundred kilometers, at least. Nor for a hundred kilometers north or south. Only 'more of the same,' as I told you the first time we ever talked."

"Is it all one lake, then? One huge inland sea?"

"I don't know, Erich. Perhaps. I've never explored beyond those islands out there. Perhaps we can take a picnic there one day. We could take off our clothes and go swimming and nobody would see us."

"Some day I would like to take a boat around to the far side of the island where you live, where all those channels and streams come together. I've only seen that side of the lake once, on the night we went to hear the rune-singer. I got very disoriented. This time I shall bring a compass, so I'll be able to find my way."

"I'm not sure a compass would help. It's sometimes . . . different . . . over there. I can find my way because I was born and raised here—some part of me always points to our island, like an internal compass. Maybe I carry a lodestone in my heart."

"What else do you carry in your heart?"

"A fullness. For you."

Their hands joined. He would have embraced her, but he did not want their first embrace to be as delicate and wary as it would have to be in a boat.

"Row me to our island. I want you to see the other side from the top of the ridge."

He followed her up the same bramble-strewn path he remembered, up the humped and glowering ridge which he did not remember as being this steep, this rocky. Its crest, an open saddle of rock framed by sparse trees, cut the sky in half. He walked across a tilted bowl of black marble, vaulted by banked and smoldering fires, as though the very waters beyond the ridge had turned to embers. Unhesitatingly, her footing as sure as if they were walking under the full blaze of noon, she led him through the last screen of trees and out onto the island's spine.

The sky fell away above him, the earth in front of his feet was a bed of coals. Made dizzy by the way both light and space leaped against his eyes, he steadied himself against her shoulder. Far to the west, the planet's very rim was a crumbly vagueness; the ruby half-light made each tree on the escarpment below them seem painted with old fire, old blood. The watery maze beyond was, once again, impossible to trace; the eye, beginning confidently at the near foreground, lost its way utterly in the middle distance. He saw no bonfires in this direction, either, only a trackless and unbounded wilderness.

But he saw them in her eyes. When he gazed at her face, some trick of optics conjured flame in her glance. He could feel a heat coming from her skin, as if it were now yielding up that secreted essence it had soaked in earlier from the mid-summer sun.

They fell together into a bed of moss—she seemed to know it was there—and became joined at mouth, breast, and hips. Crushed beneath them, the lichen gave off a cool, secret, minty smell, and the sun-soaked rocks were warm around them. She pulled off his clothing and mounted him in a series of imperious, fluid moves. The moisture at her core was both scalding and sweet. He shut his eyes against the intensity of feeling that flooded him at the moment of penetration. Then she began to rock slowly on him, crooning and moaning, breath blowing and hair a wild eddying cloud against the organ-fugue colors of the sky. He peered through half-closed lids, thunder in his temples, and saw her in silhouette: she seemed enormous, sleek, powerful, towering toward the sky, cracking its smoothness with the force of her thrusts. Where their loins met and pivoted, there was a fulcrum that kept the sky and the forest and the waters in balance. She had taken him to the exact center of this realm and anchored him there with the strength of her desire, and when he burst inside her he too offered a cry to the forest and heard it echo—as though a hundred men were yielding their seed at once—from lake to lake, until some faint and moaning reverberation reached the sun itself.

Later, his ribs gone soft and his legs spongy, he let the boat drift back toward shore while she lay against his belly, some hint of crushed moss mingled with the hot-wheat smell of her hair. The bonfires were dying now; the last one—a skeletal tepee of pine branches—collapsed even as they drew near, sending a glittering coil of embers down the blue-velvet throat of the sky. Colors were changing—in an hour, the sun would be back above the horizon.

As the boat touched shore, Kylliki said: "Will you jump through the flames with me, Erich?"

"I will."

"Do you know what that means? It means a promise—that you will always come back to me, here in the forest."

At that moment, to keep her love, he would have walked through the fire on his hands. His sense of sweet depletion, of having been drained off into her, was so intense that he felt shriveled from the waist down. Jump through the fire with her? Yes, surely he would, if his legs still functioned.

Sibelius spotted them as they approached. Aino was nowhere to be seen, having evidently retired not long after the fire-lighting ritual. To judge from Rautavaara's bleary appearance, many toasts had been consumed since Erich and the girl had left. As they neared the circles of dying fire, Sibelius rose shakily to his feet, Anna-Liisa quick by his side, hand under his elbow, and held out a glass in their direction.

"To the lovers of Midsummer's Eve! May they look before they leap, but may they leap nevertheless!"

Erich took a hefty swallow. The *aquavit* burned, yet gave him a flush of renewed vitality. Sibelius began to clap and chant; Rautavaara drunkenly followed suit. Anna-Liisa, eyes sharp and sober in the dimming firelight, stood straight and watchful as the two lovers clasped hands, backed up for a running start, then plunged downhill together. A weird, ululating cry came from Kylliki as her legs passed through the soft, granular heat of the embers; Erich merely stifled a curse as he hit the ground awkwardly on his bad foot and felt a twist of pain in his ankle. Publicly proclaimed now as lovers, he and Kylliki embraced in full view of the others for the first time.

"Bravo, bravo!" Sibelius cackled. He had shed his coat and tie and flung away his hat, and seemed animated by a tense, unnatural energy. His hands fluttered like claws and his profile, turning restlessly in the ruddy light, was sharp and bird-like. "My turn now," he cried. He advanced out of the shadows and stood close to the fire, one trembling outstretched hand lined up with Anna-Liisa's face, like a rifle sight. Erich heard Kylliki's breath draw sharply inward.

"Come on, Tuonetar! Come on, forest daughter! Now it's our turn. Give an old man a taste of the glories of his youth and jump through the fires with me."

"Old man," replied Anna-Liisa in a voice stretched to brittleness, "if you try to jump through the fires, you will fall and hurt yourself."

The composer's voice grew shrill and querulous: "I am the master here and you are the servant and I say we shall jump the fires together. I want to know what that feels like, one more time before I die."

He advanced toward her, his outstretched hand plucking, talon-like, at her blouse. Now Anna-Liisa's voice came from the heart of winter:

"Old fool, if you force me to jump the fires with you, you will die this very morning."

"Better a death in the fire than the silence I have endured! Why have you cursed me so?"

"I have not cursed you, old man. That silence comes from within your own soul—you opened the door and let it in when you walked away from this place half a century ago. All I have done is care for you, as I always have and always will."

Sibelius lunged for her, lost his balance, and ended up falling against her in a heap. She bent only slightly from the impact, pushing him upright with arms that seemed corded with iron. Her face, however, was ashen. Sibelius leaned against her, racked with dry, coughing sobs, his hands pawing feebly at the folds of cloth that covered her breasts.

Recovering from the shock that had nailed him in place, Erich dropped Kylliki's hand and sprang forward. "Major, let's get him to the house—he's had far too much to drink and he should have been in bed hours ago." Together, he and Rautavaara gently levered the composer uphill to the lodge's front door. He seemed half-delirious, yielding himself utterly to the strength and loyalty of the young men who carried him. At the door, Aino greeted them, wrapped in a robe, her grave, quiet face filled with anger, pity, and love. Mostly love, Erich decided, studying her expression by the light from the foyer.

"He's had some sort of spell . . . too much to drink . . . too much . . . I don't know," stammered Rautavaara, gently connecting the limp old man with his wife's arms.

"I know what has happened. At his age, too much stimulation can cause the line to blur between fantasy and real memory. Thank you, gentlemen, for your concern. He can be an obstinate fellow sometimes."

"Obstinacy is a function of genius," rumbled Rautavaara thickly, as the door closed. "Nietzsche said that, didn' he? Didn' he, Ziegler?"

Erich threw an arm around Rautavaara's hulking shoulder and together they stumbled back down through the trees, toward the shore, where six faint fairy rings of coals glowed like beacons.

"He may very well have, Major—he said a lot of horse shit in his time."

Rautavaara evidently thought this was the funniest remark he'd heard in days. They were both laughing so hard by the time they reached the fires' remnants that they scarcely noticed that both women were gone. Only one rowboat remained, the one Erich and Kylliki had gone out in; the other one bobbed at the end of the dock in front of the sisters' cabin. Rautavaara prodded one of his passed-out troopers; the man merely snored louder. The sun would soon be up again and the sky's color had changed completely, to a clean, creamy apricot. The lake was the color of lead, and the light against its shoreline seemed to come through a thin plate of bone china. They found an unfinished bottle and killed it. Rautavaara finally passed out in mid-syllable and slid to the ground, snoring before he landed. Erich was the last conscious soul, sitting alone by the final smoking embers of the fires, his body tingling—beyond tiredness now, for a while.

" 'Our revels now are ended . . .' " he mused aloud, waving languidly at whatever invisible band of fairies was departing, in accordance with the time-honored script of Midsummer's Eve. Too much magic can wear you out, he thought. What he longed for now was a good night's—make that *day's*—sleep, followed by a hearty and thoroughly down-to-earth breakfast. He watched the sky change color as the dawn matured; a fresh breeze brought the smell of water and trees. He was about to drop off when the same wind brought the faint sound of a scream.

It seemed to come from the sisters' cabin. He struggled against a cresting wave of fatigue and climbed into the boat. Kylliki's scent lingered, where she had been lying; the faint suggestion of her presence caused a lazy, serpentine quiver in his crotch. He shook his head in weary rejection: enough was surely enough, for one night at least. Still, he had to learn the cause of that outcry—if indeed he had really heard it, and it had not been the distorted call of some dawn-waking bird, or even, given his condition by this time, a simple auditory hallucination.

It proved not to be. As he drew abreast of the cabin, he clearly heard Anna-Liisa's sobs and the gentle counterpoint of Kylliki's soothing tones. Erich felt acutely embarrassed; this was probably none of his business; best to leave it alone, now that he had established that no one was injured or in danger. Sibelius had all but propositioned the older sister in full view of the household; had made a fool of himself and created a tense, unpleasant ending to an otherwise idyllic occasion. Cause enough for Anna-Liisa to be upset, true, but hardly, in Erich's foggy estimation, sufficient to cause the outpouring of grief and wretchedness which he was hearing. The intensity of Anna-Liisa's response was a mystery, and if he had not been so tired, so drained, so half-witted with drink, he would have sat down somewhere and pondered it for a while. Maybe later.

He did yield to another impulse, however. He thought that he had enough energy left to climb the ridge and watch the sunrise spread over the landscape on the western side. He had it in mind to find the patch of moss where he and Kylliki had made love and simply curl up there to sleep beneath the morning sun. It seemed a properly mystical gesture to make, following an occasion so steeped in legend and supernatural significance. Besides, climbing the ridge one last time would take less energy than rowing back to the mainland.

Near the top of the climb, a great weight started to push against him, as though his advance were meeting with purposeful resistance. It's surely the effect of my exhaustion, he thought, but it seems external, like a force emanating from beyond the ridgetop. He swam through it, annoyed at first, then made hesitant. Forcing himself the last hundred steps, he finally reached the summit. But the light up there was harsh and bright enough to make his eyes ache. He could not find that bed of moss—the rocks' configurations seemed strange, their shapes wild and barren. Nor did the rest of the landscape appear as he remembered it. Beneath a hard and glairy sky, the land seemed more rolling, less defined and broken by waters, luxuriantly overgrown with trees of enormous size and almost tropical density. No, this was definitely not the same landscape as the one he had gazed upon only hours before. But that was impossible. Something was familiar about it. Perhaps this was the same and only his perceptions were different. Perhaps it was different because he was here alone. He just could not be sure, and the strain of staring made it all swim before his vision until nothing seemed fixed any longer. He felt out of place. No longer welcome. Incongruously against the morning's high glare, a harsh, chilling wind began to grow, and through the chinks in fallen pines, he imagined that he heard the flutter-tongued moan of cold flutes.

Away to the west, where the landscape again seemed to fragment and dissolve into an overlapping, unfocused quilt of reflections—all silver and pewter and tin, all outlines broken, shifting, elusive—a black thunderhead rose like an anvil above the middle distance. He could hear cyclonic winds gathering force . . . out there. He looked in vain for a house, a cabin, a road, a curl of smoke rising from a hidden chimney, but all there seemed to be, from the rock on which he stood to the white-tile void of the farthest sky, was a wind-inhabited desolation where no man dwelt or even drew breath. He felt as though he stood upon an invisible boundary whose existence—or perhaps the existence of something beyond—had generated that force which had opposed and slowed his climb and which now filled him with foreboding.

Cold wind struck his face like a long, drawn-out slap. As he watched, the trees began to bend in great oscillating patches, starting at the horizon and gradually drawing nearer, the trees undulating, their tops bent level to the ground in a single fluid motion, their greenness changing from dark emerald to a dusty grass color as the wind exposed the underside of their foliage, then righted them again as it moved on. A seething of gooseflesh erupted on Erich's body: viewed from this distance, from this vantage point, the effect was exactly as though a vast invisible being were advancing relentlessly toward him, trampling the forest under its stride. He turned and fled pell-mell down the slope and back into the boat.

Twenty-one

As soon as the rain stopped, Erich made his way to an old mortar pit a hundred meters behind the main line of resistance; its crew compartment was roofed over and the interior was dry—a good place to take care of what he thought of as his "letters home." The rain had been heavy, and had stripped some of the foliage from the deciduous trees. Wet spruce trunks shone black and gleamy, as though rubbed with oil, and the evergreens' smell had a winter-tasting edge to it.

This was not a long report; little had changed on this part of the Northern Front since the first winter of the siege of Leningrad, but in one respect at least, matters had taken a disturbing turn. A long period of static trench warfare was not good for any army, and the Finns were no exception. They felt as though they had been reduced to scarcely more than groundskeepers, while the war resolved itself elsewhere, mostly by virtue of German retreats. Most of Pajari's men were convinced their turn was coming soon, and that the results were a foregone conclusion.

Their attitude was not exactly one of defeatism—Erich was positive these men would fight when the Russian offensive finally came—but their mood was fatalistic almost to the point of lassitude. *Victory* was now a meaningless word; the only question was whether or not Finland would be wiped out of existence when the storm finally broke.

"Captain Ziegler, where are you?"

Erich quickly flipped over the half-written letter to his uncle which he always kept folded over the pad he used for writing his summaries to Klatt. He nibbled the end of his fountain pen and pretended to be deep in thought.

"I'm over here."

An orderly with muddy boots bent over the edge of the pit, saluted, and said: "General Pajari's compliments, sir. He wishes the captain to join him at divisional headquarters at the captain's earliest convenience."

"Thank you, Sergeant. I'll be along in a few minutes. Any idea what this is about?"

"Some orders came through for you, sir; from Helsinki. From pretty high up, to judge from the general's reaction. That's all I know."

Pajari welcomed Erich with the gruff respect that had characterized their relationship ever since Erich had distinguished himself in the *motti* battles. At times during the past few months, since Erich had returned from his midsummer visit to Tapiola, the two men had found themselves more and more drawn into conversation—about the wider aspects of the war, about the dwindling strategic options of the Axis powers, about the perilous tightrope Finland was walking. Pajari had plenty of time for such conversations now, for his division had been manning a static defense line for a year and a half, and aside from flare-ups of patrol action, there had been very little fighting. Like his men, the general was losing his edge.

"Coffee, Ziegler?"

"Yes sir, thanks. The rain put a bit of a chill into the air."

"My orderly tells me you were off in the woods again, writing one of your reports . . ." There was a trace of humor on Pajari's lips, so Erich tried to match it when he responded with what both of them, evidently, knew to be a lie: "The usual letters to my family, General."

"Quite so. Tell them to send me a dozen eighty-eights and as many Jagdpanzers as they can spare. To tell the truth about it, at last, your reports have been useful to me, Erich. Now, when the Russians actually turn their attention to this front, and I scream bloody murder for antitank weapons, it won't be my voice alone crying in the wilderness. Where the hell else will I get such weapons, except from Germany? And whoever makes those decisions in Germany will be able to look into his file on Finland, and find there your on-the-spot assessments, confirming the need. Maybe we'll get enough heavy stuff to hold our own—Hitler wouldn't want us to fold up the way the Italians are doing now, or the way the Hungarians did at Stalingrad."

"Why is the general speaking so candidly?"

Pajari laughed and actually clapped Erich on the shoulder, a gesture of comradeship so rare as to seem hugely out of character.

"Because you are leaving us, my dear fellow. Orders came through this morning from Helsinki, reassigning you to the German Embassy staff there as . . . let me see how it's worded . . . ah, yes: 'Liaison Officer for Cultural Affairs and Music.' Quite a wonderful mouthful, isn't it? You must have made some friends in high places, Captain. Are you sleeping with Mannerheim's granddaughter when you make those trips to the interior?"

"Actually, no—just the housemaid of the Sibelius family."

Pajari laughed at the presumed joke. "Well, you won't be missing anything here except trench rot, boredom, and a long winter. But don't take the soft life in the capital for granted, because if the Reds ever get serious about this part of the front, you'll probably find yourself back in the line as a combat officer."

"Will it come to that, General?"

"Almost has to. What options do we have now? If we make a separate peace with the Russians, we'll probably suffer the same fate as Latvia and Estonia—total Bolshevization. We could, I suppose, switch sides and *join* the Russians, but the dishonor of that course would be too much for the nation to swallow. Right now, as I see it, the government's policy is just to sit tight, keep the army intact and dug in, and see how the situation develops. I suspect they're hoping the Reds'll be too exhausted after crushing the Germans to stomach another major operation up here. Maybe they'll offer us terms we can live with. Maybe we'll be able to lay down our guns, give them back this miserable patch of forest, and go home. Or maybe the whole structure of Europe will just collapse one day and the only thing left intact will be us and our little army, far away up here in the north. In the meantime, we need food and raw materials from Germany just to maintain the status quo. Wait and see, wait and see. We drift, Erich, the whole nation of us, in a frail boat surrounded by whirlpools. But there's not much room left to drift in, and there are a lot of reefs ahead. If the Russians launch an all-out attack on us, they won't stop as readily as they did in 1940. They won't want anything equivocal about this victory."

"Finland will live, General, one way or the other."

"Help us to do that, Ziegler, if you can. Send me something to stop tanks. Tell anyone in Helsinki—or elsewhere, for that matter—who will listen."

Pajari leaned across the table and grasped Erich's arm in passionate importunity. Erich knew that Pajari had witnessed the Reds' human-wave assaults during the Winter War. What the man feared now would be even worse.

"I'll do what I can, sir; I promise."

Erich's orders turned out to have impressive weight. He was able to requisition a car, ration chits, and a top-level security clearance. His official duties in Helsinki began in one week, which left time for a brief visit to Tapiola.

This time, the sentry at the forest gate glanced at Erich's documents, smiled a greeting, and waved him through without the usual phone call to Rautavaara. Erich felt as if he was coming home. When he reached the lodge, Rautavaara was there to greet him heartily, take his cap, coat, and sidearm, and usher him into the family room, where Aino took his hand and the composer emerged from his study to embrace him.

It became obvious, from hints dropped during that first afternoon, that Sibelius's intervention had obtained the Helsinki appointment for Erich. After lunch, Erich went into the study with the composer and remained closeted with him all afternoon. The two men had reached a level of understanding such that overlaying their personal warmth was a tacit agreement to acknowledge and speak openly about more practical matters—those areas of endeavor where each man might be of some use to the other.

It was now a given between them that Sibelius had selected Erich to be his postwar champion on mainland Europe, even as Beecham had been his champion in Great Britain and the celebrated Koussevitzky and Stokowski were the custodians of his remarkable American popularity. Remote as he was by nature and temperament from the upheavals of contemporary musical aesthetics—a condition compounded by the war, his age, and his sheer geographical distance from the cultural centers of the Western world—Sibelius believed that Germany would, after the war, regain the eminence she had previously enjoyed in music and musical performance, and that her conductors, soloists, critics, and theoreticians would once again set the tone for all Europe, as they had done for the previous one hundred and fifty years.

Privately, Erich had some reservations about the scenario that seemed to have crystallized in the old man's mind. However much he personally identified with the Sibelius aesthetic, he understood the retrograde position it occupied in the worldwide scheme of things. He doubted seriously that a return to rugged romanticism would emerge as a dominant trend in postwar music. Even before the war, most contemporary composers, and a great many critics, had come to view Sibelius as a living anachronism, a brandy-soaked old pike swimming against the powerful currents of taste. In that sense, to be designated the composer's sanctioned champion might be almost irrelevant in some of the capitals where Erich's postwar reputation would have to be made.

On the other hand, the ordinary music lovers of America and Great Britain—where, Erich suspected, a smart postwar conductor would seek his fortune—still loved the man's music. And, as Furtwängler had confirmed, the spotlight of the

whole musical world would be focused on the man who gave
the first performance of the Eighth Symphony.

If Erich had read the signs correctly, it seemed only a matter of time now until Sibelius chose to reveal the Eighth in its
entirety. What else could all this be leading to? By what other
stroke could the composer hope, after so many years of silence, to regain the world's attention, if not by presenting audiences with a great and solitary work which would cap his
entire career and silence forever all speculation that he was
written out, empty, too far sunk in gloom and alcohol and tottering age? And how better to present such a work than to
hand-pick its first, all-important interpreter?

That their relationship might be cresting toward the moment of revelation—when, as Erich imagined it, the composer
would thrust into his hands the full orchestral score of the
Eighth—also seemed implicit in the subtle changes he detected in the nature of their conversations. Seldom now did
the composer indulge himself in epigrams and vignettes from
the past; their discourse these days was the interchange of
true colleagues. From Sibelius, Erich learned who was who in
the musical establishment in Helsinki—who mattered in concert life, in academia, in the state-run radio network. There
were also, of course, pleasant digressions concerning the hotels, restaurants, and theaters of the capital city. After two
days of such conversation, combined with what he had already
absorbed during his previous, ill-fated visit to the city, Erich
felt very content about the prospects of his new posting.

His relationship with Kylliki had acquired subtle new colorations as well. During his time in Russia, the memory of
her had become an icon glowing against the night that had
encroached on his heart. During that period of exile, his first
few trysts with her in the forest had become enshrined in
memory as a private Eden from which he had been cruelly
cast out. The Midsummer's Eve homecoming had been like
the astonishing fulfillment of a cherished dream.

In the more ordinary nights that followed, their lovemaking continued to satisfy him as much as it had on that first extraordinary night; her sheer physicality was as natural, as

spontaneous, as totally without shame, as the wind that bent the trees.

But now that his future had acquired at least a preliminary sense of texture and definition, there were moments in the afterglow of passion when he was no longer entirely satisfied just to float with her on the receding tide. He desired the parallel satisfaction of drawing her, conversationally at least, into that speculative future, to take her by the hand and lead her, in the context of a shared daydream, out of her forest world and onto the streets of some of those fair cities whose orchestras he intended to conquer.

"I should really like to do what Hitler could not," he mused, on their second night together, as he sat up and lit a postcoital cigarette.

"However do you mean that, Erich?" she asked, stretching lithely on the bed. The last flicker from his cigarette lighter gave back a quick wink from the moisture on her loins.

"Conquer London! I've always wanted to see London, maybe even more than Paris. And I'll wager we get to see it in style, too, once I write to Sir Thomas Beecham and tell him about my connection with Sibelius. He loves Sibelius's music, you know."

Kylliki giggled and squeezed him playfully on the thigh. "Do people in England really have names like that?"

"Like what?"

"Sir Whatchamacallit and Lady Thingamabob?"

"Well, yes, if they've been knighted."

"Knights and ladies. Do they wear armor and ride horses?"

"A lot of them ride horses, I suppose, but they only wear the armor in private," he laughed. "Tell me, where would you like to go first when we get to London?"

"Oh, Erich, I belong *here*, you know that."

That was not the answer he expected. Taken somewhat aback, he pressed the matter: "No, seriously, Kylliki, what would you most like to see in London? The Tower? Buckingham Palace? The British Museum?"

"It doesn't matter," she said rather absently. "I'm sure they're all lovely."

Erich pressed harder. What was the matter with her?

"How about the palace, then? If Sir Thomas takes me under his wing, we might actually get invited to the palace. We might even be presented to the King. I would love to show you off to royalty! I would introduce you as the daughter of Tapio, king of the forest."

"Now you're making fun of me, Erich. I can't help being what I am."

"What you're being is very strange, Kylliki," he responded with just a hint of vexation showing through. "Here I am talking about the possibility—the very real possibility, mind you—of meeting the King of England, and you act as though you couldn't be bothered. It's just not normal, that's all."

"How normal is this, Sir Knight!" Abruptly, with that startling physical strength of hers, she threw him back down on the bed and began doing a number of lascivious things to him which quickly turned his mind away from the King of England.

From that moment on, whenever he spoke in a similar vein about London or New York or Rome, and about the wonders they might experience there together, she listened with wide-eyed, indiscriminate acceptance—not as though he were describing odysseys to far Cathay, but as though she would have listened with the same passive, spongelike acquiescence had he been discoursing on the future of the stock market or research in theoretical physics.

These were not strictly monologues on Erich's part—Kylliki's empathy seemed boundless—but it gradually became clear that her responses were merely echoes of his own enthusiasms and fancies. There was no curiosity behind her questions, no real eagerness on her part to share in any of these future experiences. Not once did she so much as hint at the possibility of marriage, which fact alone brought Erich up short with caution when the impulse was on him to ask her. Gradually, Erich came to a conclusion as to what her response would be: that she belonged "here," and not in those cities or in the world they represented.

Erich tried another approach, one closer to "here."

"Sibelius has told me about some new restaurants in Helsinki. He even gave me the managers' names at two of them, and told me to use his name. Just as soon as I get settled, you'll have to come down on the train and spend the weekend—we'll find the best dinner in Finland, I promise you."

"But we have such good food here, Erich . . ."

"That isn't the point, Kylliki! The point is that it's simply a lot of fun to get dressed up and eat in a classy restaurant, where they wait on you hand and foot and you don't have to wash the damned dishes afterwards."

He tried to elicit enthusiasm by mentioning the department stores in the capital, the theaters, the cinemas, the nightclubs. Always, her response was somewhere off to the side of what he brought up, as though he were broadcasting on a wavelength she simply could not receive at full strength.

He tried hard not to let her responses irritate him, but the strangeness of her attitude bewildered as well as disappointed. A young woman of her intelligence and passion, who had known only the forest world all of her life, should by all rights be devoured by curiosity, if not actually desperate to leave this rustic setting and satiate herself with the stimuli of modern, urban life. Yet, for all the unfeigned caring in her eyes and voice, she responded in exactly the same predictable, self-effacing manner to every subject Erich introduced, from grand hotels to ocean liners; lovingly, politely, she reflected at him his own interests, without ever displaying the slightest personal passion for any of the things he described.

At first, he was merely puzzled, but the more he probed, the more specific and detailed his reveries about the future became, the blander and more uniformly passive became her responses. What had once seemed innocence and sweet naïveté now began to see more like willful, superstitious abnegation. She really did believe that she was forever destined to remain here, in the forest, and their relationship was destined for regular renewals whenever Erich returned to these latitudes—like periodic visits to a spa, he supposed—with the same spontaneity and passion that had characterized it up to this time. She took much for granted, and assumed, with a faith he found simultaneously touching and just the slightest bit irritating, that he did too.

There grew in his mind a strong resolve to force the issue by devising some stratagem that would compel her to leave the forest and join him in Helsinki. Once she had taken that step, he was certain that the city's myriad enticements would sweep away her provincial hesitation.

On the morning of the fourth and last day of his visit, Sibelius invited Erich to take morning coffee with him on a flagstoned terrace overlooking the lake. It was a cusp-of-autumn morning in late September, and the air was as taut and keen as a violin string waiting to be bowed. The lake was a sheet of buffed steel, its surface strewn with the loose change of fallen birch leaves.

"Did I tell you that I heard from some colleagues in Helsinki that the orchestra enjoyed working with you? They're a pack of mules for most guest conductors, including me, so you can take that as a compliment indeed."

Erich acknowledged the praise with a bow of his head. The composer's remark did of course make him feel good, though it was beyond guessing why he had waited until this last morning to hark back to that frustrating experience.

"They were a good orchestra to work with. And they deserved better than von Golzer."

"Oh, yes, I have heard about that fellow, indeed I have. A regular ocelot. He'll land on his feet, no matter which way the war winds blow, mark my words. Now we must see to it that you, too, end up on firm ground. The war will last a long while yet, and there will be a period of chaos before and after the termination of it—that's when all the sorting out will take place, just as in 1918. You'll be safer here, away from the worst of it, and, who knows, you may even have time and opportunity to carve out a modest reputation for yourself in Scandinavia."

"Perhaps if that concert had been allowed to go as planned, Maestro, I would already have a modest reputation."

"Opportunities seldom come but once; it is merely that we are too busy to recognize all of them. I have something special in mind for you, Erich."

At the abrupt change of subject, Erich's stomach tightened. Perhaps this was the moment.

But no, not yet. Sibelius merely shifted to refill his coffee cup, tap cigar ash onto the flagstones, and offer Erich his best profile.

"On December sixth, there will be a special concert in honor of my birthday—I'll not mention how large that number is—and the sponsoring committee have asked me to select both the program and the performers. If I turned the entire concert over to you, there might be a scandal, since people's feelings toward Germany have become, let us say, ambivalent. So I have chosen a Finnish conductor and soloist to do the Violin Concerto, on the program's second half. I leave the first half up to you. I have already notified the orchestra of my choices and they have agreed, most of them with enthusiasm, so I'm told. The concert will also be broadcast, both here and in Sweden."

Erich was not displeased. If this were not the same as the premiere of the Eighth, it was a good consolation prize, putting him more or less back where he had been before being sideswiped by von Golzer. Curbing his larger impatience, he accepted this charge, his mind already racing ahead to select, from among the shorter tone poems, something bright to open the concert and give contrast to the performance of the Fourth Symphony that would be its centerpiece.

Late that afternoon, his mind buzzing with a sense of opportunity, he strode nervously back and forth along the ridge, swirls of falling leaves stirring in his wake, the score of the Fourth open in his hand. The sky, still almost cloudless, was a steeped, scorched blue, and sunlight pierced the ragged leaves in thin, hard shafts. Sometimes he moved his baton arm while he worked out a passage. After a while, he loosened his tunic, reveling in the sensation of his own sweat—this might be the last day of the year for such warmth.

Winded after an hour of such "rehearsal," Erich seated himself on a split-log bench at the edge of the terrace where he had earlier talked with Sibelius. He had not seen the old man since the midday meal. At some point during the last ten minutes, deep in the elusive second movement, Erich had become aware that he was trying to re-create the shape and shading of the performance he had conducted in his mind two years earlier, while he lay beneath the pile of frozen limbs and waited for the Altaic shaman to come into his rifle sights. Ever since he had given himself to the forest, events had manifested strange connections, web strands. Perhaps it really was as the *Kalevala* would have it, for if this interpretation made the impression he expected it to, if it went as deep into the score as he believed it would, then surely those qualities could be traced back to the interpretation's genesis. Where did Herr Ziegler get his inspiration for this performance? the critics might ask. And Herr Ziegler might answer—but of course, would not—that it had come to him while he was lying, frostbitten and hallucinating, under a stack of amputated arms and legs, waiting for the chance to slay a Tartar magician. Oh yes, there could be plenty of mystery, and power, in the origins of a thing. The old Finnmark wizards had learned a trick or two from that principle, he was certain of it.

The day's first wind moaned over the lake and combed the trees; birch leaves, scraps of gilded parchment, brushed his hair and face, and the wind brought gooseflesh to his overheated skin. An involuntary shiver. The first verse of winter, written in hieroglyphs of spinning leaves that danced along the flagstones with the papery whispers of goblins.

And from the wind, emerging as it subsided, came music. Erich turned from the act of lighting his cigarette and saw that the window of the composer's study was open. This in itself was unusual; although the old man managed to get in his daily perambulations in all except the vilest weather, his hypochondria with regard to indoor drafts was such that the study window usually remained closed even on the warmest days.

Erich let his cigarette smolder unheeded, scarcely daring to breathe. What he heard was a transformed version of the scrap of music he had carried in his mind and heart all the way across Russia. What had been the merest suggestion was now altered from what had been a minor key into a bold and virile C major, augmented by rich, strong chords. In this new guise it had tremendous stride and power—as though Erich were now overhearing an excerpt from the finale, and the part he had heard earlier might have been from a slow and sorrowful adagio. This music was instantly identifiable as Sibelius, for if Erich listened closely, he could hear the composer's earlier works referred to, in passing, through strokes of orchestration and harmony that passed like undercurrents through the main discourse. Yet, Erich realized, the orchestration was in his own head, conjured from the bare-bones outline of themes and harmonies adumbrated by the composer's piano playing: there, the trombones' declamation! There, a soft rumble of timpani; there, a spiral flight of flute and piccolo, intertwined like lovers' limbs. There was no excess rhetoric in the development he was hearing; the themes moved with the lithe inevitability of a Beethoven symphony, with the same sense of absolute rightness of progression. And there was no fat on this music; it could not even properly be called romantic, for it did not look backward, made no sentimental claims to nostalgia, made no apologies for being what it was. As the music marched proudly toward some kind of coda, Erich felt a thrill of joy uncoil along his spine.

At that instant, he resolved to act, to go to the window and confront the composer, allowing him to see the tears that had now gathered in his eyes, and beg him to release the score, beg him for the chance to conduct it; not even thinking, at that moment, in terms of his own career, but rather in terms of what it could mean for all mankind.

Wild with excitement, Erich crushed his cigarette and sprang up. He had taken two strides in the direction of the window when the music suddenly ceased in mid-bar. Two clawlike hands reached out, grasped the window sash like grappling hooks, and slammed it shut. Erich halted as though he had run into a stone wall. Around him, the wind was restive and cold; leaves washed around his ankles, giving off a smell of rich decay.

Later that night, in the sauna hut on the sisters' island, where they had gone to bathe and stayed to make love, Erich tried to describe the moment for Kylliki.

"Why does he hesitate, even for a day? The work is a masterpiece! Anyone with ears can hear that!"

"He is an old, old man, and he has been silent for a long time. Perhaps he has listened to so much silence that he has lost faith in his own voice."

Erich leaned back on the hot wooden bench, inhaling steam, waiting and wishing for the sauna process to work its usual therapy, to ease his tension and confusion. But tonight, the steam was not doing its job. Neither was the girl, to his way of thinking. He needed sympathy from Kylliki, reinforcement, not some kind of philosophical argument, and his mood was turning sour.

"Kylliki, it's just not right that such a work should be withheld. It would mean so much, to so many people."

"What would it mean to you, Erich?"

He tilted her face, its long sweet planes now glazed with perspiration, so that the firelight could dance on her lashes, glow hotly on her swollen lips.

"It means everything to me, now that I've heard it."

"Maybe that's why you can't have it."

"Don't speak in riddles to me, damn it."

"Is it such a riddle? Search your heart and find what really matters there. Is it more important to give that symphony to the world, as a gift, or is it more important for Erich Ziegler to have the fame that would come from giving its first performance?"

A large irritating dollop of sweat had gathered on the end of his nose and refused to fall off. Angrily he flipped it away, but it was immediately replaced by another. God, how he longed for an ordinary, civilized shower bath!

"But if he doesn't want me to conduct it, why has he let me hear some of it? Is he tormenting me?"

"It may only be a mark of favor, of intimacy. I have lived close to the Master since he arrived here, and I have never before heard so much as a single note of this work you describe. He may have shared it with you because he burns to share it with *someone.*"

"Then why does he simply not share it with the world? To keep such a score locked up, hidden away, is madness, almost a crime."

Kylliki's eyes flashed. She showed no sign of backing down in the face of Erich's increasing vexation.

"He is not mad. Perhaps he has simply come to a boundary he cannot cross. Don't you think he must have strong reasons for not letting go of that manuscript? With your own eyes, you've seen how he hungers for approval, even adulation. How he devours every scrap of news from the outside world concerning the status of his reputation. Haven't you seen him in that study, glued to the wireless, listening over and over again to performances of his own works, no matter how distorted they sound over the shortwave band? He is so desperately vain about his achievements, and so easily hurt by the snide remarks of those who see him as the symbol of something used up and irrelevant . . . Oh, Erich, you know all these things as well as I do, better, in fact."

"But he can refute all of that with this one score! I know he can."

"You believe that because the music has so great an effect on *you*. What if it were performed for an audience that was already conditioned to be skeptical, even to dislike it? You know how perverse people can be."

Now he was on his feet, gesturing angrily at her.

"Don't lecture me about concert audiences, Kylliki—you've never even seen one. I could fill a city with bravos if I conducted that work." What did she know—what *could* she know—of the culture that had produced Erich Ziegler?

"Even if you could, he will not release the music."

"But why not?" Erich was growing angry, for the girl's responses kept weaving a slippery noose around his logic, his clear-cut sense of mission. And indeed she did not answer him directly, but rose tensely to a sitting position, shadows flowing over her shoulders. Her eyes were smoky and full, her hands tenderly traced the lines of his mouth.

"What have they done to you, my Erich? What pain has taken root in you and made you so desperate? Even on the night I leapt through the flames with you, I sensed a harshness inside you that had not been there before. When I first came to love you, when I first gave myself to you, you were much more open to wonder, much more at home in the forest. Try to be that way now, try to see how wonderful it is that Sibelius is moved to share the deepest secret of his heart with you; how remarkable it is that you alone are privileged to hear his final work. Don't you see the glory in that honor? Your friendship must mean a great deal to him, that he shares with you both the wonder of the music and the burden of keeping it secret. Erich, try to be worthy of that trust—take it as one more, one final gift, from the forest."

"Leave the fucking forest out of this! The goddamned forest has nothing to do with it!"

She drew back from the violence in his voice, covering her cheeks as though he had aimed a blow at her. Then Erich saw inside himself, like a cell gone over to cancer, the darkness she had already spotted. He spread his hands helplessly and sought refuge in her eyes; enormous and impossibly wise, they had seen the blackness inside him before he had even recognized its presence.

"Forgive me, Kylliki. Too much has happened to me. I've been pulled back and forth too hard. The war, the things I've seen and done, how could they not affect me?"

He sat down resignedly, shoulders slumped, suddenly very weary. Things which had seemed certain had become slippery, their edges ill defined.

"I wanted very badly to return to you as the same man I was when you first met me, but I am changed by what has happened to me and no man could be otherwise. Nothing ever remains as pure and inviolate as it seems in the beginning, not even in peacetime. And in war . . ."

She was holding him now, breasts grazing his heart, the sweet pulp of her mouth tracing runes across his brow, neck, shoulders. It was true, as she had divined, that something dark and knotted had formed within him, and it was true that he longed to be rid of it. But what did she know of the horror he had seen, and whose dreadful portion he had consumed before he had been able to find his way back here to Tapiola?

A coldness gripped the underside of his heart, as persistent in its way as fear had been in the front lines. And its hold was not lessened by music, not anymore—indeed, at the very thought of the Eighth Symphony, it tightened into a fist. Only the girl's presence seemed to help.

"Kylliki . . . on Midsummer's Eve, after you had gone, I climbed back up to the ridge where we made love, to watch the dawn, I suppose. But the landscape looked different, alien, almost hostile. And then a storm came up and . . . well, I was tired and pretty drunk by that time, but it looked somehow *personal*. The way the wind flattened the trees was unnatural, frightening, it looked as though an invisible giant was striding toward me—maybe coming *for* me, I don't know. I felt real terror . . . I ran . . . I . . ." He shook his head, but the images refused to become unjumbled in his mind, and his tongue faltered in the telling.

Gently taking his hands, she leaned her golden head against his knees.

"You must be stronger than the darkness inside you. If you bear such a darkness into the forest, it may attract a kindred kind of darkness. Maybe what you saw was a reflection of the darkness moving inside you."

Helplessly, he reached for her and cupped her face. "Would I have seen that if you had been with me?"

"I don't know. The forest can be cruel sometimes, the same way the sea is cruel—by being true to its nature."

"Kylliki, I need you here and I will need you out there, if I am to put that darkness behind me. You're like a bridge over all that time in Russia—when I'm with you, I can cross over that time and still make a connection with the man I was before the war. Do you understand how hard that makes me need you?"

She seemed to understand that his need for her had never been so total, so close to the verge of violence. She nodded to him and uncoiled from him in a series of wanton, feline motions. She lay open before him on the rya rugs they had strewn before the fire, her skin shimmering. The apex of her loins, already flooded by him once, was an open orchid— firelight had soaked into her golden thatch and the slow-flowing ichor between her open petals. When he entered her, the heat was scalding and his nerves were so tightly strung that every motion of her hips made him moan. She seemed to want to purge him, make him cry, as though tears would cleanse the darkness within him, but some harsh and stubborn reflex hardened his feelings, sought to turn his hardness into a weapon, a thing for battering and subjugating. But her heat was vast and deep and she gave him all the quenching, liquid patience she had within her. In the end, a few seconds after her own climax, he came in a harsh, rat-tailed spurt: muscular, twitching, and puny in relation to the wealth of flesh she had spread to enfold him. Their energies extinguished, they passed into sleep beneath a single blanket, gymnasium smells drying in the darkness. They were acutely aware, even as they dozed, of the angles, stubbles, and flaws of each other's flesh. In the morning, when Erich woke, Kylliki had already gone over to Tapiola. The shadows inside the sauna hut were cold, and he could hear the autumn wind blowing off the lake.

Twenty-two

Erich's driver pulled up behind the Daimler they had been following for several blocks. As Erich had supposed, the car belonged to one of the government ministers in the trackside delegation that would soon be welcoming Sibelius to the capital city that was mobilized to celebrate his birthday. How much attention the average Finn would pay to all the commotion, Erich couldn't say—his duties no longer permitted much contact with enlisted men or common citizens. If the radio broadcasts were to be believed—and after all, he had helped to write some of them—the whole city was using the composer's birthday as an excuse to have a party. There was certainly not much else to celebrate at the moment.

But if there was an undercurrent of excitement passing through the uniformed and overcoated citizens who thronged the plaza in front of the railroad station, it was certainly not visible. On this bright December day, people flooded randomly into the plaza and, once there, sorted themselves into columns and followed the lanes that had been swept through last night's heavy snowfall—a series of spoke-like paths that converged at the great round portico of the main entrance, where the pedestrian traffic passed between the thirty-foot granite giants that flanked the entrance. Beginning as art deco columns, fluted with wavy lines and precisely incised rectangles, the statues turned into brawny stern-faced demigods from their rib cages up. Elbows flush against torsos, each figure held in its outstretched hands an immense globe, lighted at night. The statues' faces had always struck Erich as ambiguous: not especially heroic or guardian-like, but severe, puritanical, mildly disapproving—as though one day they might behold someone or some act too disreputable to tolerate, would raise their stone-thewed arms and hurl their spheres into the square in a Jovian gesture of condemnation. The figures fascinated Erich, for he found them symbolic of everything that was, to a foreigner, enigmatic in the Finnish character. Observing the statues at various times, Erich had conceived of them as coldly Olympian, absurdly phallic, bizarrely whimsical, or simply vulgar. Yet ever since the great architect Aalto had erected these centerpieces, the people of Helsinki had identified with them.

In glowing leather and glinting brass, a staff colonel representing Mannerheim cracked open the door for Erich, two topcoated diplomats, the vice-chancellor of the university, and a handful of ambassadors with nothing better on their schedules that morning; in a group, they passed into the station, between the glowering stone giants. Inside, the sense of vaulted space was colossal. Radiators hissed merrily in stone sconces behind rows of benches, but the shuffle and push of trains on the lower levels and the constant opening and closing of the main doors filled the air with currents of outdoor chill. Loudspeakers positioned in the concourse gave train information in Finnish, Swedish, and German. Like every other train station in Europe, this one was filled to bursting with young men in woollen uniforms, strapped, roped, and strung into webs of packages, knapsacks, bedrolls, and extra clothing—the luckier ones on their way home for Christmas furloughs; others, with sadder expressions, returning to their units. Erich and his colleagues moved as a separate formation, through the hollow cloud of sound formed by a thousand pairs of bootheels scraping on polished granite, parting the sea of pedestrians with the palpable sense of Official Business that surrounded them.

Erich had made this walk several times in the six weeks since he had taken up his new duties, in order to welcome visiting artists and dignitaries. Last week it had been Gieseking, here to perform a program of Beethoven sonatas for the state radio; Erich had found him a brusque, moon-faced gentleman possessed of a very naive view of the way the war was going and still certain, or still wanting to seem certain, of Germany's ultimate victory.

Erich's duties included the arranging of guest appearances by artists and writers from the Reich and its allies. He also supervised the exchange of broadcast materials, the publication of journalistic features and notices favorable to whatever point of view seemed mutually agreed upon by the Finnish and German governments from week to week. Usually the changes in tone were subtle, and he had spent a good portion of those six weeks making contacts who could assist him in divining the fluctuations of the wind. If what he was doing was, at bottom, little more than disseminating propaganda, it was at least—with artists such as Gieseking—propaganda of a very high order.

The other part of his duties remained unchanged. Indeed, Klatt—when informed of Erich's new posting—had been pleased. Now that Germany was on the defensive, reports on front-line conditions in the Finnish Army were largely irrelevant, but in Helsinki, near the center of political authority, Erich might sniff out something useful.

Passing through the decorated maw of a tunnel entrance, then clip-clopping down a wide terrace of steps, the delegation entered the platform area. Steam and oil filled the cold air with electric, humid smells; mechanical noises were magnified and given dignity by reverberation. They passed through clumps of waiting passengers, sudden jets of unleashed steam, like the exhalations of great beasts, fogging the polish of their boots, and emerged on the other side of a police barricade on a loading platform beside a short length of switching track, empty of people except for a small honor guard already dressed to perfection by their commanding noncom. Overhead, an ornate wrought-iron clock proclaimed the time: 11:28. Erich peered over the platform's edge, following the glowing rails into the mephitic darkness of the far tunnel. At the remotest visible distance, a train lamp appeared, grainy and wavering in the steam currents. At this moment, according to the timetable he had memorized two days ago, the private car carrying Sibelius, Rautavaara, and two of his security men would already have been detached from the original train, coupled to a switch engine, and routed, by turntable, onto this secure private siding. As befitted the living symbol of the nation.

There was, Erich supposed, still some chance that Kylliki might emerge from the train as well, but he had steeled himself against disappointment if she did not. As he had driven away from Tapiola the morning after their last night together, he had experienced more than just the ache of parting—he had felt an open wound inside, a certainty that something had been torn by their last conversation and by the ferocity and frustration of that final coupling; something that had to be fixed, patched up, smoothed over.

He wanted her here, to show her off, to have her present in the hall tonight when he led the orchestra. He wanted to take her to Stockmann's Department Store and buy her the sort of clothes she might, as a girl, have dreamed about. They could go to a good restaurant, then back to the hotel room he had booked for them, where he would undress her slowly, then ease her down onto a huge bed with crisp sheets and make love to her in a style that had never been possible in their rustic couplings on the pine floors and benches of her sauna hut. If he could do those things, things she would surely enjoy—my God, she *was* a woman, was she not?—then surely the wariness he felt would dissipate, and they could renew their relationship in a fresh and more sophisticated context.

On the morning of his departure for Helsinki, Sibelius had bade him goodbye heartily and given him a farewell bear hug during which he said, too quietly for anyone else to hear: "So you too have to leave your forest woman, eh?"

"It is different with me," Erich replied.

"Yes. Of course." Sibelius smiled distantly as he stepped back to stand beside his wife.

Erich was determined not to replay the old man's youthful love affair, even if the old man, for whatever enigmatic motives, wanted or expected him to. He would win Kylliki over, and on his terms; then all would go forward as he had planned.

He had written her six letters, each more imploring than the last. He had started the correspondence with some dignity but gradually, by the end of the last letter, he reached a level of open pleading. He said he needed her, longed for her to be there for his debut, could not conceive of enjoying the experience without her—although, even as the words went onto paper, he knew that he would manage. If the evening was successful, he would wrest considerable pleasure from it, whether she was there or not.

Finally, three days ago, a reply had come. In a surprisingly spidery and timid hand, far clumsier and plainer than her speech, she had said that she missed him, loved him, but could not come to him. The Master would surely not approve. Anna-Liisa was against it. The thought of the big city terrified her—she did not belong there but here, at Tapiola, in the forest. She was sorry to disappoint him and wished he were with her, for the winter nights had become long and lonely. She felt as distant from him as she had when he was in Russia, and she begged him to remember that they had leapt the flames together on Midsummer's Eve.

The letter had stirred conflicting emotions in Erich: a swordstroke of desire that startled him with its intensity, a flush of anger at her provincial phobias, resentment at her older sister's renewed meddling, and curiosity with regard to what Sibelius's true feelings might be in this matter, given the obsessive way the old man kept referring to his own long-ago affair.

Piercing and grotesquely festive in this subterranean setting, the train whistle tooted at the trackside delegation. The honor guard's bootheels popped smartly, the diplomats assumed more erect postures, and a pair of hovering journalists readied their cameras to record the next moment for posterity and the morning edition. They were careful to include Erich in the frame, with his Wehrmacht uniform and the Iron Cross at his throat, for the photos would be sent to the German wire services for reproduction in the Reich, as tangible proof of the continued closeness between Germany and her Nordic cobelligerent.

The photographers got more than they bargained for. When Sibelius descended the stairs from his compartment, assisted at one elbow by a ruddy and officious Rautavaara, he immediately strode over to Erich, clapped the startled man in a spindly, two-handed embrace, and cried: "Ah, Erich, tonight you'll show them all how the Fourth is really meant to go! I know it in my bones!"

If Erich had not been nervous about the concert before that public declaration of faith, he became so at that instant. The composer's remark, delivered in front of the press, made him realize just how much was being wagered, both by himself and by his patron. If Erich succeeded, if he led that harsh, recondite, enigmatic symphony with as much expertise and understanding as he believed himself ready to do, then thresholds could be crossed; it could possibly lead to the Eighth. By the composer's own reckoning, he had heard few truly convincing performances of the Fourth, although he unhesitatingly labeled it his greatest symphony.

By the time they shook free of the press, Erich was perspiring freely, as nervous as a neophyte. You've done this before, he kept telling himself; you just walk out there and wave your little stick.

Not this time, "Maestro" Ziegler. Not this time.

His apprehension became so great that he excused himself, pleading other duties, as soon as the composer's entourage had been settled in the Hotel Vaakuna's presidential suite. He then ordered his driver to head southeast, to a warehouse on Mikonkatu Street, near the University Concert Hall. Leaving the engine running and the driver smoking a cigarette, Erich extracted a set of keys from his coat pocket and opened the

front door on an unmarked, vaguely commercial-looking
structure, one of the many old Imperial-style buildings still in
this neighborhood; once, he supposed, it had been the home
of some minor branch of the Tsarist bureaucracy. Inside, he
passed through a hallway, switching on lights, and unlocked
an inner door that led to the instrument storage facility of the
Helsinki Philharmonic Orchestra.

Inside the room it was warm, dry, a bit musty. Arrayed on
all sides were mummy cases for double basses, packing crates
for harps, shrouded humps of timpani, and in the center of
the room, protected by dust sheets, the set of tubular chimes
that had arrived from Germany, after an odyssey of remarkable complexity and duration, only days after Erich himself
had arrived to take up his new post. He walked over to the instruments. He flung the coverings off as though he were dis-
robing an eager woman, then stood back to scrutinize them.
They stood almost five feet tall and weighed more than two
hundred pounds. Their color was slightly duller and more
mottled than the silvery luster of the chimes one normally saw
in percussion sections—a result, no doubt, of the peculiar al-
loys and admixtures that had gone into their casting.

In a case to one side, resting on the lid of a piano, were
mallets of various kinds. Erich picked up the nearest one and
struck a random interval on the chimes. They produced the
coldest, most penetrating bell sounds he had ever heard.
Sibelius would be startled, and probably very pleased, when
he heard them tonight. The chime notes seemed to hang in
the air, faint overtones still trembling in the shadows. Erich's
doubts receded; the effect, he thought, would surely be as he
envisioned. With that thought came renewed confidence that
the entire performance would go well.

That night, the University Concert Hall was filled with a
glittering audience. Marshal Mannerheim and President Ryti
were there with their staffs—the former's men looking stern
and Prussian in their tunics and polished straps, the latter's
cabinet, dressed in out-of-date diplomatic cutaways, looking
like so many provincial imitations of Neville Chamberlain.
Sibelius occupied a special box, bordered on all sides with flo-

ral tributes. Microphones hung above the stage and thick cables snaked up the aisles to replay transmitters that would broadcast the program live in both Finland and Sweden and feed the signals to a bank of hulking Magnetophon tape recorders recently imported from Germany. The first half hour of the evening was given over to speeches, tributes, and the reading of a singularly pompous ode in honor of the composer, who seemed to soak it all up indiscriminately, sitting erect and eagle-faced in his box, carefully presenting his classic profile to the newsreel photographers.

In a knife-creased dress uniform, Erich paced the backstage area like a caged leopard, slapping his baton against the palm of his left hand as though the implement were a swagger stick. The speeches seemed to last forever. Onstage, the orchestra moved restlessly in their seats. Rehearsals had been grueling but very satisfying—the men had not forgotten Erich, and their willingness to dig deep for him had been both touching and unique in his professional experience. He had been cunning enough to reserve one surprise for them, however, for during rehearsals he had used the orchestra's regular chimes. Tonight, he had substituted the new set. He had taken one percussionist into his confidence, even escorting the man to the warehouse and permitting him to try the new instruments privately. After playing a few scales, the man looked at Erich strangely and said: "For the Sibelius Fourth, these are perfect. Whoever made them was an artist."

During that interminable wait, Erich had time to wonder what the reviews would be like in the morning. He had observed the critics, seated in a cluster within sight of the Sibelius box. He wanted to believe they would be fair in their assessment, but he knew there would inevitably be subtle colorations to the way in which he was regarded, for his appearance on the scene had been occasioned by political, diplomatic, and private considerations, even more than artistic ones.

Now one of the engineers saw a green light flash on. He settled a pair of earphones over his head and waggled a finger at Erich: one minute to go. On stage, the president of the university finished his encomium, bowed to polite applause, and ambled self-consciously from the stage. As soon as he was off, the radio technician made a chopping motion with his hand. Erich took a deep breath and walked out into a sudden loudness of clapping, into a charged field of expectancy.

He did not begin with the Fourth, but rather with an earlier and more lighthearted work, the tone poem *Pohjola's Daughter,* a rollicking description in sound of one of the hero Väinämöinen's many amorous encounters. Substantial enough not to seem a makeweight, the composition was as warmly colored as the Fourth would be stark and cold. At the start of rehearsals, the orchestra had tended to play the work in a blowsy, full-blown manner, as though it were early Richard Strauss. Erich had worked on it, however, and by the final rehearsal, he was conjuring from them a sonority that was leaner, finer-grained, full without being fat. In terms of rhythm, he tried to impart to the work's phrases the kind of lilt he had heard from the ancient rune-singer, as though a many-tongued voice were chanting the music.

When the tone poem was finished, Erich took his first bow, then strode rapidly offstage and peered surreptitiously into the hall. To a man, the critics, even the most respected, were stealing glances at Sibelius, gauging the old man's reaction before committing themselves. Sibelius himself was wreathed in smiles and was flapping his hands together like a seal. The audience's applause renewed itself. Erich smiled to himself cynically: the Helsinki critics were no more immune to taking their cues from on high than were the critics in Berlin . . .

He waited a suitable interval for the applause to die down and for an optimal silence to settle over the hall; then he went back onstage. As he did so, every muscle in his body tense and his right foot throbbing, he reflected that nobody, not even the most embittered, world-weary critic, could accuse him of seeking a cheap success with the next part of his program. Although it had been composed as long ago as 1911, the Fourth was still the shunned wallflower of the composer's *oeuvre,* rarely performed, recorded only twice, and seldom greeted with any reaction more demonstrative than polite applause. Opening with brutal severity, closing on a note of quiet stoicism, it offered nothing in the way of crowd-pleasing excitement. Hearing this music was not necessarily the most pleasant forty minutes one could spend in a concert hall; it would never be greeted with bravos. And yet it was the composer's most original and singular work, and in its unadorned, yet also unafraid, contemplation of a landscape without warmth, an existence without pity, amelioration, or idealism, Erich found a kind of bedrock heroism. To get inside the Fourth, even as a listener, meant a kind of direct, unblinking, private confrontation with a bleakness few people cared to discover within themselves.

Erich knew. He had been to the places, both physical and psychological, where this music was born; had crouched in atavistic terror at the sight of imaginary giant footfalls crushing down the forest, coming for him. He had learned that Hell was a place not of boiling flames and capering demons, but a vast plain of granite, scoured by shrapnel bursts of ice, a place where one was always alone and where one's soul simply existed, without referents of comfort or certainty. In this work at least, Sibelius had transcended himself and become more than just a composer; in this score, as in no other, he had become a prophetic voice. The perfect performance of it—the interpretation that would finally make people understand what the Fourth was all about—would be greeted with stunned silence.

During his rehearsals of the work, Erich had tried to get the orchestra to play as though they were a chamber ensemble. He had insisted that each man *listen* as well as play; not only to the weave of musical argument, but also to the pools of silence the music had to thread its way through, and the vaster spiritual silence that surrounded the work as a whole. Only when the ensemble's playing had achieved cogent intimacy and utter transparency did he loosen the reins and allow more spontaneity, rhythmic thrust, and drama. He knew from the downbeat that, tonight, it had all come together.

The chimes were silent until the fourth movement—music

which would in any other context seem grudging and dour, but which did bring a kind of grim resolution to the symphony's emotional progression. Not triumph—that cold, empty plain still framed all human thought and feeling—but at least a kind of acceptance. The *Glocken* were there to punctuate the last movement's expressions of vigor; when played on the conventional instruments, the effect was of a sudden glint of sunlight, bright but still chilly.

The moment had come. Erich cued the percussionist and the man struck with his chosen mallets. A new sound pierced the orchestral fabric. It was still a sudden brightening of color, but it no longer necessarily suggested sunlight; it was harsher, colder, the color of bone under moonlight. Instead of brightening the mood, it stabbed through it, and in the midst of the symphony's brightest and most affirmative pages, it adumbrated something nocturnal, almost charnal. Erich could see its effect on the faces of the orchestra members, who knew instantly that they were hearing a timbre that had never been produced in this music before, yet one that was unarguably correct. As Erich had wished, the chimes' unique tone was a powerful stroke; it subtly altered the character of the fourth movement, setting up a stern tension between the music's outward impulse toward warmth and resignation, and the rest of the symphony's attitude of comfortless endurance. When the movement ended—in a spartan diminuendo that seemed to say: enough, the journey is finished, ask for nothing more—the effect was disturbing, not simply resigned.

In the uneasy silence which followed the final bars, Erich bowed stiffly and walked offstage. Scattered applause began. He peered into the hall and looked toward the composer's box, noticing that every critic in the hall was openly staring at the old man, waiting for some cue as to how to respond to Erich's interpretation. Sibelius himself sat like a statue carved from basalt. Timid, hesitant hand-claps rippled up and down the hall, not yet conjoined into a real wave of applause. Slowly, Sibelius turned, eyes hidden in shadow, seeking out Erich. Never had the old man looked so monumental, never had he played his public role with such timing or poise. Finally he rose, with the gravest deliberation, and in a grand, sweeping gesture he flung out his arms toward Erich. As though drawn by a puppeteer's strings, Erich walked back onstage and heard the first "Bravo!" uttered in a cracked, emotional voice from the composer's own lips. Now the entire hall was on its feet, the critics wreathed in benedictory smiles, some of them bent over, furiously scribbling notes on the margins of their programs. Flashbulbs popped as the composer, assisted by Rautavaara and a uniformed aide, made his way to the stage and clasped Erich in a tremulous embrace.

"*Wunderbar!*" he whispered in the younger man's ear, "*Ausgezeichnet!* In God's name, where did you find those bells?"

"I had them cast in the underworld, Maestro, in Tuonela, and they are my birthday present to you."

In response to the prolonged ovation, the two men joined hands and bowed in unison.

At the reception which followed the concert, in the banquet hall of the Esplanadikappeli Restaurant, Erich found himself seated far from the composer, next to Rautavaara, at the end of the table; he might indeed have scored a conducting triumph this evening, but when the sun rose tomorrow, he would still be a comparatively minor functionary in a large wartime bureaucracy. Nevertheless, before the toasts to Sibelius began, the composer himself insisted on honoring Erich with a short speech, a toast, another embrace. There followed a great many other toasts, and Sibelius, basking in the attention, joined most of them. Rautavaara kept score on the back of his place card and when the composer had reached a certain limit, diffidently approached and suggested that the day had been long. Erich could hear, all the way down at his end of the table, the high-pitched quarrelsome note in the composer's response, a sure sign that the old fellow was past his limit. Like an equerry bringing bad news to an ancient despot, Rautavaara was angrily banished. Sibelius rose, somewhat unsteadily, and shooed the major back even farther. "Maestro Ziegler will see me home, thank you!" he barked peevishly. Erich saw that the composer's arm was dramatically thrust in his direction—a royal summons if ever he'd seen one—and he accepted the inevitable by mumbling his apologies to the Swedish diplomat seated on his left and the university trustee across the table.

Rautavaara stoically assisted Sibelius into his overcoat. "I'll have the driver bring the car around," he said when Erich joined them.

"That won't be necessary," Sibelius insisted. "Maestro Ziegler can drive me alone."

While the composer fumbled with his hat and scarf, Rautavaara whispered urgently into Erich's ear: "Be careful—as of today, the blackout regulations are in full force. We've had some alarming intelligence reports of a buildup on the Red airfields in Karelia. I'll follow in a staff car about a block behind you, and if there's any trouble, just pull over, let me get in front of you, and I'll lead you to cover as quickly as possible."

Erich had been too preoccupied with his concert to pay much attention to the recent war news, but as soon as he began to drive he saw that Helsinki was indeed a darker place than it had been earlier in the week. Blackout regulations were always technically in force, for the city was within easy striking distance of many Soviet airfields, but because there had been no raids on the capital for two years—in keeping with the general torpor that had settled over the Finnish front—their enforcement had grown very slack. Now, as he turned the car onto Aleksanderinkatu and obtained a wider view than was possible from the cramped nineteenth-century streets around the university, Erich saw that Helsinki was dark again.

Sibelius noticed it too. The cold air, the sudden plunge into silent, snow-shrouded streets empty of traffic, past government buildings where greatcoated sentries paced with loaded Suomis across their chests, sobered him somewhat. He struggled to extricate a cigar from his coat pocket, drew smoke, exhaled a long melancholy sigh.

"I understand the Americans have been sounding out the Russians on the possibility of a separate peace treaty with us.

Top-secret business, of course, but some drunken politician came up to me this evening and *thanked* me for it—said it was largely because of me that America still gave a damn what happens to Finland! Imagine that—at my age, I turn out to be a secret weapon! The Reds won't do it, of course. They have all that humiliation from the Winter War to expunge. Stalin will want his victory clear-cut and highly visible. I only pray it will be enough for him to humble us, not crush us utterly.

"In a sense, Erich, you're lucky to be German. Germany will live, even if it is totally defeated, even if only in some truncated form, because it is too important a part of Europe, and its continued existence, in some tamed and chastened form, is necessary to too many other nations. Finland, on the other hand, is necessary to no one, not even the bloody Swedes. We could be snuffed out. All that would be left would be the legend of the Winter War and my music."

It occurred to Erich that there was considerably more to Finland's national identity than those two ingredients, but after all, the old man had just spent two days being treated as the living embodiment of the state and no one could blame him, not after such a triumphal day as this, for choosing to regard himself so highly.

They reached the hotel without incident. Rautavaara made certain that Sibelius was ambulatory and that Erich would need no assistance taking him back to his suite, then departed. By the time they reached the top-floor presidential rooms, their ambience made slightly more confining now by the heavy blackout curtains that had been drawn across the windows, Sibelius seemed to have gotten a second wind. His movements were livelier and his voice had dropped in pitch. On a damask-covered table in the center of the room—a comfortable distance from a log fire so cheerful in its blaze that Erich had a quick vision of elves, dressed in hotel livery, rushing out to light it at the instant their car pulled into view—stood a bottle of excellent brandy and a ring of glasses.

"Ah, I see they've been looking after things in my absence. Join me in a nightcap, Erich. You've earned it." It seemed a command, not a request, so Erich opened the bottle and poured. For a time, there was only the sound of the fire, crackling against a buffer of leaden silence that seemed to have crept in from the dark, inert city outside.

"Your performance tonight . . . it was deep and clear, like an arctic river. The bell tones were sublime, and I thank you for them. You have a great gift: you have ability coupled with imagination, which is a combination not found as commonly as you might suppose. My instinct about you was right."

The composer raised his snifter as though toasting his own perspicacity. Erich knew there had never been a better moment to ask him a direct and unambiguous question about the Eighth Symphony, but he was also aware that Sibelius was coasting on alcohol and a charge of nervous energy, precisely the conditions under which he was at his most unpredictable. This "good moment" would have to pass; probably the composer himself would choose the time and place to bring up the Eighth. So the subject remained in the air close to them both, a ghostlike presence on the periphery of their dialogue. Both men knew it was there, yet each—for different reasons—pretended it was not. Erich poured some brandy on the anxiety in his stomach, that muscle which knotted whenever the subject of the Eighth drifted into range and yet could not be addressed openly.

"Your performance," Sibelius continued, "had emotion, but no sentiment. That's good, because sentiment can make you weak, while emotion can make you strong. You have passed beyond mere sentiment where the girl Kylliki is concerned, have you not? And yet the emotions still run strong?"

"I haven't spoken of it, Maestro, because it seemed indelicate to do so." Erich leaned forward, a bewildered expression replacing weary contentment on his features. Why had the old man changed to this subject? "I haven't sensed disapproval from you, so I saw no need to belabor the obvious . . . I hope our behavior hasn't been indiscreet."

"Oh no, quite the contrary!" A bawdy grin creased the old man's features. "Considering the degree of lust you must feel for her, you've managed to keep your trysts both private and unobtrusive. And I *am* aware of how much desire you feel for her, Erich—I am not so old that I have forgotten what that kind of intoxication is like."

Now Sibelius was smiling at him with the presumed intimacy of an old drinking partner. Well, Erich thought, if they were going to go man-to-man now, he would follow along. He raised his glass and toasted the composer with a self-conscious gesture of camaraderie. Sibelius leaned forward unsteadily to clink glasses. Inwardly, Erich winced at the contact.

"I wrote to her several times and asked her to come to Helsinki for the concert. She did not want to risk your disapproval."

"I am," stated Sibelius with all the inebriated dignity he could muster, "the last man on God's earth to disapprove of healthy copulation. Her reasons were more subtle than that, I'm sure, for had she asked me, I would of course have invited her to accompany me in my railroad carriage. At my age, I would certainly not turn down the chance to be seen with such a woman; think of how delicious the gossip would be!" Erich watched with muted displeasure as the old man smacked his lips indecently.

"Why didn't she come, then?" he said, striving to maintain a bogus mood of conviviality.

"Imagine yourself born to the forest world. Knowing nothing but that world. Raised to believe that some fated, predestined lover would come to you *in* the forest, and that your mutual passion would flourish within the context of the forest . . . for that, I believe, is how see sees her life: all verging on her encounter with you, as though that were a part of the forest's grand, inscrutable design."

Sibelius waved his empty glass; Erich grudgingly poured a refill. "She sometimes talked of that," he said, placing the bottle out of the composer's reach. "At first, it sounded charming, but after a while, it just sounds stiflingly backward and primitive." His eyes implored Sibelius as if to say: we are men of the world, you and I, so surely, if you *must* prattle on about this, you can help me deal with it coolly, rationally. But Sibelius was not about to oblige.

"That's because she is essentially a pagan creature, your

Kylliki, like . . . like other forest-dwellers I have known. What has happened between you two was meant to happen *there*, for that is where she dwells and where she will always dwell. She knows nothing else, seeks nothing else, and would be wretched, perhaps even ill, if she spent a prolonged time any- where else. For her, it is as though a kind of magic surrounds your intimacy while you are in her world, a world into which you have gone more deeply than most strangers ever could. That magic would fail, or twist inward upon itself, if the re- lationship were transplanted to another environment."

"For God's sake," Erich blurted out, rising and pacing over to the window. "I'm not asking her to change her reli- gion, just to come visit me here in Helsinki, a place I would have thought she might be curious to see after a lifetime of living in the backwoods! Is the idea of having a good time so painful to her?"

"You miss the point, still," Sibelius mumbled, waving his free hand over the top of his drink. "It's true that like all country girls, she's fascinated by the idea of the big city, and on one level, I'm sure she aches to be in your company. But on a deeper level, she feels that there is a risk of violating the balance inherent in your relationship, and that between your relationship and the world in which it has flourished. Call it superstition if you like, but do not dismiss the power of such beliefs. If such a person believes something hard enough, it is not necessary to prove objectively that it is true—things hap- pen as if it were, and that is all we need to remember."

Sibelius sighed and drained his glass, rested his forehead against the claw of his hand, losing energy now, coming down. Then he raised his face and Erich was surprised to see an expression of pain. He leaned forward and took Erich's arm.

"You do still love her, Erich? It's not only physical desire that impels you to summon her? You understand what it meant when you leapt through the flames with her on Mid- summer's Eve?"

Erich nodded, although the thought flared in his mind

that, to judge from the composer's present agitation, perhaps he had not, at least not entirely.

"She understands, I think, that you simply cannot go off into the woods and live in a cabin with her for the rest of your life; it was not that kind of commitment that was required. But it *was* a bonding that established the permanency, and at times the primacy, of her love in the context of your future. It was a promise, on her part, that she would always be there, ready and eager for you, living harmoniously in her world, ready once again to open its doors for you, any time you choose to pass through them. And on your part, it was a promise that you would always return, that she and the forest would be your heart's center of gravity, no matter how long or how far you had to be away. It was not exactly a betrothal, yet in some ways it went deeper than one. For she will still be there, still as much in love with you as she is today. She *will not change*, Erich, not in that respect!"

Sibelius staggered to his feet, a fierceness in his eyes. For a moment he stood, trembling, in front of Erich, with an expression of such inner turmoil that Erich feared for his heart. Then, abruptly, he turned away and leaned tiredly against the mantel.

"Perhaps if she did come here, you would see that these things are truer than you now believe. I don't know what will happen, but for your sake, and for hers—and for the sake of my music and the difference you can make in its acceptance—I shall persuade her, order her, whatever it takes, to come here to see you, after Christmas. I'll have Major Rautavaara communicate the date and time of the train's arrival. Now please go; I'm very tired."

It was a dismissal. Confused, groggy, not quite sure what had been said to him or why, Erich rose and bade the composer good night. As he bent to replace the top of the decanter, he glanced up, at a firelit angle, and saw that the old man's eyes were full of unshed tears.

Twenty-three

Whether Sibelius had persuaded Kylliki to come to Helsinki, or had simply commanded her to, she arrived on a morning train two weeks into the new year of 1944. Rautavaara had telephoned Erich several days before and said: "The girl is coming," followed by a train number, date, and time of arrival. From Kylliki herself, there had been no communication, and now, as Erich watched the train's headlight fill the tunnel, then suddenly spill out into the main terminal, he felt as anxious as a young suitor waiting for his first date.

She descended the stairs hesitantly, peering through a veil of steam with a shy expression on her face. She saw Erich, waved, ducked back inside for her bag, then walked toward him with a brisk, tense stride. She was dressed for winter, in a roughspun woolen coat, her neck nicely framed by the folds of its retracted cowl. Her hair formed two shining wings the color of winter sunlight; her face was pale, but her eyes, seemingly enormous, were their darkest color, almost damson. Seeing her thus, he was swept by such desire that he wanted to run forward and plant the city at her feet, as though he were a great warlord bearing the spoils of a fallen capital. The nagging sense of something being out of sync was banished by the simple fact of her presence.

When they embraced, he could feel tension flowing through her, felt himself absorb some of it.

"You didn't write . . ." he began.

"I only knew I was coming a few days ago. I would have gotten here before the letter. Besides, Erich, we were not meant to talk on paper, only together."

The thought occurred to him—it tallied with the hesitancy, the childlike scrawl, of the one brief letter she had sent him—that she probably did not have much formal education; country school rudiments, probably, but surely nothing more. He reminded himself to go slowly at first on this visit. This woman not only had no experience with cities, she was convinced that she belonged in the forest and nowhere else.

Very well, then, it was time for her education to commence. He thought they made an attractive couple, in any case—she so strikingly crowned by her glorious hair, himself erect in spotless dress uniform, his boots glossy, the Iron Cross at his throat, his breast splashed with colorful campaign ribbons, his face hard and fit, its martial cast offset by the compressed sensuality of his mouth. Erich had stood with many dignitaries, had bowed to many audiences, yet on this morning, at Kylliki's side, he luxuriated in pride as never before. He would show her the city royally, as though unrolling it for her like a fabulous scroll. In a sense, it would be like taking another kind of virginity from her, and he found that idea curiously exciting.

His first pleasures with her, that morning of her arrival, turned out to be simpler ones. He was surprised at the joy he derived from such mundane acts as driving the car and holding the door open for her, and he reveled in the envious glances of other men when he and Kylliki traversed the lobby of his hotel. He had traded his own Spartan room, requisitioned under wartime regulations, for a spacious suite; it had cost him a month's pay and a bribe to the desk clerk in the form of some extra gasoline ration coupons. But what delight it afforded him to open the brass-bound lobby doors for her, allowing her to sweep past him like a princess. Her eyes widened at the sight of the marble and gilt and leather of the interior. A few moments later, after a ride in a brass-trimmed elevator piloted by a factotum whose uniform was even more elaborate than Erich's, he threw open the door to their suite and heard her gasp at the sight of the large white ruffly bed, the chandeliers, mirrors, pile rugs, and gleaming porcelains.

She was more than willing to make love right then and there. Shedding her coat, she thrust herself on him, jamming her breasts against his chest and sealing his mouth with the sweet heat of her own. Although he was strongly tempted, he finally, gently, disengaged her, assuring her that there would be plenty of time for lovemaking later, after they had seen some sights, enjoyed a dinner. Not that he wasn't tempted—his body's response confirmed how starved he was for her touch. He caressed her while they kissed, finding each breast and greedily tugging each nipple to engorgement. Then he pulled back, cocked his head teasingly, and made a gesture of caution. He laughed when she misinterpreted it and looked nervously over her shoulder, as though someone might be watching.

"Let's wait until tonight, my love. I have the whole day carefully, shall we say, 'orchestrated,' and it would never do to perform the finale before the scherzo."

"You don't want me now?" she pouted, a little breathlessly.

"I want you desperately. But by tonight, after the wonderful day I've arranged for us, and the sublime dinner we'll be eating, I shall want you a thousand times more."

"What if it's only a hundred times more?" she said, touching her hair and dress, but smiling again.

"Then I'll owe you nine hundred."

"I was never very good at arithmetic, so I guess I'll just have to trust you."

They were interrupted by a knock on the door. Erich opened it to find the coffee and fresh rolls he had ordered from room service while checking in at the front desk. He poured a cup for himself and enjoyed it while Kylliki prowled the room, her face lighting up with naive delight at the sight and feel of furnishings, curtains, even the supply of stationery in the bedside drawers. Finally, she left off her pacing and joined him for coffee and rolls. Insisting that she needed no other meal until evening, she now seemed eager to fall in with him and follow wherever he chose to lead.

He parked on the edge of the great *kauppatori*, the city's open-air market district on the edge of the South Harbor. As always, even in winter, the market was thronged. It was the city's heart, and on this clear but icy day it was an oasis of warmth and color; moving among the throngs of people there, from one oil-drum bonfire to the next, it was easy to forget the cold. Erich and Kylliki held hands, as though they were young students skipping class for the day, and together they moved through the crowd, listening to the singsong of a dozen Finnish dialects, some of them so thick that even Kylliki had trouble understanding them.

Along the quays, a hundred fishermen displayed their catches. They had been out on the harbor ice since before dawn, sheltered in tiny stove-equipped shacks, tending lines dropped through holes into the inky waters below, and had come back in to catch the afternoon's pedestrian traffic. Their fish lay on the bows of boats—now beached and canvas-shrouded for the season—in beds of shaved ice, so freshly caught that the ice was pink beneath their open mouths, while housewives hefted them, plumped them knowingly with ap-praising hands, and haggled vigorously with the leathery fish-ermen who stood, wreathed in pungent tobacco smoke, behind their displays. In the sun, the long line of fish, spread in a thin ring around most of the seafront, looked like an im-mense silver necklace.

Other tables and stalls, facing the row of fish vendors and stretching back toward the downtown district, displayed baked goods, candy, tobacco products, thread and lace, sauna-whisks and wooden ladles, chickens and boots, cabbages and Swedish magazines, and tall steaming samovars of coffee and tea. To satisfy her whim, Erich bought them each a waxed-paper cone full of steaming French-fried potatoes, sweet, mealy, and glittering with coarse grains of salt. She burned her tongue on one, her eyes popping from the pain as she bit into its fiery center. He showed her how to nibble the potatoes from one end, how to blow on the next part before biting into it. She laughed wonderfully even at this mundane ritual.

Not until the afternoon was waning did she finally tire of the market and agree to accompany him several blocks north, to Senate Square, where she was as overwhelmed by open, formal space as she had been just moments before by crowds. When, after rounding a corner, they first came in sight of the great central plaza, she clapped her hands in a burst of childlike glee. Her delight was contagious—Erich could almost see the sights through her eyes. He joined her in a dance around the base of the bronze statue of Alexander II. Best of all, she liked the huge open vista of gently rising steps, a whole hillside of them, that led upward to the snow-white facade of the Cathedral of St. Nicholas. Against the azure sky, the configuration of its elegant copper domes hinted at some faint northward percolation from Byzantium.

"Let's go inside," he suggested.

Kylliki stared at the building as though it were made of gold, raising herself on tiptoe, then leaning first to one side, then the other, as though she were trying to engrave every detail of the scene on her memory. "No," she finally said, "let's just walk around it from this distance. The interior could not possibly be grander than what we're seeing."

"But it is," he insisted. "It's filled with icons and gold and stained glass, with hundreds of treasures."

"I don't care, Erich. This is exactly how I want to remember the sight." They circumnavigated the cathedral from that distance. And while they explored the great square, she clutched his arm tightly, as though she might at any moment be struck by vertigo.

There were still a few restaurants in Helsinki where it was possible to obtain a fair imitation of a prewar dinner; they were not frequented by the general public, however, and it required some phone calls on Erich's behalf by a highly placed Finnish politician—a music lover, as it happened, who had been at the Sibelius birthday concert—to secure reservations for them. She sat on the edge of her seat, nervous as a fawn, her eyes bright. Twice during the meal, important-looking men in well-tailored clothes came to their table and exchanged greetings with Erich, with the obvious intent of getting a better look at the striking young woman he was with. Erich had planned to cap the evening with a trip to the theater, but so intense was Kylliki's delight in the meal and its exotic rituals of service that they lingered until well past curtain time. When they finally did leave, they walked the distance back to the hotel, through streets that looked as though they had been glazed with sugar.

Heavy blackout curtains had turned their bedroom into a stuffy enclosure. Once the lights were off, they retracted the curtains, permitting a diffuse snowy glow to seep in from the streets below. Erich made love to her by that cool, pearly light, but the tranquility of the illumination seemed to generate in him a chafed, contrary mood. He changed positions frequently, as though prodded by a fever of restlessness, unable to savor her in one configuration without soon wanting to try another. Rather than the epic encounter he had envisioned this morning, it was a compulsive and athletic coupling, and although it siphoned off the pressure that had been building between them since morning, he felt it was too febrile to unite them closely. The climax left him gasping, sticky, mildly irritated that it had not been better and more luxurious. He tried to be philosophical: perhaps, now that all that urgency had been damped, they would rest, talk, try again later, with superior results.

Erich's cigarette bobbed in shadow. On the other side of the bed, nearer to the big French windows, Kylliki sat up in a wash of silver-white refraction, tracing the line of his breast with her fingertips.

"I have to tell you something, a little bit of a confession," she said. He rested his free hand on top of hers, feeling the rounded motion of its tendons. The movements reminded him of piano strings in vibration, and the rhythmic pattern of her caress suggested Debussy.

"Now is a good time for it."

"I asked Madame Sibelius if I could listen to your concert, on the night of the Master's birthday. She said yes." She straightened and her hand motions ceased; in Erich's mind, the Debussy quotations continued to flow, cool as alabaster. "It was almost as if I could feel you entering the room over the airwaves. You had a power that night, Erich, and I could feel it, even transmitted over such a distance. I had been missing you dreadfully, and it was almost as though I were touching you again, at least while the music was playing."

She shook her head and rose to a kneeling position, breasts now painted with silver, hair platinum in the strangely vaporous light. "And after the concert was over, after the applause had faded, I thanked Madame for sharing the wireless with me, then I hurried back to the island, while I still had that feeling of closeness, and I shut my bedroom door and took off my clothes and lay down and pretended you were beside me, and I touched myself the way you sometimes do. It was over in a moment or two, all sharp and bittersweet, and on the crest of it, I called out to you, as though you could receive my feelings over a wireless here too. And when it was all over, I grew sad very quickly."

Erich thought of her, giving pleasure to herself with the echo of his concert still in her mind, and felt himself stirring once again. Hands on her thighs, she was bent over him, her face sunk in shadow. All he could see were the lines of her shoulders, the hair like silk woven from ashes. As she finished speaking, he extended his free hand and cupped the cuttlebone sharpness of her pubis, kneading the hot moss he found there. Automatically, she began to roll her hips. It felt as though his hand were being kissed; the hair on the back of his wrist mingled with the down inside her upper thighs, a sensation of oriental subtlety.

He felt relieved, convinced now that their first groping, all-at-once encounter had merely been an overeager, almost adolescent, discharge. The real lovemaking, the experience that would set a seal upon this day, was yet to happen. Because he wanted her to be pleased, to drift in that same direction with him, he said: "I think perhaps I did feel something, a sudden burst of desire, while I was changing into fresh clothes after the concert. It stopped me with one shoe in midair," and having said it, he began to convince himself that he had.

"Tell me about the bells, Erich. That's all the Master could talk about when he returned from Helsinki—about how wonderful the bells were."

He rolled farther into the snowy light, wanted her to see the pride in his face. "I had them cast especially for the Fourth when I was in Germany. I wanted to reproduce for him the sound he had in mind—the sound you showed me in the forest. Tomorrow, if you like, we can go to the place where they're stored, and you can play them."

Her face lit with anticipation. Excitingly, she rubbed against him like a length of hot silk, suddenly kittenish, playful, laughing and tossing her head.

"I had a fearful row with Anna-Liisa before I left this morning. If the Master had not ordered me to come, I would have had to yield to her demands."

"Well, what does she demand of you? That you stay cooped up in the woods forever?" He kicked free of the sheets, strode forcefully to the window, and gestured at the city. "There's a whole world out here, Kylliki, and you can sample as much of it as you like, without losing your roots in the forest. She can't expect you to live your life like a nun, even if she seems content to do so."

Kylliki drew her knees up to her chin, reflexively covering herself with the sheet. Erich returned to the bed, suddenly apprehensive at the change of mood. They had seemed to be on the verge of renewed desire, and then Older Sister had managed a long-distance intrusion. It was time, he told himself, to regain the initiative and to keep it.

"My sister said: 'You don't belong in the city. The balances are shifting again, and it is dangerous for you to leave at such a time.'"

"Good God," growled Erich, shifting his weight so that his hand could find the spot it had recently occupied.

"Erich, she is also worried about you."

"Nice of her to be concerned." He laid a string of half-moon kisses from her knee to her hip. Kylliki let him finish, even shifted to accommodate him, but then she disengaged once more.

"She knows—we both know—that you can't just come dwell in the forest, that your work has to be done elsewhere. But during the times when you can come back to me, there's always a kind of transition to be made. She's afraid that circumstances are working against that, making it more difficult, afraid that you will stay away for longer and longer periods of time . . . and that eventually the connection will become too feeble to bind us anymore."

Worry lines broke the moon-smooth plane of her brow. Damn her sister!

"The connection that binds us is not feeble," he declared, his voice close to anger. He explored her insistently with his hand now; deep wet muscles fluttered against his fingertips.

"Indeed they are not, especially since we jumped the bonfires together. And you see now why you must honor that ceremony—because something wonderful has already come about for you."

Erich saw no causal connection between something that had happened one night in June and the opportunity that had opened for him in December, but if it pleased her to believe that there was, so be it.

"And how do I honor it, my love?"

"You see?" she chided him, wagging a long white finger before his nose, "if we were still in Tapiola, you wouldn't have to ask such a question—you'd already know. You honor it by returning to me, at least once a year, to renew the pledge of our love that you made that night. Is that too much to ask of you?"

"I couldn't stay away from you for a whole year and you know it."

As he spoke the words, he meant them, even though some detached part of his mind remained aware that the war would not last forever and that his career, once successfully launched, might well take him far away for even longer periods. There was no conscious doubt about it right now, however: she was worth making a journey for. Pleased at his words, she pivoted gracefully away from his hand and slid down, with a sigh of sheets, her buttocks marbled in the snowlight, until her head was level with his hips. Slowly and magnificently, he felt himself being engulfed by an avid cone of heat.

They worked some kind of magic on each other that night, Erich thought when he woke the next morning, on a flood tide of renewed love for her. That second time had been the one he'd been fantasizing about for weeks, allowing him fully to rediscover her sweetness, the bounties of her heat, after a long period of being distanced from them. He had breakfast sent to their suite and he sought to treat her with the utmost delicacy and consideration. But Kylliki seemed to wake unrefreshed, with soft shadows under her eyes and a nagging cough that frequently interrupted her meal. She picked at her toast, ignored her coffee until it was cold. Her manner was still affectionate, but seemed touched with some nebulous discontent which she would not acknowledge and refused to discuss. Perhaps she had not slept as well as he had, after they had finally reached the condition of satiation they had been working toward all evening.

Erich dressed briskly, whistling; outside, the morning was overcast but tolerable-looking. He was ready to go out long before she was. She seemed to dress in slow motion, as though there were weights on every limb, and his bright enthusiasm for the coming day evoked in her only a tepid response.

Because it was not far away, he took her first to the warehouse on Mikonkatu. Once inside, he cut on the lights and ceremoniously threw back the dust sheets that covered the chimes. They glowed coldly. Proudly he handed her a mallet.

"Here—play a few scales or something. Wait until you hear the quality of the sound."

But she seemed reluctant to take the mallet, as though he were offering her a gun or a knout. Glancing down at it tensely, she frowned, seemed to struggle against some internal current. Finally, with a thin, forced smile, she permitted her fingers to close around the handle. Her forearm stiffly cocked, she approached the chimes as though she were about to strike a large insect. Erich watched with a feeling of dismay and bewilderment. Then she let the mallet drop to the floor. She shuddered, covered her mouth with her hands, and backed away.

"Erich, I cannot touch it. It sings of death. Can't you hear it?"

"No, God damn it, I can't! What's wrong with you?"

Anger flared quickly in her eyes, then was gone. "Forgive me, but I just cannot touch them. Be angry with me if you must, but I can't. How can you not feel it?"

"Feel *what*?"

The only thing he could feel was a rift opening between them at that moment which was capable of negating all they had shared in the past twenty-four hours. Kylliki must have sensed the same thing happening, and to stop it, she refused to say anything more about the chimes, but tugged imploringly at his sleeve, begging his forgiveness again.

They both tried hard to repair the morning. After relocking the warehouse, Erich suggested a trip to the big Olympic Stadium, hoping that such a spectacular sight might rekindle the fascination she had felt the day before when seeing the city for the first time. She maintained a resolute smile during the tour, but the immensity of the empty stadium made them feel puny, as though they were crawling on the rim of some gigantic meteor crater. When Erich tried to take her up into the 235-foot observation tower, whose topmost deck afforded an unexcelled view of the city, he was politely stopped by two uniformed sentries at the elevator entrance. Even as he showed his papers and talked with them, he saw the elevator disgorge a team of technicians carrying spools of cable. From their insignia, Erich recognized them as air defense troops; the tower had been commandeered as an air-raid warning outpost. When Erich had first checked on the possibility of going up into the tower, a week earlier, he had been told that it was still open, just as in peacetime. Now, all his training, all his instincts, told him that something new and ominous was in the air, and he made a mental note to keep his eyes open for other signs.

After a strained lunch back in the downtown district, he escorted Kylliki to Stockmann's, Helsinki's largest department store. Here at last a flicker of yesterday's enthusiasm returned to her. He purchased for her a pendant of amethyst on a chain of gold—to match her eyes, he said. He also bought her a dress, a silk scarf, and—while she looked away with mingled delight and embarrassment—a Swedish-made nightgown copied from the best prewar Hollywood styles.

She wore it for him that night, after a dinner that stretched out longer than it should have, as though both of them were wary of the night to come. Back in the suite, she took the nightgown box and her handbag into the bathroom, closed the door behind her, and stayed there for what seemed an inordinately long time. Erich heard sharp noises from time to time, as though objects were being nervously clicked against porcelain. He poured a drink, then another, and smoked a cigarette with each. He did not hear the bathroom door when it finally opened—he merely looked up, a scowl of impatience on his face, and beheld her standing in the doorway. She had donned the nightgown, painted her lips, darkened her brows and lashes, and pinned her hair back in a clumsy attempt at styling. The effect was gawky, adolescent, yet touching: an attempt at sexy sophistication made by a young woman whose only contact with the whole idea must have been dog-eared copies of out-of-date movie magazines.

"Do you like me this way?" she whispered, shyly opening her arms.

In a perverse way, he did. The sight of her nipples pushing against the nightgown's silk, the cling and slither of the material on the slope of her hips, was crudely, fetishistically, arousing. The tarty makeup coarsened her features, made a bright, bawdy parody of her mouth. He seized her roughly, tumbled her on to the bed with the lights still on, and began to kiss away her decorations.

As familiar music changes character when transposed to a new key, so did their passion take on an edge that was foreign but compelling, an element of masquerade that Erich found both liberating and slightly sinister. The sight of her smeary red mouth curled back with excitement stimulated him tremendously, and it seemed an invitation from her to be dominated on this occasion. So he shaped her to his whims, using her to explore idle currents of erotic speculation as he might with a high-priced whore. The friction of this unaccustomed role seemed to excite her as well, for she climaxed several times, with cries of unprecedented abandon that seemed to come from another woman's throat. Afterward, dazed with exhaustion, they bade each other good night with a tenderness that was almost apologetic.

In the morning, however, Kylliki awoke with stale traces of makeup on her face and her hair, still bobby-pinned here and there, tangled like a bird's nest. She looked as though she had been drawn upon with crayons, and her mood was sullen. He sensed that any jocular references to last night's scenario would be resented. There was the potential for a painful argument, palpable as a bad smell, should they choose to poke at each other hard enough to activate it. They chose not to, but the price was a prickly silence as Erich dressed. He had taken much time from his duties already, and he had to attend to at least a morning's worth of work before he could get free again. He spoke solicitously to her, ordered breakfast for her—certain as he did so that she would not eat it—and left her with an ample sum of money, in case she later wanted to explore the shops near the hotel.

He found it hard to concentrate on his work that morning. If Kylliki was simply out of sorts and perhaps disoriented by the environment itself, the change in her had influenced some of his own calculations. He had had no trouble with the idea of returning to her periodically, of going back to the forest. He had done so at every opportunity, had dreamed about it nightly, hourly, all the time he was in Russia. She had loomed in his mind as a creature of enchantment, a kind of wood sprite. Now, however, seeing her sad and confused amid mundane urban surroundings, he could relate to her simply as a real, albeit exotic, young woman with whom he happened to be in love.

But now that he saw her in that light, he also felt, as he never had when he was with her in Tapiola, that there could be stormy misunderstandings between them, compromising the instinctive clarity they had previously enjoyed. He did not want to lose her, nor to see her tired, angry, haggard. And in truth, until she had come to him here in the city, he had never seriously considered any of these possibilities. Perhaps this was the lesson Sibelius had sought to teach him by ordering Kylliki to come.

Suddenly convinced of a course of action, Erich asked for three days' leave of absence and made arrangements for them to take the morning train northward together.

As he walked back to the hotel, he noticed that military traffic had increased dramatically in the past twenty-four hours. Twice he watched convoys pass with towed Bofors guns, hulking searchlights, and once an enormous cluster of parabolic sound detectors; obviously, a major reinforcement of Helsinki's antiaircraft defenses was under way. Thinking back over his morning, Erich realized that the Finns in his bureau had seemed unusually tense and preoccupied, as well as somewhat guarded in conversation with their German allies.

He found Kylliki still in bed. She had drawn the blackout curtains, and the room was cloudy with cold grey light. Her skin was taut against her cheeks and there were pouches beneath her eyes; her lips were drawn and pale. Shocked by her appearance, he took her hand and pressed it.

"You didn't go out at all today?"

"I'm sorry, my love, but it's no good for me here anymore. Anna-Liisa was right. Can you forgive me?"

"Only if you'll go with me to the dinner party at the Hungarian Embassy tonight."

"Don't tease me, Erich. I cannot possibly go. I will not go."

"Would you if I told you that we are going back to Tapiola together, tomorrow morning, on the first northbound train? I've already phoned Major Rautavaara; he'll send a car to the nearest station."

Her very bones seemed to soften with relief and gratitude. She hugged him with thin arms and cried against his chest. He stroked her for a long time, and when she was finally quiet again, her flesh felt firmer, more vital, against him.

"If I put on a touch of makeup, can I still go to the embassy? I know I'll look like I've just been released from a hospital, but I'll try to make you proud of me."

There was a gallantry in her offer that touched him. He kissed her eyes—still hot and sunken—and told her that he could not fail to be proud of her, ever.

By the time they reached the embassy, not far from the university district, she had recovered her spirits and most of her looks. As she passed down the reception line with Erich, exchanging handshakes with diplomats and officers, she was treated with the deference that is the perquisite of great beauty, and she seemed to relish it. They danced, drank champagne, and exchanged private observations about various people in the room. Perhaps, Erich reflected, this was what it would be like for them if they were married. He decided that the prospect was altogether pleasing, and began thoroughly to enjoy himself.

He realized something was wrong when an *aide-de-camp* entered the room and cornered two Finnish generals for a whispered conversation. An uneasy current began to flow in the room. The generals thanked the messenger, then moved to speak with the ambassador himself. A moment later, that gentleman mounted a chair and waved for silence. Before he could speak, however, the banshee wail of air-raid sirens preempted his announcement. There were stunned glances—Helsinki had not been bombed in more than two years.

"Erich, where shall we go?"

"You should go to the basement, with the others. You'll be safe there. I need to see what's going on, though, and the balcony here is as good a place as any. Don't worry—I'll take cover if the raid gets close."

"I want to stay with you."

"Why?"

"So that at least on this one night, I will have been to war with you."

Her expression was touchingly earnest.

"Brave girl. Well, then, let's go watch the show."

Was this a false alarm, a token raid, or a major escalation? The only way to learn was to watch it happen, and it was his duty to do so—Klatt would want a firsthand account of this business. Erich led Kylliki out onto a balcony overlooking the southern harbor district, carefully closing the blackout curtains behind them. The sirens were eerie in the clear, frosty air. Searchlights probed the night in the direction of Estonia, for it was that vector—the Finns had learned in 1939—that afforded the optimum bomb run over Helsinki. There was a bomber's moon tonight, sure enough: a swollen white grape hanging over the frozen Baltic. It was impossible to hear the planes' engines above the sirens, but they must have been close because the heavy guns—100-mm batteries out on the city's perimeter—suddenly began slamming shells skyward. Searchlight beams oscillated, trembled, backtracked; then several beams closed in on a glint of wing, pinpointing the formation. Now Erich could see that this was not a nuisance raid but a serious air strike, for he counted at least twenty planes—Petlyakov Pe-2s—approaching in a quartet of V-formations.

The range closed now and the planes flew steadily into a sudden froth of Bofors fire, the sky below them lathered with firefly swarms of tracers. One plane took a hit and spiraled into the ice; several others rocked out of formation from near misses, but kept coming anyhow.

"Looks like they're going after the docks."

"Are we safe here?"

"We are if the bastards know how to aim properly."

Mushrooms of fire suddenly boiled among the warehouses, wharves, and loading facilities of the harbor. A small coastal icebreaker, trapped in a narrow lane of unfrozen water, took a bomb on the bow and immediately began to list. The bomb pattern crept inland, pounding the edge of the outdoor market, creeping toward Senate Square. Erich suddenly cried out in alarm.

"Christ, they're going to hit the instrument warehouse!" The thought of his chimes, the tangible symbol of his waxing fortunes, being destroyed by a bomb spurred him into frenetic action. Without waiting for the all-clear to sound, he raced outside to his car with Kylliki breathlessly in tow. They drove recklessly through streets lit by flames, pulling over several times for ambulances and fire engines, detouring twice around barricades of steaming rubble. A block from the ware-house, he was forced to pull over, for one of the old Tsarist-era buildings had taken a direct hit, spilling its masonry, lath, and woodwork into the street. Beyond that debris he saw a film of smoke in front of the storage building. He could not tell whether the smoke came from somewhere else, or from within the building itself.

"I've got to get those chimes out in case the fire spreads. You wait for me here."

He had only taken a few steps before her scream stopped him. Stumbling over a smoldering length of wainscoting, she grabbed his coat fiercely.

"Don't go in there, Erich! There is death in there!"

"Kylliki, for God's sake, the air raid is over, the planes have gone! Let go of me! I'm not in any danger!"

"Yes, you are! I tell you, there is death in that building!"

Lit by yellow flames, her face had changed: he could see the play of vulpine sinews, a subsurface of harsh planes and skull-tight lines, all softness and vulnerability vanished. One second she seemed older, the next she seemed ageless and somehow distorted, the familiar contours of her face wavering like a tone played with too much vibrato. The abrupt alienness of her visage, and the ferocity with which she glared at him, sent a charge of fear through him. She seemed less like a woman than a fury, her teeth bared and her nails out-stretched like claws. For an instant he was terrified of her— something was alive within her that he could not define, some savage, atavistic energy. "All right," he said quietly. "All right.

I'll wait here with you for a while. We can go back into the car, if you like."

At once, her features seemed to coalesce and the succession of mask-like variations he had seen, distortions no doubt conjured by firelight and adrenaline, jelled once more into the face of the young woman he loved. But she was no longer looking at him—she was staring at the sky.

Straining to look in the same direction, he saw nothing at first, then saw a streamer of candle flame in the darkness, a few strands of tracers groping wildly for it as it came down: a damaged bomber, losing power, falling from the sky. Erich grabbed Kylliki and threw her over his shoulder. Staggering from the weight, he clamored over rubble and lurched toward an alleyway between two intact buildings—the safest spot he could find in the seconds that remained to them. He threw her into the shadows, then took one last look before crouching over her in a protective knot: the Petlyakov was trailing banners of flame from both engines as it clipped a set of wires and spun into the warehouse, one wing collapsing in a shower of burning petrol, right over the entrance where Erich would have been standing, fumbling with his keys, if he had ignored her warning.

In the firelight, her hair was flame itself. Her eyes were still enormous and their pupils devouring vortexes, still showing some reverberation of the metamorphosis he had perceived in her face as she summoned the strength to hold him back.

"You saved my life," he gasped.

"Our lives," she said, loud above the crash and roar of the bomber devouring itself, "for I would have followed you into the fire if you had gone."

"How did you know?"

"How did you hear a rune-song that no one chanted? You told me how being in the forest had awakened new senses in you, after only a few months of being in my world. You did not doubt the reality of those senses, or their usefulness, did you?"

"No, but this is . . ."

He could again feel time dilating around him, could feel each separate constriction of his heart, could hear the vast progression of his own blood, and in the inferno where his beloved chimes were melting, the bomber's ammunition began to explode, each slow and rhythmic bang summoning back into his mind the sound of the shaman's drum.

"Different? You were going to say, 'This is different'?" Kylliki threw back her head and howled with wild, barbaric laughter. "Oh yes, Erich, because what you sensed after a few months in the forest, my people have had bred into them for the ten thousand years we have lived in the forest and been its seneschals!"

She embraced him with arms he could not have escaped from with all his strength, and they clung together at the mouth of Hell, her words reverberating like thunder in caves of his heart.

When at last they stumbled into their hotel room, they ripped the clothes from each other and made love with their flesh still redolent of flame and cordite and the tincture of molten bells. They clawed and bit and cried out so loudly that at one point, two hours before dawn, an employee of the hotel knocked on their door and demanded that they stop disturbing the other guests. Erich Ziegler met him naked at the door with a Luger in his hand and threatened to blow his head off. No one bothered them again.

The next morning, all leaves were canceled. Erich escorted her to the train and held her wordlessly until it was time for her departure. She looked, as she entered the passenger car, as gaunt, as filled with beaten-down sorrow, as any refugee.

"I will come to you," he said, "as soon as I can."

Twenty-four

In July 1943, in the hot rolling wheatfields of the Ukraine, on the flanks of a westward-bulging salient that would forever after be remembered by the name of Kursk, the drab provincial town that lay at its center, the Wehrmacht made its last attempt to regain the initiative on the Eastern Front. The Red Army met them with 1.3 million men and 20,000 cannon. In the resulting apocalypse, the Wehrmacht's offensive power was shattered forever. Punching a sixty-mile-wide hole in the Germans' now-feeble line, the Red Army unleashed a torrent of reserves and sent the battered Wehrmacht reeling.

By the start of 1944, two-thirds of the territory captured by the Wehrmacht during the victorious campaigns of 1941 and 1942 had been retaken by the Red Army: Kiev, Smolensk, Kharkov, Orel, Novgorod—all had been liberated. Mussolini had fallen ignominiously, and the collapse of his regime sent a shock wave through the other Axis satellites and cobelligerents. Not only Finland, but Hungary, Bulgaria, and Romania were all feverishly trying to reopen diplomatic doors that had been shut for two years, each nation balancing a terrible equation as it sought the method and timing which would enable it to avoid, on one hand, Soviet conquest, and on the other, Nazi reprisals against betrayal. For the Germans, though no longer strong enough to win in the East, were still powerful enough—as the Poles would learn that summer—to crush rebellion behind their own lines.

Finland too was in a period of frantic *sub rosa* negotiations, having reopened, through Stockholm, its diplomatic contacts with both America and the United Kingdom. The January air raids on Helsinki had been a signal to the Finns that unless a separate peace agreement was reached soon, their turn was coming.

Depressed and angered by the destruction of the chimes, frustrated that his last days with Kylliki had been so troubled, Erich remained in Helsinki, carrying out routine duties. But he was reminded, by every westward movement of the red pins on the maps of the Eastern Front, that he was still a Wehrmacht officer, and that his medical record was no guarantee that he would not be called back to front-line duty in a national emergency.

His first summons, however, was not to combat, but to a mid-February conference in Narvik, as part of a Finno-German planning group that met to discuss ways of coping with the Russian offensive which would surely be unleashed as soon as the ground was dry enough to support armor. Erich was taken aside, the day after his arrival in the bleak Norwegian port, and formally reactivated as an intelligence operative by the durable and long-suffering Klatt. This time they greeted each other almost as old friends; the fastidiousness of manner that had vaguely irritated Erich during their first meeting had been worn away by two years of demanding service. Klatt knew how lucky he was to be stationed in the remotest corner of the war, and it was obvious by now that his first priority was to ensure his personal survival. Klatt had access to a constant flow of top-secret material, so he was able to confirm what Erich had long suspected: for Germany, the war was as good as lost, even if the fighting was far from over.

"As soon as Ivan can spare the men and material needed to tidy up his flanks, there'll be some convulsions on the Finnish front, that's for sure," said Klatt, while the two men ate dinner at a Norwegian restaurant. "And we in the intelligence branch are frustrated as hell by the Finnish government's business-as-usual attitude. Surely, behind that facade, there must be all sorts of feverish maneuvering going on."

Erich lifted another forkful of excellent broiled fish and gestured with it for emphasis. "On the contrary, Colonel. The Finnish government is virtually paralyzed, no maneuvering room left in any direction. All the Finnish leadership can do is brace itself for what's coming, assure the population that all is well, and pray desperately that some kind of opportunity arises out of future developments."

"Be that as it may, I want you to go operational again. Keep your eyes and ears open about conspiracies, *coup* plots, overtures of separate peace to the Allies—the usual menu of symptoms."

"Can I stay in Helsinki?"

"I'm afraid not. I need to know what the officers and men are doing and thinking, not the politicians. I have other ways of keeping tabs on them. No, Erich, I'm sending you back to your old comrades in the Third Division."

"Oh, shit."

Klatt opened the bottle of *aquavit* a waiter had just deposited on their table and poured Erich a glass.

"Now, now, be reasonable: the farther out in the field you are, the less likely it is that somebody will try to transfer you back to Germany. And besides, the Third Division is a lot closer to your friends at Tapiola."

Erich coughed on a swallow of burning liquor. "How did you know about that?"

"Dear chap, I am a bloody intelligence officer, after all."

"Well, all right, then, but there's one problem I should tell you about."

"And that is . . . ?"

"General Pajari is aware of my double role, and probably has been since the beginning. That's going to compromise my effectiveness, don't you think?"

Klatt chuckled and reached for his briefcase. He opened it and ruffled through a sheaf of papers.

"We've already asked General Pajari if he had any objections to your return. Quite the contrary—he seems eager to welcome you back. I believe he thinks you might be valuable to him *because* of your intelligence-gathering function, not in spite of it. Among all these damned papers, Ziegler, I have a list of prominent Finnish officers whose political sympathies indicate that they might be disposed to take action, on their own, against a civilian government that attempted a sell-out to the Russians. Your General Pajari is on that list. An on-the-spot connection with Wehrmacht intelligence might come in handy for him in several ways. I also have the impression that he had a certain amount of personal fondness for you—something the old bastard rarely feels for foreigners of any stripe."

Well, thought Erich, I'll be damned. He felt a touch of real affection for the gruff Finnish officer.

"How do you keep the players straight in all of these games, Colonel?"

"Ha-ha-ha! Trade secret, Captain: sometimes the idea is not to keep them 'straight' at all."

Erich remained in Narvik for a week; it was a dismal, fog-bound place, but at least it had an officers' club. He and Klatt drank a good deal together and speculated about the future. For the first time in their long, albeit sporadic, relationship, they also talked about personal matters. It was Klatt's opinion that, however the war turned out, the permanent presence of Russia as a dominant world power would mean lucrative employment for a good intelligence man; Klatt hoped he could go to work for the Americans, since he had a great fondness for Detroit automobiles. Erich, for his part, confessed that he had acquired a fiancée, a Finnish girl who lived in a remote part of the lake district. As a result of this exchange of confidences, Klatt arranged, at the end of the strategy conference, for Erich to have two extra days of grace stamped onto his travel documents, enough time for an overnight visit to Tapiola. He accompanied the liaison team to Oulu by train, then requisitioned a car and drove eastward.

The foreboding that the new year had brought to Helsinki had spread to the interior: the first thing Erich noticed was that Rautavaara's easygoing security squad had been beefed up into a platoon. The ineffectual candy-cane gate had been augmented by two log blockhouses equipped with machine guns, and the security check was much more thorough than the cordial wave-through he'd grown used to over the past two years. Rautavaara, however, was his usual extroverted self, pumping Erich's hand and forcing him out of the car long enough for coffee and a catch-up on news from the capital. When Erich remarked on the increased security, the major said that there was no specific intelligence about any possible Russian raid on the lodge, but given the increased political tension, the raids on Helsinki, and the general state of affairs all along the Eastern Front, it had been decided to reinforce the Tapiola garrison just in case. Sibelius, he went on, had insisted on throwing a party for all the new troops—a function which severely overtaxed the kitchen facilities at the lodge and which ended badly when a loutish Ostrobothnian corporal had attempted to take liberties with one of the serving girls. Erich's face reddened with anger at that bit of news, but Rautavaara quickly reassured him: "Not the one you're seeing. The older sister."

"What did she do?"

"Pulled a carving knife on him. Tough old bitch, that one."

"Sounds like Anna-Liisa, all right."

Rautavaara had promptly notified the lodge of Erich's arrival, and during the time he spent socializing with the major, the family prepared a table of welcome for him. Both Aino and Sibelius met him at the door, proffering cigars, brandy, coffee, even a tray of Fazer candies. Erich, acutely aware of how little time he had, wished they had chosen another occasion to welcome him like the prodigal son, but he was hungry after his journey, and their attention, their demonstrations of affection, surrounded him with a delicious sense of warmth. He wished in passing that all official records on him might be bombed out of existence so that he could just sit out the remainder of the war right here. Sibelius was ebullient, at moments almost manic, as though it were a birthday party and he were keeping an extra-special present hidden just offstage, waiting for the perfect moment to produce it. Erich had arrived in the late afternoon, and the party shaded over into supper. When both servants appeared bearing trays of food, Erich took the first chance he could to sidle close to Kylliki and whisper: "I'll meet you at your cabin as soon as I can get away from all this. At the rate he's drinking, he can't last too long."

"Don't be too sure. How long do we have, Erich?"

"I'm back on active duty, I'm afraid. We only have tonight."

She faced him with an openly bawdy expression, permitting her tongue to roll moisture across her mulberry-colored mouth.

"If all we have is one night, then I'll make sure it's a night you'll remember."

Not long after this exchange, Erich heard Sibelius snap at Anna-Liisa, who had committed the sin of removing a bottle not yet empty. Once again, as he had done on Erich's very first visit to Tapiola, the composer called her by the name "Tuonetar." This time, Erich knew enough to translate that as "Daughter of Tuoni"—the infernal river that marks the boundary of the *Kalevala's* underworld—and the flash that arced between Sibelius and the older sister was more than the irritation of master toward careless servant. Aino also caught the exchange, and when it was over, she regarded her husband with an expression of mingled love and pity.

The incident created a blemish on the hitherto carefree texture of the evening. A few moments later, Sibelius stood up, red-faced and blustery, and announced to the room at large: "If you will all excuse us now, please, I have some very important business to discuss with our guest. Private business, and rather urgent."

And so, in a matter of a few awkward moments, composer and conductor found themselves sitting together alone, under a bank of cigar smoke. As soon as Sibelius was satisfied that the others had truly gone, he exhaled a tremendous sigh and turned to Erich with a gentle smile.

"Reach into the pantry there, Erich, and bring us a full bottle. We may need lubrication before we're done. Then come into my study."

When Erich followed him into that Spartan room, Sibelius closed and locked the door behind him. He gestured for Erich to sit. The composer remained standing, a frowning portrait of himself looming over his left shoulder.

"Where will you be stationed at the front?"

"Where I was originally: with the Third Division—they're still dug in in the same part of Karelia they captured two years ago."

"Good. Much safer for you there than on the isthmus. That's where the storm will break, and break it will—anyone can read the signs. We humiliated Stalin during the Winter War, and this time around, Uncle Joe will want his revenge. I'm prepared, you see, if they do drop parachutists on us, to join up with Rautavaara's men and do my bit."

He opened a closet door and Erich saw the old Mosin rifle inside, draped with a gleaming bandolier full of 7.62-mm bullets. Erich remembered that confused, dramatic day of his first visit, when the old man had shot at a flight of Russian bombers. It was overwhelming, the distance he had come since then, and the changes that had been wrought on his relationship with Sibelius.

"I hope it doesn't come to that, sir."

"But it might. There may be nothing left of Finland in six months' time but a legend of heroism. If that's the case, I should like to be part of that legend too."

"You already are, Maestro."

"And, in an adoptive way, so are you too, my young friend. I am not nearly as morbid as my detractors claim that I must be on the evidence of my music—that, you already know—but nevertheless, there is at least a statistical possibility that this could be our last meeting. I want to distinguish this moment by extending to you a privilege—something you can tell your grandchildren about, if you survive this war and I do not."

With that, he turned his back on Erich, swung open the

portrait—which Erich could now see was actually hinged on the wall, not hung from it—and twirled the dial of a wall safe hidden behind it. The steel door opened. Sibelius rummaged to his elbows in darkness, then brought forth an inch-thick manuscript. Without another word, he handed it to Erich.

The inscription at the top of the first page read: "Symphony No. Eight, Op. 117."

Erich's hands trembled. The room spun around him.

"I was an ambitious young man once myself, Erich. I know that you've wondered long and hard about this piece, and you've had the good breeding not to badger me about it as so many others have. Furthermore, you have proven that you understand my work and identify with it deeply, perhaps as no other conductor in my experience has done. In gratitude, therefore, I am going to satisfy your curiosity."

Erich stammered something, but was cut off by a chop of the composer's hand.

"No! Hear me out before you say a word, because there are conditions. While I am alive, you must tell no one that you've heard this. If you do, I'll deny having played it for you and make you out a liar. And *all* I can do is play it for you, as best I can, on this piano. What you are holding is the only copy of the score in existence. You'll just have to put it all together in your head while I play it, supplying the orchestration with your imagination. As you may have suspected, I've played snatches of this work before, when you were within earshot, but always I have broken off, because I was suddenly afraid of revealing too much of it. At last, however, I've realized that I simply cannot keep it bottled up inside me forever, that I must share it with someone, someone with a deep understanding not only of my work, but of my situation, of the conditions which surround me now.

"The other condition, Erich, is that if you agree to hear this work, you must do so in the knowledge that it can never be performed; that I cannot, will not, release this score to the public. This music must remain here, in Tapiola. Do you accept these conditions?"

Erich nodded dizzily, but his mind was already racing far

ahead. After all, with Sibelius, what held adamantly true on one afternoon might be totally superseded on another day. Over the course of two years, the composer had gone from flatly denying the existence of an Eighth Symphony to actually playing parts of it for Erich. His mind suddenly filled with numbers: dates, ages, life expectancies, the length of time it would take for the war to end and his career to resume. In another two years, even if it required infinite patience, flattery, and a willingness to put up with the composer's moodiness and temper tantrums, who could say what further change there might be in his attitudes? Erich tapped his fingers thoughtfully. Sibelius was already quite old; would he not, as a farewell gesture to the world, ultimately release this swan song, when the certainty came to him that he would not even be around to witness its critical and popular reception? So Erich nodded his agreement, still too stunned to speak: for the moment, of course, the conditions were acceptable.

"Good. Pour us a couple of drinks and pull your chair around to face the keyboard. I'll need you to turn the pages for me at certain places."

Then he began to play.

Like many music lovers, Erich had often spent idle moments speculating on what it might have been like to be present when Beethoven was thrashing out the details of the *Eroica,* or to have been in Wagner's silk-lined study when the Master of Bayreuth was fine-tuning the chromatic fevers of *Tristan und Isolde.* From the moment Sibelius patted the piano bench for him, from the instant he sat down and bent forward to follow, as closely as he might, the progression of abstract marks on the lined paper, nothing in the world existed for Erich except this room and the experience he was undergoing in it.

Heard in its entirety, the Eighth did not disappoint. In moments of depressing speculation, Erich had several times theorized that the composer might be guarding the work so tightly because it was simply inferior, or weakened by too many unresolved problems. But it was not inferior to his other works: it grew organically from them and expanded upon the techniques explored in the best of them. Although it adumbrated images of vastness, yet it was constructed from the most economical materials, developed with a sureness of touch that bespoke a lifetime's ascent to this level of craftsmanship. The transformational techniques of *Tapiola* were raised here to heights of power, expressiveness, and formal logic beyond even that work's level of attainment. As the fragment he had already heard suggested, it was a symphony both noble in spirit and transparent in gesture—as clean, as balanced, as shapely, as anything by Mozart. Themes coagulated from sparks, dust motes, atoms-into-molecules, as though the music were literally coming into being through the agency of the listener's presence.

In keeping with this sense of organic creation, the symphony was cast in a single flowing movement, tempered now and again with silences which were themselves critical parts of the discourse, its overall somberness relieved by a mercurial, gnomic scherzo-dance in the center of the work. After that, the character of the piece altered, subtly at first, from the highly personal motivic style that was Sibelius's own to a more formal, monumentally abstract style: brass sonorities piling up above dark swells of bass and celli—wild, leaping arabesques, pagan and ecstatic, in the woodwinds, in counterpoint—an earthy timpani/bass drum crescendo that stretched over fifty bars with some changes in dynamics that were going to be hell to realize in rehearsal—and finally, the whole symphonic argument coalescing into a stark, monolithic triple fugue. This in turn culminated in a peroration for full orchestra that brought in a startling countertheme which harked back, for one shaggy, fist-shaking moment, to the turbulence and raw passion of the youthful symphonies. At the very end, there was a colossal detonation from the percussion, augmented by full brass and screaming woodwinds, which shattered into small glittering motivic fragments that drifted, like particles of ice, onto a plane of final silence.

Fire and ice, the symphony was a culmination of impulses hinted at by the noble Seventh; in it, Sibelius had unambiguously triumphed over all of his own earlier stylistic weaknesses and inconsistencies; had summarized, recapitulated, and transcended his own life's work. One page of this symphony gave the lie to all the rumors, some of them decades old, that the composer was written out, too enfeebled by age, obsolescence, and alcohol ever to write good music again.

Yet the impact of the Eighth went much farther. By its very existence, it proclaimed that the age of masterpieces was *not* over, nor ever could be as long as pieces such as this were being written. It could become the center of gravity for an entire species of creative impulse—the emotional, personal, and vatic-metaphysical—that had been decreed obsolete in the face of twentieth-century imperatives and catastrophes. Here was a standard around which the musically disenfranchised might rally. It could not be suppressed, this work, and oh, Erich thought with some delight, what a row it would cause among the Bright Young Men who set the tone of musical fashion! Its potential effect, once released, was incalculable—it would reopen debates, alter attitudes, destroy comfortable assumptions. Whether or not history ultimately proclaimed this work a masterpiece, it would certainly cause the history books to be rewritten.

It took Sibelius more than an hour to play through the piece. He made sure that Erich heard or saw everything in it, playing the melodic line first, then doubling back to pick out the counterthemes, accompaniments, and harmonic embellishments, trusting that Erich, with his skill and training, could put the whole thing together mentally. By the time the last chords had thundered and decayed into silence, it was not far from midnight. Erich drew breath to voice his intense reaction—indeed, had he been in a concert hall, he would have been on his feet, shouting "Bravo!"—but the composer waved him to silence.

"Just listen to me, Erich, and don't attempt to change my mind or argue any of the points I'm trying to make. I am tired and drunk, and it's taken a lot out of me to play this for you."

Sibelius rose, joints creaking, walked unsteadily to the shelves that lined one wall of the study, and removed from one of them a pair of stuffed, bulging correspondence files.

He opened one of them and placed it in Erich's lap. Erich riffled through the documents: telegrams, letters, clippings from magazines and newspapers, inquiries from conductors, music publishers, record companies, journalists, agents, and ordinary music lovers in all walks of life. The subject of all of them was the same: When will we hear the Eighth Symphony? . . . What will your Eighth Symphony sound like? . . . How will the new Eighth Symphony compare with the others? The litany went on and on; postmarks on some of the envelopes were recent, but others went as far back as 1920. The weight of this material against Erich's flesh seemed immense.

"But it's a great work," he stammered, "the crowning work of your entire career . . ."

"Oh, I know it's good. But is it good enough to satisfy twenty years' worth of that kind of speculation? I'm sorry, Erich, but I don't think anything could be, including this score. And never forget that there is another, invisible 'file,' so to speak: it consists of already-written reviews and scathing deprecations tucked away in the minds of every critic, composer and pedagogue who has a vested interest in seeing music continue down its present course. There's a colossal ambush waiting for this symphony and I don't want to give them the satisfaction of walking into it."

Erich leapt to his feet, his face transformed with the look of a man who had just discovered a Cause. "But there are so many, many more people who will embrace it, adore it! It will bypass those critics and speak directly to the music lovers!"

"Yes, but they are out of power too. They are not the ones who will write the reviews, the articles, the dissertations. Their time, like my own, and like this symphony's, has passed."

"Still, it would be *played*! Look at all the conductors who are standing in line, begging for a chance to direct it. And it will be recorded, too—look at this proposal from HMV in London, or this one from RCA in America. And once it's released on records, its true worth can't be suppressed. No matter how long it takes, audiences always make up their own minds—and in time, they will acknowledge this as a true masterpiece."

"And I will be long dead, having endured calumny and insult in my final years. I've been tinkering with this score, fussing with it, for quite some time, and I've drawn a great comfort from the fact that, as long as I'm still working on it, I am not yet truly finished as a composer. Don't you see: if I send it out into the world, I will cut myself off from that feeling, and I will become very vulnerable to all those reviews that will begin by saying: 'Well, this is not quite up to snuff, not what we expected from the old fellow at all!' or 'Poor old Sibelius has produced another exercise in musical reactionism, one which suffers in comparison with his earlier works . . .' et cetera, et cetera. I can hear the whine of their voices now and it sickens me."

Observing the look on Erich's face, the old man stopped his monologue in mid-gesture and laid a hand on his shoulder.

"Erich, I did not play this for you in order to torment you, but to give you the last, deepest gift I could bestow—knowledge that I have shared with no other living soul. To play this for you, and then tell you that it must never leave this house, that has given you a measure of pain, I know. But I also wanted to give you peace of mind, to end the constant speculations that have troubled you."

Peace of mind? Erich thought, stepping forward, about to interrupt. Again, this time more forcefully, Sibelius cut him off with a gesture.

"You do not need the artificial boost your career would get from conducting this work—in fact, if the initial critical response to it were as condescending as I fear, you could do yourself actual harm by being so intimately identified with it. You have a gift for conducting Brahms too, I am sure, and Beethoven, and even our tarty little friend Stravinsky, and when you want to perform some Sibelius, you have my entire *oeuvre* to choose from. Your career is already launched—and launched from here in Finland, not in the Reich, and not through the kind of toadying to power that has brought fame to swine like von Golzer. When the war is over, Germany will turn first to artists who were not tarred with the brush of the Nazi regime. You fought for your country, yes, but only as a simple soldier; you will not be identified with the genuine monsters, and there will come a time when such facts carry great weight in determining who gets to perform and who does not. In short, Erich, you do not need my symphony nearly as much as you think you do."

Erich knelt at the composer's side, grasping the arm of his chair.

"I think mankind needs it, Maestro."

A veil descended over the old man's features, and his frame sagged from weariness. "Indeed? Well, how lofty of you. Mankind is welcome to its seven sisters, but not to this one. This one stays here in the forest. What damned difference will one more so-called masterpiece make?"

Sibelius closed the score and stood, his shoulders slumped and his face grey. Erich moved to assist him.

"I am very tired now, Erich, and I need to rest. Please do not attempt to argue with me, or I shall grow very cross and be sorry that I took this step with you."

He replaced the score in the wall safe, locked it. Erich helped him to his bedroom. At the door, the old man turned and embraced him, kissing his cheek with lips so thin that they were defined only by the warmth of the brandy that had soaked into them.

"Good night, my boy."

"Good night, Maestro. And thank you."

Striving to remain outwardly calm, Erich donned his greatcoat, pocketed a flashlight, traced the path down to the lake. Once he was outside the lodge, he gave vent to his raging frustration by kicking at rocks, swiping at tree branches with his flashlight. The night was still and clear and his footsteps chimed on the ice as he crossed to Kylliki's island. Anna-Liisa was not at the cabin, having discreetly vanished, as she sometimes did on nights when the two lovers could meet, presumably to one of the "other dwellings" that Kylliki sometimes mentioned, but had never shown to him.

Kylliki was dressed in the gown he had bought her in Helsinki; here, on her own ground, she looked poised and alluringly confident.

"He played it for me," Erich snarled, removing his coat.

"The symphony?"

"Yes."

"I thought perhaps he would do something like that. I've been hearing snatches of unfamiliar music from his study all week. I guess he was practicing. Well . . . what did you think of it?"

Erich slammed his fist down on a table, jarring the lamp upon it and sending ripples of tense flickering shadow against the wall.

"It's magnificent! And he refuses to let the score out of his hands. At least for now." He drew a deep breath and tried to regain his composure. "I mustn't be discouraged—look how far I've come with him by being patient. In time, he'll come around. He must! He . . ."

"Erich!" She stopped the movement of his lips with her fingers. "You cannot resolve these things tonight. And you and I do not have much time."

She enfolded him and for a moment he was irritated at having his attention diverted from the earlier experience. But of course she was right: this ever renewing sense of an erotic continuum flowing through and around them like a magnetic field—this, at least, was a mystery he could explore.

He sank gratefully to his knees, arms around her hips, face tight against the silk that covered her little drum of a belly, wishing he could burrow into her flesh.

When he realized, sixty minutes later, that in spite of all her ministrations, he was going to be impotent on this night, he blamed it on the frustration that had racked him earlier. Kylliki said that she understood, and he was thankful for the kindness she showed as she stroked him into a guiltless sleep, her eyes focused sadly on a far distance.

Twenty-five

There were no trees overhead and it was hot. Stripped to the waist, Erich scooped sweat from his forehead and bent over to grasp one end of a treetrunk. At intervals along the log, fourteen other men bent with him. At the front end, an engineer officer called a cadence: *"Yksi . . . kaksi . . . kolme!"*—One . . . two . . . three! On the final number, the men swung together. The log rose in an arc and crashed down in a welter of pine chips, filling up the space assigned to it. General Pajari was putting his command bunker closer to the front, less than five hundred meters behind the main line of resistance, and he wanted it to be strong. By the time Erich and his comrades were finished, it would be.

The main highway between Viipuri and Leningrad rolled through the Karelian Isthmus about nine kilometers southwest of their position, but that was another division's responsibility. A secondary road, however, went right through their sector and the most elementary military logic told Pajari that the Russians were sure to focus much of their attention on this part of the line. The ground on either side of the road, out to a distance of several hundred meters, was dry. Three weeks of summery weather had sucked all moisture from the shallow bogs that covered the same terrain during spring and autumn—now it was good tank country. Farther to the left and right, out toward the Third Division's flanks, the land grew steeper and more wooded, crisscrossed with small lakes. Tanks could still be used there, but not *en masse*, the way the enemy preferred to use them.

So Pajari, wanting to exercise control over as much of the defense as possible, was digging himself in on the reverse side of a low ridge that overlooked the road. When the bunker was finished, he would be able personally to see the most vulnerable section of his front, and would not have to rely on someone else's judgment about when and where to commit his limited reserves. The isthmus topsoil was thin—a meter and a half below the surface, the engineers had struck red granite, which they had dynamited until there was enough room for a multi-chambered fortress walled with solid rock. The roof consisted of six layers of crisscrossed logs, the last of which Erich had just helped put into place; these, in turn, would be covered with three or four meters of packed earth and sandbags—thicker, if the Russians gave them enough time.

Technically, Erich did not have to perform manual duties, but since he would probably be spending most of his time in close proximity to Pajari, he felt a vested interest in building the bunker. Besides, the Third Division had become "his" unit by now—he had spent more time under fire with it than any of the fresh-faced recruits who had replenished its ranks over the past two years. In early May, the Third had been pulled out of the East Karelian salient it had occupied since the war's first Christmas and had embarked by rail for the Karelian Isthmus. It and another division had been inserted on the right flank of the secondary defense line across the isthmus, about twenty kilometers behind the main line of resistance.

From the day they arrived, Pajari made it known to every man in the division that he expected them to be in the thick of things not long after the Russian offensive started. Erich was a bit shaken by Pajari's pessimism—after all, he ventured during a conversation with the general, the Finns had withstood stupendous Russian attacks along much these same lines during the Winter War, and this time there had been two years to prepare the defenses.

"Doesn't matter," Pajari had responded, "because it's a different army now. Look around you, man. Half of my division is made up of eighteen-year-olds who've never been in anything worse than a patrol skirmish, if that much. The same thing holds true for those divisions in the line in front of us. The entire Northern Front's been static since January of forty-one. The edge has gone from the Finnish Army, Captain. If these men don't fall apart when the shelling starts, they'll become veterans quickly enough, but the shock up there on the main line is going to be like nothing most of them have ever imagined in their worst nightmares. Oh, they'll still put up a fight, most of them, but they'll hold for a matter of days, maybe hours, not weeks like it was during the Winter War. And don't forget that back in 1940, it was the Red Army that was raw and inexperienced—you can hardly say that now. If our intelligence reports are correct, they've even transferred several Guards divisions from the Baltic Front to the isthmus—the best troops they've got, in other words. All we can hope for is that the forward troops take some of the steam out of their attack; I don't expect them to stop it."

"Can we?"

Pajari's eyes were hard as he replied: "If we don't, they'll be in Helsinki within a week."

For the next twenty days, the men of the Third Division did everything they could to strengthen their positions. Pajari pushed the troops hard, trying to condition them, physically and mentally, for what was coming. Pasty youths who had managed to put on weight during their months of lackadaisical service in the Karelian forest turned brown in the sun, sweating off the pounds and stretching their muscles to agony as Pajari bade them dig trenches, bunkers, tank traps, and gun emplacements. Barbed-wire entanglements a hundred meters thick were cinched around the division's lines like a belt; thousands of mines were sown; telephone cables were buried deep in rock-lined slit trenches laboriously hacked from the stubborn Karelian soil. And out between the wire and the minefields, like some elaborate druidic monument, rose a belt of granite monoliths, hulking reddish menhirs arrayed four deep. They were not tall enough to stop tanks outright—the division lacked the manpower to quarry rocks of sufficient size to do that—but they would slow the tanks and force them to climb at steep angles, exposing their thinly plated underbellies—the only part of a T-34 that could normally be penetrated by the Lahti antitank rifles that were still, despite their glaring obsolescence, the Finns' primary defense against Red armor.

All of Pajari's artillery support was spotty, but with regard to antitank weapons the situation was close to perilous.

By this stage of the war, almost half the division was equipped with captured Soviet weapons—Tokarevs and PPSh submachine guns, mostly—while the number of Finnish automatics per company was at least double what it had been at the start of the war. Artillery support was spotty, and the situation with regard to antitank weapons was marginal at best. To defend the road sector, Pajari had a handful of 37-mm Swedish Bofors guns—good weapons in their day, but too weak to do much more than knock the treads off the newer Soviet tanks—and a few reconditioned Russian 76-mm field guns, captured back in 1940, whose ammunition had been converted, in small Finnish workshops using hand tools, to solid shot.

To back up these orthodox weapons, Pajari's sappers had manufactured hundreds of satchel charges, wired together bundles of stick grenades, and rigged mines on the ends of long poles, so they could be thrust between the treads and bo-gie wheels of oncoming vehicles—close-range weapons that required icy nerve and exquisite timing to be of any use at all. During the last few days, Pajari had sent several of his steadi-est Winter War veterans around to each platoon to indoctri-nate the new men in antitank tactics. They always ended their lectures with a firm admonition: If the tanks break through, let them. Don't panic, stay in your holes, look to the front, and try to repel the infantry that are sure to come after the tanks. The Red Army rarely sent its armor very far ahead of its infantry; eventually, the tanks that did break through would run out of gas or ammunition, or get stuck in a bog where they could be picked off at leisure. At least, that was how things had worked in 1940, and everyone knew the Reds had gotten a lot better since then.

On June 4, the command bunker was declared complete. Erich had just finished helping to arrange camouflage netting over the top layer of earth. Winded and sweaty, he was sitting on top of an observation slit, draining a canteen and swatting at midges when, from the corner of his eye, he saw the sky ripple. Out of the lemony haze of morning sun came a six-plane wedge of ground-attack aircraft, red star insignia bright on their wings. Erich had never seen this particular type of plane in Finnish air space before, but from his service inside Russia he knew instantly what was coming at them: Shturmoviks—lean, fast, armor-plated sharks mounting a 37-mm cannon, machine guns, and rockets, airborne sledge-hammers capable of punching through a Panther tank's roof armor with a single burst. Such aircraft, Erich knew, were reserved for the most vital sectors of the Eastern Front. It was at that moment of insight, with a sudden spasm of pure dread, that he understood just how big an attack might be moving against them.

The Shturmoviks raked the area thoroughly, making three passes in all, and flew away through a hail of tracers without losing a plane; four times Erich saw Finnish ground fire strike, and simply bounce off, the planes' armored bellies.

By noon on June 8, rumors were flying through the division that there had been an Allied landing in France. Curious, Erich went to Pajari and asked for confirmation. Yes, the general told him, there had been a landing in France. So what? Erich mulled this response for a moment, then shrugged: so what indeed? France was . . . somewhere in another universe. Yet the news did occasion some wistful speculation among many Finnish officers. How pleasant it would be to have the Americans land near Turku, to happily surrender to them, and then to be able to rely on their mighty protection against the Bolshevik hordes. But, as Pajari also confirmed, the only word that came from America now consisted of diplomatic warnings to negotiate with the Soviets before it was too late. Finland would make no separate deals with the West at this late hour.

At dusk on that same day, a runner brought fresh aerial photos to Pajari's bunker. The general slit open the message pouch, carried it to his map table, and spread the contents under a light. There was a loud gasp from the circle of officers gathered around. Erich peered over a battalion commander's shoulder and saw a large glossy print covered with white grease-pencil marks, little horseshoe-shaped hieroglyphs that denoted Soviet artillery batteries. These markings were so numerous that they blotted out all details of the terrain they stood on. Pajari began counting, gave up, consulted a sheaf of data that had come with the pictures. Then he spoke quietly to the room.

"Gentlemen, these photos show the ground approximately six kilometers in front of the Finnish main line of resistance—that is to say, about twenty-six kilometers east of where we're standing. They were taken this morning. As you can see, the number of Russian guns has multiplied fantastically in the past twenty-four hours. This intelligence summary suggests that the enemy has arrayed against us almost four hundred cannon per kilometer of front."

Another officer, who had bent down with a magnifying lens to study the details, raised his head and shook it slowly.

"They're just lined up out in the open, wheel against wheel; they haven't even bothered to camouflage them. Why doesn't the air force take them out?"

"Because the air force is outnumbered thirty to one and what you don't see in these pictures are the hundreds of fighter planes covering these positions. Three reconnaisance planes went up to get these little snapshots, and only one of them made it back."

There was no escaping the tension that night. The sudden cessation of the Russians' nocturnal harassing flights seemed ominous. Pajari admonished his officers to put a resolute face on things, but everyone, whatever his rank, sensed that a curtain would soon be rising on a very personal and terrifying drama. Few men slept well, if at all. They talked in clipped, muted voices, chain-smoked, wrote letters and wills.

Erich attempted to draft a just-in-case letter to Sibelius, and when he failed at that, he tried the same thing for Kylliki, but he got no further than a few labored sentences. A looming enormity pressed down on his brain, his hand, and the words crawled, then died. Finally, after 2 A.M., he passed into a superficial doze peppered with flaring, unsettling dreams. It was a state of not-quite-sleep which permitted him to be aware of the drift and content of his own dreams. He knew the white bear was waiting somewhere in those thickets of imagery, and he struggled to wake before that apparition could manifest itself. As he did so, he seemed to hear a crescendo of drums, a tattoo heralding his rise to full consciousness.

He sat up, scalp prickling, instantly and fully awake. The drumroll did not diminish, but grew louder and more focused. It rose like a wave from the dark tree line to the east. Erich went to the nearest observation slit: a kilometer beyond the wire, on the far side of those undulating brushy fields where the tanks would surely come, the forest was a steel-hard black, stenciled against a yellow, pulsating aurora—the entire horizon was being drowned in fire. Concentric overlapping rings of light pulsed and thumped, shaking the blue-black curtain of the summer sky as though it were only painted canvas. Concussion hammered up through the earth and punched rhythmically into the soles of Erich's feet. Every man in the bunker was at the slits now, faces outlined quite distinctly. It was impossible to differentiate individual explosions: the sound rolled liquidly back and forth across the sky, without a seam, without a break. Pajari turned and shouted something, but his voice was remote, tiny, indecipherable; only then did Erich realize, even at a distance of twenty kilometers, how loud the bombardment really was.

When the Russians finally opened their isthmus offensive, two hours before dawn on June 9, 1944, the preparatory bombardment could be heard in Helsinki, 170 miles away. Every half-kilometer of the Finns' first defensive line was swept by 300 shells per minute. With the coming of daylight, 800 Soviet aircraft joined the bombardment, flying sortie after sortie against railheads, road junctions, supply depots, gun emplacements, and anything with a discernible radio antenna. Outnumbered twenty-five to one in fighters and thirty-five to one in bombers, the Finnish Air Force did what it could, its pilots performing prodigies of valor as they dived repeatedly into enormous formations of enemy planes and shot them down by the dozen.

Sporadic shellfire fell on the Third Division's positions, but it was probing, tentative, nothing like the thousand-gun flail that stirred the earth to the east. Late on the ninth, reports from the front lines began filtering back: most of the defensive works so painstakingly constructed on the main line of resistance had been pulverized—bunkers had been caved in, concrete blockhouses lifted intact from their foundations and thrown out of alignment, telephone lines ripped to confetti. By the end of the first day's action, however, and at a cost of thousands of casualties, the Russians had only succeeded in overrunning a few isolated positions.

On June 10, the enemy's artillery was further augmented and the number of aircraft operating over the isthmus rose to more than a thousand. Three Guards divisions, supported by hundreds of tanks, massed that day against a single Finnish regiment and tore it apart, opening a six-mile-wide hole in the forward line. Things came unraveled fast after that.

By late afternoon, ranging fire had begun to probe the Third Division's sector, random clusters of shells that spewed grainy earth-fountains from the stubbly fields and sent shrapnel singing through the barbed-wire garlands. Through the smoke and the geysers of fire-laced earth came a flow of desperate and haggard men—a trickle at first, then an undammed torrent. Some carried weapons, others were weaponless and half-naked, some clung to trucks and horse-drawn wagons, some had open wounds, some stumbled like zombies, their eyes rolling in their heads. Pajari's medics went out and helped the injured, and he sent his best officers out, with drawn pistols if necessary, to stem the panic, regroup the stragglers, rearm them, and parcel them out in the Third Division's lines.

Erich went out to see these wild-eyed scarecrows for himself. He encountered a grizzled middle-aged sergeant, blood caked on his temple beneath a filthy bandage, eyes red in grimy sockets; he was supporting a younger man, a lieutenant, who appeared to be unwounded but whose head lolled, whose eyes were unfocused, whose limbs were loose and floppy. Dried mucus covered the lieutenant's mouth and chin, and when Erich stooped to assist the sergeant, he noticed two thin lines of dried blood tracing a path from inside the officer's ears all the way down to the gaunt hollows of his shoulder blades.

"Where's this man hit, Sergeant?" Erich shouted above the explosions.

"Hit? Hit?"

The man did not appear to understand him, so Erich shook the sergeant and pointed again to the officer.

"Sergeant, where is this man wounded?"

The sergeant shook his head through infinite weariness, focusing for the first time on Erich's insignia. "He's not 'hit' anywhere, you fucking German pig! His brain's been turned to mush from the concussion, that's all. Now leave me the hell alone so I can get him away from these shells!"

As the sergeant struggled to pass Erich, the lieutenant was seized by a violent spasm. He screamed, arms flapping wildly, and his eyes rolled back until only the whites showed. His jaws crashed together in a series of contractions so savage that the tip of his tongue fell to the ground and foam boiled from his lips. At that moment, a cluster of shells fell close by: hot yellow flashes covered Erich with a wave of stinging dirt and filled his lungs with bubbles of fiery gas. He was hurled to one side, and several minutes passed before his head cleared sufficiently for him to stand. When he did so, the sergeant and his burden had vanished.

Survivors struggled through the Third Division's sector

well into the night. The first groups were the most panic-stricken—men whose stamina and sanity had been undermined by the bombardment and who had finally broken. Later on came the more organized groups—men who had stayed as coherent units and fought as long as they could. Some of them grimly took up positions with Pajari's men; others, burdened with wounded or lacking weapons, were sent farther to the rear, where someone, somehow, would try to regroup them, rearm them, and form them into reserves.

At one o'clock in the morning, June 11, the Third Division's turn came on Golgotha. Erich had spent six hours out in the lines, helping to sort out the stragglers. Enemy shelling had dwindled, which probably meant Ivan was in the process of moving his guns forward. At midnight, Erich had returned to the command bunker for food and a nap. An hour after he lay down, something kicked him in the stomach, lifted him bodily, and hurled him to the floor.

He opened his eyes on a scene filled with madness. The bunker felt as though it were being beaten with titanic sledgehammers. All around him was a single gigantic Sound: grainy, viscid, actually tactile. It enveloped him, licked his flesh like cats' tongues, filled his skull and stuffed his head with hot nauseating gases. He felt his eardrums verge on bursting, his sinuses inflate and pop, his eyes bulge, pushed out in exophthalmic bubbles by the pressure within his own skull. His lungs and stomach seemed hooked into a bellows as he strove painfully for normal breathing amid a vortex of violently changing air pressures. It was not possible to hear any one single explosion; they formed a continuum. A vast, writhing, sharp-edged light burned over their positions, a single vivid garland of flash, the points and edges and interstices of each explosion linked to the next in huge snow crystals of fire. If he attempted to move in one direction, fists of force would shove him back to his starting point, while other shock waves beat against his back, legs, ribs, liver, balls, and heart.

After an hour of this, he began to feel as though he hung, floating, on pillows of hot gritty smoke. His eyes burned, his throat was dusted with alum, the joints of his hips and shoulders throbbed, and after one particularly brutal detonation—a direct hit on the bunker roof that cracked one of his teeth and filled the interior chambers with choking fumes—he urinated in his pants. After two hours of this bombardment, the men with him gave up any pretense of performing their duties and all of them, including General Pajari, curled up into balls, white-knuckled, clutching pieces of furniture, weapon stocks, personal charms, and talismans—the choices seemed arbitrary and capricious, a smorgasbord of rosaries—their eyes fixed on the sagging, dust-leaking roof above their heads, each man coping as best he could with the certain knowledge that one or two more hits like that would bury them alive.

Pajari had been the last man to yield to the shelling. For much of those two hours, when he was not sprawled on his back from concussion, he moved from switchboard to radio set, striving to form a picture of what was happening to his command. Every report gave the same picture: the shelling was heavy beyond any precedent, even greater in its weight and fury than the breakthrough bombardments the Reds had unleashed in 1940. No enemy ground movement had been reported yet, but damage to the defenses was mounting by the minute. Finally, no more reports had come in: all the division's radio sets had been battered into silence and all the carefully laid telephone wires had been cut, no matter how deeply buried.

As though a conductor had cut off the sound with a chop of his hand, the shelling halted at thirty minutes before dawn. In that sudden vibrating silence, Pajari instantly began to function as a commander once more, dispatching signalmen to repair wires, runners to ascertain the condition of various sectors, marking on his maps, as the information was returned to him, the location of strong points that had been knocked out by the bombardment. Watching him, Erich recalled the time when the general had said to him, just before the start of the *motti* campaign: "Now you'll see what the Finnish Army does best." It was ironic that now, two years later, they were both about to see what the Red Army did best.

Erich knew he would fight—not from a sense of duty to

any army, not even from loyalty to Pajari, although he admitted to feeling such an emotion. He would fight this battle because his contribution might make some difference in his own prospects of survival. At one point during the bombardment, he had thought about simply saying "to hell with it" and running away, but no one in the open could have survived that rain of shells. Now it was too late to do anything but fight.

He went to the wooden gun racks near the bunker entrance and picked up his Suomi. He inserted a seventy-round drum, stuffed one more drum and a handful of twenty-five-round clips into a satchel, and poked two stick grenades into his belt for good measure. Then he shook the dust out of his helmet, seated it on his head, and ducked outside into the reeking darkness.

He emerged onto a lunar escarpment. Overlapping shell craters, still puddled with eddies of smoke, had altered the familiar landscape, in many places beyond recognition. Long segments of trench line had vanished; a heavy-weapons bunker off to his right looked as though a meteor had fallen on it. Dazed and deafened men shuffled through the smoke like wraiths. He saw noncoms counting heads, medical personnel struggling over the broken ground with stretcher cases, signalmen draped with spools of wire scuttling like crabs, ammo parties hastening to the forward positions with cases of grenades and Maxim belts: the myriad arms and legs of the divisional beast trying to right itself and move effectively again. The murk around him was pricked by moans and occasional screams—and somewhere in a clot of darkness at the bottom of a caved-in trench, a heartbroken sobbing that went on and on and on.

There was a good field of fire available from a foxhole about twenty meters to the right of the command bunker—indeed, the position was dug there to prevent Soviet sappers from taking the bunker from the rear—and since the Degtyarev gunners who had occupied it were both dead, they made no objection when Erich joined them. He levered the corpses out of the hole—no time now to be fastidious—and hastily replaced several leaking sandbags that had been knocked down by concussion.

The ground sloped gently from where he was, leveled out for a hundred meters or so, then rose to form a lower plateau along which Pajari had established his main line of resistance. It was still too dark to make out any details, but it appeared that those positions had taken just as much punishment as the ones in Erich's immediate vicinity—he could see fires licking at logs, and the darkness twitched and jittered as men worked frantically to evacuate the wounded and make whatever repairs and preparations they could in the few minutes' grace between the end of the bombardment and the start of the attack.

Farther east, beyond the Finns' most advanced positions, the low rolling fields and scattered trees were hidden by mist as well as darkness. A roughening of texture beneath the fog indicated the extent of the barbed-wire belt, and beyond that the tips of the antitank rocks were just visible—dwarf children of Stonehenge. Through his binoculars Erich tried to pierce the gloom beyond, but all he could discern was the distant tree line to the east, sharp-cut against the first wash of dawn. As he was slowly swinging the glasses, he was distracted by a firefly flicker just outside their field. He lowered them, rubbed his eyes, saw nothing. He raised the glasses again—a spark floated in the murk as he did so, and he quickly refocused on it. It was much closer than the tree line. Another spark, to the left of the first one. Another. Several all at once. Inside the fog. Out by the rocks.

"Sappers at the rocks!" Erich cried out, simultaneously with four or five other warning voices in the front line. Two Maxim guns opened fire together, joined raggedly by several lighter automatics. A spray of tracers splattered against the rocks, ripping the ground fog to shreds. There was a single shrill cry as one burst found a target, then the weapons' chatter was obliterated by a stupendous chain of explosions that flashed along a five-hundred-meter strip of the rock barrier. Chunks of granite the size of small cars could be seen tumbling like wooden blocks; others were knocked askew like broken teeth.

Summer dawn gathered quickly now beyond the distant trees, and with it could be heard the rusty squeal of tank treads, sounding from all parts of the horizon. Through his glasses Erich saw the edge of the tree line begin to stir, like liquid on the verge of boiling. Moment by moment, the woods seemed to swell with incipient motion; the tree line became granular, fluid—coming toward him. As light grew over the trees and fields, the black, bobbing mass resolved itself into machines: T-34s, Stalin-Is, a few packets of brute, hulking, SU-152 self-propelled guns—and men, thousands of men, flowing over the undulant terrain like a spreading oil slick. Now he could hear their chant: *"Uuuu-RAH! Uuuu-RAH!"*, and he could see squads of shock troops clinging like spiders to the backs of the tanks.

Finnish artillery opened fire. The contrast between its measured, rationed volume of fire and the prodigal deluge the Soviets had unleashed amply illustrated the disparity between the resources of each side. Every fold of ground had been pinpointed by the Finnish gunners long ago, but there was really no need for fancy shooting: a shell dropped anywhere between the tree line and a point halfway to the wire was going to hit something. Bodies spiraled against the brightening sky, spinning like bats in a sudden beam of light. Erich held his breath as the Red armor went into the minefields. A T-34 struck an antitank mine on the road shoulder and vomited a long unwinding strip of tread, smoke gushing from its turret. Other tanks rolled through the orchards of antipersonnel mines, popping the devices beneath their weight like so many balloons, dirty fans of smoke spewing sideways from beneath their grinding treads, clearing paths for the infantry. But many of the infantry did not bunch together and follow the tanks—with a fatalism no European army could afford or was psychologically capable of, hundreds of Russian foot soldiers simply walked into the minefields, clearing the mines by the brutal expedient of detonating them. Men dropped all along the front ranks, legs suddenly gone beneath them; it looked to

Erich as though someone had turned a giant shotgun on them at knee level.

Now the Red tanks opened fire, their turret guns' salvos carrying a plunging, whiplash sonority quite distinct from the deeper cough of artillery. The tanks were at the rocks. Some zigzagged through paths blown by the sappers, others simply steamrolled over the barriers. He watched one T-34 nose up, tracks spitting mud, shock troops spilling from its hull like disturbed cockroaches. The Lahti gunners waited until its underside was exposed, then fired—astonishingly sharp, vicious cracks—and Erich could see the cherry-red 20-mm rounds banging into the tank's belly, hanging in the shadows there like coals thrown down a well; some of those rounds went through, and the turret was instantly full of little molten comets, caroming wildly from side to side, ruining flesh, and finally striking the ready ammo. The tank shuddered to a halt, canted wildly atop the rocks, treads roaring without purchase, and fire spouted from its hatches, vents, and observation slits, a dragon's tongue of flame roaring from the barrel of its big turret gun. The top hatch was flung open and two crewmen bailed out, afire from head to foot, screaming pitch balls that fell and rolled wildly along the ground, scattering the infantry that had been trailing their vehicle through the rocks.

Now the tanks were into the wire, grinding it flat, and the infantry was swarming forward, through the minefields at last, rolling against the sheet of fire that poured from Pajari's trenches to meet them. Erich saw more hundreds fall, but he knew the attack had too much weight and momentum to be stopped. The forward Finnish positions were submerged in a brown, howling wave. Erich beheld a melee both intimate and chaotic, as men fought with grenades, entrenching tools, pistols, rifle butts, knives, and fists. The enemy tanks, channeled by the wreckage choking the minefields, funneled onto the road and its shoulders and kept pressing forward, shedding vehicles every few meters from mines and antitank shells, firing constantly as they moved. A great ponderous turtle-backed Stalin tank loomed out of the smoke some thirty meters from Erich's hole, its cannon pointed at him like the mouth of a cave. A Finnish private leapt at the tank from a nearby hole, two smoking satchel charges in his hands, and paced the tank like a long-distance runner, getting its rhythm. With exquisite timing he slung his explosive packs into the vehicle's treads, then dove clear. One charge bounced off and exploded harmlessly; the other, perfectly positioned, blew out a shower of bogie wheels and tread segments. Immobilized, the tank was struck quickly by a half-dozen shells and reduced to blazing scrap.

The earth shook as a dozen T-34s, each weighing twenty-nine tons, rumbled past Erich, probing deep behind Finnish lines. He fought down a sense of panic and remembered Pajari's tactical doctrine: ignore the tanks, but stop the infantry at all costs.

A wavelet of Russian soldiers, washing up-slope from the teeming madness in the forward positions, rose from the ground in front of the command bunker. Glancing in that direction, Erich saw that the barrel of one of the bunker's three machine guns was already glowing red-hot. Then he was too busy to see anything except the brown-clad men wavering in front of his Suomi's blade-sight, too busy to feel anything except the bruising plunge of the gun against his shoulder, the forms in front of him bucking and spinning and dropping, dwindling in numbers as they got closer. Changing magazines just in time, Erich dropped the last man at such close range that he could see the stains on his teeth.

He rose to peer over the rim of his hole, moving like a man walking through glue, and saw that the tanks' break-through had been stopped by the sudden appearance of his old friend *Vanha Mikko*, which had steamed up from a well-camouflaged hiding place and taken a backstop position on a spur of track five hundred meters in the rear. Firing over open sights, the train's gunners slammed round after round into the dense formation of armor, stopping the tanks cold. Now, with no additional tanks moving on them from the east, some of Pajari's Bofors crews wheeled their lighter weapons 180 degrees around and began throwing shells into the thinly armored rear ends of the tanks, striking them in their engines, their spare fuel tanks, locking them in a crossfire. The tankers' morale finally broke, and every vehicle began to extricate itself as best it could.

Distracted by the noise and violence of the spectacle, Erich did not see the T-34 until it was dangerously close to him. Its driver was intent only on retiring in one piece, and the tank roared eastward, bouncing from hummock to hummock, crushing dead and wounded alike in its path. It was fifty meters away and coming in a direct line with Erich's position when he spotted it. His first impulse was simply to run, but the tank's machine-gunner drove him back with a burst that ripped the ground inches from his feet.

The geometry of the moment was desperately clear: the tank, if it held to its present course, would pass directly over Erich's position, its treads straddling the sides of his foxhole with inches to spare; if it swerved, even a few inches, he would be crushed like an insect. Erich took a great gulp of air and made himself as small as possible, while the tank—the biggest thing he had ever seen—filled every corner of his sight. He covered his ears to shut out the terrible grate of metal on metal. Hot diesel fumes scorched his nostrils. The walls of the foxhole closed around him like a vise and he was pushed to his belly, face jammed into the dirt. He could feel the bow-curve of his ribs as they were driven inward: his lungs were being crushed. Then came the worst physical sensation he had ever experienced: the cold, python slither of the T-34's treads as they grazed his back, crushing him deeper into the dirt. He could no longer breathe against the hideous pressure. He tried not to scream, not to waste one second's worth of oxygen, but as the stars behind his eyes became novas and his sternum began to creak, he did scream, bellowing like a bull, his tongue burrowing into soil. Somewhere far above him, there was an enormous clang, as though a huge ball-peen hammer had struck the tank. That was the last thing Erich heard before he passed out.

When he regained awareness, it was late afternoon and he was being helped onto a litter by two exhausted-looking Finnish soldiers. They examined him, exclaimed at the vast purple welt that covered him from shoulders to buttocks, then rolled him face down on the stretcher. One of the litter-bearers later informed him that if his foxhole had been one inch shallower, or if the tank had deviated an inch from its path, they would have had to scoop Erich out with a shovel. The tank itself, Erich was gratified to learn, had taken a solid-shot round from a 76-mm piece, rolled a few meters farther, and blown up. As they carried him away, he could see its enormous turret ring, discarded on the slopes like a giant's wedding band, and next to it a smoldering, gutted hull.

Pajari's division had beaten off three assaults that day, each one of decreasing ferocity. The terrain in front of the Finnish lines was carpeted with Soviet dead—it would have been possible to walk the entire kilometer and a half from Pajari's bunker to the tree line without once touching the ground itself. He also learned that the valiant *Vanha Mikko* had finally met its fate from a vengeful Shturmovik attack late in the afternoon—the locomotives had been rocketed to pieces and the train's artillery cars strafed into scrap iron. Survivors from the crew had taken up rifles and joined Pajari's reserves as infantry. Erich hoped that Segerstam and his other former comrades from the train, if indeed they had still been with it, were among the survivors, but he never learned for sure.

It hurt terribly for Erich to move his arms, to breathe, to urinate, but the astonished medics quickly ascertained that, aside from the gigantic bruise, he was basically unharmed. They wrapped him with elastic bandages, smeared him with ointment, gave him a couple of pain pills, and sent him to bed. He went, gratefully.

In the morning, the Third Division's ordeal began all over again. Overnight, the Russians had massed light and medium guns at the tree line, firing flat-trajectory salvos directly against the face of any surviving Finnish pillboxes. One by one, the strong points which had so far given spine to the defense were isolated, smothered with fire, and silenced. At noon, a fresh Red division, supported by sixty tanks and self-propelled guns, rolled forward and crashed into the battered Third. This time, Pajari's men reached their limit. After inflicting more than six thousand casualties, destroying more than thirty pieces of armor, and enduring either heavy shelling or direct assault for almost forty-eight hours, the Third Division began to waver. Pajari could not stop the disintegration, knew it, and ordered a retreat while the unit still remained under his control.

This happened on June 12. For the next three days, the Third Division conducted a fighting withdrawal, turning to offer resistance when the terrain was favorable, planting mines to slow down the enemy, licking its wounds. All over the isthmus, resistance was crumbling; the Russians had everywhere struck with the same overwhelming density of men and machines. The attackers' casualties had been immense, staggering—one Guards division lost sixty percent of its effectives in a single morning—but they kept coming. The Soviet commanders knew that ultimately they could replace their losses and the Finns could not. It was not a subtle strategy, but it was undeniably effective, and Stalin was not a commander to shrink from paying a butcher's bill.

On June 15, Mannerheim ordered the complete evacuation of the East Karelia salient north of Lake Ladoga, land that had been won at great cost in 1941 and that had been Finland's last remaining bargaining chip. The defenders there withdrew to shorter, more easily held lines along the old national border and several divisions of troops were freed for duty elsewhere. These were entrained and sent south hurriedly to reinforce the disintegrating isthmus front.

On June 17, the Third Division reached the last line of prepared defenses between Helsinki and the Red Army: a line of earthworks and pillboxes that stretched from Viipuri to Kupasaari to the inland port of Taipale on Lake Ladoga. Intelligence estimates of Russian strength on the isthmus now listed twenty infantry divisions, ten armored brigades, four regiments of self-propelled artillery, two thousand wheeled guns, and more than a thousand tactical aircraft.

For the Finns, the blackest day was June 20. The city of Viipuri—which the Red Army had not been able to capture in two weeks of savage fighting during the Winter War—fell after a few hours of desultory resistance by inexperienced and badly led Finnish troops. Erich had been inside a bunker with Pajari when the news of Viipuri's surrender came in over the radio; that was the only time Erich ever saw the general cry.

At bay now, with little but raw courage left to interpose between the Red hordes and the nation's heartland, the Finnish Army turned and made its last stand. The shock of Viipuri's collapse went through the army like an electric current; officers and enlisted men alike, its ranks were swept by a dark and powerful emotion, an amalgam of shame, rage, and renewed determination that the nation should somehow, even now, survive. Mannerheim's bold gamble of stripping the front north of Ladoga began to pay off as comparatively fresh troops detrained and were inserted into the line, thickening the defense and providing local commanders at last with reserves that could be used to plug the inevitable breakthroughs that the Russians scored, almost hourly, with their armored thrusts, but which they were still too slow and clumsy to exploit properly.

By the time it stopped retreating, the Third Division had lost almost a quarter of its strength. But it had brought its heavy equipment out of the caldron and it had become, once again, a battle-wise veteran unit. That fact was proven during the last week of June, when the Third Division was pierced by no fewer than sixteen armored spearheads. In every case, the Finns stayed in their positions and threw back the infantry. But the Third Division too was bleeding, its strength diminishing by a few hundred men each day, and no replacements could be expected—every man Finland could spare was already in the line. Cumulative exhaustion was taking its toll as well, and the men's response to breakthroughs became more sluggish. They looked like wraiths, their eyes rimmed with black circles, cheeks gaunt, mouths chipped and pale; they made mistakes now that they would not have made a week ago. When the Russian shells stopped falling, when the infantry's cries of *"Uuuu-RAH!"* sounded, the officers blew whistles and shouted and ran up and down the trenches, kicking and cursing the men to their feet. And the men responded—some in numb silence, others with obscenities, some openly weeping, but still, so far, they responded. Erich could feel the weariness, amounting almost to fatalism now, creeping through his own bruised limbs and aching head. Hour by hour, they were turning into skeletal zombies. And still the Russians came, pouring across the fields and bogs and woods, climbing the windrows of their own dead.

On the final day of June, eight German Sturmgeschütz III-D assault guns, low-slung armored vehicles mounting powerful cannon, arrived in the Third Division's sector, sparkling in their factory-fresh paint. Pajari positioned them hulls down behind the most vulnerable sections of his front. The next Soviet attack was stopped in its tracks: the German tank destroyers picked off fourteen T-34s and two Stalins before they got within five hundred meters of Finnish lines, and the Red infantry never appeared at all. The next morning, several truckloads of Panzerfaust antitank rockets arrived and were distributed, after sketchy training lectures, to the most experienced tank hunters in the division. These crude shoulder-fired weapons proved to be murderously effective: a hit on the turret of the T-34 usually blew the whole vehicle apart, lifting the entire twelve-ton turret into the air atop a boiling geyser of flame.

All along the final isthmus defense line, the eleventh-hour arrival of fresh troops and modern German equipment turned the balance in favor of the Finns. The weapons had arrived too late to save Viipuri, and without Mannerheim's cold-blooded decision to shift troops out of East Karelia, they would have been too little. Together, these two factors stabilized the situation, not in time to save the nation's most historic city, but in time to save the nation itself. The ferocity and frequency of Russian attacks gradually tapered off, and by the end of July, intelligence reports indicated that the Guards divisions, the best troops the enemy had, were being taken from the isthmus and redeployed to add weight to the offensive that was crashing toward Poland. For Stalin, Finland had once again become a sideshow—it had been eliminated as a potential threat to his northern flank, and its army, though still strong on the defensive, could never again mount a serious attack. And the contemptible ease of his victory at Viipuri had gone a long way to palliate the humiliation of his defeat, on that same ground, during the Winter War. No one in the world was making jokes about the Red Army now.

On the morning of August 20, Pajari asked Erich to go for a walk with him. The two men, bonded by all they had witnessed together, strolled through a strangely peaceful forest, where the music of streams could again be heard. Sunlight, like strokes of pastel chalk, sliding through a glossy canopy of green, patterned the earth at their feet. Their boots turned dewy and were dusted with bits of fern and wildflower. Pajari took deep, savoring breaths of the scented air. Erich could tell what was going through the general's mind: this soil, this forest, would remain Finnish.

"Erich . . . you've been more than an ally, you've been a valued comrade. Even your spying was useful to me—your reports may well have influenced the decision to send us those Panzerfausts. The men are fond of you, as am I. But the time has come for me to send you away."

"Away? Back to Germany?"

"There is nothing for you in Germany now except danger. And soon there will be nothing for you with our army, either. Peace talks are under way with the Russians. It's likely that they will permit us to exist, unoccupied, as long as we retreat behind our old borders and utterly sever relations with Germany. It could be a week, two at the most, but one morning you and I will no longer be allies. We may even be enemies. There are still thousands of German troops in Lapland, and if they don't withdraw over the border into Norway, the Russians will undoubtedly insist that they be thrown out."

"Would that mean fighting between Finnish and German troops?" Erich felt his stomach lurch at the thought of this final macabre irony.

"I pray not, but there's a real possibility of it. Hitler will regard our separate peace treaty as an act of betrayal. We already have some sketchy intelligence reports that the Germans in the north are fortifying their supply depots with trenches that face south rather than east. The Russians are insisting that the removal of German forces from Finnish soil is to be Finland's responsibility, and if we don't do it before the end of autumn, they will simply march in and do it for us, and that will be the same as Russian occupation of the top one-third of our country. You know as well as I do that once the Russians occupy territory, it usually leads to outright annexation. We cannot permit that, even if it means turning our guns on our former allies. As a soldier, I am ashamed to have to tell you this, and I do not expect it to happen without serious dissent, but in the end, our men will obey their orders, for it will gradually become clear to them just how much is at stake."

Pajari took a pack of cigarettes out of his tunic and offered one. Erich found it hard to meet the general's gaze.

"Where does that leave me, General?"

"Free from any further duties with my command, and rather in limbo, I'm afraid. If you stay here, eventually we will have to intern you. If you go north and rejoin the German troops there, sooner or later you'll be forced to fight again, either against the Russians or against us. There is, however, a third alternative, and I advise you to take it while you can. Go to your friend Sibelius, and put yourself under his protection. With hostilities in that part of Finland winding down, the security there should be lax. You ought to be able to wait out the end of the war—it can't be too long now. By the start of winter, one way or the other, Finland will be at peace again, and no one will have any reason to bother you. And when all of this shit finally settles, come look me up and we'll go get drunk together."

So on August 21, 1944, dressed as a Finnish officer, lavishly equipped with travel and identity documents, still armed with his personal Luger, Erich Ziegler, with the full knowledge and connivance of his commanding officer, became a deserter.

On September 2, Finland broke diplomatic relations with Germany.

Two days later, an armistice was signed with the Soviet Union. One of its provisions called for the total expulsion, by force if necessary, of all German troops from northern Finland.

Twenty-six

Erich arrived back at Tapiola on the first day of September. He experienced no trouble getting in. Major Rautavaara had been called away to lead troops in Lapland—although there had as yet been no fighting between Germans and Finns, the situation was, at last report, very tense. His security troops had been replaced by a couple of MPs, both of them youthful draftees who were eager, now that peace had been signed with the Russians, to go home. Erich did not even try to evade them, although it would have been child's play; he simply drove up to the checkpoint on the road, arrogantly took the boys' salutes, and proffered his papers—high-clearance documents which identified him as Seppo Läppäläinen, military intelligence, on special assignment from General Pajari. The guards treated him obsequiously, checked him out with a quick phone call to Pajari's headquarters, then waved him through and never bothered him again.

Once he passed through that gate, Erich found himself back in a realm detached from the outside world and its concerns. The forest closed in around him, thick and comforting, with all its vivid strangeness as freshly revealed as it had been on his first visit. Given the harried state of his nerves when he arrived, the sensation of being absorbed by the environment was balm and benison.

Sibelius welcomed him, as Erich had hoped he would, with no questions as to his status and no limitations placed on the length of his stay. With Kylliki he was, at first, sullen and uncommunicative; the strain of the isthmus fighting, the collapse of Finland's cause, the recurring nightmare of being buried alive under a tank, all of it had left him drained. But her joy at seeing him had been so eruptive, so welcoming, that in a matter of days he had regained both his passion for her and something of his own mental equilibrium. He felt that he had found what he needed here: the out-of-time ambience of Tapiola had healed him before, and now it did so again. Or so it seemed.

While the days of late summer lasted, under jade-blue skies and deciduous trees swollen with verdure, awaiting the first cold tincturing winds, he and Kylliki spent their days as well as nights together, for Sibelius had thoughtfully excused her from most of her household duties. She did not broach the subject of her visit to Helsinki. Simply by returning to her beloved forest, she seemed to have erased that awkward episode from her memory. Erich had no wish to bring up the subject either, for he saw no way they could even discuss it without spoiling the purity of the days they were enjoying together.

They spent several days in a rowboat, with a picnic hamper, exploring the skerries in the far reaches of the lake. While in the boat, they seemed suspended between two blue hemispheres, two mirrors of preternatural clarity and depth. They visited islands that would have graced a Chinese painting, so perfect was their harmonious balance of shape and placement: pines, granite crags, and pebbled coves all juxtaposed against the water-sky with the exquisite compositional elegance of a bonsai arrangement. On one of the last really warm days, as they were rowing back toward Tapiola through a sunset that made everything seem viewed through sheets of transparent gold, Erich had shipped the oars—still tipsy from the *aquavit* he had drunk after lunch and still tingling from the twisting intensity of their lovemaking on the beach they had chosen for their picnic—and impulsively unfastened his wristwatch.

"When I am here with you, there is no time," he proclaimed, dropping it into the slag-bright water.

She was not as taken by the gesture as he had expected.

"When you want to step outside of your own time again, Erich, don't throw away your watch—just come back to me here."

"But I want to stay here always."

"On a day as fine as this one, it's not a lie to say such a thing. But this is the last day of summer—I feel it too strongly to be wrong—and soon, you will feel trapped here by the winter. And then the war will end, and it will be time for you to leave and pursue your career."

"I tell you, I don't *want* to leave you, or this."

"Not the way it is today, no, but sooner or later you will; you must. I've known that, I think, from the start. Yet I believe you *will* come back to me, when the changes ring on your spirit too hard and fast. And that will be enough to keep alive the pledge we made together on Midsummer's Eve."

Erich resumed rowing, the oars clattering in their locks, the boat lurching ahead so abruptly that Kylliki fell forward, flailing for balance and cracking her knees smartly against the empty seat between them. For an instant, all he could think about was the loss, through what turned out to be a barren little gesture, of a perfectly good wristwatch.

"I made no pledge," he grated, fists knotting on the oar handles. "I recited no oath that I can recall, yet you keep telling me that I did."

Her face went white and for a second, Erich saw her struggling to contain a reaction far greater than his own sudden irritation. Her appearance echoed that illusion of metamorphosis he had perceived by the firelight of the exploding bomber, the immolation of his precious chimes: the planes of her face seemed to dilate and contract, her eyes to darken and grow fierce, even as her mouth and hands made the reflexive gestures of someone hit by sudden drastic pain.

For a blind, wild instant, Erich wanted to press on and wound her even more, wanted to purge from her this cherished delusion, so that he could just speak to her *as a woman*, not some kind of woods nymph.

"You seem to know every detail about some kind of arrangement between us whose very existence I can't even pinpoint!" He was actually yelling at her now, and his words seemed to strike like a whip, causing her to flinch and moan. He pressed on, an almost sadistic fire in his blood.

"I too had an arrangement in mind, Kylliki! In the civilized world, it's called a marriage proposal. I wanted you to be my wife, to come with me into the real world. I would have laid that world at your feet. By God, I would do it still, but you couldn't even stand a few days in Helsinki without getting the vapors and pining for the goddamned forest! My arrangement, my pledge, operating in my world! I'll make it now, in simple words: will you marry me and come away with me?"

Tears flowed down her cheeks. They might as well have been blood, from the way she twisted and dug her nails into her hands.

"I am already betrothed to you, Erich. In the way of the forest, we were united as one on Midsummer's Eve." He could hardly understand her words now, so harshly was she racked by sobs. "I have promised to be here for you always, in my world, ready to open its doors for you any time you choose to pass through them."

The boat was still now, the last angry splash of oars rippling away to nothingness. Even the wind's own breath had stopped.

"And my part, Kylliki? Spell it out for me, please, for I'm tired of chasing fairy dust. What is my part of this little pagan arrangement? If I'm giving a concert in London on Midsummer's Eve, do I have to sacrifice a goat before mounting the podium . . ." His words were cut off by a shriek.

"Oh stop, please won't you stop?" She was pleading now, hands wrung together, shoulders swaying as she keened. And her face seemed to age with sorrow, as though a hundred winters were trying to leave their imprint all at once.

"... or maybe I should pull the livers out of a pair of doves when I go backstage at intermission, and dedicate them to the god Tapio?" He pressed his words home like bayonet thrusts. "Spell it out for me, girl! The rest of it! What did I 'pledge' when I singed my ballocks jumping drunkenly through a bonfire with you?"

Quietly now, in a flat, broken-backed voice, she said: "Only that you would come back to me when you can, only that this place in the forest would remain the sacred center of your heart, no matter how long or how far you had to be away."

"Oh, well, that's fine, just like the 'arrangement' old Sibelius is always moaning and groaning about! But I wonder about the correct protocol, and since neither Sibelius nor Tapio is here to advise me, I'll just have to ask you. Am I supposed to remain chaste and celibate while I roam the orchestral capitals of the world—I mean, a man can get awfully horny in between visits to the subarctic forests, you know!"

She sprang at him like a jungle cat, slapping his face so hard he could feel blood spring free in his nose, and then, in an astonishingly powerful continuation of the same feline leap, she dived cleanly into the lake and swam away, toward the island where she lived. Erich fumbled with the oars and tried to follow, but she was so swift, her strokes so powerfully athletic, that he gave up hope of catching her.

He sat, dazed, in the boat, smoking cigarettes, for an hour, before he realized that shadows were lengthening on the lake and the air was growing chill.

So suddenly had this breakup come upon them, so massive and irrevocable seemed the damage, that he could not yet feel its pain.

He had lost her. Just that quickly. The idyll in which they had been living, these past few glorious days, had proven hopelessly fragile, sustained only by their mutual wills. One crack, and it had all shattered.

I will start hurting soon, he thought as he rowed slowly back toward the lodge, *and it will be terrible when it comes.*

Very well, then. He would live with it, as he had learned to live with so much else the war years had inflicted.

He still had his friendship with Sibelius. He still had the Eighth Symphony almost within his grasp. That was the core of his destiny, the foundation of his future.

Dinner that night was a tense affair. Kylliki was nowhere to be seen, and when Anna-Liisa served the food, she avoided even glancing at Erich's place at the table. She already knew, he concluded. Every time the older sister passed behind him, on her way to and from the kitchen, the air seemed to grow cold along his shoulders, as though an unseen hand were about to plunge a knife into the top of his spine.

After supper, Erich excused himself, took a bottle from the liquor closet, and drank it outside, alone, sitting on a rock overlooking the island where the sisters lived. No light showed in its windows. Erich had nearly finished the bottle and was about to surrender to the cold and go back in when he heard the kitchen door close, and Anna-Liisa's footsteps rounding the back side of the lodge.

In the last, deceptive breath of twilight, he watched her row across to the island. In gathering darkness, he finished the bottle and rose unsteadily. At last, he saw a light on the sisters' island, and he followed its progress from inside the cabin to the boat landing. The lantern's reflection now appeared in the lake, and from the shapes it defined, Erich could see both sisters, heavily cloaked against the cold, get into their boat. The lantern remained lit, so Erich could follow their course around the left side of their island, and off into the far dark reaches of the lake. He watched until the light grew faint, wavering, hallucinatory, wondering where they could possibly be going and why. At the exact moment when distance and night finally extinguished the light, Erich began quietly to weep.

Helping himself to Sibelius's liquor stock, Erich went to his room and drank himself into oblivion. When he woke late on the following morning, he had a sickening hangover and a mood overlaid with grief and resentment. His mood was recapitulated by the morning: a keen grey wind beat down the birches and tore at their leaves—the summer was dying.

Sibelius sought him out that morning, bringing coffee to his room.

"It's over between you and the girl, I take it?" the old man said quietly.

"I suppose it is, Maestro. And I don't really know what happened."

"Aristotle once wrote: 'Nothing that is vast enters into the life of man without a curse.' Perhaps you'd care to spend the day, after you've had your coffee, of course, in the company of an old musician?"

Through his layered misery, Erich felt grateful.

"Thank you, sir. I'd like that."

Although the days remained fair, the nights became touched with iron. As September died, the wind from the north turned keen above the fir-clad ridges, stippling the lake with hard white chop. The coming of autumn, and news reports of the harsh and grudging terms of Finland's new peace treaty with Russia, both seemed equally to affect Sibelius, plunging him into a prolonged siege of brandy-fueled melancholia which Erich shared totally.

He spent most of his time with the composer now, watching Sibelius count off the final days of September as though they were his own last hours, as though the oxidization of each leaf mirrored the deterioration of his own aging cells. The old man's identification with nature, hypersensitive at the best of times, became obsessive, close to morbid.

Every afternoon, with Erich by his side, the composer grasped his walking stick, tucked his great domed head into a wide-brimmed hat, and went forth to walk the shoreline, always at the same fading hour. And every day, not long after he arrived beside the water, a flight of chalk-white cranes came gliding past from the marshes north of the lake, where they fed every day, to their nests far out in the skerries that jumbled the horizon.

Always, just as the birds passed the old man, they gave voice to lonely piping cries, frail ideograms inked on the wind. Erich observed this ritual half a dozen times, knowing that Sibelius believed the cranes were speaking to him, and not altogether certain himself that they were not. Sibelius's eyes grew cloudy as he watched the birds sweep past, as though they were trying to impart to him some final runic bars of music. Once, as the distant cries came to him, chilled by their passage over water, Sibelius lifted his free arm and reached out, fingers cupped and gnarled, supplicating, as though begging the sound to remain in the air long enough for him to touch it, caress it, crush it to his breast. As he made this gesture, a look of despair seized his features—as if the very beating of his heart depended on his capturing that final passage of music. And each afternoon that this barren ritual was repeated, the old man's vast and granite heart seemed to crumble a little more.

Finally, on the last day of September, the birds did not fly at all. Sibelius waited for them—scowling, motionless, propped up on his walking stick—until he was only a black outline against the hard, sad orange dusk; until, from Erich's vantage point, he looked like an old troll brooding over lost treasure. When Erich finally approached him, gently cupping his elbow, he saw the composer's face held by a rictus of yearning so intense, so devouring, as to be indistinguishable from pain.

The cranes, of course, had simply flown south for the winter, like all sensible creatures that could, but the mystical significance that the composer attached to their departure was symptomatic of the atmosphere that now dominated Tapiola.

Sibelius did not go out for a walk on the day after the cranes left. Instead, he summoned Erich to his study and, quite without preamble, began to discuss with him the problems and challenges of conducting the Eighth Symphony.

So in the end, it proved to be just that simple, Erich thought, satisfied that the old man had changed his mind. Suddenly he was entrusting to Erich the secrets of a piece of music whose mere performance would assure Erich of instantaneous worldwide fame. There could no longer be any question about whether or not the composer would permit him to conduct the work; only when. It seemed clear to Erich that Sibelius still did not want the work to be released during his lifetime, but the composer was, after all, seventy-nine years old; how long, when one took a realistic look at it, would Erich have to wait? So sure did he become of the composer's intentions that he was able to enter wholeheartedly into the discussion of interpretation. At one point, halfway through the development of one of the work's more impressive climaxes, Erich even had the boldness to suggest a change in orchestration.

"Maestro, here—three bars after the brass comes in: could you perhaps double the clarinet there? That counter-melody is important, and as it stands, the brass must either play too softly, or if they do not, the clarinet's line will be smudged, maybe unheard. A good balance would be impossible to achieve."

"Ah . . . perhaps so . . . yes, let me try it." Sibelius turned to the piano and tried the passage at the dynamics indicated in the score, then played it again with the clarinet line stronger. The difference evidently convinced him, for he clapped his hands in childlike glee: "Bravo, Erich! It does work better! It's really a pity we shall never hear it done that way."

"I shall do it justice, Maestro, as though you were standing by my side."

The composer's hands froze above the keyboard.

"When will you do this, Erich?" he asked gently.

"Why, later . . ." Erich stammered, ice suddenly coating his belly. "Later, when conditions have changed and it's all right to perform this score."

"When I'm dead, you mean." Sibelius sighed and placed a hand on Erich's arm. "Erich, my friend, my colleague, I wish with all my heart that it could be so, but it cannot be."

"God damn it!" The angry shout flew from his lips before he could stop it. Flushed with embarrassment, furious with a sense of betrayal, Erich was on his feet, fists knotted, glaring at the composer, who continued to speak in regretful yet placid tones.

"How long do you think I have had this score written

down? Fifteen years, a decade? No, Erich. I've started things I called eighth symphonies before, a hundred times, and always torn them up after a few days or a few weeks. But this, *this* was completed only a few days before the first time I showed it to you. It was all written here, in Tapiola, in the forest, and here it must remain.

"When I first moved here, when the outbreak of war was imminent, I asked, I pleaded, I begged, to be allowed to write it—just to prove to myself that I *could*. To prove that it could still come from within me. Your coming here, my boy, was the final catalyst that enabled me to do that. Can you possibly understand what it means to me, after twenty years of silence, to find such music still inside me?"

Erich felt the earth shifting under his feet, a yawning crevasse opening where he had been about to place his weight. "It's always come from within you, old man!" he cried desperately. "Where the hell else did it come from?"

"You're wrong. It had not always come from within me. Not only, not just, not always. This place, you see, is more to me than just the site of some pleasant youthful memories. I'll try to tell you what it is, but it will not be so easy to accept, not even for you—and you have experienced the power of the forest for yourself. Perhaps what happened to me, and what I learned about the forest, is really 'true' in some objective sense, or perhaps it is only 'true' for me, and for the rare few like me, and like you, who become attuned to it."

Sibelius motioned Erich back from the piano. He poured liberal drinks for both of them, then carefully eased himself into an armchair. Erich remained standing, his legs tensed as though he were preparing for a sprint.

"Do you remember how, in our discussions, I have often mentioned the fact that no one really knows for certain just where the Finns came from? The best guess is that they wandered into this part of Scandinavia in the late Dark Ages from somewhere in central Asia. But is it not possible, even logical, that those first nomadic tribes who settled here found these forests *already* inhabited? Not heavily populated, mind you, but . . . inhabited."

Sibelius put down his glass, placed both palms on his knees and took in a deep breath, raising his head briefly toward the ceiling.

"Those others would have been the *true* forest-dwellers. They would have known no other world but the forest, worshiped no other gods save its gods, and, by our standards, they would have been on unthinkably intimate terms with their environment, symbiotic with it, almost living kin to the trees themselves. They would have been animists, perceiving a life force indwelling in every aspect of nature, and their culture would have been carefully tuned to the forces of nature, both benevolent and malign. They would have dwelt in the deep forest as fish dwell in the sea, responsive to and shaped by every wind, every current, every nuance.

"They may well have been living in total symbiosis with the forest for thousands of years, and if you or I were to meet one of those people today, we would have no more in common with them than with an ancient Egyptian. Think what secrets they might have woven into the fabric of their reality! Their knowledge of the forest would be intimate beyond anything we could know. They would be its acolytes, its intermediaries *vis-à-vis* the world of ordinary men."

"All right, so Kylliki and her sister are descended from the original race of forest people. I don't care if she came from Mars, and I don't see what the hell any of this has to do with your Eighth Symphony!"

Erich poured himself a recklessly strong drink, then dropped into a combative crouch on the edge of the armchair opposite the composer, glaring at the old man defiantly.

"You will," Sibelius snapped at him, "and until I finish, I damned well expect you to continue showing me some courtesy!"

Erich tightened his mouth sullenly, but acknowledged the demand with a clenched nod.

"Very well: when I first arrived here, I knew no more of these things than you did. My mind was full of daydreams about composing music, just as yours once was with dreams of conducting it.

"Soon after I arrived here, while walking one morning by the lake, I met a woman whose beauty and spirit enslaved me utterly. She was a virgin, and I was not too long beyond that state myself, yet the passion that ignited between us was deep, seasoned, knowing, and full of sweet nuance. With her, I learned all that any man needs to know about human love—all, at any rate, that this one man could stand to learn. When I was with her, I could not imagine ever wanting or needing anyone else, any place else. The power of that love awakened the artist within me. I began seriously to compose, in the truest sense of the word, right here, in the forest, in Tapiola. This turn of events delighted my lady—she intimated that my taking this step evidently coincided with the wishes of the forest itself. I pretended to take her seriously, humoring her.

"But soon I was not so sure. As our weeks together went by, she took me to strange and splendid places deep, deep in the woods, taught me new ways to see and listen, so that my heart became swollen with unwritten music. My brain was inflamed with so many impulses and connections, stuffed with so many ideas, themes, germ-motifs, that it took two or three symphonies, as you well know, before I could settle down and do my more disciplined, more mature work."

Sibelius lit a cigar. Erich saw that his hands were shaking.

"I have come to believe that this woman was one of that ancient race of forest-dwellers. The things she knew, the things she showed me—all on another plane entirely from folk wisdom, from mere superstition. She could only have been something . . . other. I myself became so open to the forest's emanations that I eventually came to believe that I was writing my music, at least in part, as a kind of homage to the land and its spirits. More than that: I came to feel that I was somehow fulfilling its wishes, its design, by writing as I was starting to write.

"But in exchange for all that the forest had given me, there was something besides music that I had to give in return. After the woman and I leapt through the fires on Midsummer's Eve, I learned what it was: I was expected to return to her, back to the forest, at periodic intervals, as long as I lived.

"And I did come back, Erich, a few times, up until about the time I completed the Third Symphony, but then I rebelled. I had become a success, an international figure, not to mention being a married man with daughters to raise. The woman in the forest had by then become just a symbol of youthful passion, an object of nostalgia, but on my final visit here, the woman sensed that she had lost me, and she warned me. A 'bargain,' she insisted, had been made between us, or rather between the forest and myself, with her as the midwife, and I owed continued allegiance. Full of arrogance and pride, I denied it. I grew angry. Finally I cursed her, and swore I would never see her again."

Impatient at first with the old man's monologue, Erich now felt each word strike home upon himself.

"At the sound of my anger, my declaration of independence, she grew pale and trembled, as though I had set in motion some terrible force which was buffeting her, yet whose winds I could not—not yet, at any rate—feel. In a small cold voice, she pointed at me and said: 'Seven strings upon thy harp, seven and no more,' then she turned without another word or glance, and vanished into the trees."

Sibelius lowered his voice; Erich had to lean closer to hear the rest.

"As you know, *Tapiola* was my last significant composition. I think I was . . . allowed . . . to write it, because of the subject matter; otherwise, the Seventh Symphony marked the end of my active career as a composer. For years, I struggled to write another symphony which would surpass it, tantalized by fragments that teased at my brain but would never hold still long enough for me to put them down on paper. If I go to Hell when I die, Erich, it will seem like a pastoral landscape compared to the sight of sheets of staff paper with no music written on them."

"Your life is not my life, your love affair not my love affair, and your fate will not be mine," Erich interrupted.

Sibelius went on as though he had not heard, or—much

more irritating to Erich—as though what he heard was completely irrelevant. "When the war came, and the government sought to find a safe refuge for me in some forgotten place, I suggested coming here, hoping somehow to find a way to redeem myself, if not in the world's eyes, then at least in my own. The forest seemed to understand why I had come, and it was granted that I should be given this much release: the music could come if it *would* come, and I was free to write it down if I could. But what resulted would be, in the end, my gift back to the forest, my offering, my atonement. Here in Tapiola, I could compose, but here in Tapiola the music must always remain. That was the essence of things; that was the bargain I eventually knew I had made."

"Damn this talk of bargains!" shouted Erich. "I have made no bargain!"

"Yes," said Sibelius, very quietly. "You have. You have been given insights and connections enough to launch your career. You have experienced your life's greatest passion here, and you have shared with me a great and powerful mystery. Whether you accept it or not, Erich, what has happened to you in the forest has deepened you, strengthened you, and given you the origins of your greatness as an interpreter. You owe it your allegiance, and you owe your forest woman, your Kylliki, some portion of your life, from now on. Do not learn from me just what you *think* will be useful to your career— learn from me everything that I have to teach you. This knowledge I have given you, out of my love for you, out of my belief in your abilities, and out of my need for you as a spokesman for my art. It is a gift more valuable to you than this symphony manuscript. In time, you will see that."

Erich could not restrain himself. He sprang from the chair and pointed his finger at Sibelius, all but shouting: "All I see, old man, is that you've dangled before me the opportunity of a lifetime, tormented me with it, then snatched it away from me and justified your senile sadism on the grounds of a lot of demented mumbo-jumbo! For God's sake, if you care so much for me, then let me conduct that symphony! If not now, then later, when it can't possibly matter to you anymore."

"Whether I am alive or dead is not relevant. No one may conduct it," repeated Sibelius, his head sunk into shadow.

"Why did you write it, then?"

"I've told you: so that I myself would know it was still within me to compose such a work. So that I can die without a heart full of silence. In time, you *will* understand."

"I understand only that I've had a bellyful of these stupid games!"

"You haven't believed anything I've said, have you? You think it's just the raving of a drunken old fool. Very well, then: do you want to know the name of the woman I leapt the fires with, *half a century* ago? It was not the grandmother of those two servant girls, or even their mother—it was Anna-Liisa! Anna-Liisa herself! Only the god of the trees knows what her true age is!"

Erich cursed and slammed his glass to the floor, then stormed from the room.

"You're mad!" he shouted over his shoulder, as he stalked through the house and pushed his way out through the front door.

Bursting with anger and frustration, feeling that he had been seduced, toyed with, and rejected, he walked blindly down the path to the lake, paying no heed to the branches that slapped his reddening cheeks. He had had all he could stand of the Finns and their damned mysticism. The forest and its gloom, the interminable winters and their unending darkness, the brooding steeped-in melancholy of these people . . . Dear God, he had had enough of it all! He had fought for this nation as hard as any of its native sons, and with a great deal more enthusiasm, as it happened, than he had given to his own. Now he felt betrayed by that very commitment.

Cursing again, he flung a stone into the lake, then another, shattering its mirrored surface, furious at himself for ever having been seduced by this mindlessly monotonous landscape, for having become infatuated with these dour, provincial people. Suddenly, like a flood held in abeyance for years, he was filled with a passionate longing for the *real* Europe: for boulevards and cathedrals, cinemas and bistros, brocaded opera houses and grand hotels and women who wore lipstick and silk stockings.

Perhaps it was not, after all, too late for him to make his way to the far north, rejoin a German unit, and retreat into Norway. Once there he would probably be safe—there could not be much direct contact anymore between the Reich and its Norwegian forces, and it was clear that Hitler could not last very far into the new year, if that long. Once in Norway, Erich could wait out the final debacle, then slip home and resume his career. It would be grim in Europe, for a few years yet, but compared to this godforsaken wilderness, it would all seem like Paris to him.

Gradually, the certain understanding that, one way or another, things were finished for him here created a pocket of calmer resolve in his mind. He forced himself to breathe deeply, to stop throwing rocks like a petulant, thwarted child, to regain his self-possession. He would apologize to the old man, make up with him, acquiesce in his fantasies, and make sure that before he left, he had suitable letters of introduction and recommendation. The British, in particular, should be interested in a conductor with personal accolades from Sibelius. He would cold-bloodedly salvage what he could from this experience and not look back.

Daylight was fading by the time he had regained control of his emotions and was retracing his steps along the shoreline. The lake and its islands had become an abstraction of yellow and ebony, a chill arrangement of sunset and silhouettes, without charm or grandeur for him now. He paused to light a cigarette. Then he heard the soft, hesitant crunch of footsteps.

Down the shore, in a clearing beside the water, stood Sibelius. In one hand he held a bottle, and in the other he held what could only be the manuscript score of the Eighth Symphony. Seeing Erich, he waved tipsily and said: "Come over here with me, Erich, and I'll let you take part in something you can tell your colleagues about till the day you die. Come over here and help me make an offering."

Help him? The composer was both drunk and demented—

he seemed to be working himself up to the act of destroying the manuscript. Having spoken, Sibelius turned, sat down on a rock with the score limp in his hands, and stared moodily at the last wash of light on the water. Waiting, perhaps, for the cranes to tell him what to do next.

Erich turned away in disgust, in actual physical revulsion, and fled back up the slope toward the house. Halfway there, he suddenly realized the magnitude of what was about to happen on the beach. An illumination struck him motionless: all this time he had misread the nature of his destiny, or had divined only a portion of it. His mission was not only to conduct the Eighth, but first of all to save it. Never mind what the loss of the Eighth would mean to Erich Ziegler, said the voice of his destiny; leap from the selfish contemplation of that to the much larger and more horrifying implications of what this meant in terms of the European civilization he had just been reflecting on with such nostalgia.

Erich knew he had reached the pivotal moment of his life, knew without any doubt that this was why he had been sent to this place, why he had undergone such a strange and sometimes terrible odyssey. He alone in all the world, except for the composer himself, knew what a masterpiece Sibelius had written; not just the crowning achievement of one man's career, but one of the pinnacles of musical creation in this century—perhaps the last great romantic symphony. And only he, Erich Ziegler, knew that this masterpiece was about to be destroyed by its creator, on the strength of a deluded, alcoholic fantasy. Surely, fate had placed him here, at this exact moment, for the purpose of intervention.

The air had turned chilly with the deepening of dusk, and his sweat felt like beads of cold lacquer by the time he reached the door of the lodge. He plunged into the entrance hall, threw open a closet door, grabbed his coat and his pistol belt, then ran back down the slope toward the lake, praying that he was not too late. His purpose was now blindingly clear, heroic, as though every moment of the past three years had been propelling him toward this time, this place, this act.

He staggered onto the shaley beach just as the composer,

having finished lighting a cigar, was about to touch the dying flame to the corner of the title page. Erich's hand moved like an instrument of God: fingers curling around the checkered butt of his Luger, he drew the weapon and pointed it at the composer's heart.

"Forgive me, Maestro," he said, surprised at the resolve in his own voice, at the power and sense of focus pouring through him at this moment. Alone, and by an act of his personal will, he was about to alter the history of music. "Forgive me, Maestro, but I cannot and will not allow you to destroy that great work. I do not do this for selfish reasons, but in the name of all those for whom your music has meaning. Please hand me that manuscript. Do it now."

Sibelius coolly permitted the match to drop; it hissed briefly in a pool at his feet. The last breath of light from the water glowed along the Luger's barrel. The composer no longer seemed flesh and blood: he had become impossibly solid and monolithic, a figure carved from basalt. When at length he spoke, his voice was weighted with great sadness.

"So, Erich . . . you too turn out to be the sort of German who points guns at artists. Does this gesture mean so much to you that you could even fantasize about shooting me? I know you better—if you did kill me, your next act would be to put a bullet in your own brain . . . then the girls could find us here together in the morning, nibbled on by small animals. God, what an undignified death scene that would be!"

Now the old man was actually laughing, a sad, sardonic rumble.

"Very well, Erich. In the end, it will be the same. I have told you that this music cannot leave, will not be allowed to leave, the forest. If you attempt to take it away by force, not only will you fail, but you will awaken a great slumbering anger somewhere out there . . ." He swept his hand in a wide arc, encompassing the lake, the island, the forest itself. He handed Erich the manuscript, a ghost of refracted light dancing on the tears that filled his eyes. Then he sat down on a rock, raised his bottle in mock salute, and tilted it to his lips.

His laughter—hollow, taunting—followed Erich as he ran

down the shoreline, the score clutched to his chest, the pistol still in his hand. The enormity of what he had just done filled him with excitement, mingled with apprehension: did men always feel this way when they defied the gods, or was this *his* delusion, even as the tale of wood sprites and forest-dwellers had been that of the composer?

He could not leave without seeing Kylliki first. He had to explain what he had done, why he was fleeing, to promise her that he would—he really would—return to her as soon as . . . as it was feasible. But the thing he was carrying now, the importance and immensity of his burden, required that he get far away, to safety—both for himself and for the treasure he had just . . . was it "stolen" or "saved"? In either case, the act was done; he knew he could not have done otherwise.

He rowed rapidly to the sisters' island, praying that Anna-Liisa was not around, with her grim expressions of disapproval. This meeting with Kylliki, part reunion and part farewell, was going to be delicate enough for Erich without his having to face down whatever recriminations the older woman would hurl at him.

When Kylliki opened the door and saw him, she jumped back as though struck in the chest, her mouth open and her eyes wide. Erich noted, with relief, that she seemed to be alone.

"Erich, what's happened?"

He was winded, disheveled, and his eyes were wild.

"He was going to burn it! He was drunk, and he was just going to stand there and watch it burn! But I saved it, Kylliki, I saved it! It's with me now, it's safe now."

"The symphony . . ." Her voice blanched into a reedy whisper as she realized what it was that he carried. "Erich, my love, you don't know what you've done. You must return that."

Fully committed to his course now, he laughed scornfully at her. Brushing past her shoulder, he entered the cabin, his eyes searching every corner.

"I need something to wrap it in, for protection against the elements. Look, Kylliki, please don't worry—I'll come back for you after the war. I promise. And as for Sibelius, he'll thank me for this when he comes to his senses, you'll see."

"No, he will not! Nor ever forgive you. Listen to me, Erich: you must return that manuscript. It cannot leave the forest."

"Oh no? Watch it go, my darling love, watch it go with me! Is he going to summon trolls and goblins to stop me? A dragon perhaps? Cast a spell on me? Have me struck down by lightning? Christ, I'm sick of living inside a story by the Grimm Brothers! This music is real, Kylliki, the product of that composer's genius, not the product of his senility and delusions! It is magnificent and I have saved it from being destroyed by a drunken, self-pitying old man! Ah, there's what I need!"—He had spotted an empty burlap sack, once full of flour, folded in a cupboard. Throwing a broom handle roughly aside, he opened the sack and thrust the score inside, wrapping the excess material around the manuscript several times. Folding the entire package into a U, he jammed it into the pocket of his coat.

"If you do this terrible thing, Erich, you can never come back. Do I mean so little to you?"

"And do I still mean enough to *you*, after what happened out there on the lake, for you to want me to come back?"

"Yes," she whispered passionately, her eyes deep and more beautiful, he knew, than the eyes of any woman he would ever meet.

He shook her by the shoulders and the intensity of his grip made her wince.

"Then believe me when I tell you that neither one of us means anything next to this piece of music, don't you understand? I'd have torn it from his hands, I'd have struck him, if necessary, to save it from his pathetic little immolation scene."

"How did you get it from him?" she said in a broken voice. "By trickery or by theft?"

Fiercely, almost proudly, he straightened, shoulders braced, then opened the flap of his holster and brandished the Luger in his fist.

"I took it with this!" he cried defiantly.

Kylliki regarded him for a long moment: he was glazed with sweat, lips drawn and feral, his eyes gone cold, fanatical. The pistol gleamed like a fetish carved from anthracite, an instrument of power and coercion that seemed now to grow from his hand like a talon.

Then she slowly raised her hands, wove her fingers deep into the rich sweet gold of her hair, and tore two bloody fistfuls of it from her scalp, a scream ripping from her throat in an explosion of rage and pain. She fled through the cabin door and into the darkened woods. Strands of her hair—filaments of gold mottled with scarlet—settled slowly through the air like feathers from a startled bird. Gripping the bundled manuscript tightly, Erich ran after her.

She did not run up the ridge. He followed her screams around its base, along a path whose existence he had never suspected, which led eventually out on the far side of the island, and across the threshold of that wild and jumbled landscape he had glimpsed several times from the ridge, that he had traversed under her guidance on the night of the runesinging, but that he had never been able fully to comprehend. Now he did. He knew: the exact instant when he passed an invisible border between the mundane forest he knew so well and that other forest world whose existence he had suspected, whose paths he had wandered in dreams and some few nightmares, but only once in the flesh, and that with Kylliki's protection, on the night of their visit to the rune-singer. This, he knew, was the *true* forest: a place where time was different and reality was richer, older, wilder, vaster, more chaotic at times, yet also a place where each leaf and fern and rock and pond was interconnected by invisible ganglia whose electric agitation he could, even now, distinctly feel as he passed into their ambit. The forest was alive around him, and the tree branches no longer simply brushed him or whipped across his face— they felt him, analyzed him, struck and groped at him with the reflexive, purposeful motions of living sinew.

Despite his growing apprehension, still he followed the woman's cries, deeper and deeper, splashing through viscid bogs that sucked at his boots, crossing the floor of a vaulted pine barren, skirting thickets of tropical density and oppressive, suggestive darkness. If his instinct was right, Kylliki was fleeing to the cabin of the rune-singer.

Quite suddenly, as though a curtain had been drawn back from a stage proscenium, he saw the cabin's windows glowing, as though the light came through parchment. He forced himself to slow down, breathe evenly, approach in silence. There was a sudden flare of light, and he saw Kylliki's outline as she threw open the door and rushed inside, howling like a wounded animal. The door remained ajar, and there was no need, given her hysteria, for Erich to approach in stealth. Closer, he heard another woman's voice: the old crone's, filled with alarm and shock, and both women speaking hurriedly and emotionally in what seemed to his ears an archaic and florid dialect that was not Finnish—all he could understand were the repetitions of his own name. Close enough to see inside now, he beheld Kylliki's back, heaving, her hair wild and torn, hands clawing the air as she sobbed her tale to the ancient, bent-over witch who stood before her, countenance hidden in shadows.

Erich knew he should run back the way he had come; knew that some great and formless peril seemed to be growing all around him, getting stronger by the moment. But there was something about the tableau inside the cabin that arrested him, compelled him to come a step closer, then another, and then his boots crushed a branch, which announced itself loudly during a gasp for breath in Kylliki's raving narrative.

At the sound, the crone's face came up into firelight, sharp and sudden, with a grim predatory ferocity in her eyes, and Erich found himself staring into the age-ravaged features of Anna-Liisa. The crone-sister's eyes flared as she saw him, and her arm rose—one thin, claw-nailed finger pointing at his breast in accusation, a coarse ejaculation of rage bursting from her lips in a shower of spittle. Erich felt as though the nails had pierced him, fastening him to the spot; as though the twig he had trod upon had metamorphosed into a sawtoothed trap fastened on his ankle. At her sister's scream, Kylliki turned toward him and as the firelight swept her tear-stained face, he saw that its flesh had gone slack. The mouth he had never grown tired of kissing had become thin, cracked, incised with the furrows of late middle age. The lustrous lavender eyes had grown milky, pouched with sagging flesh, and her hair—her split-pine, sun-gold, fragrant hair—was coarse, tangled, grey as frost.

Screaming, his mind an inflamed boil, Erich ran through the forest. Blindly, instinctively, he bore east and north, toward the northern end of the lake, in the direction of the road. At this moment, the generations of rational, educated people who had produced Erich Ziegler yielded their primacy to more distant, atavistic kin. His mind may well have directed him toward the road simply because that was the most rational course, but something ancient in his blood had also turned him in that direction, for the fully wakened primal part of him truly believed that if he continued plunging west, into that shifting and multidimensioned wilderness, he would never—not if he ran for a hundred years—reach a place of safety.

He ran, it seemed, for eternity, his feet swelling, ballooning inside his boots, his lungs engorged, eyes on fire and swimming with will-o'-the-wisp lights that might be inside his head or might be gathering around him like a swarm of agitated glowing wasps. Behind him was a growing shadow. He felt the forest stir, fully awakened now, sentience rolling across its dark and brooding face like a storm shadow.

A crack tore across the sky and a bitten thumbnail of a moon appeared. Gradually, impinging on Erich's awareness of the noise his own body made as it tore through the underbrush, he heard a much larger, wider, disturbance—a crashing. Glancing over his shoulder as he ran, he glimpsed something vast, a shadow whose dimensions and source were not visible, a fluid and powerful outline—now muscular, now unstable and tumescent, wildly pulsing, as though its form, already huge as a thunderhead, were still incomplete, growing. In front of that rushing darkness, a tempest wind preceded, raking the trees and bending them to the ground. The hair on

Erich's neck crackled. He voiced a cry of unreasoning terror and forced his body on, faster, racked now with enormous pains and blood-bombs that erupted across his vision, spurred to the verge of a bursting heart by the sure and bone-deep knowledge that his very soul was now in hazard.

He found the road by tripping over it. Suddenly, there were no more vines and creepers and thorns tentacled around his legs, and this abrupt freedom from obstruction threw him off balance and pitched him forward. His face grazed the roadbed's grit, peeling skin and pulping his lips, but he hugged it close, sobbing for air, as he heard, behind him, a great wind diminish into a sigh, replaced by the sudden pulse of utter silence.

Twenty-seven

Rautavaara heard the Lapp guide calling from just below the crest of the hill. Putting his maps back into their leather case, he hoisted himself from a crouching position and ambled forward. The guide had found tracks—mere ghosts of imprints, already nearly obliterated from the groundwater that was seeping up through the tundra. Whoever was leading these Germans, he was good—so good Rautavaara's men might have lost their quarry if the Lapp had not been helping them. The Lapp was a reindeer herder of indeterminate age who had been recruited several days ago at a trading post. He probably did not have the remotest idea of where "Germany" was, but he did know that, in burning the trading post to the ground, the retreating Germans had also burned the food supplies his village had depended on to get through the coming winter.

That was the sort of vindictive mischief the Germans had been making ever since their withdrawal started in the first week of October. When Rautavaara had been assigned to command this detachment—taking over from an officer whose pro-Nazi sympathies were much stronger than Rautavaara's own, and whose discipline, evidently, was considerably less—he had wondered just how zealous his men would be. Most of them, after all, had served on the same front with the Germans from the Norwegian Command, and the sudden shift of politics against their comrades—at the behest of their traditional and recent enemies—had struck all of them as a rotten and two-faced deal. The officers had been balky and some of the men openly insubordinate when they embarked on transports at Oulu and headed north to Tornio, on the Swedish border, where they executed an amphibious turning movement that inserted them behind the right flank of the retreating Germans, multiplying the pressure on them.

The Finns' reluctance lasted only until noon on the first day of that operation, at which time they were severely bombed and strafed by Stukas from Norwegian airfields, then briskly shelled by German shore batteries whose garrisons resisted stubbornly, apparently not afflicted with the same doubts the Finns had about turning their guns on former allies. Prepared to go ashore and accept a decorous, bloodless surrender, Rautavaara's men had ended up having to shoot their way in, sustaining more than a hundred casualties before it was over.

Whatever pro-Wehrmacht sentiment might have survived that initial contact faded quickly as the Finns moved after the retreating Germans and discovered that their former comrades were exacting a ruthless revenge on every part of Lapland they passed through. Every bridge, culvert, and drainage pipe had been demolished with explosives; every farmhouse and post office had been burned to the ground; the great hydroelectric plant at Ivalo—source of power for an area nearly as large as Belgium—had been dynamited to rubble. On October 16, in conjunction with two Finnish divisions that had marched overland, Rautavaara's unit took part in the capture of Rovaniemi, capital of Lapland. That pretty white town had been razed to ashes; all that stood was a concrete clock tower near the ruins of the railroad station, a structure that had proven too stout for the charges laid against it.

The next week had been spent advancing toward the border town of Muonio, at the base of the "lion's paw" formed by Finland's most westward provinces. Having by now been driven some two hundred fifty miles from their starting points, the German formations were losing coherence with every mile. It had been three days since Rautavaara's patrols had encountered any organized resistance—just bands of wet, exhausted stragglers wandering in the general direction of the Norwegian border, most of them only too happy to surrender.

When they first arrived in Lapland, they had advanced through the final days of autumn, through a landscape that, in peacetime, had attracted hikers from all over Scandinavia: the tundra's moss and shrubs were a deep burnt orange, topped with birches dipped in antique gold, framed by bare, massive, cloud-mottled hills; a land generously veined by cobalt-blue rivers so clear and pure that a thirsty man need only bend down and drink from them. But those colors had died in a single hard night, replaced by miserable grey washes of rain that stripped the trees, flooded the creeks, and washed the hills down to their bleak, dun-colored cores. And last night, the first dusting of snow had come down. Because the snow held footprints in the soil even after it had melted, the guide had finally found the tracks of the small German party they had been following for two days, and had lost for the past twelve hours. There were five or six men, the guide told Rautavaara, heading northwest, roughly paralleling the south bank of the Ivalo River. If they had crossed this hill in the earliest morning hours, when the snow still lay fresh, they would only be a mile or two ahead, and this close to the Norwegian border they would probably be taking the paths of least resistance, skirting the forest, whose last northward reaches filled the low tarn-spotted valleys between here and the border, keeping to open terrain, probably high up, trying to avoid all the water that had filled the land in recent days.

"Can we catch them before they reach Norway?" Rautavaara wanted to know.

It turned out that they could. The guide led them on a crazy, zigzag march through rock-strewn moorlands and over wind-scoured fells, and revealed to them a reindeer migration path that was unmapped and probably unknown except to this man and other members of his tribe. Rautavaara made some quick calculations, estimating their pace over this relatively easy track and comparing it to the presumed head start of their quarry. There, just before the forest ended for good at the edge of the great heaths: that was where they should intercept the Germans. Rautavaara would have preferred to let the poor bastards go—over the border and out of harm's way. But his orders were firm on that point: pursuit was to be conducted right up to the border itself, if necessary, and Major Rautavaara, whatever his personal inclinations, was an officer who obeyed his orders. Besides, the Germans' scorched-earth policy had made it politically expedient now to harass them without mercy.

Ziegler had ordered his children to break camp before dawn and had pushed them hard ever since. That was how he thought of them, although he was careful to treat them like men, hoping that if a crisis came, they would reciprocate by acting like men. But they were babies, really, maybe two of them old enough to shave on a daily basis; draftees still in their teens, dropped into this God-shat-upon wilderness only a few weeks after the whole German effort in the far north had collapsed and the great withdrawal had started. Ziegler had shown them what he could about keeping warm and dry, but they were not very good at it, and truth to tell, the vileness of the weather was such that no amount of woodcraft could do more than ameliorate the worst extremes of physical misery. None of them had been truly dry, or comfortable, for nearly a week. Their food, now reduced to a few tins of rations, would just barely last until they reached Norway. At the midday halt, during which they had grimly spooned cold rations into their mouths while huddled beneath a tattered square of camouflaged tarp, Ziegler had gone to the crest of the nearest ridge. First scanning the terrain carefully to make sure it was as empty as it looked, he had seen what he believed to be Norway through his binoculars: a low range of sullen folded hills, raw and purple as an old bruise. It looked as though they could be reached with just another day's march—if the weather held; two days if it snowed again. Hard to say, really; distances were not easy to judge in this landscape of mists and moorlands. He would tell his charges that it was Norway, in any case, because if it wasn't, it still had to be close, and the knowledge that they were within sight of safety would surely put some vigor back into their sodden feet.

His scouting duties complete, Ziegler enjoyed the luxury of privacy. He scuttled below the skyline, into the cover of a nest of rocks, and lit one of his last cigarettes. It was beginning to look like they would make it. The well-being that coursed through his nerves at that thought, and at the touch of nicotine, inspired him to open the dispatch case hanging over his shoulder and verify, for the hundredth time, that the score of the Eighth was still there, securely wrapped, untouched so far by rain or mud. He was going to bring it off. In time, what he was doing would be recorded in the history books: how he had taken a terrifying moral leap and saved a masterpiece from destruction at the hands of its besotted and hallucinating creator. He did not think, would not permit himself to think, about what had seemed to happen afterward, deep in the forest—or had it been deep within the "other" forest? He had, after all, been terribly overwrought. Christ, he was tired of this country; it would be good to leave it all behind and get on with his life.

Ziegler had left the main body of retreating German units almost two weeks ago. He had been ordered to take part in the demolition of Rovaniemi and he had refused, point-blank, to obey. The officer who had ordered him to assist in the destruction hadn't even known his name, so there was scant risk of any repercussions. He had simply wandered away into the smoke from the explosions, collected a knapsack full of rations, a couple of maps and a compass, and set off on his own, hitching rides when he could, otherwise walking. He had run into the Lost Boys a few days later, shivering and hopelessly disoriented—marching in the wrong direction, in fact—and he had taken them under his wing. He wished them well, but he would be glad to be rid of them too; if he had still been on his own, he would have been in Norway by now. But if he hadn't taken the responsibility for helping them, they would have ended up dead from exposure or locked up in a Russian prison camp, which was probably worse.

Anyway, in a few hours, it wouldn't matter. Finished with his cigarette, he took one more look at the terrain ahead of them. It would be safer to follow the middle elevations of the ridges, away from the skyline yet still above the valleys where any pursuit was likely to come from. But he estimated that they could cut hours off their traveling time if they brazenly crossed the highest slopes—the rockier, elevated terrain would be less cut up by fresh, flooded streams, and therefore much easier to walk on. There had been no sign of pursuing Finnish troops for more than twenty-four hours. So be it. He stood up and walked back to his "command."

An hour later, halfway across the first series of slopes, Ziegler looked down at the border of the forest half a kilometer distant. A great northward-thrusting tongue of trees extended up this far, washed against the hills' lower slopes, then yielded to open tundra: the continental terminus of the tree line, just like the shore of an ocean.

He remembered that hideous march down from the Arctic Front, the first winter of the war, and how glad he had been to see the trees, for they had signified shelter, firewood, safety. How much else the forest could signify, he had learned later.

Soft curtains of rain brushed over the trees while he watched, imparting to that barren vista an almost oriental delicacy of aspect.

"I am beyond you now," he whispered to the distant trees. The soldier just in front of Ziegler tripped, arms akimbo, and sprawled on wet gorse. Then Ziegler saw the red hole in the man's thigh and simultaneously heard the remote flat crack of the rifle shot that had taken him down. Instinctively he rolled to his left, down-slope, just as another bullet sang overhead. The Lost Boys froze in their tracks, and even as Ziegler rolled clear of the fire-beaten slope, he saw them, with mingled expressions of fear and relief, drop their weapons and raise their hands.

Scrambling to his feet, Ziegler ran toward the forest; he

would be safe there. He would make it to Norway tomorrow, moving swiftly and without encumbrances now. Norway wasn't going anywhere.

Splashing through numberless shallow tarns of frigid water, his breath raw and heavy with moisture, Ziegler reached the forest without another shot being fired at him. If the Lost Boys had not pointed out his escape, the chances were good that he hadn't been seen. He stumbled into the trees, feeling them close in, dense and comforting, behind his exposed back. He resolved to go deep into the forest, to find a place where he might build a small fire, thaw out, maybe dry his last pair of socks.

An hour later, when he judged himself truly safe from pursuit, he slowed down and took stock of his surroundings. He was in a grove of evergreens, evenly spaced, the ground between them carpeted with springy moss. He saw water gleaming and realized how thirsty he was, and how empty his canteen had become. Through immaculate silence he walked forward, came upon a clear, rushing arctic stream, drank and refilled.

As he turned his attention from the water to the rest of his surroundings, he noticed something strange about the glade in which he found himself. Scattered about—lumps of chalk on emerald green—lay the bleached skulls of reindeer who had died there in winters past. The eye sockets, pooled with secrets, regarded him as he trod softly away from the stream and deeper into the woods. Ahead of him now was a large tarn, thickly scummed with greenish muck. The skulls were more numerous here, and they had been carefully arranged in pyramidal cairns. In such remote places, he had heard, the Lapp nomads still practiced shamanist rites that had faded into myth in the towns and villages. What unthinkably ancient rituals were still observed in this hidden place, this utterly silent cathedral of trees where the reindeer came to die in greater numbers than coincidence might explain?

Ziegler shook his head ruefully: this country! This damned forest!

All the same, a crenelation of dread had started to kink the muscles of his spine. This was not a place he should have run to, not now. Perhaps two months ago, he could have come to such a place as this with his sense of wonder kindled to the point of awe—but now he sensed only a heaviness in the air, as though he had arrived at a place where his very presence was inimical. The boggy tarn, its outline broken by tendrils of mist, seemed to give off a coldness against his skin, and the chalky cairns reminded him unpleasantly of the skull poles outside the Russian *motti*, and of the wounded shaman who had turned, just before vanishing, and stared into his soul. He had been presumptuous indeed to think he could ever find a place for himself in this world, or that he could even, for very long, comprehend it. In any case he no longer felt welcomed here, and the certainty of that caused him to take a step backward, repelled by a sudden burst of dread.

Tickling his ears at first, on the barest threshold of hearing, came the soft susurrus of distant bells. As though something far, pale, and infinitely fragile had been displaced by the wind; as though his presence in this place, whether it be sacred ground or accursed, had set a thing in motion in the depths of the forest.

Suddenly, he knew what that thing was. Fifty meters away, a tree was uprooted and flung into the air. A low bestial sound—a wet, phlegmy growl—filled the glade, drowning the elfin bells, mocking them.

The white bear came at him. Eyes red, jaws drooling mucus, it lumbered with astonishing speed through the last screen of trees, as though it were the furious guardian of this place.

He screamed and backed away, slamming into a tree. He would not get far if he ran—back across the stream, perhaps, before the animal was upon him, but no farther. Not sure whether he was confronting a fury sent against him by the forest god, or a real animal of flesh and blood, Ziegler tugged his Luger from its holster, sighted on the bear's heaving chest, and emptied the clip as fast as he could pull the trigger, sending rolls of thunder across the forest, conjuring wide prismatic echoes from the distant hills.

The bear, its chest torn and its heart pierced, hissed with pain and fell dead, five meters from Ziegler's feet, its hind paws sloshing into the pond scum. Slowly he approached it, examined it, then threw his head back and roared with laughter.

It was an old, sick bear, and he had probably disturbed it as it was scouting, crankily, for a place to spend the winter. He inspected its muzzle and learned that it was nearly toothless. Its fur was patchy, discolored, and hung in loose, diseased-looking folds from its bones. Ziegler kicked the animal's shoulder, laughing even harder: this embodiment of doom, this archetype his mind had thrown out at him, in times of stress, as a harbinger of death, had turned out to be a toothless, wheezing, rheumy-eyed derelict.

Their attention drawn to the forest by the pistol shots, Rautavaara and the two men with him tracked the German easily, first by the hasty trail he left as he ran into the trees, then by the wild laughter they could hear echoing deep in the woods ahead of them. They were brought up short by the sight of their quarry, doubled over with laughter, beside the corpse of a freshly killed bear. The man seemed demented. When the corporal beside Rautavaara raised his Suomi to fire at the German, Rautavaara at first made no objection—the last thing he needed now was a lunatic on his hands. Then he caught a familiar timbre in the laughter. Peering more closely, he thought he recognized the way the fellow carried his shoulders; it looked like someone he had seen laughing before, under much pleasanter circumstances.

Rautavaara raised his hand to stop the gunner, saying: "Don't shoot—I think I know the man!" in time to prevent Ziegler from being killed, but not in time to stop the gunner from triggering a three-round burst that grazed Ziegler's rib cage, drawing copious blood and shattering the leather straps of the dispatch case that dangled over his shoulder. The contents of the case erupted in the greyish light: leaves of paper, fluttering like dove's wings, blown by the force of the Suomi's big slugs into a cloud that settled very slowly on the trembling surface of the bog.

Without even looking to see who had shot him, Ziegler ran forward into the pond, shouting in alarm, groping wildly for each sheet of paper. He clutched them to his chest after plucking them, one by one, from the surface, advancing ever deeper into the water as he did so: knees, thighs, crotch, hips, then suddenly halting and staring at the viscid substance with comprehension and terror.

"Ziegler! For God's sake, don't move any more! It's quicksand! I'll get a tree branch and we'll pull you out!"

But Ziegler did keep moving, kept reaching out for each leaf of paper he could save, and every motion worked him deeper, added to the inexorable suction that was pulling him down. Rautavaara, unable to find a big enough branch on the ground, ordered his men to cut down a birch tree with gunfire; the forest shook with hammering thunder and the air filled with the keen sweet smell of birch pulp.

By the time they extended the shaft out over the surface toward Ziegler, one of his hands was already covered with muck.

"Drop those damned papers and grab hold of the tree!" Rautavaara screamed.

But Ziegler, eyes bulging, seemed determined to retrieve the last few pages before turning toward the life preserver that had been thrust at him, and there was not quite enough time for him to do both. When he realized that, he attempted to fling the papers away, but by that time the surface had already risen to his neck, and his arms moved slowly, slowly, elbows gummed and shoulders dipping below the surface.

Now he seemed paralyzed with horror. He opened his mouth to scream and the surface flowed into it, choking him. Each struggling motion drove him a little bit deeper. One of his hands touched, barely, the trembling tip of the extended tree, but then—too heavy, too oppressed by weight and suction—the hand flopped heavily into the muck and vanished. All that now remained above the surface was the top of

Ziegler's head, his eyes protruding as though they would burst.

"He's done for, Major, poor bastard."

Rautavaara read the plea in Ziegler's eyes, one last message between old comrades, drew his own pistol and fired three times, accurately—the only mercy within his power to bestow. Suction and the weight of Ziegler's body carried most of the papers down with him.

Using the birch pole, Rautavaara and his men worked to fish out a few of the surviving pages. He was curious to see what kind of document was valuable enough to be worth the risk of such a monstrous death. Something, surely, that Finnish intelligence would be interested in.

He was able to retrieve a few sodden pages from the bog. After glancing at them, however, he wadded them in his fist and tossed them back with an angry and bewildered shrug, for there was nothing whatever of military value on them—only a few lines of barely legible music.

Historical Note

Finnish composer Jean Sibelius published his last major work, the tone poem *Tapiola*, in 1926. He continued to live, however, on his estate at Järvenpää until his death, on September 20, 1957. During the last decade of his life, he was carefully shielded from criticism by friends, colleagues, and the Finnish press, and only a handful of important guests were granted personal audiences—ordinary music lovers had to be content with distant glimpses of his home, or with busts and postcards purchased at the official souvenir kiosk. Before being ushered into the composer's presence, even such distinguished guests as Eugene Ormandy and Leopold Stokowski were admonished to ask no questions about the Eighth Symphony.

Speculation about an Eighth Symphony remained rampant throughout Sibelius's life, and has continued to this day. Although numerous eyewitnesses claimed to have had glimpses of the score during the thirty-year "Silence from Järvenpää," not so much as a single page has ever come to light.

That the composer, profoundly afraid that the work might not live up to expectations, may have destroyed the manuscript by his own hand was a theory suggested to the author by Professor Erik Tawastjerna—one of the executors of the composer's estate—during a conversation in Helsinki in the spring of 1965.